T0062510

A
TREASURE
WORTH KEEPING

MARIE PATRICK

Crimson Romance
New York London Toronto Sydney New Delhi

CRIMSON
ROMANCE

Crimson Romance
An Imprint of Simon & Schuster, Inc.
1230 Avenue of the Americas
New York, NY 10020

Copyright © 2013 by Donna Warner.

All rights reserved, including the right to reproduce this book or portions thereof in any form whatsoever. For information address Crimson Romance Subsidiary Rights Department, 1230 Avenue of the Americas, New York, NY 10020.

CRIMSON ROMANCE and colophon are trademarks of Simon & Schuster, Inc.

For information about special discounts for bulk purchases, please contact Simon & Schuster Special Sales at 1-866-506-1949 or business@simonandschuster.com.

The Simon & Schuster Speakers Bureau can bring authors to your live event. For more information or to book an event contact the Simon & Schuster Speakers Bureau at 1-866-248-3049 or visit our website at www.simonspeakers.com.

ISBN: 978-1-4405-7569-3
ISBN: 978-1-4405-7568-6 (ebook)

This is a work of fiction. Names, characters, corporations, institutions, organizations, events, or locales in this novel are either the product of the author's imagination or, if real, used fictitiously. The resemblance of any character to actual persons (living or dead) is entirely coincidental.

To my critique partners, Lexi and Ann, who are definitely treasures worth keeping; to my son, who continues to inspire me every day; and to my husband, my hero—this journey wouldn't be nearly as much fun without you.

Chapter 1

Charleston—1850

Music, raucous laughter, and light spilled onto the street as soon as Tristan Youngblood, captain of the *Adventurer*, opened the door of the Salty Dog. He stood still for a moment and let the atmosphere of his favorite tavern in Charleston wash over him.

The *Adventurer's* crew filled the room with the exception of Coop, who stood watch aboard ship, and Jemmy, Tristan's son, who was too young to join the celebration. A more trustworthy, patient, experienced group of men he'd never find. He loved and respected them all, found comfort in their company, and trusted them with his life—and his secret. To the world, he was Captain Trey, treasure hunter. To those who shared his confidence, he was Tristan Youngblood, Lord Ravensley.

They had reason to celebrate this night, even if he did not. After months and months of searching, they'd found the legendary lost treasure of the *Sierra Magdalena*, a Spanish galleon savagely torn apart in a hurricane almost two hundred years ago off the coast of Hispaniola. Each and every one of them thought they had found heaven—or at least a little part of it.

Pockets bulging with pieces of gold, they turned, almost as one, and raised their tankards toward him. "Captain!"

"Tippy." He signaled the tavern owner. "Drinks are on me."

Loud cheers met his pronouncement as Tippy lined up clean tankards on the bar and proceeded to fill them one by one with thick, foamy ale.

Tristan accepted his crew's slaps on the back and handshakes as he made his way through the crowded room to drop a small pouch of gold coins on the bar.

Graham Alcott, the *Adventurer's* navigator as well as Tristan's second in command and oldest friend, sat at a table in the corner, his arms around the two winsome barmaids perched on his knees. A cigar smoldered in the brass tray surrounded by the remains of a hearty meal.

Tristan grinned as he strode toward his friend. It never failed. No matter where in the world the *Adventurer* put into port, Graham found the loveliest, most willing ladies.

He cleared his throat. Graham took his eyes off the tantalizing bosoms presented to him and glanced up. His smile could have charmed the birds from the trees—or the drawers from even the most discerning young woman.

"Tristan," Graham acknowledged as he nodded to the chair opposite him. "Sarah, my love, get the captain a glass of your finest rum." He gave each girl a sound kiss on the cheek and a promise to meet them later, then he patted both behinds to usher them off his knees. With squeals and giggles, the women rushed to do his bidding.

Tristan dropped into the chair and stretched out his long, leather-booted legs, crossing them at the ankle. He grabbed a serrated knife and cut a piece of bread still warm from the oven, then slathered it with sweet, creamy butter and took a bite.

"Well?" Graham prodded as Sarah delivered two heavy-bottomed glasses and placed them on the table. Tristan grinned as Graham's merry brown eyes followed the gentle sway of her hips.

"Well what?" Tristan replied after he swallowed.

"Don't play games, Tristan." Graham rested his elbows on the table. "I've known you too long. I was there when Tippy gave you the letter. I know the family seal when I see it. Was it your father? Is he here?"

Tristan stared at the light amber brew in his glass as he chewed the last of his bread. "No, my father isn't here. He sent his henchman, the honorable Theodore Gilchrist, Esquire. If we'd made port in Jamaica, I would have met Paul Farnsworth, another in my father's employ. Apparently, Father has all my regular haunts covered. The earl was bound and determined to give me the news." The information Mr. Gilchrist imparted made his stomach churn, made the bile rise in his throat, made him want to disregard convention and lose himself on the high seas. Brown eyes twinkling with curiosity, Graham sat up straighter. "What news?"

Tristan pulled a half-smoked cigar from his vest pocket and used the candle on the table to light it. As he exhaled, blue-grey smoke swirled to the ceiling. "I have a little less than four months to put my affairs in order, go back to England and then—"

"Then what?" Graham lifted his glass and took a long drink.

"I am to be married."

"Married!" The navigator choked on his rum as he spit out the word. He coughed into his hand, his face red. For a long time, he stared and said nothing. "I would offer congratulations, but I gather you don't regard this as good news."

Tristan twisted the signet ring on his finger while he looked around the room—at the hunk of bread on a plate in the middle of the table, at the cigar smoke drifting around him—anywhere but at his shipmate. "No, I do not." He stopped twisting the ring long enough to rake his fingers through his hair; then he picked up his drink.

"You can't be surprised." Graham leaned back and folded his arms across his chest. His black-booted foot rested on the empty chair next to him. "Your father has been trying to marry you off for the past five years. Every time you go home, he introduces you to another eligible young woman. Perhaps he sees this arrangement as the way to get the deed accomplished."

Tristan tossed back the rum as if it were water and ignored the burning sting the liquor left in his throat before he gave voice to his concerns. "God help me, I don't want a marriage like my parents'. They barely tolerated each other before my mother passed."

He twisted the ring on his finger and caught the glitter of the lion's amber eye. "There was never any love between them. I doubt there was even fondness." He lowered his voice. "My father has had the same mistress since before I was born and my mother … my mother went through lovers like … well, like you and I go through bottles of rum."

Sarah sashayed to the table and refilled both glasses. Tristan nodded his thanks but didn't offer her a smile, as was his wont. The news of his impending marriage settled like a rock in his stomach.

"Was your parents' marriage arranged?" Graham swept his tongue over his lips in anticipation then reached for his refilled glass.

"Of course. It's the way it's done." Tristan let his breath whistle between his teeth and crushed his cigar in the tray, frustrated by his father's announcement. "I don't want to marry a woman I don't know, have never met. I believe—"

"But you don't have to, Tristan. You're an adult. Almost thirty. Tell your father no."

Tristan snorted. "If it were that easy, I would. You don't understand. Your parents met, fell in love, and married, the way I would like to, but … marriage is expected." He lowered his voice to a whisper though he doubted his words could be overheard in a room full of laughing men and women. "For a man of my position. As the next Earl of Winterbourne, I have an obligation to make the most advantageous match, which means marry for money to fill the family coffers and produce future earls. And as my father's solicitor informed me, though my younger brother and his wife have been married for nine years, there are no children from the union." He rubbed his fingers over his freshly shaved face and found he missed the beard he'd grown during his last voyage. "Father wants heirs."

"You jest."

"I wish I did."

Graham leaned back in his chair and studied the liquor in his glass. A smile crossed his face after a moment. "What about Jemmy?"

Tristan shrugged. "Father doesn't know the adoption papers have become final, but I don't think he would accept Rielle's son as his heir. She was my friend and I loved her as such, but Jemmy isn't of Youngblood ... blood."

The navigator nodded, and Tristan knew he understood more than his spoken words. Graham shook his head. "No more treasure hunting. No more sailing around the world at a moment's whim. No more getting stinking drunk and spending our time with willing women." He grinned to reveal a compliment of pearl white teeth beneath his shaggy beard. "I pity you, my friend."

"Four months," Tristan repeated, his tone and mood somber until an idea grabbed hold and wouldn't let go.

Izzy's Fortune. If he could find the infamous treasure of Queen Isabella, he could fill the Youngblood coffers with more than enough gold to last several lifetimes. He wouldn't have to marry a woman he didn't know, wouldn't have to spend the rest of his life with a woman he didn't want. He could have the time he needed to find what he wanted most.

Love.

Passion.

A woman who could share his dreams.

Who am I trying to fool? There is no such woman.

But Izzy's Fortune. That, at least, had a chance of being real.

And if he found the treasure before Wynton Entwhistle of the *Explorer*, so much the better. An open rivalry existed between the two men and had from the moment they met some years ago when they'd both gone after the same fortune. Since then, Tristan had managed to stay one step ahead of the scheming seaman, much to Entwhistle's regret and frustration.

Tristan glanced at Graham, smiled, then started to chuckle. "Four months is long enough to try one last time to find Izzy's Fortune." His gaze darted around the room to the crew in the midst of their merriment. "Do you think they'd mind?"

"Hell, no!" Graham slammed his glass on the table. "When do we leave?"

"Three days. No, four. We'll need that long to gather supplies. Once we leave Charleston, I don't plan on coming back—at least for a long time. Remember, I'm expected in England to—" Tristan choked on the word "—marry."

"Again, you have my pity." Graham laughed. "Who is this woman? Is she at least pleasant to look at?" He waved his hands in front of his face as his grin grew wider. "She isn't some ugly beast with rotten teeth and pitted skin, is she?"

"I have no idea. I didn't even ask her name." Tristan wasn't surprised he had not asked a most important question. He supposed the announcement that his marriage had been arranged without his knowledge or consent had shocked him into not thinking at all. "I should find out, shouldn't I?" He tossed back his drink in one swallow. "I'll pay another visit to Gilchrist in the morning, but in the meantime, I'm going back to the ship." He stood and flipped a gold coin on the table. "I'll relieve Coop so he can celebrate with his mates."

"Are you certain?" Graham rose as well, although he never released the glass of rum in his hand, nor did he take his gaze from Sarah MacNamara and Rosie Flint. "I could just as easily take the watch."

Tristan shook his head. "No, you stay." He glanced at Sarah wending her way through the tavern's rowdy customers. Her hips rocked back and forth as she sidestepped with innate agility the various hands aiming for her backside. She met his stare and grinned. "Sarah and Rosie would be disappointed if you didn't keep your promises."

Tristan made his way through the men, and again accepted their congratulations and well wishes before he handed another small leather bag filled with gold to the barkeep. He saluted his crew. "Drink up, me hearties! You've earned it." He resisted the urge to tell them to keep their eyes, as well as their hands, on their gold.

"Aye, Cap'n!"

His men would be in sad shape tomorrow, sporting colossal headaches, perhaps still drunk from this night's revelry, so he gave them a reprieve. "I expect you all to be onboard the *Adventurer* in two days."

Again, their rousing chorus of "Aye, Cap'n" met his ears.

He grinned as he pushed through the door and left the deafening din of the Salty Dog. A senseless whistle escaped him as he strode over the cobblestones toward the three-masted clipper at berth.

His shoulders relaxed as his stride grew longer. He inhaled and caught the scent of a hearty beef stew as it simmered in someone's pot. Warm light spilled through the windows of the homes he passed and he heard the telltale sounds of people settling in for the evening.

He loved harbor towns—the charming, quaint villages of England, the rowdy, yet oddly cosmopolitan ports like Charleston, the rough and tumble atmosphere of Port Royal. The sight of the ships from all around the world lined up side by side, their colorful flags waving in the breeze, comforted him as nothing else ever could. He would miss these ports when he obeyed his father's command and married the woman the earl had chosen—a woman whose name he didn't even know.

Beneath the glow of a street lamp, he stopped and shook his head.

An arranged marriage. God, he hated the thought.

Shoulders tight once again, he kicked at a rock on the cobblestones and scowled. The earl had given him no choice.

If the truth were known, Tristan didn't object to the idea of marriage—he just hated the idea of being coerced into it, forced to give up the life he loved.

Part of it was his own fault. All the years he'd searched for treasure, he could have and should have searched for a wife. He could have remained in England and attended the debutante balls where most of the eligible bachelors of his class chose their future wives from the best families.

But marriage and the responsibilities of the earldom wasn't the life he wanted.

The sea called to him, lured him, begged him to feel its power and glory. From the moment he'd first stepped foot on a ship, he'd known he wanted to sail for the rest of his life. The warmth of a woman's hand on his cheek could not compare to the cool touch of spindrift on his face. The tedium of running the Winterbourne estates could never measure up to the exhilaration of riding out a storm on the high seas while the sky raged around him. In those moments, Tristan knew he truly lived.

He glanced up as he drew closer to the *Adventurer*. A shadow passed before the windows of his cabin, back and forth, as if someone waited for him with great impatience. It couldn't have been Jemmy. The boy had been fast asleep when Tristan had left to see his father's solicitor.

It wasn't Coop Milliron, either. His faithful crewman paced the length of the deck from bow to stern, his footsteps heavy on the wooden planks. They grew louder in the still night when he climbed the stairs to the quarterdeck. Moonbeams lit his path. He had no need of a lantern to guide his way.

Tristan studied the shadow and grinned. The silhouette belonged to a woman—he couldn't deny the full thrust of her breasts or the long skirt that twitched with her step. His grin widened, but only for a moment.

Who was she? What was she doing aboard his ship?

There could be two reasons a woman would be on his ship at this time of night. Either she was a strumpet … or a thief.

If she was looking for the spoils from the *Sierra Magdalena*, she'd wasted her time. Though it was common knowledge in Charleston that he and his crew had found the treasure, only a fool would have kept it on board. Tristan had never been a fool.

The other alternative pleased him much more. If she was looking for a night of pleasure, well then, she'd come to the right man.

Tristan quickened his step and bounded up the gangplank. Cooper jumped, startled, and pulled his cutlass from the sash around his waist in one easy, practiced move. The sharp blade glinted in the moonlight.

"Coop!" Tristan raised his hands and sidestepped the weapon.

"Cap'n, ye scairt the hell outta me!" The crewman lowered the cutlass and shoved it back into his sash then patted the handle for good measure. He stood as tall as his short stature would allow which made the white cotton of his shirt strain against the roundness of his belly. "Doncha be knowin' not to sneak up on a man? Coulda got yerself killed!"

"Who is the woman in my cabin?"

"She dinna give me her name, Cap'n. She been waitin' on ye fer pert near a hour." His grin spread from ear to ear then faded as his bushy eyebrows disappeared beneath the red kerchief tied around his forehead. Tufts of dark brown hair, peppered with grey, spiked around the square of cloth on his head. In the moon's glow, his cheeks were ruddier than normal and his bulbous nose, a result of years of heavy drinking, shined like a beacon in the middle of his face. "Were ye not expectin' her?"

"No, I was not."

The crewman mumbled beneath his breath words Tristan couldn't quite make out before he apologized. "I'm sorry, Cap'n. It ain't unusual fer ye to have a woman in yer cabin, though it ain't happened in a while."

"It's all right, Coop," Tristan said. "Why don't you join your mates at the Salty Dog? You shouldn't miss the celebration."

The seaman's sharp brown eyes disappeared in the wrinkles of his face as he grinned. "Aye, Cap'n!" He needed no further urging as he scurried down the gangplank.

Tristan watched him for a moment then strode across the deck, the hard soles of his boots loud in the silent night.

At the end of the hallway, his door stood wide open. Candles lit against the darkness created a warm glow on the mahogany paneled walls. He glanced around the room. All the built-in cabinets were ajar. Maps littered the floor, some flat, some curled into long tubes, which rolled back and forth as the ship moved. Perturbed, but not angry, his jaw clenched but only for a moment as he took in the sight before him.

The woman stood at his desk, her hands flat on the surface as she studied a map. Covered in yards of pale blue silk, her backside wiggled as she shoved the current map out of her way to study the one beneath it.

The glow from the candles brought out the golden glints in her hair, which curled down her back in wild abandon. With a well-practiced flick of her hand, she pushed long, light brown hair away from her face then reached for the snifter of cognac on the desktop, finishing the amber brew in one swallow.

Tristan leaned against the doorjamb and twisted the ring on his finger as he admired the tantalizing view before him, no longer bothered by her uninvited presence. A new feeling took hold, one that filled his veins with desire. It had been a long time since he'd had a woman. "Are you finding my maps of interest?"

"Oh!" She gave a guilty start and whirled around. A pretty shade of pink colored her face and contrasted with the pale blue of her gown. Her eyes, the color of the deep blue sea, were wide and twinkled in the candlelight. "I'm … I'm . . ." She paused to breathe. "You must be Captain Trey."

"I must be." He took two steps into the room. She backed into the desk, unable to retreat further. "And you are?"

The muscles in her throat moved as she swallowed hard. "I . . ."

"If you're looking for the *Sierra Magdalena's* treasure, you won't find it here. Nor will those maps help you."

She drew herself up as his words hit her. "I beg your pardon. I am not a thief."

Tristan smiled as wicked thoughts careened through his mind and took another two steps into the room. He stood only a breath away from her, close enough to see the faint scar on her forehead, close enough to notice her eyes weren't merely sea-blue, but had flecks of green in their depths as well. Long dark lashes fluttered as she stared into his face and licked her lips.

He knew an invitation when he saw one. Without hesitation, he wrapped his arms around her, lowered his head, and tasted those tempting, moist lips.

The woman stilled in his embrace, then melted against him. She tasted of brandy, warm and intoxicating, while her perfume filled his senses and surrounded him with the clean scent of a forest after a rain. The combination of her taste and smell tantalized him; the heat of her response excited him and made him realize one kiss was not enough.

His mouth slid over hers, gently at first, then with more force. Her lips opened beneath his, and beyond the initial taste of brandy, he detected the cool freshness of mint.

"Captain," she breathed as she turned away and his lips touched the softness of her cheek. Small, dainty hands pushed against his chest. "I am not a common … strumpet here for your pleasure."

Tristan grinned. Oh, she was a beauty with the color of roses in her cheeks and the sparkle of indignation in her sea-blue eyes. Contrary to her words, she had responded to him. Her body still trembled within his embrace.

"My apologies." He released her and she staggered. "When a man comes aboard his ship and sees a beautiful woman who claims she is not a thief, he can only think one other thing."

Those beguiling eyes flashed, and for a moment, Tristan battled with himself to keep from falling into their fathomless depths. He pulled a chair away from the table before slumping into it and crossing his legs. "If you're not a thief and you're not a harlot come to fulfill all my carnal desires, then who are you?"

"My name is Caralyn McCreigh," she said and waited, as if she expected him to recognize the name.

He wasn't listening. He couldn't tear his gaze away from the beauty of her face, the wild curls of light brown hair held back from her small features by a ribbon the same pale blue as her gown, or her full figure emphasized by the cut of her dress.

"I … ah … I have a proposition for you," she blurted and raised wide eyes to him.

In that moment, Tristan was lost. Still intoxicated by her taste and smell, he now had to contend with desire sweeping through him with incredible speed and urgency.

"I want to hire you to help me find Queen Isabella's treasure."

Tristan said nothing, although his fingers drummed the tabletop. Was it possible? Had she overheard him talking with Graham? How did she know about the treasure?

Of course, everyone knew about the treasure, but how did she know he had searched for it and planned to search for it again? Was it coincidence?

Before he could voice his concern, she said, "You know my father, Daniel McCreigh of the *Lady Elizabeth*." She smiled with obvious love for her father. "He told me he'd met you in Kingston. He thought you were an honorable man."

Recognition dawned for Tristan. He did, indeed, know Daniel McCreigh, the fine, upstanding man who captained the *Lady Elizabeth*. They had both been in Finnegan's Crooked Shillelagh, commiserating that neither could find Izzy's Fortune, though each had searched for quite a few years. He remembered sharing an enjoyable evening with the man, hoisting tankards of ale and regaling each other with tall tales of life at sea. At one point, they'd even compared notes on where the treasure was not.

Tristan studied her, looked beyond her beauty, and saw the resemblance. "Many have searched for the treasure, Miss McCreigh, and yet, no one has found it. Queen Isabella's treasure may not even be real."

"Yes, that is true, but I believe it is." Her voice lowered to a whisper. "I know, in my heart, the treasure is real."

As did he, but he couldn't tell her that. They'd just met. "What makes you think you will succeed where others have failed? Your own father couldn't find the treasure."

"I know, but I have these." She reached for the soft-sided valise on the floor beside the desk, which Tristan hadn't seen when he'd come into his cabin. She pulled an oilcloth wrapped package from the depths of the case and laid it on the table in front of him. Her fingers trembled as she tugged the string and moved the protective covering aside to reveal a journal before she pulled out the chair beside him and sat.

The leather binding was cracked and brittle. As she lifted the cover with her gloved fingers exposing pages fragile and delicate with age, Caralyn said, "My father was never serious about finding the treasure. For him, it was a lark, an adventure he and I could share, but I was raised on stories of Izzy's Fortune and I . . .I always believed. Even when I found this journal, Papa refused to come out of retirement to find it."

Tristan looked from the book to her face. Her eyes were animated and sparkled in the glow of candlelight. Pink stained her cheeks. Enthusiasm colored her voice. He said nothing as he watched her, but his thoughts ran riot.

"This is the journal of Alexander Pembrook," she said. "He sailed with Henry Morgan."

She lifted one page after another with a touch so light, so dainty, Tristan's body responded as if she caressed him. The fine hair on his arms rose as he imagined her fingers on his skin. Excitement rippled through him, and his heart beat a little faster in his chest.

She stopped about a third of the way through the journal. "Here." She pointed to the page and pushed the book toward him. "Start here."

He moved the candle closer and started to read. The journal entry, dated June 1670, described separating the *Santa Maria* from her two flagships and overtaking her in a battle, which left the ship with gaping holes in her bow and her crew in bloody heaps. The passage further related how Morgan's men transferred the treasure to their own ship, set the *Santa Maria* on fire, and watched her sink into the ocean.

"This is all very exciting," Tristan commented as he slid the journal back to her, "but is it true?"

"I believe so." She stared at him, and in the depths of her fathomless eyes, he knew she did. With great care, she searched further through the journal and stopped at another page. "Morgan didn't trust very many people, and he moved the treasure several times. The last time he did, Alexander was one of the men he selected to help move the treasure and swore to secrecy."

Tristan rose from his seat. He grabbed her brandy snifter from the desk, found another one for himself in the cabinet over his head, and poured them both a draft of fine cognac. He swallowed his without even tasting it then refilled his glass.

"According to his journal, Alexander moved the treasure once more—stealing it from beneath Morgan's nose the year Morgan was arrested and sent to England for breaking a peace treaty between England and Spain."

She tapped the journal with her forefinger. "The final resting place of Queen Isabella's treasure is the Island of the Sleeping Man. He describes the island quite well, but I have never been able to locate it on any map. I can tell you where it is not because I've accompanied my father on several of his adventures." She took a sip of her brandy. "After he hid the treasure, Alexander … *reinvented* himself, I suppose would be the correct term. He changed his appearance, changed his name, changed everything about himself and settled in Jamaica, but he never stopped writing in his journal." She turned more pages and pointed to various paragraphs, but she never read from the writings themselves, so he knew she had committed certain things to memory.

"He married Mary Collins, a plantation owner's daughter and lived happily at Sweet Briar in Saint James Parish before Henry Morgan returned to Jamaica as the lieutenant governor." Her fingers smoothed over the written words.

"Alexander became very ill after Morgan returned. He didn't leave the plantation, wouldn't see visitors. I have the impression he spent a lot of time in a little chapel on the plantation, praying. I don't know if part of his illness was due to his constant consumption of rum, but I know he believed he'd been cursed for stealing the treasure. He believed Morgan would come for him at any moment." She paused and took a deep breath before continuing in a rush.

"His writing reflected his illness and his fear. Many of his words are gibberish, out of context, and make little sense, even though I've read this over and over. His last entry is August 10, 1680. I imagine he died a short time later."

Fascinated, Tristan watched her take another sip of brandy then lick her lips once again.

"To my knowledge, Izzy's Fortune is still hidden on the Island of the Sleeping Man."

Anticipation surged through Tristan's veins, and yet he couldn't allow himself to show it. Why should he trust her? She was simply a woman he'd found on his ship, going through his maps. Perhaps she'd made it all up, wrote the journal herself, but to what purpose? Was she bored with her life? Did she long for adventure?

He studied the book, noticed again the brittle pages, the ink so faded in places he had trouble reading it, and knew with certainty, the journal wasn't forged.

He felt her intense stare and looked at her.

"You don't believe me," she blurted, as if she'd read his thoughts. "I have this." She reached for her valise again and laid a wooden box beside the book, slipped the lock, and lifted the lid. Nestled in a bed of black velvet lay a golden goblet encrusted with precious gems. Rubies and emeralds sparkled in the soft glow of the candles and created rainbows on the dark mahogany walls. "It was with Alexander's journal. I found them both hidden in the false bottom of an old grandfather clock my father had purchased many years ago. I don't think they were ever meant to be found. If an earthquake hadn't toppled that clock to the floor, I never would have known."

Stunned, Tristan swallowed hard. He'd never seen anything so beautiful in his life, aside from the woman next to him. He said nothing as he lifted the goblet from its bed of velvet and inspected the gems, the perfection of the craftsmanship, the tiny inscription at the base.

"I will finance the expedition on the condition I am allowed to join in the hunt and we split the treasure—half for you and your crew, half for me." She held her breath and waited for his answer.

He came to a quick decision. There were those, he knew, who would think him insane, unstable. A superstitious group, his crew would regard him as quite mad and would object to a woman on board the *Adventurer*, but he had to take the chance—on her. On the journal. On the golden chalice in his hand and the possibility of finding Izzy's Fortune.

"I accept your proposition. We leave in four days."

Chapter 2

Caralyn let out her pent up breath in a long sigh. Relief washed through her with such speed, she wanted to cry. She couldn't believe he'd agreed without an argument. She had been prepared to beg, and if that hadn't worked, she'd been prepared to offer … herself.

The first part of her plan to gain her freedom had gone off without a hitch, but it was only the beginning. They had to find the treasure, just had to—her future happiness depended upon it.

She'd come to the *Adventurer* alone and waited for him with the knowledge he might deny her request with a simple shake of his head. And yet, he hadn't. He hadn't been irate to find her in his cabin, hadn't been disturbed she'd gone through his maps. He seemed more amused and curious than angry.

Though her father had spoken of Captain Trey many times, hearing about him had not prepared her for meeting him. She had expected an older man, but the man who sat before her couldn't be considered old in any way. Young and vibrant, raw energy and blatant sexuality oozed from him, which both frightened and excited her more than she dare admit.

She hadn't expected him to be quite this handsome, either. He looked like a pirate. Or at least what she imagined a pirate would look like. Dark hair, brushed back from his forehead, formed a queue at the back of his neck, and was held in place by a length of leather. High cheekbones emphasized remarkable, unusual sherry-colored eyes, which bore holes through her and heated her blood. He possessed a beautiful smile, which he flashed at her, and the softest lips. Her mouth still tingled from when he'd kissed her.

Broad shouldered and muscular from years at sea, his long, lean body carried not an ounce of fat. She glanced at his hands and held her breath. Not the hands of a dandy or someone who only used his strength to open a brandy bottle. These hands had known hard work, and yet she detected an inherent gentleness in his long fingers.

"Why have you brought this to me? Why hasn't your father taken the journal and goblet and set sail?" His fingers touched hers as he handed back the items. A suffusion of heat sizzled from her fingertips all the way to her toes.

"Father said he's too old and tired to chase rainbows. He said it was time for both of us to give up the fantasy of Queen Isabella's treasure." She left out the part about his plans for her marriage. An arranged marriage to a man she didn't know, a man who would take her away from the home she loved on Saint Lucia, a man who would expect *things* from her. "He retired and sold the *Lady Elizabeth*."

Caralyn didn't tell him how much it hurt to know her father had sold the ship to a complete stranger. She'd always assumed he would give it to her. After all, she was the only one of his children who loved the *Lady Elizabeth* as much as he did.

With nimble fingers, she wrapped the journal in its protective oilcloth, placed the goblet in its box, and tucked them away in her valise. "There is one other thing." She pulled out an envelope. "It's a contract, specifying the terms of our agreement."

Captain Trey took the envelope and removed the contract and its duplicate. Once again, Caralyn held her breath. Though he had verbally agreed, he could still change his mind. The possibility all her plans were for naught still weighed heavily on her heart.

He said nothing as he read the document, but his eyes wandered to her several times. Again, his grin spread from ear to ear. "I am to take you to London by April twentieth, whether we find the treasure or not."

"Yes."

"That doesn't give us much time, Miss McCreigh. It's the middle of January." With a frown, he dipped his pen into the inkwell but didn't sign. Instead, he stared at her. His remarkable eyes seared her to her very soul. "Did Entwhistle send you?" he asked as his gaze swept over her. Her heartbeat quickened as excitement rippled through her.

She took a deep breath. "I assure you, Captain, I came on my own. No one sent me. Perhaps it is foolish, but no one knows I came to see you."

He continued to stare at her. Caralyn didn't blink, didn't turn away. She kept her gaze steadily on him, praying he wouldn't back out of their agreement.

"Finding this treasure is important to you." He wasn't asking a question. It was a statement of fact and the deep tenor of his voice filled her veins with warm honey.

"Yes. More important than you'll ever know." She didn't elaborate, didn't tell him the proceeds from her share of the treasure would be enough to buy her out of a marriage she didn't want. Nor did she tell him how frightened she was to fail in her quest or how much the thought of high adventure filled her with excitement.

"For me as well, Miss McCreigh." He signed his name in bold slashes on the bottom on the pages before he handed her the documents and the quill.

"Shouldn't we have a witness?" More nervous than she could bear, Caralyn couldn't resist asking the question.

And wished she hadn't.

The captain's cool sherry-colored gaze settled over her. He said not a word for a very long time while his unrelenting stare played havoc with her senses.

"If we are to be partners in this venture, you'll have to trust me."

With a slight nod and trembling fingers, Caralyn wrote her name beneath his on both pages, although her signature wasn't as bold. She blew on the ink to make it dry faster, handed one copy to him, then folded hers and stuffed it into the valise.

"It's done, then. In four days, we set sail. In four months time, whether we find Queen Isabella's treasure or not, you will deliver me to London." She held out her hand and waited, her heart in her throat. She would say her vows on April twenty-fifth, according to what she remembered from before she'd ceased listening, but she wanted to give herself time to find her future father-in-law and offer him gold in exchange for her freedom. Tristan grinned as he stared at her hand then gave her his own and shook.

"It's a pleasure doing business with you, Miss McCreigh." His eyes twinkled, his teeth gleamed pearl white, and the burnished highlights in his hair danced in the candlelight. He did not release her hand. The warmth of his touch traveled from her fingers all the way up her arm. Her heart beat an insane tattoo in her chest and she wondered, perhaps too late, if she had made a mistake. How in the world would she be able to maintain her balance, her equilibrium, if she was to spend all that time with this handsome, charismatic man?

"Might I see you home? Or were you planning to stay aboard the *Adventurer* until we sail?" The expression on his face told her he wouldn't mind if she stayed.

"I have a carriage waiting, but I'll see you in four days. I'll send my maps tomorrow."

Tristan rose from his seat to tower over her. Caralyn wondered if he would kiss her again. In truth, she would rather like it. The touch of his mouth had been electrifying, intoxicating, unlike anything she'd ever experienced. She stared at him, mesmerized by the luminous shine in his eyes and the smile on his face.

"Come. I'll escort you to your carriage." He offered his arm. Without hesitation, Caralyn slipped her fingers into the crook of his elbow.

• • •

As the carriage made its way toward a townhouse on the other side of Charleston, Caralyn tried to keep her excitement at bay. With little success. Her head swam with thoughts of the supplies their quest would require, the clothes she would pack, the maps she would send along. Most of all, she thought of the treasure and the freedom it would give her.

She hugged herself and would have squealed with delight if the hour hadn't been so late.

When the carriage stopped in front of her brother's three-story home, Caralyn stepped out and stood on the sidewalk for a moment. The light from a lantern beside the door sent a glow over the darkness and turned the shadows of the bushes into hulking monsters. She eyed those bushes with suspicion as she made her way up the walk and wondered if one of her nephews would jump out to scare her.

She chuckled, realizing how ridiculous her fears were. The hour had grown late. Surely, her rambunctious nephews were fast asleep or at least pretending to be.

With great care, she twisted the knob and pushed the door open. The hinges squealed in protest and she stopped, hoping the sound hadn't been as loud as she imagined. She took a deep breath, closed her eyes, and let herself into the house.

"Where have you been?"

"Oh!" Caralyn jumped and tightened her grip on the handles of her valise.

Her brother sat in a chair beside the grandfather clock in the great hall. The single lamp above his head created a halo of sorts and highlighted the abundant grey, which streaked his light brown hair.

Charles, her senior by only five years, but in attitude and thought, so much older, glared at her with obvious annoyance.

He rose from his seat and stalked toward her, the echo of his hard-soled shoes on the marble tile reminiscent of a death knell. A white ring formed around his mouth as his lips pressed together in anger and color suffused his usually pale cheeks. "No, don't tell me. You've been down to the docks. Again. Without Mrs. Beasley to accompany you." His nose wrinkled. "I can smell you from here."

Caralyn said nothing as he drew closer and stood within arm's reach. He towered over her, as did most people, and glared at her. Her gaze rose to his face—his angry face—and she drew in a deep breath. It wouldn't be unexpected for him to reach out and slap her. She'd seen him do it to his own children. She'd also seen the fear in their eyes and wondered what had happened to the carefree young man she had once idolized.

"When I said you could stay with me, I expected you to obey the rules of this house, not traipse all over Charleston in the middle of the night." His brows drew into a frown and his breath wheezed in and out of his lungs. "I am responsible for your safety, though God knows it's a thankless, impossible task."

Caralyn ignored his words and pasted a smile on her face. "Not to worry, brother dear. My plans have changed and you will no longer be responsible for my protection. I'm leaving."

"Where are you going?"

"Home." Just to be flippant, she added, "To plan my wedding."

His expression changed and his features softened. The white ring of anger around his mouth disappeared, as did the glare in his icy blue eyes. He looked once more like the brother she adored.

"Good. It's about time you came to your senses. I agree with Father. You are twenty-four years old. You should be married." He pointed a finger at her and shook it in her face. "Perhaps a husband and children can turn you into a proper lady, not the hoyden you've become. Father spoiled you overmuch, I think, letting you run around in boy's trousers and sail with him on the *Lady Elizabeth*. Marriage will change that."

His barbed words stung and tears blurred her vision. Caralyn swallowed against the growing lump in her throat and fought back the only way she knew how—with sharp words.

"Is that what happened to you?" She drew herself up to her full height of five foot one. Shoulders back, chin lifted, she returned his unrelenting glare. "Marriage changed you from the sweet, funny boy who used to lift me up on his shoulders to the cruel, tired, unhappy man I see before me."

Charles opened his mouth but she interrupted him before he could utter a word, even as redness crept up his face, in spite of his rigid stance and balled fists.

"If this is what marriage is—" She paused and struggled for composure. "Then I don't want any part of it, Charles. Your poor wife. I feel sorry for Vanessa. All she does is try to please you and what does she get for her trouble? You, snapping at her. I've seen you make her cry with just a look."

She continued, giving voice to the opinions she had formed over the past few years. "You're the same with your children. They, too, do everything in their power to make you happy and they get the same treatment from you. When was the last time you told Vanessa you loved her? When was the last time you spent the day with your sons? Or hugged your daughters?"

"How dare you criticize me when you have no idea what my life is like," Charles bellowed. His voice shook the rafters and echoed down the long hallway. Even the crystal chandelier overhead tinkled with the vibration.

"I'll dare a whole lot more, brother dear." With angry tears blurring her vision, she stood up to him. "At one time, you were in love with Vanessa. What happened? Is it too hard to be a kind, gentle husband? Are the obligations of fatherhood too much for you?" She reached out and laid her hand on his arm. His muscles were tense beneath her fingertips. "The first year you were married, I saw such happiness, but now, I see resentment and anger. I don't want that to happen to me."

Her fingers smoothed the muscle throbbing in his cheek and her voice softened. "I want a marriage like Mama and Papa's. I want to still be in love after thirty years. Don't you want the same?" She removed her hand from his face and turned, striding purposefully down the hallway, hopefully leaving her brother with much to consider.

She stopped on the first landing and concentrated on breathing. One obstacle managed. Now all she had to do was make it to her room without running into Mrs. Beasley, the very suitable companion her brother had hired the day after she'd arrived in Charleston alone, having traveled from St. Lucia by herself.

Since then, Caralyn had found imaginative ways to become separated from the prim widow who insisted on accompanying her everywhere she went and imparting lessons on how to be a proper lady.

No lights appeared beneath Mrs. Beasley's door. Caralyn forced herself to tiptoe past, just in case the woman was lying in wait as she had done on other occasions.

Smudge met Caralyn at the door to her room on the third floor, her meow of welcome making her long whiskers twitch. The cat circled then rubbed her body against the hem of her gown. Caralyn laid her valise on the small table beside the door, picked up the cat, and cuddled her next to her chest. She smoothed her chin along the feline's soft fur as her fingers scratched the patch of white between the black ears. Smudge's eyes closed as she purred.

"Are you ready for a great adventure, Smudge?" The cat purred louder and moved her head so Caralyn could rub the perfect spot.

As she scratched the cat's head, she looked around her room and frowned. Her nieces and nephews had been in here, she knew. And they'd left a mess.

The jar of cream she used on her hands was left open. Gobs of the thick salve coated the handles of her brush and comb, and face powder was sprinkled on every available surface of the vanity. Greasy little fingerprints smudged the mirror. Hair ribbons created a colorful rainbow on the floor amid her shiny hairpins.

The armoire doors gaped open to reveal—nothing. Her gowns were scattered on chairs, on the bed, on the floor. One shoe peeked out from beneath the bed, the other unseen.

The cat leapt from her arms and jumped on the bed to stretch out alongside a bump under the quilt, and blink her big yellow eyes.

Caralyn grinned. She couldn't help it. One of the culprits was still here. Four-year-old Elizabeth, named for Caralyn's mother, snuggled beneath the coverlet, her light brown curls spread out on the pillow. She wore one of Caralyn's nightgowns, its frilly lace collar hiding her slim neck, and clutched a bright yellow ribbon in one hand. White powder dusted her cheeks and forehead. She slept as only the young did—full of peace, exhausted from a day of chasing her older siblings and getting into mischief. Her long eyelashes fluttered on her cheek while she sucked her thumb.

Caralyn sighed as she arranged the quilt around the child's shoulders and wiped some of the powder from her face. "Betsy" murmured around her thumb and burrowed deeper into the bed, but did not awaken.

Out of all her nieces and nephews, Betsy was her favorite, the one who reminded her of herself the most. She would miss this girl.

"Sleep, my angel." Caralyn kissed Betsy's forehead then removed the ribbon from her hand. "Tomorrow brings another grand adventure."

She straightened and adjusted the blanket once more, almost hiding the girl's angelic face. Caralyn grinned. "If you're an angel, we must do something about those horns." She resisted the urge to chuckle as she set about cleaning the mischief her nieces and nephews had created in her room.

Finished, she washed her face, slipped into a nightgown, and then rubbed cream into her hands. As she slid beneath the covers, Caralyn cuddled up to her niece and closed her eyes, but sleep eluded her for a long time.

The ugly scene where her father broke his promise to her and announced that she would be married replayed in her mind. Her reaction had been less than mature; it embarrassed her now. She had cried and begged to be released from the agreement he'd made, and when he denied her, she had run to her room, locking herself in, refusing to speak with him, even after he mentioned through her closed door that she might be able to buy her freedom. To this day, she could only remember that she was to marry the son of the Earl of Winterbourne and where she was to go in London to marry him.

Her throat constricted and tears stung her eyes. She regretted making her mother worry, but she'd been so angry, felt so betrayed that she hadn't cared when she'd left a note and then boarded the first ship for America she could find.

Despite her father's now broken promise that she could marry a man she loved, despite everything, she did not regret the adventure about to begin. Excitement churned through her veins. When she did finally fall asleep, it was to dream of a fortune in treasure and the handsome man who would help her find it.

Chapter 3

Thaddeus "Porkchop" Bing snuck out of the Salty Dog and scurried through Charleston as fast as his bowed legs and over-large breeches would carry him. Filled with excitement, he could hardly contain himself and grinned like the idiot his crewmates often accused him of being.

Captain Entwhistle would be very pleased by the news he couldn't wait to impart. He rubbed his hands together then reached down to pull up his trousers, which threatened to puddle around his ankles. Not for the first time this night, he admonished himself for not having the foresight to wear a belt, or at least a length of rope to keep his pants up.

The *Explorer* waited, not in Charleston Harbor proper, but a short distance away by rowboat. This positioning was no accident as Captain Entwhistle preferred to keep his whereabouts unknown until he chose differently.

With a sigh, Porkchop climbed into the small dinghy, picked up the oars, and began to row. In no time at all, his breath came in short gasps and his muscles trembled with exertion, but he didn't pause until he reached his destination and the rowboat bumped against the side of the ship.

"Who goes there? Announce yerself!" a surly voice yelled from the deck.

"Shut yer rotten mouth, ye scurvy scum," Porkchop mumbled under his breath. "It's me, Porkchop," he called.

He maneuvered the boat toward the rope ladder hanging over the side of the two-masted schooner then climbed aboard. His shipmate didn't offer a hand in assistance, but Porkchop didn't mind. He wouldn't have offered a hand either. That was just the way of it aboard the *Explorer*. More scavengers than treasure hunters, each man on this ship looked out for himself and himself only. Loyalty belonged to one man—Wynton Entwhistle, the man who kept gold in their pockets, though not as much as Captain Trey kept in those of his men.

"Is the captain here?"

"Where ye think he be?" Johnny Campbell snarled and lowered the lantern in his hand. "Buggerin' idjit, 'course he's aboard."

Porkchop ignored the nasty jibe and stomped across the deck. He stopped long enough to tug at his trousers then knocked on the captain's door.

"Yes?"

As Porkchop swung the door open, the quill in Captain Entwhistle's hand paused in mid-air over the map spread out on the desk. Covered in tiny tick marks, the edges of the parchment curled and threatened to roll into one long tube. The captain looked up but did not rise from his chair. His eyes narrowed and his face took on a reddish hue, which Porkchop could see quite clearly in the glow of candlelight.

Porkchop swallowed hard and after a moment's hesitation, announced, "He's goin' after Izzy's Fortune." He kept one hand on the doorknob, the other held up his trousers. "Jes' like ye said, Cap'n."

"When does he leave?"

"Four days." Porkchop glanced around the captain's cabin and compared his own meager living quarters with the opulence before him. Teak paneled the walls here, and the bunk contained a real feather mattress, while he slept in a hammock strung between the ship's side and a large wooden column, his worldly possessions stowed in a locked box below his makeshift bed. Jealousy surged within him, but only for a moment.

If nothing else, Porkchop knew his limitations. He knew he wasn't smart or savvy enough to command his own ship, although he often dreamed of such. There wasn't a man alive who would take orders from Captain Porkchop. He swallowed his disappointment and said, "Least-wise, that's what I heard 'im tell his man."

The captain grinned but Porkchop wished he hadn't. It wasn't a good smile and only meant one thing. He and his shipmates would get no rest, and they surely deserved a rest after the weeks they'd spent following the *Adventurer* and Captain Trey. Even in Porkchop's limited experience, he knew the *Explorer* could never match the *Adventurer's* speed. To add to their misfortune, they hadn't been able to outrun the sudden storm that almost capsized the ship. By the time they'd caught up, Captain Trey had already claimed the treasure as his own, much to Captain Entwhistle's fury.

Porkchop and the rest of the crew had no choice but to watch as the booty was loaded onto the other ship while Entwhistle cursed Captain Trey's luck. At the time, he had been afraid the captain would order them to board the *Adventurer* and take the treasure for themselves.

Entwhistle stood and began to pace the confines of his cabin, the plume of the quill fluttering in the breeze of his own creation. "Did you happen to hear the course they're setting?"

"No, sir."

"No matter. We'll be waiting for them when they leave port." He stopped pacing long enough to look out the small window. "Gather the crew. I want everyone back on board before dawn."

"Aye, Cap'n." Porkchop backed out of the room and closed the door. He heard the snick of the lock slip into place, tugged at the waistband of his trousers, and quickly obeyed the captain's orders. He knew the penalty awaiting him if he did not. Captain Entwhistle was not above keelhauling a man if his orders were not carried out with the utmost speed.

As he climbed down the rope ladder, he realized he'd forgotten to impart the most important news—Captain Trey's impending marriage. He shook his head, debated with himself, and decided that tomorrow morning would be soon enough to tell Captain Entwhistle.

Chapter 4

Tristan stood at the window, hands clasped behind his back, and breathed in the salt air.

"What have you done, Father?" He spoke the words aloud, knowing there would be no answer. His jaw clenched as resentment toward his father and his still unnamed bride—Gilchrist had left town before he could ascertain that information—made his stomach bubble with bitterness.

He exhaled his pent-up breath as he studied the sunlight shimmering on the water and forced himself to relax. His jaw unclenched. The burning in his stomach eased.

Unbidden, the image of Miss McCreigh popped into his mind and made the corners of his mouth twitch. Miss McCreigh's eyes sparkled like the rays of the sun on the rippling ocean. And her smile—well, that could melt even the coldest man's heart.

From the moment he met the lovely Miss McCreigh, he couldn't get her out of his mind. The battle he waged within himself had no end—promised to one but attracted to another. The thought of her made him as giddy as a young boy, and yet he knew he shouldn't be thinking of her in such a way, even though she *did* have marvelous eyes, and they *did* twinkle brighter than the stars in a black velvet night.

He shook his head, chuckled with the irony of the situation, and moved toward his desk. *I am most decidedly mad and belong in Bedlam!*

Still, he couldn't help but be impressed by Miss McCreigh. She certainly knew how to stock a ship for a journey. All morning, a steady stream of supplies had arrived. Angus MacTavish shouted orders and the men rushed to obey as no one wanted to rile

Mac's ire. The quartermaster had a legendary temper. His tongue-lashings had scarred men for life.

Kegs of water, barrels of flour and oats filled the hold, enough for a good, long journey, although Tristan did wonder how many men Miss McCreigh thought she'd be feeding and if she didn't know they'd be putting into port often.

A small ship by most standards, the *Adventurer* was built for speed and her crew numbered only twenty-four, not including his officers or Jemmy.

Chickens squawked and if he wasn't mistaken, he thought he heard the plaintive bleating of a goat. His grin widened. They'd have fresh milk. Bright yellow bananas, scarlet apples, and other colorful fruit filled several wooden boxes and kept company beside sacks of potatoes and rice. Coffee beans and small tins of tea had been packed in the galley. Crates of wine and other spirits were delivered, too, packed in such a way as to survive even the worst of storms. Beef and ham, smoked and packed in finely ground charcoal, rested beneath sausage links suspended from hooks in the ceiling.

No detail went unnoticed. She'd even thought of cords of wood for the stove in the galley and a small, brass hipbath.

Though he hadn't seen her since the night he'd found her on his ship, he'd heard from her in the form of short notes written in her beautiful penmanship, all scented with her unique perfume. Her maps had been delivered the day after they'd met and he'd studied them—to his utter frustration. He compared hers to his, making tick marks on the islands already searched, but no matter how long he stared at said maps, he couldn't find the Island of the Sleeping Man. It simply did not exist.

Izzy's Fortune. If the island didn't exist, then perhaps the treasure didn't either. And yet, he still believed. He'd seen the jewel encrusted goblet, hadn't he?

Am I just on a fool's mission to avoid the inevitable? Should I sail home to England and at least get to know my future wife before we're expected to fall into bed and produce an heir?

He shook his head to clear his thoughts and focused his attention on the maps spread out on his desk. The shouts from the men continued, the creaking of ropes and pulleys in need of lubrication as the supplies were lowered below deck sounded loud even in his cabin with the door closed.

He drew his finger across the island of Tortuga, Morgan's base of operations for many years as well as a safe haven for other pirates who roamed the Caribbean. Was it possible Morgan knew what Alexander Pembrook had done and retaken the treasure?

Yes, anything was possible. And who knew what had happened over the past one hundred and sixty years. Time and Mother Nature were fickle mistresses. Earthquakes, fires, and hurricanes changed the landscape. Entire towns, or a grand portion of them, tumbled into the sea, which had been Port Royal's fate in 1693, and although rebuilt, some things were lost forever.

And yet, anticipation swept over Tristan. His pulse quickened. Every nerve in his body quivered with excitement. He couldn't wait to begin this adventure. Even the knowledge that this was his last one before he settled into married life couldn't put a damper on his growing enthusiasm.

The shouting of the men changed in tone, then all sounds ceased. An eerie silence settled around him. He heard nothing, not even the creaking of the ropes. With a sigh, Tristan rolled up all the maps in one long, thick tube, placed them in a cabinet above the desk, and smothered a curse when he stubbed his toe on Caralyn's trunk resting by the door.

On deck, the men, almost every single one of them, stood in a circle. The faces he could see were a mixture of awe, suspicion, confusion, and derision. They mumbled among themselves, whispered comments and opinions Tristan couldn't quite hear.

Graham Alcott and the ship's physician, Brady Trevelyan, uninvolved in the disturbance, leaned against the brass railing on the opposite side of the deck. Tristan caught Graham's eye, but the man only grinned, held up his hands in mock surrender, and shook his head. Tristan would get no help from that quarter.

"What is all this?" Irritated, stubbed toe throbbing inside his boot, Tristan stalked across the deck, pushed aside several crewmembers, and entered the circle. And then he knew what had caused the sudden, deafening silence. Irritation quickly turned to amusement and his heart lightened in his chest.

More beautiful than he remembered, Caralyn McCreigh stood as tall as her petite stature would allow, shoulders back. Her eyes sparkled and her cheeks flushed as she turned in a slow circle and stared each man down. A light breeze fluttered the tendrils of sun-kissed brown hair around her face. "I have permission to board this ship." Her voice rang out clear as a bell and sharp as diamonds as her gaze fell upon him. "Tell them."

This may well prove to be the grandest adventure. The thought fluttered through Tristan's mind and made him more anxious to begin their journey.

He grinned and swallowed a sudden burst of laughter. If the crew thought they could intimidate her, they'd be sadly mistaken. One look at Caralyn's flashing eyes should tell them she would not be bullied. Not even by MacTavish, the bandy-legged Scotsman, who stood almost toe-to-toe with her, his bushy mustache a white slash in the middle of his red face.

Tristan cleared his throat, reached out, and took her hand, drawing her closer to him. Heat sizzled up his arm and his heart skipped a beat only to resume with a painful thud. "May I present Miss Caralyn McCreigh, our benefactor for this treasure hunt?" He smiled at her then noticed the metal cage in her grip. "And who is this?"

Caralyn held up the cage. "This is Smudge, my mouser. I cannot abide mice or other vermin aboard ship." The cat blinked her huge, yellow eyes then stretched one paw from between the metal bars and showed everyone her long, menacing claws. The tight circle of men loosened, each one backing up a step or two. Tristan stared at the cat and smothered a groan. Though he didn't share them, he understood his men's superstitions. The cat might be more trouble than having a woman on board, and yet the sight of the feline didn't dampen his excitement.

"Why don't you wait for me in my cabin?"

"Of course." Caralyn gave a slight nod, then head held high, skirts swishing around her, she swept past the men and disappeared through the doorway beneath the quarterdeck. As soon as she was gone, the circle tightened again, leaving Tristan in the middle this time.

He turned slowly and faced each one of his crew until he came face to face with MacTavish. "Is there a problem?"

The Scotsman returned his stare without flinching. His face reddened even more and his body stiffened, prepared for confrontation. Though shorter than the rest of his crewmates, the man's barrel-chest and thick, muscular arms made him appear larger. "We canna sail with a woman aboard ship." MacTavish's mustache twitched as he said the words in his heavy Scottish brogue. "'Tis bad luck, as ye well know."

Tristan eyed the quartermaster and forced his clenched fists to relax. He understood. He truly did. The men had their beliefs. However, the *Adventurer* was *his* ship. *He* captained her. If he decided to allow a woman on board, then so be it. "I'm sorry you all feel this way. Miss McCreigh has great knowledge of Izzy's Fortune and she has provided us with the provisions you loaded into the hold today. Perhaps you can overcome your superstitions in light of that."

MacTavish rocked on his heels and crossed his arms over his wide chest. As the unofficial spokesman for the group, he had a lot to consider. After a moment, he held up one finger and turned to the rest of the crew.

Tristan left the circle and leaned against the ship's brass railing as MacTavish spoke with the men. After a series of soft-spoken questions and many hand gestures, the quartermaster joined him at the rail. "The woman we can abide, I suppose, but that … that black demon . . ." He shuddered. "A black cat, Cap'n, is worse than a woman on ship. The men refuse."

Tristan's jaw clenched. The beat of his heart elevated and pulsed in his neck. He rubbed the back of his neck to relieve the building tension. "That's their decision. They're more than welcome to leave now." He took a deep breath to still his anger and exhaled slowly. "I am captain of this ship. Miss McCreigh is my guest … as is her cat."

The Scotsman's face drained of color. "But, Cap'n—"

Tristan cut him off, his words clipped, his voice commanding. "Make the decision, Mac. We set sail in less than thirty minutes. I suggest you make preparations."

He turned on his heel and noticed Jemmy for the first time. The boy clung to a rope swinging from the main mast, but his eyes were on the doorway where Caralyn had disappeared. Tristan tried not to smile. Jemmy seemed truly and utterly smitten with their guest, if he were to judge by the wide eyes, toothy grin, and long sigh that escaped the lad.

All of eight, bearing the silky blond hair and cornflower blue eyes of his mother, Jemmy faced him, saluted and as agile as a monkey, climbed higher on the rope. A blend of pride and fear overwhelmed Tristan and his heart swelled with love for the boy he'd adopted. He couldn't resist the urge to call out a warning. "Be careful, Jemmy."

The boy saluted once more and disappeared into the crow's nest.

Tristan traversed the short corridor that separated his cabin from his officer's quarters and entered his room to find Caralyn unpacking her trunk and hanging day dresses in the built-in cabinet. Smudge purred from her perch amid the pile of clothes—his clothes—on the bunk. The cat's huge, pale yellow eyes opened and closed slowly, almost hypnotically before she stretched out a paw and began to bathe herself.

He cleared his throat.

Caralyn gave a short, startled squeak then whirled around to face him, eyes wide and beguiling. She held a frilly petticoat up to her chest. "I beg your pardon. I would appreciate it if you would knock before entering my cabin."

More amused than angry, although he should have been, Tristan leaned against the doorjamb and grinned as he twisted his ring around his finger. "I see you've made yourself at home."

"Yes." She shook the wrinkles from the pristine petticoat in her hand as her eyes darted around the rich mahogany-paneled cabin. "I believe I shall be quite comfortable."

His gaze went from her and the lace-trimmed undergarment in her hand to the pile of silk stockings and frilly drawers on the chair. "You should be comfortable, milady. This is, after all, the captain's cabin. My cabin, to be more specific." His smile grew as wicked thoughts swept through his brain and a surge of desire heated his blood. "Were you planning on spending the voyage with me?"

A blush crept up her neck and stained her face. Her eyes widened even more and turned a slightly darker blue. Her mouth opened and closed several times before she whispered, "But my trunk was here. I thought . . ."

Those enticing thoughts careened through his brain faster and faster. To spend time with a beautiful woman—this woman—making love couldn't have appealed to him more. He imagined how silky her skin would feel beneath his fingers, how her face would flush as he brought her to climax time after time. His body reacted as blood flowed from his brain to his groin. The cabin became too warm, too stifling, as the evidence of his arousal pressed painfully against his trousers. "You're more than welcome to stay."

Caralyn stood motionless. Energy radiated from her in heated waves. The blush that stained her face and neck darkened as she stared at him with huge, glittering eyes.

As soon as he said the words and saw her reaction, he wished he could take them back. *What the hell am I thinking? She's a lady and I'm betrothed to another.* And yet, he couldn't stop the thoughts once they'd taken root. For an insane moment, he wanted to grab the petticoat from her hand and fling her across the bed, clothes piled high or not, and taste, once more, the sweetness of her mouth, feel the softness of her body beneath his.

Before he could apologize, a chorus of voices rose from the deck.

"Now what?"

The issue of who would take the captain's cabin would have to wait while he unraveled whatever new drama unfolded on deck. "Stay here." He slammed the door as he left his quarters; however, the door did not remain closed. It swung open almost as fast. The breeze ruffled his hair.

Caralyn grabbed his arm, her fingers hot where they touched his skin. Her voice trembled as she said, "We are equal partners in this venture."

Her boldness didn't surprise him. After all, she'd been brash enough and confident enough to wait for him on his ship in the middle of the night and propose this adventure. He liked women who were self-assured and forthright, and the impulse to kiss her and find out if her daring extended further overwhelmed him, but the noise from the deck grew louder as his men hurled belligerent responses to whoever had them in such a state. Above it all, he heard one woman's strident voice, demanding to see the captain.

"Sweet Mother, what is that?"

Mouth open in an O, her face as pale as the sails which powered his ship, Caralyn stared at him. A small sound escaped her as her body stiffened, and if he wasn't mistaken, tears glimmered in her wide eyes. Her mouth closed with an audible snap of her teeth and her chin trembled. The urge to console her—for what he didn't know—surged to the forefront and he took a step toward her, his arms open, ready to draw her into the comfort of his embrace, and yet, he couldn't allow himself to touch her, hold her. If he did, he might not be able to let go.

He turned on his heel and hurried down the short hallway toward the deck.

The most amazing scene met Tristan as he stepped through the doorway and stopped short. His men stood in a half circle while the feisty woman they faced held them at bay with the sturdy umbrella she brandished like a sword. Tendrils of vibrant chestnut hair poked out from the straw hat upon her head. Her stance as a fencer seemed at odds with the somberness of her black dress, though he could see touches of white lace at the cuffs of her sleeves and collar.

As with many women, Tristan couldn't hazard a guess regarding her age. Face unlined and smooth, except for the small wrinkles created by her frown, she appeared older than Caralyn, but not by much. A few years, perhaps, but certainly no more than ten. "I'll break this over someone's head if you don't move back and let me board." A jab of the umbrella punctuated every one of her clipped words.

As a group, the men backed up another step.

Caralyn, right behind him, didn't stop when he did. Instead, her momentum pushed him further out onto the deck, her soft body pressed to his. For a moment, Tristan lost his balance. Though his steps were as sure-footed as always, his mind and body betrayed him. The warmth of her pressed against his back added to the improper thoughts he'd had earlier and desire sizzled through his veins. He became hot and cold at the same time, his heart pounded in his chest as if he'd run miles, and he wished she weren't wearing her bright yellow gown so he could revel in the heat of her naked body.

Tristan shook his head and took a deep breath to steady his wandering thoughts. "Who is that woman?"

Voice choked with what he assumed were repressed tears, she said into his back, "My companion, Mrs. Temperance Beasley." She whispered the words so low, he had a hard time hearing them, but the inflection in Caralyn's tone conveyed her disappointment to perfection. He glanced at the woman on deck and then turned so he could see the woman hiding behind him. An involuntary groan escaped him. One woman on a ship was hard enough for his crew to accept, but two?

"I demand to see the captain." Mrs. Beasley's voice became more shrill and reminded Tristan of a fishwife hawking her wares.

Before he could make a move, amazement and wonder made Tristan purse his lips in an attempt not to grin as Brady Trevelyan adjusted his silver brocade vest, stepped away from the railing, and pushed his way through the men surrounding the woman. The most reserved and shy of the crew, Brady seldom spoke to women—let alone strange women—so it surprised Tristan the physician would act so out of character.

"Are you the captain?"

"No, ma'am. I'm the ship's doctor." Without effort and with his usually calm demeanor, he removed the umbrella from her grip then grabbed her hand as he bowed and kissed her gloved knuckles. "Brady Trevelyan. And you are?"

"Temperance Beasley."

"A pleasure, Miss Beasley." Once again, he kissed her hand. "How may I be of service?"

"My charge is aboard this ship. I must see her immediately," she huffed as she pulled her hand away from him. Her body was stiff, yet her eyes widened behind the lenses of her glasses, and the grim line of her mouth relaxed a little. Tristan couldn't be certain, but he thought he saw the hint of a smile.

"Of course." Brady said something else, words Tristan couldn't hear, before he turned and faced the crew. "Get back to work."

Trained to obey the commands of a senior officer, the crew dispersed and went about their duties although several of the men cast suspicious glances in the doctor's direction.

Tristan watched it all with something akin to awe. He'd never seen Brady behave this way. Ever. Over the many years they sailed together, he'd come to know Brady, knew the man had been deeply in love with his wife and loved her still, despite her passing almost a decade ago. Until this day, this moment, the doctor hadn't looked at another woman the way he now gazed at Mrs. Beasley.

With a slow shake of his head, Tristan glanced at Graham, who remained against the rail. The navigator cocked an eyebrow and gave him a crooked grin before he saluted and jogged up the stairs to the quarterdeck to take the wheel.

Hand tucked into the crook of his arm, Dr. Trevelyan escorted Mrs. Beasley across the deck. "Captain, I believe this young woman would like a word with you and Miss McCreigh."

Tristan bowed but didn't attempt to grasp her hand and bestow a kiss upon her knuckles as Brady had. He didn't say a word as he took one step to the side.

Caralyn didn't move a muscle. She stared at her shoes, her small hands clenched into fists at her sides, as if preparing for an oncoming battle.

"Miss McCreigh, I am appalled and outraged by your behavior. Look at me when I'm speaking to you," Mrs. Beasley demanded.

When Caralyn glanced up, the woman wagged a finger in her face. "What in the world were you thinking? Did you think I didn't know what you were planning? Did you think you could leave me behind to face your brother's wrath? I think not. We are leaving this ship immediately and boarding the next ship bound for England." Mrs. Beasley grabbed Caralyn's arm and tried to pull her along but Caralyn was having none of it. She twisted her arm free and remained rooted to the spot.

Tristan stared at Mrs. Beasley then at Caralyn and wondered where Caralyn's earlier bravado had disappeared to, but he didn't have to wonder for long.

Right before his eyes, she straightened to her full height and threw her shoulders back. Her eyes narrowed and her mouth tightened into a grim line. In a strong voice, she said, "I'm not leaving. And you have no right to speak to me in such a fashion. You, Mrs. Beasley, are my companion, paid for by my brother—"

"To keep you out of trouble."

Caralyn winced but continued as if she hadn't been interrupted. "Not my mother nor my father nor my keeper. I have struck a deal with Captain Trey and I intend to accompany him on his search for Izzy's Fortune." Her voice softened and she reached for Mrs. Beasley's hand. "Please understand, Mrs.—Temperance. This is my last chance."

While the two women faced each other in hostile silence, the crew unfurled the sails, untied the thick ropes, which held the ship tight against the quay and hoisted the anchor. Several of them used long poles to push the *Adventurer* away from the dock. The sails billowed and snapped as they stretched with the wind that filled them. The clipper rocked beneath their feet.

"Welcome aboard the *Adventurer*, Mrs. Beasley." Tristan grinned. "I hope you have a pleasant journey."

"What?" The woman glared at him, her dark brown eyes narrowed.

"We're under way, ma'am." Dr. Trevelyan drew her attention to Charleston slipping away.

Mrs. Beasley stomped her foot, folded her arms across her chest and pinned Tristan with a glare. "But ... but I have no baggage. I . . ." She drew a deep breath. "I demand you turn around or whatever it is you do and take me back."

Though her stare might frighten others, it failed to intimidate him at all. Tristan had faced more threatening foes, his father included. He glanced at Caralyn. Hope lit her eyes to an even bluer blue. Although he could take both women back to Charleston, the simple fact remained he didn't want to, and as captain, he made the decisions. Besides, perhaps Caralyn would bring him luck and they'd find the treasure. "I'm afraid I can't do that, ma'am. Miss McCreigh mentioned this is her last chance. 'Tis mine as well."

Mrs. Beasley huffed and turned her attention to Caralyn. "Well, you've gotten your way once again, Miss McCreigh, but your brother will hear of your antics as soon as possible. I'm certain he won't be happy."

Caralyn didn't respond. She didn't even spare a glance at her companion. Her eyes, brilliant blue and shiny with tears, remained on him. She mouthed the words *thank you*. Tristan's heart swelled.

"And you, young man, I'll be watching you. I know your kind." Her eyes narrowed again as she grabbed Caralyn by the shoulders and started to push her toward the doorway beneath the quarterdeck. "As long as I am on this ship and Miss McCreigh is under my protection, you will keep your distance." She turned to face him and blinked behind the lenses of her glasses. "We may be on a ship filled with men, but the proprieties will be observed at all times. Do I make myself clear?"

Tristan nodded. "Yes, ma'am." He winked at Caralyn, grin still in place. "The question of who should have the captain's cabin has been settled. You and Mrs. Beasley shall take it for the duration of our journey. Now, if you'll excuse me, I believe I have a ship to guide and a treasure to find."

Chapter 5

Calloused hands tight on the thick rope, spyglass tucked safely in his sash, Porkchop scrambled from his perch in the crow's nest. "Cap'n Entwhistle," he called out long before his feet touched the deck. In his haste, he tripped over a coil of rope and sprawled on his stomach. The loud guffaws from the rest of the crew cut into him like a whip crack against his back. Face hot, Porkchop cussed his shipmates beneath his breath, hauled himself to his feet with as much dignity as he could scrape together, and glared at Johnnie Campbell and Toothless Will. Laugh all they want, he had important information for the captain.

With one last tug on the waistband of his trousers, he knocked on the door and swung it open before he received any response.

Captain Entwhistle paused in the process of lighting his pipe. The flame on the end of the long, slender stick he used died in a puff of smoke. Porkchop found himself on the receiving end of an ugly, hateful stare. Fear, lightening fast and sharp as the edge of a cutlass, made his mouth dry and his hands shake.

Porkchop swallowed hard and tried with all his might to quell the rapid beating of his heart, the quaking of his knees. The uncomfortable knowledge Captain Entwhistle could kill him without the slightest bit of remorse for disturbing him raced through his mind. He slid his knit cap from his head and bowed at the waist. "Beggin' yer pardon, Cap'n. The *Adventurer* be leavin' port." The words left Porkchop's mouth in a rush. "She's got women on board."

Captain Entwhistle gave a slow nod. The knowing smile, which split his lips, appeared worse to Porkchop than the deadly glow in his eyes of only a moment before.

"Ah, very good." Entwhistle placed his pipe in the brass tray on the desk and rose to his full height of six foot four, his tall lanky frame filling the small confines of the cabin. Without another word, the captain swept past him. Porkchop let a sigh of relief escape and followed the captain through the doorway onto the deck.

"Step lively, men. The chase begins."

• • •

Caralyn hung the last day dress in the cabinet, closed the trunk, and rubbed her hands together, all beneath the heat of Temperance Beasley's angry brown eyes. The woman sat in the desk chair, body stiff, hands folded in her lap, knuckles white. The serviceable straw hat she'd worn earlier perched atop the desk. Lips pressed together, forehead furrowed, she had yet to utter a word, but Caralyn knew the silence wouldn't hold for long. A tongue-lashing the likes of which she'd never forget was in the making—she just wondered when it would take place.

"I am sorry, Mrs. Beasley." Caralyn took a deep breath and walked the few steps to stand in front of her chaperone. Remorse for her actions weighed heavily, but the idea of an arranged marriage sat like lead in her belly.

The woman raised her head. The iciness in her glare made Caralyn take a step back. She shivered but not with cold. Fear and uncertainty made gooseflesh break out on her arms, and she rubbed her skin briskly to get rid of the bumps. "It was never my intention you should be stranded on this ship with me, but you must understand. This is my last chance for true happiness."

A knock on the door interrupted her apology or anything Mrs. Beasley might have said. With a sigh, Caralyn permitted entry.

Dr. Trevelyan's muscular frame filled the doorway. His glance went from her to Mrs. Beasley, and a smile graced his features to light up his whole face. Light brown eyes sparkled with undisguised pleasure as he stepped into the room. He approached

Mrs. Beasley without another glance in Caralyn's direction and offered his hand. "Your presence is requested on the quarterdeck."

Caralyn bit her lip to hide her grin. Faced with such courteous behavior, Mrs. Beasley didn't quite know what to do, as evidenced by the confusion flickering in her eyes and the tenuous smile tilting the corners of her mouth. She blinked, several times, behind the lenses of her glasses. With a slight nod of her head, she gave her hand to him and allowed him to escort her from the cabin.

Almost as an afterthought, Dr. Trevelyan said over his shoulder, "Captain Trey would like you to bring the journal, Miss."

Quick to obey, Caralyn dug the journal from the bottom of the small valise next to the desk, removed the protective oilcloth and followed them out to the deck. Before she climbed the stairs to the quarterdeck, she paused at the rail and gazed into the distance. The sight astounded her, as always.

The Atlantic Ocean spread before her in undulating patterns of blues, greens, and white-crested waves as far as the eye could see. A powerful wind filled the sails and caused her hair to escape the pins holding the heavy locks in place. In moments, the silky tresses whipped around her face. As Caralyn pushed the errant locks behind her ears, she inhaled and caught the fresh scent of salt water. Pure joy made her smile widen, made her want to giggle and hug herself at the same time.

She belonged on the water. Nothing in the world compared to being on a ship as it cut through the waves at a smart clip. The gentle sway of the deck beneath her feet soothed her, relaxed her tense muscles. Her smile grew as her father's words rang in her ears. "You're a child of the sea, Cara. My mermaid."

She drew away from the sight and climbed the steps to the quarterdeck. The crew of the *Adventurer* stood at attention, bodies stiff, chests puffed out. Their attitudes were so different from when she'd first stepped aboard, at least on the surface.

Caralyn did catch one or two men glare at her as she made her way to Captain Trey at the wheel. Beside him, Mrs. Beasley stood with her hand tucked in the crook of Dr. Trevelyan's arm. The frigid chill of her gaze bored into Caralyn, yet the woman said not a word.

Despite the coldness of Mrs. Beasley's glare, a thrill Caralyn couldn't deny surged through her to make her stomach quiver even more. Not only was she right where she wanted to be, but the sight of Captain Trey added to her exhilaration. Long, muscular legs slightly apart, he stood tall, in full command of the power of the ship beneath him. The wind ruffled the sleeves of his loose white shirt and caressed his dark hair. He held the wheel as she imagined he'd hold a woman, his grasp light yet firm, easy and relaxed. Knowledgeable. Sensuous.

Impulsive by nature, Caralyn struggled to control the desire to run her fingers through his hair and feel its silkiness by hugging the journal closer to her chest. He turned to her and grinned. Her mouth went dry. Gooseflesh pimpled her skin as a rush of warmth infused her entire body.

"I believe a formal introduction is in order." Tristan released the wheel to a slim man whose bald head gleamed in the sunlight and took her hand. "Miss McCreigh, Mrs. Beasley, this is Mr. Wyvern."

The man nodded in greeting but his eyes never left the horizon and his hands remained steady on the wheel. "Me mates call me 'Mad Dog,' ma'am."

Amused, Caralyn couldn't help but comment, "That's an interesting nickname. Why do they call you Mad Dog?"

A blush crept up his face, his ears, and covered his entire bald head. "I'd rather not say, ma'am."

Tristan led her away and introduced her and Mrs. Beasley to the rest of the crew.

They met Aaron Willis, the cook, whose round stomach and apple cheeks gave testament to the fact that he sampled everything he prepared and enjoyed every morsel. He shook her hand with plump fingers and winked. "Call me Hash. Everyone does."

To her delight, most everyone they met had a nickname. Thomas Milliron, the ship's cooper who kept all their barrels and crates in shape, was naturally called "Coop." Jared Singleton, the carpenter, went by "Woody," and so it went. Even Doctor Trevelyan had another name. The crew called him "Stitch," which made him flush.

"Ah, Miss Cara, ye've grown into a fine young woman." A tall, lanky man grasped her hand and held it. "A far cry from the hoyden who ran around in hand-me-down trousers and insisted on climbing the rigging." He grinned and revealed white teeth beneath the heavy beard covering the bottom half of his face. Caralyn tilted her head as she studied his features. His eyes, chocolate brown, twinkled as his smile widened. His voice lowered and he winked. "I'm disappointed ye don't remember me. What did ye always want to learn?"

"Knots. I wanted to learn how to tie knots," she whispered as recognition slowly dawned and pleasure swelled within her. Socrates Callahan had sailed with her father aboard the *Lady Elizabeth* and patiently taught her how to tie knots, among other things. He hadn't changed much, though it had been a long time since she'd seen him. "Socrates?"

"One and the same." He took off his hat to reveal a wealth of fire-red hair.

"Oh, it's been too long, Socrates." Caralyn giggled and threw herself into his arms. "I haven't seen you since … since I got this scar on my forehead. Papa never forgave you for that, even though it was my fault."

"And yer father was right." He wagged a finger in the air and tilted his head as he cocked an eyebrow. "Ye had no place climbin' under the bowsprit so ye could kiss the mermaid."

Caralyn rubbed her fingers over the scar as memories assailed her. Vivid visions of clinging to the bowsprit's ropes so she could press a lucky kiss upon the *Lady Elizabeth's* figurehead flitted through her mind and caused a shiver to race up her spine. She hadn't expected a rogue wave to nearly drown her.

If not for Socrates's timely intervention, she'd have lost her life. Though in the process of his pulling her to safety, she'd nearly cracked her head open on the ship's brass railing.

Daniel McCreigh had been livid and Socrates had left the ship. A wave of sadness washed over her for her part in the man's misfortune. "Where did you go after you left the *Lady Elizabeth?*"

He shrugged but his grin remained in place. "I traveled here and there, signed on a couple different ships before I met Cap'n Trey. Been lookin' for treasure ever since."

"I see you two know each other," Captain Trey stated in normal tones, yet Caralyn heard a tinge of something else. Jealousy, perhaps? She glanced in his direction and found her suspicions justified. The captain held himself rigid, his beautiful sherry eyes narrowed as he observed his crewmember.

Socrates bowed slightly. "Miss Cara and I are old friends. I sailed with her father for many years."

"I still know how to tie knots." She squeezed his hand one more time and moved on to meet the last member of the *Adventurer's* crew.

"My second in command and navigator, Graham Alcott."

"A pleasure, dear lady." Mr. Alcott kissed her hand.

Though she'd never met the man before, she'd met many like him. Charming, good-natured, always with a smile, his eyes twinkled with merriment and humor. Those like him were fortunate to know the secret: Life is an adventure and should be lived to the fullest. He grinned as he released her hand and she knew, without a doubt, he'd never want for anything.

"Last, but not least, my son, Jeremiah." Tristan's hand squeezed the boy's shoulder. Caralyn caught the gleam of undisguised love in Tristan's eyes. The glow repeated in the boy's eyes. "We call him Jemmy, isn't that right, son?"

Taken by surprise the captain had a son, one who appeared to be about seven or eight years old, Caralyn's eyes widened and her stomach tensed. A child usually meant a spouse. She recovered quickly by holding out her hand. "Very nice to meet you, Jemmy."

Jemmy glanced at his father. After a slight nod from the man beside him, the lad extended his hand and shook, though his face turned the brightest pink, and a silly smile parted his lips. The wind ruffled his silky blond hair as well as the sleeves of the loose shirt he wore. Cornflower blue eyes twinkled—with mischief, if Caralyn wasn't mistaken.

Charmed by the young boy, she grinned. "I have a nephew your age. You must call me Cara."

Again, the boy looked to his father for reassurance.

"*Miss* Cara," Tristan corrected as his gaze met hers over Jemmy's head. He reached for the journal in her hand. "May I?" Their fingers touched and a surge of warmth tingled up her arm. Her heart pounded in her chest from the unexpected heat rushing through her limbs. She inhaled and raised her eyes to his only to exhale in a rush. Never had she met someone who exuded such raw energy, such restrained power, or had such unusual eyes and so dazzling a smile.

He held the leather-bound book high. "This is the journal of Alexander Pembrook. He sailed with Henry Morgan and took part in stealing Izzy's Fortune from the *Santa Maria*." He moved with feline grace as he paced before his men, his steps certain as his long legs ate up the distance from one side of the quarterdeck to the other. His deep, rich voice touched every nerve in Caralyn's body until everyone else on deck blurred in her vision and there was only him.

"He recorded everything, even the fact he stole Izzy's Fortune from beneath Morgan's nose." He paused for effect and eyed each of his crew in turn.

The men started whispering among themselves, the buzz of their voices becoming louder and more intense, their gestures more animated as their enthusiasm for treasure hunting intensified. The captain turned toward her and captured her in the warmth of his gaze. The world as she knew it ceased turning.

That's when Mrs. Beasley pinched her on the arm. Caralyn jumped and stifled a yelp.

"Get that dreamy look out of your eyes, girl," the woman demanded in a harsh whisper. "He is not the one for you. Might I remind you of your wedding in April?"

"I am well aware of what my future holds," Caralyn snapped and rubbed her arm. "I need no reminders of my fate."

She would have said more but her attention was drawn once more to Captain Trey as he continued to address the crew.

"According to this journal," he said as he held the book high once more, "Izzy's Fortune is buried on the Island of the Sleeping Man. Have any of you heard of this island—the name, a rumor, anything?"

The men glanced at each other, their voices raising as they all spoke at once, but no one, not a single soul, had heard of the Island of the Sleeping Man.

Disappointment rushed through Caralyn, made her stomach drop, and a sigh escape her through lips that seemed frozen into a fake smile. Sudden tears blurred her vision and a lump rose to her throat. *It was all for nothing. It doesn't exist.*

Captain Trey approached her and tilted his head. A slight smile curved his lips. "Have faith, Miss McCreigh. Just because the name doesn't sound familiar doesn't mean the island doesn't exist. I believe. Do you?"

Her breath hitched in her chest. "Yes. I believe."

His hand brushed hers when he gave her the journal. Shocked by the intense heat that singed her fingers, Caralyn jumped and dropped the book. It landed face down on the deck. The spine split and the leather cover cracked even more, tearing away from the rest of the book. Several pages came loose and scattered on the deck.

With a horrified cry, she dropped to her knees and picked up the book but not before a single sheaf of paper, caught by the wind, floated across the quarterdeck and out to sea. Several more would have taken the same course if Mrs. Beasley hadn't had the foresight to step on them to keep them in place.

Captain Trey dropped to his knees as well and retrieved the pages from beneath Mrs. Beasley's shoe. Caralyn studied his face, so close to hers. Those sherry-colored eyes bored into her and made her insides flutter.

He started to hand the papers to her then stopped and withdrew a folded piece of parchment from the pile in his hand. "Well, what have we here? This must have been hidden between the leather cover and the book itself." He unfolded and stretched the parchment across his knee. "I believe we now know what this mysterious island looks like."

The parchment contained a sketch of a small, idyllic cove, tall palm trees, and a rock formation above the cove that faintly resembled a man, flat on his back with his hands folded across his chest. His belly rose higher than his feet. It was the most beautiful thing Caralyn had ever seen. "Oh," she breathed as she took the sketch from him with shaking fingers. "The Island of the Sleeping Man. It is real!"

Tristan rose to his feet then held out his hand to help her. Caralyn slipped her fingers between his as if it were the most natural thing in the world. She clutched Alexander Pembrook's journal to her chest with her other hand and followed as he showed each man the sketch.

"Does this look familiar to anyone?"

Hector de la Vega peered at the drawing in the captain's hand. "May I?" he asked as he took the sketch and inspected it closely. His features grew serious as he looked from the drawing to Captain Trey. "I know this place, *Capitan*."

"Do you remember where?"

Caralyn held her breath and prayed.

"*Si, Capitan*. It's one of the islands surrounding my home." He released the drawing into Captain Trey's hand and sighed. "But we cannot go there. *Isla de Caja de Muertos* is haunted."

The captain scoffed. "I don't believe in ghosts," he stated, then turned to her and cocked an eyebrow. "Do you?"

Caralyn shook her head. "No, I don't."

Tristan grinned as his voice boomed over the quarterdeck. "Mr. Alcott, set a course for Puerto Rico."

Chapter 6

"Puerto Rico!" Mrs. Beasley's high-pitched wail broke the silence. Her face paled, except for the spots of color highlighting her cheeks. Caralyn thought the woman might faint.

She grabbed Caralyn's arm and pulled her away from the captain. The book almost dropped to the ground again, but Caralyn clutched it against her chest.

Mrs. Beasley lowered her voice and hissed, "Have you taken leave of your senses? This is insanity. Utter madness." Her eyes narrowed and a white ring formed around her mouth as her lips pressed together to form a thin line. "We must be in England by April twentieth. I promised your brother, who, in turn, I'm sure, promised your father." She shook her head. "All this nonsense about finding a lost treasure is just that, Miss McCreigh. Nonsense. There is no such thing as Izzy's treasure."

"Izzy's Fortune," Caralyn corrected.

If possible, Mrs. Beasley's lips clamped together tighter. Brown eyes glittered with displeasure and glared into her. Caralyn tried to take a step back, suddenly fearing the woman would strike her, but thin fingers dug into the soft flesh of her arm to hold her captive instead.

"I understand, Miss McCreigh. I was young once," Mrs. Beasley admitted in a voice sharp with agitation. "I defied my parents to run away to be with the man I loved. Look what happened to me. Widowed at twenty-eight." Her jaw jutted out. A muscle throbbed in her cheek and she pointed a finger as she continued her tirade. "Not a farthing to my name. Forced to seek employment. Dragged hither and yon at the whims of a silly girl."

"I am not silly." With a jerk, Caralyn freed herself from Mrs. Beasley's iron grip. Anger simmered within her and made her eyes burn with unshed tears. "And the treasure does exist. It must. All I'm asking for is one more chance to find it. We will be in England by the appointed time whether we find Izzy's Fortune or not. Captain Trey has given me his word."

"And you believe him?" Mrs. Beasley's scowl deepened, her body grew more rigid.

The urge to defend the captain and his honor swelled in Caralyn's chest. "Yes, I do. We have a signed contract."

"What do you suppose your future husband will say when he learns of your … ah … adventure aboard this ship with all these men?"

Caralyn's stomach knotted. She hadn't thought of that. What would he say? What would her future husband think of her if she couldn't buy herself out of the betrothal contract and was forced to go through with the marriage?

Mrs. Beasley jumped on her hesitation. "You see, you haven't thought that far ahead. You haven't even considered what will happen once he learns what you've done. He may call the marriage off." She rushed on, pausing only to draw breath. "The scandal could ruin your chances of ever finding a good match, not to mention what the shame and humiliation could do to your father and the rest of your family."

We could live down the scandal. My parents did. And yet, she couldn't stop the little seed of doubt from worming into her brain. *What if I finally find the man who will sweep me off my feet? What if I can't ever marry because of what I've done?*

Like a dog worrying a bone, Mrs. Beasley demanded more answers. Answers Caralyn couldn't give her. "What about the danger, Miss McCreigh? This venture of yours could be fraught with peril." A deep furrow formed between Mrs. Beasley's eyes as her features pulled into an even deeper frown. "Your safety could be in jeopardy. What if you should not survive this endeavor?

Have you thought of that? What will I be forced to tell your family then?"

Caralyn reached her limit of being berated. Her own parents never spoke to her this way. "You have two choices, Mrs. Beasley. I can arrange to have you leave the ship at the next port and I will purchase your passage to England or wherever you wish to go." Caralyn took a deep breath. She stood straight, shoulders back, head high, every muscle in her body quivering with anger. "Or you may accompany me and share in the profits, should there be any. You'd never have to suffer the whims of a silly girl again. But whatever you decide, I will continue this quest. With or without you."

The woman snapped her head back as if she'd been slapped. She drew in a sharp breath and her voice shook with rage. "Mark my words, Miss McCreigh. Nothing but ill can come of this adventure of yours. You, and any chance for your future happiness, will be ruined."

Confidence replaced her nervousness and Caralyn met the woman's fierce glare with one of her own. "I will live with the consequences of my actions."

Mrs. Beasley glared at her, huffed in her breath, then spun on her heel and stomped away. Loud and heavy on the wooden planks, her footsteps conveyed her anger and frustration. She stopped at the rail in the same spot where Caralyn had paused earlier and stood looking out to sea, her body stiff, her hands gripping the polished brass.

"She isn't very happy."

Caralyn turned and came face to face—or rather, face to broad, muscular chest—with Captain Trey. A sprinkling of dark hair peeked from the open collar of his shirt. Her eyes widened, her pulse rate quickened. Mesmerized by the sight, she could only stare. She tore her gaze away, and glanced up to meet his brilliant, warm eyes. They twinkled with humor and something else. Perhaps regret for Mrs. Beasley's situation?

Her mouth suddenly dry, she licked her lips. "No, she is not and I cannot say I blame her. She did not ask for the circumstances she finds herself in. It is my fault she's on this ship at all."

"Is there something I can do?"

Caralyn shook her head and swallowed the lump that had risen to her throat. "She would like it if we could turn around and go back to Charleston. Other than that, I do not believe there is anything any of us can do."

"Perhaps there is." He gestured to Dr. Trevelyan. He and Mrs. Beasley stood at the rail together, deep in conversation. Mrs. Beasley lost some of the tension in her rigid stance and relaxed when she smiled at the doctor. "Give her some time, Miss McCreigh. She'll come around."

Caralyn shook her head. "Mrs. Beasley isn't one to forgive and forget so easily." She knew the truth of her words as her companion and the doctor strolled toward the mess hall and galley at the other end of the ship. She still smarted from Mrs. Beasley's past reprimands. "She has a way of calculating my misdeeds and reminding me of them all the time."

"I'm certain, with the good doctor's help, Mrs. Beasley will forget how she came to be aboard the *Adventurer*. Once she catches the excitement of searching for treasure, she'll soon forgive you as well." He grinned as he touched the journal clutched in her arm. "Shall we see if we can repair Mr. Pembrook's journal?"

He led her in the same direction the doctor and Mrs. Beasley had taken, except they didn't go into the mess hall. Instead, they entered the spacious galley.

Hash sliced vegetables at a big wooden table, the sharp knife hitting the cutting board with rhythmic thunks as he made quick work of slicing carrots into bite size pieces. A big bowl of potatoes waited to be peeled and quartered. Beside them, onions peeked out of a burlap sack.

The pristine white apron around Hash's waist emphasized the girth of his belly, which jiggled with his movements. He barely glanced at them as he transferred several handfuls of carrots into a big pot on the stove, his movements surprisingly delicate and graceful for such a large man.

The captain pulled out a chair at the other end of the table. "Make yourself comfortable. I'll find the glue."

Caralyn glanced at the pages and put them in order. They belonged at the end of the journal, the last thoughts Alexander Pembrook committed to paper. A few of the pages had only one or two words on them while some were filled with Alexander's ramblings, none of which made sense.

While she waited for the captain to return, she glanced around Hash's domain. Impressed by the cleanliness and order that prevailed, she smiled. Spices in small glass bottles, all neatly labeled, lined a shelf above the stove. Pots and pans in various sizes hung from hooks over the table and made soft clinking sounds as they clanged together beneath the ship's gentle sway. A floral-patterned china tea service on a handled wooden tray sat on a counter beside the stove.

The aroma of braised beef assailed her nose. Her stomach growled, reminding her she hadn't eaten a thing aside from a quick cup of tea before the sun brightened the morning sky. She eyed the loaf of bread in the middle of the table as the smell of the simmering stew made her mouth water. Her stomach made another unladylike noise. "That smells heavenly."

Before she could ask Hash for a piece of raw potato or a carrot stick or even a hunk of bread, something rubbed against her leg. She squelched a squeal of surprise then glanced at her skirts. Smudge blinked her big yellow eyes and purred as she rubbed her face along the hem. Her long white whiskers twitched before she leapt into Caralyn's lap.

"How did you get in here?" she whispered as she scratched the cat behind the ear to produce an even louder, satisfied rumble.

Hash tapped a long wooden spoon against the rim of the pot before placing the utensil on a small plate; then he turned away from the stove. The wide grin on his face made his eyes crinkle at the corner. "It's all right, ma'am. Smudge and I have become fast friends. Unlike my shipmates, I like cats and this little one is as sweet as they come."

He waddled around the table until he stood before her then reached down to scratch the smudge of white between the cat's ears. "She reminds me of Prissy, my sainted mother's favorite companion many years ago."

Smudge purred louder beneath the big man's ministrations until the teakettle whistled and drew Hash away. The cat jumped from her lap and followed Hash to the stove, weaving between his legs, rubbing her sleek body against him. The cook didn't seem to mind.

With quick, efficient movements, he prepared the tea. Matching sugar bowl and milk pitcher accompanied the cups and saucers on the tray.

"Would you like a cup?"

"I would love one, but I can get it myself. You're busy."

"Cups are in there." He nodded toward the floor-to-ceiling cabinet behind him. "I'll be back in a moment."

He lifted the tray and disappeared through another door, one which she believed led to the mess hall where the crew gathered to eat. Smudge meowed in short staccato bursts as she sauntered behind him, her tail straight up.

Caralyn rose from her seat and opened the cabinet. The cups were on the top shelf behind a decorative strip of wood that would hold them in place if the seas became too rough. She mentally calculated the height of the shelf and knew, no matter how hard she tried, she'd never reach them. She looked around the spotless galley for something aside from her chair to stand on. Beside the cabinet, she spotted a small wooden crate.

Even standing on the box, she couldn't quite reach the cups, though she strained and raised herself up on one tiptoe.

"All I want is a cup of tea," she muttered as she stepped off the crate, put it away where she'd found it, and pulled a chair over to the cabinet. She climbed on the seat and reached for the cups, but still, she came up short. Her fingertips grazed a handle. She rose on her toes and stretched, determined to get a cup, wishing, not for the first time, she weren't so blasted short.

"I found the glue."

"Oh!" Startled by the captain's deep, rich voice, Caralyn whirled around to face him and lost her balance. She reached for a shelf, for anything to stop herself from falling, but only grasped air.

She never touched the floor. One moment, she tumbled toward the wooden planks below her; the next, she landed in his arms. She inhaled and closed her eyes. He smelled of soap and spice and sea air. Beneath her hand, his heart beat almost as fast as hers.

"What were you doing? You could've killed yourself." He lowered her to her own two feet as gently as he would a child, although he held her much longer than necessary, in Caralyn's opinion. She didn't mind. She rather liked being in his strong arms.

"I wanted a cup of tea." His near proximity, not to mention having his hands on her waist, did delicious things to her insides and made it difficult to think. She feigned irritation to cover her rattled disposition and pointed to the cups on the top shelf of the cabinet. "Whose idea was it to put them so blasted high?"

Merriment danced in his beautiful eyes as he studied her. The corners of his mouth twitched. Without a word, without having to stand on tiptoe or on a chair, he reached into the cabinet and grabbed two cups.

Caralyn folded her arms across her chest. "I suppose you find that amusing."

"Not at all." Though he denied his amusement, the twinkle in his eyes told a different story. "We all come to terms with our limitations. Yours just happens to be your height." His voice lowered and took on a definite teasing quality as he added, "Or lack thereof."

Caralyn huffed and returned to her seat at the table. This wasn't the first time someone had teased her about her height but she had no rebuttal. He spoke the plain, unvarnished truth. At five foot one if she stood up straight, she was usually the shortest person in the room.

He fixed tea for both of them, placed the steaming brew on the table, then moved a chair closer to her. His arm brushed against hers as he took his seat. The simple act made Caralyn draw in her breath. Her thoughts scattered. Concentration became impossible. Every nerve in her body zinged from the slight touch.

What is wrong with me? Why does he affect me this way?

"Now that we have our tea and you are no longer climbing on chairs, we can repair Mr. Pembrook's journal." He moved the book to the side to uncover the pile of loose pages. "Did you find the places where these belong? It appears Pembrook didn't number his pages."

"I know exactly where they belong." She opened the journal with all the care and delicacy it deserved and showed him the bare binding where the pages were missing.

The captain perused the thick sheaf in his hand. "This is interesting," he remarked, then read aloud. Caralyn hardly paid attention to the words. Instead, she listened to the deep rumble of his voice, which vibrated all the way to her toes. She studied his face, riveted by the way his lips moved. A vein throbbed in his neck and that, too, caught her attention.

She inhaled his clean spice and sea air scent and hid a smile of delight behind her hand. Without doubt, he smelled better than any man had a right to.

"'Let the light of my heart guide you.'" Captain Trey paused in his recital. "Hmm. Pembrook wrote it three times in a row. I wonder why."

He turned toward her. Embarrassed she'd been caught staring at him, heat flooded her face and her heartbeat doubled in her chest. She picked up her cup with clumsy fingers and almost spilled the tea.

Stop it, Cara. He's just a man. Possibly a married man at that.

While she blew on the tea to cool it, she concentrated on bringing herself under some semblance of control. When she thought she could trust her voice, she said, "I noticed he repeated that same phrase in several places, but many things he wrote do not make a bit of sense." She tapped her lips with her finger and whispered, "Always three times though. It must mean something, but I haven't a clue what."

"No matter. We will figure it out."

Caralyn watched as the captain dabbed a thin line of glue on the edges of the pages, then she looked up at his face. His brow furrowed, his mouth set in a thin line as he focused. The tip of his tongue poked out of the corner of his mouth and rested there. She smothered the urge to giggle. So intent on making sure he didn't get glue where it didn't belong, he hardly had it anywhere it did belong.

"Hold your breath," he whispered as he placed the sheaf of pages into the book and held it there for a few minutes.

Either the glue was too old or he hadn't put enough on the pages, which she suspected, but it didn't work.

He tried again, using more glue. Still, the thick sheaf came away from the book easily. He wiped at the adhesive, removing the excess with his fingers and tried a third time.

After his fourth attempt with the same results, he shook his head and simply closed the book. "As much as I would like it to be so, I'm afraid I cannot repair Mr. Pembrook's journal." He pushed the diary toward her.

Caralyn ran her finger along the cracked leather. "Perhaps we can find a book binder when we arrive in Puerto Rico. In the meantime, I'll just put it away." She touched his arm and marveled at the tense muscles beneath his skin. "Thank you for trying."

His gaze met hers. Caralyn inhaled as his eyes darkened and his pupils dilated. Her gaze traveled down to his mouth to study the quirky half smile on his parted lips and she wondered if he wanted to kiss her as much as she wanted to be kissed. She leaned toward him, breath held, and . . .

He stood abruptly, breaking the spell she'd been under. "Please excuse me. A captain's work is never done." His voice sounded strained as he rushed from the galley, his long strides echoing on the wooden planks.

Caralyn cringed. *What must he think of me?* She took a sip of tea and nearly choked as a new thought trickled into her mind. *How on earth am I to be with this man for four months and not fall completely under his spell?*

Chapter 7

Tristan stood at the wheel, hands resting on the smooth wood, and surveyed his surroundings. Pride swelled his chest and filled his heart. For the life of him, he could imagine nothing better than this. The sails were full as the sun began its descent into the horizon behind him and the *Adventurer* cut through the ocean at a smart clip. A sigh of contentment escaped him.

As with most evenings, the men gathered on the deck to play cards, mend clothing, or regale each other with tall tales, their bellies full of Hash's cooking. Sometimes, there would be music and dancing. Those who could write wrote letters home, which would be delivered to the postmaster when they sailed into port. A few read books from the small library Tristan had collected over the years.

He spotted Jemmy sitting cross-legged on a coil of rope, his face wreathed in smiles as Mrs. Beasley read to him. Laughter escaped the lad and Tristan grinned. His son had developed a soft spot for the woman—for both women, if the truth were told, although a bit differently for each. Jemmy regarded Mrs. Beasley as one would an aunt; Caralyn, an older sister or cousin, perhaps. Given the opportunity, Tristan imagined the boy and Caralyn could find trouble.

He studied the interaction between Jemmy and Mrs. Beasley and realized a ship might no longer be the best place for his son. Jemmy needed maternal guidance and the loving comfort only a woman could give, although Tristan had done well without those things. The lad also needed an education that went beyond the common sense lessons of the crew.

Perhaps it *was* time to return to England, take the reins of the Winterbourne estates, and give Jemmy the best education wealth and status could provide.

In the midst of his musings, he caught Caralyn leaving the galley with a cup in her hand. His stomach did an odd flip and his mouth became dry. Surefooted, she crossed the deck in a hurry, although she did greet each and every man along the way. His smile returned. For a crew that hadn't wanted to take a woman aboard, they'd certainly changed their attitudes in the last four weeks. Now, they tripped over themselves for a smile or a kind word from her.

His grin widened when he noticed her bare feet peeking from beneath the edge of her pale pink skirts. She had discarded her shoes their second day at sea as had most of his crew. Smudge followed behind her, tail up, slinky body rubbing against everything and everyone. His men tolerated the cat, too, more so than he would have guessed. He'd even caught one of them slipping Smudge a morsel of meat from his plate, and if the truth were known, Tristan himself had grown fond of the feline.

His eyes drifted from the cat back to Caralyn. He liked this woman. In many ways, she reminded him of himself. Single-minded, willing to do anything, even menial chores such as polishing the brass and swabbing the deck, to achieve her heart's desire. Determination glittered in her eyes while pure joy bubbled in her laughter, and she laughed often.

Though he missed his cabin, the arrangement seemed to be working. He still had access to his day room where he kept the ship's log, and each evening he and his officers dined with the lovely Miss McCreigh and her sometime difficult, sometimes charming companion.

It was said bad luck would fall upon the ship willing to take a woman aboard, but thus far, Tristan hadn't had one lick of bad luck. In fact, their voyage had been incredibly smooth.

"Captain?"

Tristan did not take his hand from the wheel but his eyes followed her progress from the short flight of stairs until she stood by his side. "My given name is Tristan. It would please me if you would address me as such."

"Tristan," she complied. His name flowed from her lips like honey, infusing him with warmth. "My family calls me Cara." A flush colored her cheeks, which made him smile. "I brought you some coffee."

The sun hung over the indigo ocean as if on invisible strings, the pink-orange glow bathed the entire ship. Soon, stars would twinkle in an inky sky like diamonds against black velvet. Tristan sighed. What better place could he ever dream of being? And would that dream be complete without her?

As he grabbed the ceramic mug, he wondered where the thought had come from then quickly dismissed it from his mind. The subtle scent of cinnamon rose from the steaming brew and assailed his nose. The corners of his mouth twitched. Since she'd been on board, the coffee had become decidedly better than the bitter swill he'd grown accustomed to. A culinary genius with meats and vegetables, Hash couldn't brew a decent cup of coffee to save his life.

"I could take the wheel so you can drink your coffee."

He caught the hopeful expression on her face—the wistfulness in her sea-blue eyes and tentative smile gracing her lips, and without a word, took a step away from the wheel.

Caralyn grasped the smooth wood beneath her hands. As Tristan leaned against the wheel housing, he imagined her delicate yet strong hands on him, caressing him, leaving a trail of warmth wherever they touched, searing his soul. Gooseflesh broke out on his arms and a shiver chased down his spine as the visions in his mind grew.

He held his breath as he studied her small features, the slight upward tilt at the end of her little nose, the full smile curving her lips, the perfect arch of her eyebrows and the curling mass of light brown hair pulled away from her face by a thin ribbon. Caught by the constant breeze, silky tresses escaped to curl around her face. Tristan's fingers itched to tuck the errant tresses behind her ears.

He tightened his grip on the mug instead. It wouldn't do to touch her, not even a slight brush against her skin with his fingertips because he knew himself—he'd want more. Much more.

"She handles like a dream." Her mouth, moist and tempting, spread into a grin. "How long have you captained the *Adventurer*?"

Tristan concentrated on pulling his gaze away from the sight of her lips—not an easy task when the thought of tasting their sweetness flooded his mind. He took a sip of coffee in the hope the steaming brew would temper the sudden desire that made his entire body ache with longing. "Almost eight years. I bought her after the crew and I found our first treasure." He took another sip of the delicious coffee, savoring the taste of cinnamon on his tongue, even as it burned his throat.

"Now our old ship, the *Wanderer*—she was a beauty, but barely seaworthy. We almost met our end several times when she took on too much water." He gestured with his mug to draw her attention to the width and length of the ship. "The *Adventurer* is bigger, yet surprisingly faster, and Hash loves his galley."

Her gaze returned to him, her eyes wide and sparkling, her mouth parted slightly. The sun finished its descent into the ocean and illuminated her in rays of red and gold. Tristan inhaled a lungful of air. *My God, she is beautiful.* But he'd already known that, known it the moment he laid eyes on her the first time. Nothing had changed since they'd left Charleston except he'd come to know her a little better. With knowing came more beauty … and more wanting.

He cleared his throat and backed up a step. "How are you and Mrs. Beasley fairing? Has she spoken to you yet?"

"You mean a real conversation?" Her chest rose and fell with her deep sigh and she shook her head. "Other than complaining about anything and everything? No."

Her hand tightened on the wheel, knuckles white. Tristan winced. He wanted to place his hand over hers in order to relax her tight grip but he couldn't. If he touched her hand, he'd want to touch her arms, the soft skin of her shoulder, the place where her collarbone encircled her neck, the smooth silk of her cheek and . . .

Her words faded in his ears as he studied her mouth, her creamy complexion, the faded scar on her forehead, which he found utterly adorable. *Stop it*, he demanded of himself. *You are betrothed to be married.*

Caralyn's words became crystal clear once more. "She is unhappy sharing a cabin and a bed with me. She's tired of having to rinse out her clothing each night and donning damp under ... ah ... things in the morning, though I've offered to let her wear mine until we reach Puerto Rico." Another sigh escaped her.

"She is uncompromising and her list of complaints grows daily. She watches me whenever I am on deck. I feel the disapproval in her glare, but I have noticed she's quite taken with Jemmy and Dr. Trevelyan. She spends all her time with them." Her eyes drifted to where Jeremiah, Mrs. Beasley, and Stitch sat beneath a lantern on the deck. "I can't blame her there. Stitch is a gentleman of the first order and Jemmy is the most adorable boy. You must be so proud of him."

She worried her bottom lip with her teeth, as if she couldn't quite come to a decision, then blurted out, "He must look like his mother."

He studied his son, not for the first time, and saw his mother so clearly. "Yes, he does look like Rielle. Same silky blond hair, same mischievous smile, same twinkling eyes. One of the most beautiful women I've ever known. Not only on the outside, but inside, where it counted most. He has her sweet disposition, too."

The expression on Caralyn's face conveyed her confusion, and he explained further.

"Jeremiah is the child of my heart though not of my blood. His mother and I were neighbors. We grew up together and I loved her as I would a sister." He took a sip of coffee and grimaced as the liquid as well as the memory left a bitter taste in his mouth. "She'd made poor choices after the deaths of her parents, one right after the other, and fell for a man who wasn't worthy of her. I begged her not to marry him, but she was in love and didn't see Connor for who and what he was. The last time I saw her, I promised her I would take care of Jemmy if anything should ever happen to her."

His gut tightened, even now, after all these years, by the thought of what could have been prevented. He couldn't bring himself to reveal the guilt that still gnawed at him, still haunted him late at night. All the arguments he'd had with Rielle had failed to sway her. She had loved her husband and refused to leave him, despite the fact Connor Talbot was an abusive man.

"Jemmy wasn't quite two when Mr. Arbuckle, Rielle's solicitor, literally dropped him on my gangplank—for safekeeping, he'd said. It had taken him several months to locate me." He couldn't fight the sigh that escaped him, nor could he help the tightening of his jaw or the clenching of his fist.

"By that time, it was too late. When I arrived in England to see Rielle, I learned both she and her husband had died." Tristan swallowed hard to dislodge the lump in his throat. "By his hand."

• • •

She shouldn't have asked, shouldn't have delved into what was not her business, for now Tristan's entire body thrummed with tension. Not only could Caralyn see his anger in the white knuckled grip of his coffee cup, his rigid jawline, the muscle that jumped in his cheek, but she could feel it as well. Suppressed fury shimmered around him, cloaking him in a mantle of heat. His eyes darkened in the glow of the lanterns Mr. Quincy lit around the upper deck and Caralyn swallowed against the sudden dryness in her throat.

He wasn't married, didn't still pine for Jemmy's mother, but the knowledge did little to relieve her. She, herself, wasn't free. It didn't matter, though. She still wanted to smooth the throbbing muscle in his jaw with her thumb, wanted to ease his tension, his anger, his pain before her innocent statement ruined a perfectly lovely evening. "I'm so sorry for your loss. She must have been very special." She did touch him then, laid her fingers on his arm. Compared to the smoothness of his skin, his muscles were hard steel. "You've done a wonderful job with him. He's such a little gentleman."

He nodded and let out his breath. The grip on his coffee cup lessened and the rigidity eased from his jaw. The muscle there no longer jumped as he gestured toward the boy. "I can't take all the credit. The entire crew has had a hand in raising him." The warm glow of love replaced the darkness in his eyes. "And last year, it became legal. I adopted Jemmy."

The object of their conversation scampered up the steps, his voice rising as he yelled, "Papa! Papa, will you play?"

Tristan bent down on one knee and faced his son. His voice lowered and Caralyn couldn't hear what he said but it didn't matter. Such love showed on the captain's face, such adoration reflected in the boy's eyes, her heart melted. Jemmy was indeed the child of Tristan's heart. Anyone who witnessed them together could see that.

Tristan rose and ruffled Jemmy's silky blond hair before the boy dashed away. His bare feet made hardly any noise on the wooden stairs as he disappeared below deck.

"My apologies for the interruption." His eyes met hers and his voice floated over her like a warm mist.

"No apologies necessary," she murmured although her throat had gone dry. "As I said, he's a lovely boy. Sweet. Intelligent. Full of *joie de vivre*. And a little bit of mischief. He reminds me so much of my nephew."

Without preamble—they weren't even on the subject—Tristan said, "I must know. When we first left Charleston, you told Mrs. Beasley this was your last chance. Last chance for what?"

The question surprised her and Caralyn stiffened. Her hands gripped the wheel as she gazed into the horizon, at the deck, at the sails full of wind—everywhere but his face. And yet, it didn't matter she couldn't see his handsome features. She still felt his intense gaze. His eyes never left her, the glowing orbs piercing her skin to see straight into her soul.

Caralyn swallowed. *I need to find the treasure so I can buy myself out of my betrothal and won't have to marry a man I don't know.* The words were on the tip of her tongue but she couldn't utter them, couldn't drag them from her throat. In her mind, the explanation sounded horrible, terribly selfish, and discourteous. She could only imagine how those words would sound aloud.

He waited with patience. His foot didn't tap the deck, he didn't fidget, didn't gesture with his hands to draw the explanation from her. Indeed, he stood perfectly still except for tilting his head to the side as he gazed at her.

Self-doubt made her squirm beneath his steady scrutiny, made her question her motives. Caralyn opened and closed her mouth several times. How could she possibly explain so he would understand what she really wanted—not an arranged marriage but a romance to take her breath away, a man to sweep her off her feet?

A fairy tale romance and a knight in shining armor wasn't so much to ask for, was it? And yes, she could have gone to London and met her intended, given him a chance to win her heart, and probably should have, but she didn't. Instead, for good or ill, she chose to search for a treasure that may not exist, chose one last adventure, one last lark.

She didn't have to answer after all. Jemmy raced up the stairs, followed closely by Mad Dog.

"Pardon me, Miss. You're in for a treat." Mad Dog gestured first to the violin Jemmy handed Tristan then to the wheel. Caralyn relinquished her grip and took a step back.

Tristan grinned at her and tucked the violin beneath his chin. He took a breath then closed his eyes and drew the bow across the strings. The first notes were clear and so beautiful, tears misted her vision and a lump rose to her throat in an instant.

With no sheet music, he played from memory and from the heart. Caralyn recognized the tune as one she had played many times on the pianoforte, but never without music. Conversation on the deck stopped; the only sounds were the slapping of the waves against the hull, the sails snapping in the wind and the pure magic of the violin as Tristan played.

There were many things she'd learned about the captain in the short time she'd known him. He was stern yet fair, kind and compassionate, full of charm and good humor, a loving father and trusted companion; yet this was a whole new side to him, another piece of the puzzle that made Tristan who and what he was. Another reason to fall hopelessly, madly in love with him.

Caralyn stiffened, shocked by the thought. She wasn't on this adventure to find love; she was on this adventure to find a legendary treasure and save herself from marrying a man she didn't know. With a conscious effort, she pushed the niggling thought to the back of her brain, where she hoped it would stay, and concentrated on the heavenly music.

Graham bowed then straightened and held out his hand. "Madam, would you care to dance?"

"I would love to." She tucked her hand in his and allowed him to lead her to the main deck. Most of the crew just listened with dreamy expressions on their faces as the music pierced the darkness of the night to soothe their souls. A few mouthed the words to the song.

From the corner of her eye, she saw Stitch offer his hand to Mrs. Beasley, and saw the woman nod and practically fall into his arms.

"They make a lovely couple, don't they?"

Graham swiveled his head as the good doctor and Mrs. Beasley danced around them. "Yes, they do. I'm happy for Stitch. He's been alone far too long and Mrs. Beasley seems like a nice woman."

Caralyn grinned. "She can be when she isn't berating me for one thing or another. Or complaining. Or reminding me Izzy's Fortune may not exist."

"Oh, but the treasure does exist. I believe in it as does Tristan. And the rest of the crew. We just have to have patience and perhaps a little bit of luck." He swirled her around the main mast where a group of men watched them with something akin to longing in their eyes. "Are you enjoying your … ah … adventure?"

He grinned at her as if he had a secret, a tidbit he was dying to share, yet one that would remain locked away. Caralyn had a feeling the navigator and first mate retained many undisclosed confidences and could be trusted with many more.

"Oh, yes. Very much. You've all been wonderful hosts and the *Adventurer* is a beautiful ship. Sleek. Fast. She reminds me of the *Lady Elizabeth*, my father's ship." They continued to spin around the deck. "How long before we reach Puerto Rico?"

"If the wind remains true, I would think in another two or three days."

Socrates stood behind Graham and tapped him on the shoulder. He winked at Caralyn. "Excuse me, Mr. Alcott, may I cut in?"

"Of course." Graham stepped away. He tilted his head to the side. "Thank you, Miss McCreigh. Perhaps I shall have the pleasure of dancing with you once more."

The music changed in tempo as Caralyn stepped into Socrates's waiting arms. A concertina and mouth harp joined Tristan's violin in a lively reel. The men clapped and stomped their feet to keep time. Her skirts lifted to reveal her bare feet as Socrates whirled her around.

Breathless yet exuberant, Caralyn danced with one crew member after another. She'd even taken a turn with Jemmy, who glided across the deck with remarkable grace. As with other parts of his education, the *Adventurer's* mates must have taught him to dance, to make polite conversation, and to bow over her hand.

The beat changed one more time, slowing down to a beautiful waltz. The violin seemed to have a different sound but it didn't matter. Caralyn grinned and reached out for the next man in line. Her heart hammered in her chest, as much from the lively dancing as from realizing who now held her hand.

"May I?" His voice filled her veins with warm honey, filled her head with delightfully delicious thoughts, filled her stomach with thousands of butterflies.

If there was any such thing as magic, Caralyn found it the moment she stepped into Tristan's arms and they began to dance. So many things conspired to cast a spell over her: the twinkle in his eyes, the smile that tugged at the corners of his mouth, the feel of his muscular arms around her, the brilliance of the stars against the velvety black night.

An errant lock of thick black hair fell over his forehead. Her fingers itched to smooth it away and find out if his hair really was as soft as it looked. She hesitated, torn between wanting to touch him and needing to maintain her bearing. With a toss of his head, the errant lock disappeared and she lost her chance.

They didn't speak as they swirled and dipped and stepped to the music. Caralyn didn't think she could form a coherent thought if she tried, and for a moment she forgot to breathe, especially when his eyes began to smolder with warmth. A shiver raced up her spine, despite the heat of the evening and the robust activity.

This wasn't what she bargained for when she proposed this voyage. The possibility she would fall for the captain had never entered her mind, although she did admit, if only to herself, she'd found him attractive the moment she met him.

More stars sparkled in the sky than Caralyn had ever seen and each one reflected in Tristan's eyes. The constant breeze cooled her warm skin but did nothing to cool the rush of heated blood through her veins. She stared at his mouth—those beautiful lips curved in a smile—and wanted more than anything, to taste them again. And would have.

"Well, I do believe that is quite enough for this evening." Mrs. Beasley, ever vigilant, ever proper, actually had the audacity to interrupt their dance. Spots of color highlighted her pale skin, and her breath came a little faster from her own exertions. "Come, Miss McCreigh, it's time for us to turn in."

Caralyn stayed in the warm circle of Tristan's arms. "I'll just stay on deck for a while longer."

"You'll do no such thing," Mrs. Beasley insisted. "It wouldn't be proper to leave you here, alone, with all these men."

Without a word, Tristan relinquished his hold on her. Caralyn almost lost her step without the warmth and strength of his embrace but recovered quickly. "Good night, Cara." He bowed slightly, but the gleam never left his eyes.

Oh, she didn't want to leave him, didn't want the magic of the evening to end, didn't want—

Dear God, what do I want?

She knew exactly what she wanted. To find Izzy's Fortune. To be swept off her feet by a knight in shining armor in a fairy tale romance. Or, perhaps, a sea captain.

She had a feeling Captain Trey could fulfill one or both of those dreams, but not until she was free of the promises that bound her. "Good night, Captain. Thank you for a lovely evening."

Once in the privacy of their cabin, Caralyn opened her mouth, ready to give Mrs. Beasley a scathing set-down but she never had the chance to speak. The woman was humming, actually humming, and if Caralyn wasn't mistaken, a smile pulled at the corners of Mrs. Beasley's mouth as she prepared for bed.

Mrs. Beasley crawled beneath the light sheet, adjusted her pillow so she could sit up, and waited. The heat of her intense gaze bore into Caralyn's back, but if she gave the woman enough time, perhaps she'd fall asleep. The lure of the star-studded night, the gleam in the captain's eyes, the warmth of his smile all held a promise she wanted to experience more.

"Quit procrastinating, Miss McCreigh. I know what you're thinking, but you won't be sneaking back on deck after I'm asleep. You'll have to crawl over me to do it." Mrs. Beasley harrumphed. "As you know, I'm a light sleeper."

Caralyn almost choked. Good God, the woman could read her mind. With no choice, she undressed, slipped into her nightclothes, and slid into bed.

Though determined to stay awake until the drone of Mrs. Beasley's snoring filled the cabin, the sweet sound of the violin made it impossible to keep her eyes open. In moments, the soft magic of Tristan's eyes accompanied her to dreamland.

Chapter 8

"Tristan," Caralyn purred in his ear as she nibbled on his earlobe. Her breath sent shivers down his spine. Warm fingers left a trail of fire as they stroked the hair on his chest and quested lower. He inhaled and smelled fresh sea breezes coupled with the delightful scent of her own unique perfume. His body responded without effort or conscious thought. The steel-hard arousal she caused throbbed with every beat of his heart.

"Tristan," she breathed. Gooseflesh pebbled on his arms and legs. Sweat beaded on his brow as her lips left his ear. She licked the side of his neck, her tongue hot on his skin before she straddled his hips and slowly lowered herself over him. Tristan groaned, his hands at her hips, driving himself deeper into her.

He awoke with a start only to find his pillow over the nether regions of his body. "Damn," he breathed on a sigh. He threw his pillow on the floor and scratched his fingers through his unruly hair as he sat up in the bunk. Relief rippled through him. At least he was alone in the cabin he shared with Graham. "Just a dream."

But his body had responded. He remained ready and able to satisfy the lustiest maiden and though he no longer slept, Caralyn's dream voice persisted. He heard it clearly. "Tristan." Excitement made the pitch a little higher.

Despite the raging erection that threatened his sanity, Tristan thrust his legs into a pair of trousers, slipped into a shirt, and raced from the cabin. Still trying to present a dignified picture, he tucked his shirt into his trousers, which did nothing to hide the fact his body remained fully aroused. "Ah, hell," he muttered as he pulled the shirt free of his trousers and let it hang loose. He climbed the few stairs to the deck and stopped.

Caralyn stood at the bow of the *Adventurer*, face to the rising sun, a vision so lovely, so beautiful, Tristan exhaled with a sigh. She hadn't changed from her nightclothes and though the cotton of her nightgown and robe were thick enough that no light shined through, the wind pushed the material against her and rippled her hair behind her like a golden brown flag. For the first time, he saw her naturally nipped in waist, slightly flaring hips, and long legs—all of which did nothing to quell the raging erection pushing painfully against his trousers.

Her laughter, that sweet, contagious sound, broke the silence of the morning. She glanced in his direction, her face wreathed in smiles. "I know what it means," she yelled across the deck and pointed to a group of small islands in the near distance.

Tristan strode to her side and immediately removed his shirt to place it over her shoulders, hiding most of what he'd already seen in hopes his crew wouldn't see the eyeful he had. Propriety cast all concern for his own state aside in order to protect her modesty.

"What the hell are you doing, Cara?" He nodded to several of the crew who must have been awakened by Caralyn's voice. Or her laughter. They shuffled and stumbled to the deck in various stages of dress. Mr. Quincy rubbed sleep from his eyes. Mr. Jacoby stifled a yawn as he tucked his shirt into his trousers. Mr. Milliron tried to slick back the cowlick standing up at the back of his head. Not one of them spoke, no doubt in awe of the sight before them as a ray of sunlight exploded from the middle of the largest island and bathed Caralyn in gold.

"I couldn't sleep. Something called to me, Tristan. Wanted me to see the sun rise this morning." She pushed her hair out of her eyes and grinned. "I know what it means."

Tristan rested his hands on the rail and took a deep breath. He studied her—the wide grin, the flush spreading across her face, the twinkle of excitement in her sea-blue eyes—and again, the sight did nothing to ease his physical attraction to her. He took another breath in an effort to still the rapid beating of his heart, to stop the blood from pumping through his veins with such ferocity.

It didn't help that sunlight and spindrift created a shimmering radiance around her. His dream Caralyn paled in comparison to the real life Caralyn beside him.

To make the impossible harder, she grasped his arm, long slim fingers hot on his flesh. What was it about this woman that made his stability falter? Made him want to slowly caress her silken skin and explore every inch of her body? Made him want to hold her close and never let go?

Tristan closed his eyes and tried to regain his balance.

"I know what it means," she repeated a third time.

He opened his eyes without gaining the steadiness he so desperately craved. "I beg your pardon, but I have no clue what you're talking about."

"Pembrook's journal. Pembrook repeated the sentence, 'Let the light of my heart guide you' three times." She drew in her breath and her grin widened. "He was telling us there are three islands." She squinted into the rising sun and drew his attention to the largest island in the small grouping. "See how the biggest island is shaped like a man sleeping on his side, knees bent, hands folded under his cheek? See where the sun shines through? Isn't that where his heart would be?"

"I do believe you're right. That is where his heart would be, but Cara, this island looks nothing like the sketch Pembrook drew. There was no waterfall in Pembrook's rendition and the sleeping man lay flat on his back."

She bowed her head, but only for a moment. "I know, Tristan, but I also know, in my heart, in my bones, this is the Island of the Sleeping Man. This is the island we are meant to find. I think Pembrook intentionally drew the picture he did to keep anyone from finding this island. Please, Tristan. We have nothing to lose and everything to gain by exploring."

Her hand tightened on his arm and her eyes glowed with such hope, Tristan didn't have the heart to deny her request. He waved to Socrates at the wheel. "Steady the course, Mr. Callahan."

Hector de la Vega finished tucking his shirt into his trousers as he stepped forward. "Beggin' yer pardon, miss." He bowed his head toward Caralyn then turned his attention to Tristan. "Might I have a word, Capitan?"

"Of course."

"In private, sir."

Tristan stepped away from Caralyn, but he didn't think she noticed as her face was turned into the wind and her eyes were focused on the islands in the distance.

"*Capitan*," de la Vega said softly, "I must confess. This is not *Isla Caja de Muertos*, not the island I remember from my youth. We have barely passed Hispaniola and still have many miles to reach Puerto Rico."

"I understand, Hector, and thank you for telling me, but Miss McCreigh believes this is the Island of the Sleeping Man." He turned so he could see Caralyn at the rail. She hadn't moved except to raise her face toward the sun. "She believes this is the island we are meant to find and it does resemble a man sleeping on his side. Perhaps it is so, but we'll never know unless we take a moment to explore."

The crewman nodded slightly before taking a step back and almost colliding with Graham. He nodded to the navigator then excused himself.

Tristan took in Graham's appearance, the bright shining eyes, the freshness that only comes with an excellent night's rest. He himself had listened to Graham's snoring for quite some time until the steady noise eventually lulled him to sleep.

"You studied the charts as much as I, Tris. What's more, we've sailed the Caribbean for almost ten years and we've never seen these islands before."

Again, Tristan couldn't deny the obvious, but it didn't matter. If there was a chance to find Izzy's Fortune, he'd take it. He shrugged his shoulders. "If nothing else, they're worth exploring, don't you think?"

"Of course. However, I believe we should proceed with caution. Although these islands are uncharted, it doesn't mean they are uninhabited."

"I agree." Tristan excused himself and gave orders to Socrates at the wheel.

They circled the islands twice, concentrating on the largest one, the one that resembled a sleeping giant, but found nothing of interest except sandy white beaches, an abundance of tropical plants and trees, and a mountain that must have risen two hundred feet above sea level. They did see a sunken ship east of the island, its weathered masts rising above the water, but it seemed to have been there for quite some time. A decade, at least.

The islands appeared deserted as nothing stirred except the palm fronds and the three waterfalls that thundered down into the ocean. No telltale smoke from someone's fire marred the perfection of the blue sky, no sound other than the chirping and cawing of the colorful birds peppering the trees and the multitude of chickens on the ground.

By the time they dropped anchor west of the sleeping giant's knees, Tristan realized Caralyn could barely contain her anticipation. He understood, as her enthusiasm mirrored his own. He heard the excitement in his own voice as he shouted orders to the crew, exhilaration rippling through his body, causing his stomach to tighten and a smile to hover around his mouth.

While his men filled two longboats with supplies and provisions, he watched Caralyn pace the deck from bow to stern. She had plaited her hair into one long braid that bounced against her back as she moved and plopped a hat on her head—not a straw bonnet as he would have expected, but a tricorn, which gave her an air of impudence. She had changed clothes as well, giving up the nightclothes in favor of a loose white shirt and a pair of well-mended trousers tucked into serviceable leather boots. She looked like a pirate—a charming, curvaceous pirate—and he couldn't help the immediate reaction of his body.

He shook his head to clear his thoughts and hopefully get his heart back to beating normally, but he couldn't keep his eyes from straying to her time after time.

He watched her now and grinned. Impatience made Caralyn's steps quick and decisive. She chewed her thumbnail, another nervous habit she had in addition to chewing her bottom lip. Tristan tilted his head as she stopped her relentless pacing in front of Mrs. Beasley in response to something the woman said but continued to gnaw at her fingernail.

Tristan strained to hear the older woman's comment.

"What you're wearing is positively indecent," Mrs. Beasley remarked loud enough for him and the rest of the crew to hear as her gaze raked Caralyn from head to toe. "And if your brother or father were here, they'd make you change."

Caralyn grinned as she rubbed her hand against the patched trousers covering her legs. "Perhaps my brother would, but my father wouldn't. Father's crew made these for me, Mrs. Beasley, and they are more than sufficient for the exploring we are about to do. More importantly, I have very fond memories when I wear them."

In his opinion, Caralyn looked rather fetching, but he kept his opinion to himself as Mrs. Beasley turned to face him. Her lips were pressed together as she pinned him with a glare then *harrumphed* and turned away. She opened her umbrella against the rays of the sun and stood at the rail, her body rigid.

Tristan covered his mouth with his hand to hide his grin. His Cara was a spirited, sassy little slip of a thing.

Now, where did that thought come from? She isn't my Cara.

At long last, the boats were ready and lowered onto the crystal clear blueness of the water. Securely tethered to the *Adventurer*, they bobbed in the waves. From where he stood on deck, Tristan could see the pristine sandy bottom beneath the surface of the ocean. Colorful fish darted and hid between stalks of coral. A stingray, its wingspan more than eight feet, glided beneath the ship.

"Whistle for me, Mr. Anders."

The bosun complied and tooted on his whistle—three short blasts and one long one. Every crew member stopped mid-chore and lined up on the quarterdeck. Tristan strode up the steps, grin firmly in place. "I need a few volunteers to explore the island. We'll be there at least overnight, perhaps longer, depending on what we find."

Socrates, MacTavish, and Gawain Jacoby raised their hands almost before Tristan finished speaking.

"Count me in." Caralyn's sweet voice filled his head and he whirled around to face her.

He wanted to say no as he didn't know what dangers they might find, but one look at the determination in her eyes changed his mind. She had every right to accompany them. She'd certainly dressed for the occasion.

"Me as well." Dr. Trevelyan raised his hand.

"If you're going, then I'm going." Mrs. Beasley stiffened her spine as she moved closer to the good doctor. It didn't escape Tristan's notice she slipped her hand into Brady's or the blush that gave color to the man's cheeks. Nor did he miss the steady stare pinned on Caralyn, and he knew Mrs. Beasley's reasons were twofold.

"Oh hell, I'll go." Graham stepped forward, his lopsided smile contagious. "I'll hunt some treasure."

"Papa," Jemmy piped in. "I want to go."

Tristan shook his head. "Not this time, son."

"Please, Papa. I'll keep up, I promise." He crossed his heart with his finger. "I won't get in the way. Please?"

Who could resist the hope in those cornflower blue eyes? The crooked grin? Tristan was just as lost looking at his son as he was looking at Caralyn. He gave in. He couldn't help himself. "All right, but only if you follow every one of my orders. Do I make myself clear?"

The boy nodded with so much enthusiasm, he almost lost his balance. Tristan steadied him with a quick hand to his son's shoulder. The grin Jemmy gave him melted his heart. Love swelled his chest.

Tristan climbed down to one of the waiting boats first, grabbed a rope to steady himself, straddled the seat, and reached up for the next person while Mac did the same in the other dinghy.

"Are you ready for this?" he asked as he grasped Caralyn around the waist and guided her to a seat.

"I've been waiting for this all my life." Her words were breathy, as if she'd run a great distance. Her eyes were wide and her smile faltered. A slight tremor raced through her, one he could feel. Tristan wondered if she could feel the same shiver race through him as he released her, although with a great deal of reluctance. She made herself comfortable next to Jemmy.

Tristan settled himself and picked up the oars.

"Now, Cap'n, ye know ye be doin' my job." Gawain Jacoby gestured to the oars in the captain's hands.

He thought about handing the paddles over to his crewman but knew he couldn't. Not now, not after touching her and feeling the warmth of her skin through the thin clothing she wore. If he didn't keep himself occupied, he'd want to touch her again. "Today, Mr. Jacoby, I shall row." Tristan slapped the oars into the water and began to row.

The small boat, even loaded with supplies, cut through the sea easily as they rounded the huge rock outcropping that formed the sleeping giant's knees.

The thunderous roar of the water as it fell unimpeded two hundred feet into the cove below drowned out conversation. Misty vapor created a rainbow more beautiful than he'd ever seen, the colors rich and vibrant. The sight took his breath away.

Caralyn caught his attention as she pointed upward where the gaping maw of a cave opening dotted the sheer rock wall.

"What?" Although he knew she spoke, he missed most of what she said in the rumbling torrent of gushing water. He rowed the boat past the cascading cataract and into an idyllic cove surrounded by lush vegetation and sandy white beaches.

"How are we supposed to get up there?" she repeated, louder, and Tristan twisted in his seat to study the hole in the granite where the slumbering man's heart would be. Unless they could scale perfectly smooth rock, they had to find another way. "There has to be another entrance to the cave. Otherwise, sunlight would not have been able to shine through it to guide us."

He stopped rowing for a moment and just took in the sight before him. There were several words Tristan could have used to describe the Island of the Sleeping Man. *Perfect* came to mind as did *heavenly* and *peaceful*, despite the cacophony of birdsong. Perhaps even magical and enchanted, as if the island could cast a spell over him and anyone else who dared to venture on the pristine shores.

Tristan wasn't the only one mesmerized by the tropical beauty. Caralyn pointed out some of the sights to Jemmy, her blue eyes twinkling, her mouth curved into a serene smile, her infectious laughter echoing off the rock walls surrounding the inlet. In that moment, he wanted to lay her down on the soft white sand and—

He didn't allow himself to finish the thought. Instead, he rowed again, the physical exertion a great distraction as he focused on bringing the boat to the middle of the cove. Tristan hopped into the warm, tranquil water and pulled the dinghy onto the sand beside the remains of what had once been a fire-pit. Scorched stones formed a semi-circle roughly three feet across, but he could tell there had been no fire in the pit for a long time. Along the tree line, someone had built crude shelters using the bounty of the island.

He helped Caralyn and Jemmy from the boat then started to unpack the supplies with Graham and Gawain's assistance.

"Jemmy and I are going to explore," Caralyn told him as she gestured to a grouping of huge boulders where the waterfall cascaded into the cove.

"Stay within my sight. Jemmy, you listen to Miss Cara."

Caralyn held Jemmy's hand as they scampered along the edge of the water, unconcerned her well-worn boots were becoming drenched. Tristan grinned as he watched her. For a moment, the smile on her face made her look as young and carefree as his son. Her laughter left him in no doubt she wasn't a child. She was all woman, a soft, sensual, alluring woman who'd make a wonderful mother.

The thought careened through his mind before he could stop it, and he shook himself free of the implications. *What the hell am I thinking? One minute, I want to lay her in the sand, the next, I'm thinking what a wonderful mother she would be.*

With a sigh, he pulled his gaze from her and grabbed one of the canvas tents from the boat. He was just about to drop it on the sand when something made him stop. Gooseflesh rose on his arms and a cold shiver raced down his back. The fine hair at the back of his neck rose. Dried leaves crunched and crackled as if the sleeping giant had awakened and thrashed the forest in anger because his slumber had been disturbed. The piercing squawks of the birds died, replaced by a heavy silence. Tristan's stomach clenched and his eyes narrowed as he scanned the area, looking for the source of his unease. He saw nothing. No one else seemed to notice anything out of the ordinary, but the feeling of impending peril wouldn't stop.

He walked a few paces away from the boat and dropped the tent. Again, the rustling at the edge of the forest made him stop and take stock, but it wasn't until he heard the strange, eerie grunting noise that his heart leapt into his throat.

The rustling sound grew louder and the leaves closer to the edge of the forest shimmered and shook. Small saplings, just beginning their growth toward the sun, crashed to the ground, the sound deafening in the stillness of the cove. He glanced down the beach toward Caralyn and Jemmy. They didn't hear what he heard, couldn't have heard what he feared and yet, he didn't even know what he feared. So far, there was just noise, but the din was enough to strike terror in his heart.

He started running toward them while keeping an eye glued to where the sand ended and the thick copse of trees and ferns began, shouting orders to his men to get everyone back in the boats until the danger had passed. His heart pumped in his chest, but his blood ran cold as a feral pig burst through the foliage and thundered straight for Caralyn and his son. "Cara! Jemmy! Don't move!"

Caralyn stopped and turned. She waved at him, oblivious. It wasn't until she started to twirl toward Jemmy that her eyes as well as her mouth opened wide as the animal raced closer to her. She didn't scream, although Tristan wouldn't have blamed her if she had.

Her face lost all color and her body stiffened, but only for a moment. In a blink of an eye, she pushed Jemmy behind her then reached into the top of her boot and withdrew a wicked looking knife. The honed edge glinted in the sun.

Amazed, his heart hammering in his chest, Tristan drew his pistol without stopping his run across the sand, took aim, and pulled the trigger at the same time Cara flung the knife toward the animal.

The shot echoed within the small, protected cove, the sound bouncing off rock wall. Mrs. Beasley's scream accompanied the panicked shouts of Dr. Trevelyan and Graham. Blood spurted where the bullet pierced the boar's head and the pig squealed as the knife struck him between the eyes and buried itself halfway up to the hilt. The pig died instantly, yet the momentum of its breakneck speed kept the animal sliding in the sand before coming to rest a mere foot in front of Caralyn.

A wave of relief washed through Tristan with such force, his limbs weakened and his muscles had the consistency of water, but still he made it to where Caralyn and Jemmy stood. He dropped to his knees in front of them and gathered them both close to his heart. "Are you all right? You don't know what I thought when I saw that boar coming straight for you."

He pulled away and inspected them both. Even though the swine had died before it even came close to them, Tristan still had to check, still had to reassure himself. He ran his hands down Jemmy's arms, which proved to be next to impossible. The boy squirmed with excitement, his face animated, his hands moving as fast has his mouth.

"Did you see it, Papa? Did you see what Miss Cara did with the knife? Did you?"

"Yes, I saw." Torn between awe and relief, Tristan raised his eyes and met Caralyn's. Hers were wide and brilliant blue—no guile, no fear, but no pleasure or pride, either.

"We're all right," she insisted and tilted her head when she spoke. She didn't blink, didn't turn away. "Truly. Just a little startled."

Though Caralyn insisted, Tristan heard the slight tremor in her voice. Indeed, the quaver echoed in the quaking of her body—or perhaps it was his body which quivered. "Stitch should take a look at you both. Just to make sure."

"It's not necessary, Tristan." She laid warm fingers on his arm and the tingle of her touch surged all the way to his rapidly beating heart. "The pig never came that close. We're fine." She lowered her voice. "Please, let's just drop the subject. Neither Jemmy nor I are hurt. How could we be?"

He should listen to her and drop the subject, he knew, and yet, he couldn't. Tristan drew in a deep breath and let it out slowly, but the simple action did nothing to ease his tension or the fear still raging through him. Caralyn didn't understand how the thought of losing either one of them made his heart hurt. He glanced at his son, those big blue eyes wide and shiny, and realized Jemmy didn't seem at all upset over the near miss with the swine. Indeed, the lad's fascination over Caralyn's knife throwing abilities surpassed any fear he might have harbored.

Before he could utter another word, Stitch and Mrs. Beasley joined them at the water's edge, as did Graham, Socrates, and the rest of the small group. The good doctor did a very cursory examination while Mrs. Beasley expressed an opinion or two, which for once, coincided with his own. With no cuts or scrapes or bruises, both Caralyn and Jemmy were pronounced perfect.

As they walked back to the makeshift camp, Tristan placed Caralyn's hand in the crook of his elbow. "Perhaps you should take Jemmy and Mrs. Beasley back to the *Adventurer*. It isn't safe for you here. There may be more feral pigs."

She stopped and removed her hand from his arm. Tristan stopped as well and watched the physical change come over her with something akin to awe. The way she straightened her spine, threw her shoulders back and raised her chin struck a chord deep within him. He saw determination in the ramrod stiffness of her back, fortitude in her relentless stare, and persistence in the solid line of her mouth.

"No, Captain, I will not go back to the ship. I've waited a lifetime to search for this treasure. Neither you nor a wild boar will stop me."

"You realize, as captain, I can order you to return. Indeed, I can have you locked in your cabin for the entire journey. For your own good."

The blueness of Caralyn's eyes darkened until they became the color of a storm-tossed sea. Unshed tears shimmered in their depths. Her chin and lower lip quivered as she crossed her arms over her chest. "You wouldn't be that cruel."

No, he wouldn't be that cruel. He couldn't, not when she stood before him, unafraid and defiant and fighting back the threatening tears. The tricorn hat, tilted at a jaunty angle, and her attitude reminded him of Jemmy.

They stood not more than a foot apart, their eyes only on each other. The rest of the world could have disappeared. Tristan knew stubbornness, tenaciousness, and perseverance when he saw them and looking at her, right now, right this moment, he saw all those qualities. They were instilled as deeply in her as they were in himself.

He tilted his head slightly and silently admitted she'd won this battle. Caralyn accepted her win with grace.

Socrates came up along side them, dragging the dead boar, the muscles in his arms bulging. Sweat glistened on his brow. "He's a big one, Captain."

"Indeed, Mr. Callahan. Tonight, we feast." Tristan grabbed both Caralyn and Jemmy by the hand and continued on to the small boats beside the fire-pit, right behind Socrates and their future dinner. "Mr. Jacoby, go back to the ship and bring the rest of the men. Ask for volunteers to stay with the *Adventurer*, but let them know they'll not miss out on the fresh meat. Mac, please start a fire. Graham, Stitch, and I will finish putting up the tents. Socrates, I assume you'll take care of preparing the meat until Hash arrives?"

Once the men rushed to follow his orders, he turned toward Caralyn. "I could use a bit of brandy. How about you?" He pulled the flask from the boat, untwisted the top, and handed it to her. Caralyn tipped the silver bottle, but only took a small sip, as if her nerves didn't need steadying. She handed the flask back to him then started to walk away. "Where are you going? You should stay close to the boats, close to us."

Caralyn said nothing although she did turn toward him, her smile as infectious as ever. She slipped her hand into Jemmy's, as if daring Tristan to physically stop her. At the last moment, she changed direction and sat beside Mrs. Beasley on a blanket on the soft sand.

"She is the most stubborn, most inflexible—"

"Recognize yourself, do you?" Graham asked as he pulled another tent from the boat.

Tristan twisted to stare at his friend, saw the grin spreading Graham's lips, then finally smiled himself. "I'm not at all stubborn."

Graham cocked an eyebrow, smile still firmly in place, but only mumbled, "Of course. You don't have a stubborn bone in your body. Right, Mr. Callahan?"

"Yes, sir, Mr. Alcott. Not the captain. Ain't no stubbornness here," Socrates agreed.

"What are you talking about?" Stitch asked as he grabbed the sack Hash had so thoughtfully prepared.

Voice on the edge of laughter, Graham replied, "We were just commenting on the fact the captain doesn't have a stubborn bone in his body."

Stitch's eyebrows shot upward and dimples appeared in his cheek as he grinned. "Indeed. I quite agree. Not one persistent, mulish, tenacious bone. For some, perseverance is an excellent trait. For others, that same quality just causes trouble." The doctor's gaze drifted toward the blanket.

Tristan ignored Stitch's comments as well as Graham's hearty chuckles. He glanced in Caralyn's direction, not only to assure himself of her safety, but to catch another glimpse of her infectious smile. She and Jemmy were deep in conversation, the boy's face set in a serious expression, his eyes only on her.

"I've never seen anyone handle a knife like that." He didn't even realize he'd said the words out loud or that they were filled with awe until Socrates grunted. Tristan faced him and finished his thought. "Who taught her?"

Socrates grinned as he pulled said knife out of the boar's skull. "I did, many summers ago. We practiced day in and day out until she could hit the bullseye ten times out of ten. Very persistent, our Cara was. Still is from what I can see." He wiped the blood from the blade through the thick hair on the carcass then flicked his thumb over the sharp edge. His grin still in place, he muttered, "You have my sympathy, Captain."

Chapter 9

"What do you mean, we lost them?" Captain Entwhistle's face turned a peculiar shade of mottled red as he raised his cold glare toward Porkchop. "Explain," he bellowed.

Porkchop swallowed hard though his mouth had gone dry. He stood in front of the captain's desk on legs that seemed like blocks of wood instead of flesh and bone, his stomach twisted in knots, bile burning the back of his throat. The crewman opened his mouth several times, but not a word would come forth. Sunlight seeped in through the windows of the captain's cabin to warm the room but did nothing to dispel the icy fear that made Porkchop shiver.

In truth, he couldn't explain. He hadn't been the one keeping watch, hadn't been the one to lose sight of the *Adventurer's* white sails on the horizon. He *had* been the one to have the ill fortune of drawing the low card from the deck to decide which one of them would have the dreadful task of telling the captain the news. He shifted his weight from one leg to the other.

"Well?" The captain pushed out of his chair and rose to his full height. The chair toppled backward to crash into a small cabinet filled with porcelain and glass curios. Tinkling glass plinked to the floor, sounding like a broken music box. Entwhistle didn't seem to notice. His icy stare never left Porkchop's face. A muscle throbbed in the captain's cheek as he leaned forward on his desk, the heat from his hands fogging the satiny finish of the desktop.

The fury in the captain's eye, the tension in his body, made Porkchop back up a step, then two. He squeezed his buttock muscles tight, afraid the knot in his stomach would unravel and he'd soil himself right then and there.

"Speak, you bloody imbecile."

Porkchop jumped. He hated to snitch on any of his crewmates despite how they treated him, but faced with Captain Entwhistle's barely suppressed rage, he couldn't help himself. "It were Petey," he confessed in a rush. "Petey was watchin', but he were jokin' an' carryin' on like he al'ays does."

Hands balled into fists, the redness of his face deepening, Captain Entwhistle said not a word as grabbed the cat o' nine tails from the hook on the wall and slammed the door as he left the cabin.

Porkchop breathed a sigh of relief. He still stood. Still breathed. The captain hadn't killed him. He didn't want to witness what the captain would do to Petey, and yet, he couldn't help himself. On tiptoe, he crept toward the door and cracked it open as the first lash of the cat o' nine tails laid open the flesh on Petey's back. The scream that followed made Porkchop wince and close his eyes.

With each crack of the whip, each subsequent scream, the crewman jumped—ten times in all before silence reigned once again. Forcing his eyes open, he saw Captain Entwhistle grab the spyglass from his mate's hand. He held the device to his eye and scanned the horizon. As he lowered it, he drew in a deep breath. Mouth set in a grim line, he ordered, "Set a course for Jamaica." He stepped closer to Petey. "Trey has friends on the island. You'd better pray he'll visit them like he always does."

While the crew of the *Explorer* rushed to change course, Porkchop left the safety of the captain's cabin and rushed to help Petey. He untied the man's hands from the main spar and gently laid him on the deck on his stomach.

"Don' touch me, ye bloody whelp." Petey managed to utter between clenched teeth. "Ye tol' 'im it were me, din't ye?" Blood spilled from the many gashes, and the shredded remains of Petey's shirt, stained crimson, lay in tatters against the man's back.

"Serves ye right, ye idjit. I got me enough scars on me back to be takin' another whippin' for ye. Now, jes' hold still and I'll fix ye right up." He expelled his breath, thankful it hadn't been him who'd received the lashes, thankful the captain had stopped at ten and not killed Petey. "We'll be in Jamaica 'fore too long. Ye'll be right as rain by then."

• • •

From her spot on the blanket, Caralyn watched the men set up camp, her attention focused on Tristan. He'd rolled up the sleeves of his shirt to reveal tanned, muscular forearms. Heat, humidity, and exertion caused perspiration to bead on his forehead and his thin shirt to stick to his back, which emphasized every rippling muscle as he worked. Truthfully, the sight did strange things to her insides, and a shiver worked its way from her head to her toes and back.

Before she knew it, three old canvas tents surrounded the fire pit, now cleaned of debris, all without her help. A coffee pot burbled on the grate over the crackling fire Mac had prepared. The last thing the men did was move several big logs to surround the fire-pit before they trudged toward the grouping of tumbled rocks at the bottom of the waterfall they'd passed on their way into the cove. The rocks formed several serene pools away from the force of the thundering water.

"May I join you?" Tristan stood at the edge of the blanket, blocking the rays of the sun. She hadn't seen him come back as her attention had wandered to Jemmy and his fascination with a turtle. Caralyn shielded her eyes as she glanced up at him and her breath hitched in her chest.

Sunlight silhouetted his long, lean frame and reflected off the water droplets in his hair to create a halo of sorts. He looked like a Greek god standing before her. Again, a shiver raced from her head to her toes and back while a thousand butterflies danced in her stomach.

Tristan didn't wait for her answer as he lowered himself to the blanket spread out on the sand. The rest of their small group, all freshly washed and sporting the same shimmering droplets, quickly joined him.

"Jemmy, leave the turtle alone. It's time to eat." Tristan grabbed a burlap sack, placed it on his lap, and untied the rope holding it closed.

"Aye, Papa." The boy picked up the turtle and moved it closer to the blanket before he sat, legs crossed.

Caralyn hid her smile behind her hand as Tristan stopped in the middle of pulling foodstuffs from the sack. A sighed escaped him as he glanced at his son and the turtle slowly inching its way across their makeshift table.

"Jemmy, your new friend cannot join us for lunch." The boy's eyes opened wide as he moved the turtle off the blanket. "And you didn't wash your hands."

Caralyn rose to her feet and held out her hand to the boy. "Come on, Jemmy, we'll go wash our hands together." She grinned in Tristan's direction but didn't say a word as Jemmy stuck his hand in hers. They walked toward the jumble of rocks where the crew had gone earlier. Tristan's eyes followed her—she could feel the heat of his gaze on her back but resisted the urge to turn around and smile at him.

When she and Jemmy returned, a small feast was spread out on wide, glossy leaves. Hash had packed bread, cheese, and fruit in the burlap sack. He'd also added a bottle of wine and a small glass jar of milk. They drank from tin cups and ate with their fingers as if they were on a picnic in the country.

Caralyn bit into an apple. Juice dribbled down her chin, and she wiped it away with a grin. She felt like a princess from one of her favorite novels, *Arabian Nights*, although a tropical island was the farthest thing from the Arabian desert. The constant chirping and squawking of the birds, the clucking of chickens, the hypnotic rush of the waterfalls, the gentle lap of the water on the sand made this more of a paradise than anywhere else.

Nothing could have been more perfect, except perhaps, to find Izzy's Fortune. For a moment, Caralyn allowed herself to dream of the treasure they would find and what they could do with those riches.

She could stay here—they all could—and build a life far from the trappings of society. Or they could set sail for distant and exotic places, only stopping long enough to pick up fresh supplies. She wouldn't have to marry the man her father had chosen for her.

From beneath the fringe of her lashes, she snuck a quick peek at Tristan. The *Adventurer's* captain sat across from her, relaxed, joking with his crew and Jemmy but still vigilant. From time to time, his stunning eyes scanned the tree line, and then satisfied there would be no repeat incident with a wild animal, he'd rejoin the conversation.

He must have felt her staring at him because his gaze slanted in her direction and he grinned. Caralyn's face warmed, and a trickle of excitement shimmied down her back.

"We should start exploring before it gets too late." Tristan rose with the fluid grace of a jungle cat then extended his hand for her. Caralyn grasped it only to learn there were more than simply a thousand butterflies in her stomach. She put the estimate at about a million.

The rest of the party rose as well and dusted off their clothing.

"There's a small path beside the waterfall where we all cleaned up." Caralyn pointed to an overgrown footpath barely visible between the tremendous growth of ferns, trees, profusion of flowers, and sheer granite wall. "From what little I saw, it seems to follow the mountainside. That might be our best course."

Tristan stood next to her. The warmth exuding from him curled her toes. "Looks like a good place to start."

She watched with interest as he filled a sack with the pristine white sand from the beach. As he tied it around his waist, she couldn't resist asking, "What is that for?"

"A means to help us find our way back."

Caralyn tilted her head to the side as he repeated the process twice more and tied those sacks to his belt as well. "I'm afraid I don't understand."

He grinned at her. The smile curving his mouth could have charmed the birds from the trees. Caralyn simply stared, unable to draw her attention away. The urge to kiss the rakish grin from his lips, to taste his mouth, overwhelmed her.

"Are you ready?"

Caralyn pulled her focus from his lips. Despite almost being killed by a feral pig, and perhaps because of it, excitement rippled through her. "Of course."

Armed with pistols, machetes, and hearts full of hope, Tristan led them across the shifting sand and into the tropical forest, one hand clutching Jemmy's, the other wielding the long, sharp machete. Caralyn followed close behind, as did Mrs. Beasley, Dr. Trevelyan, and Graham. Mac brought up the rear. He carried a lantern as well as several thick candles and matches in a large leather pouch that strapped around his shoulders and hung down his back. Socrates stayed behind to wait for the rest of the crew and finish preparing the boar for roasting.

Birds cawed and squawked, producing some of the strangest sounds Caralyn had ever heard. Some grew silent as the group passed by then resumed screeching, as if they were admonishing the humans for invading their perfect world. Others left their perches in a flutter of colorful wings. Chickens scurried out of the way. Caralyn saw eggs scattered along the path.

Flowers bloomed everywhere—pushing up from the ground between giant ferns, dangling from trees and bushes in all the colors of the rainbow, from the palest pastels to the most vivid hues. Though she didn't know the names, she recognized some of the blooms from her home on Saint Lucia.

Vines clung to the sheer granite wall, cascading from the top of the mountain down to the forest floor to create an emerald curtain, punctuated by bold, vibrant blooms. Caralyn inhaled the sweet scent of a blossom and sighed with pleasure.

She slapped at her face, grateful for her long sleeved shirt and trousers as insects buzzed all around them. Spiders created the most beautiful and intricate webs, which shimmered in patches of sunlight. Despite the beauty of her surroundings, a shiver raced up her spine. Where there were spiders, there were bound to be snakes. Sneaky and silent, cold and scaly, snakes terrified her. She listened to the sounds all around her and shivered once more.

The farther they advanced into the interior of the island, the more rigorous the climb became. The trail they'd started on disappeared into unrelenting greenness, broken only by boulders and piles of rocks they needed to circumnavigate. Fallen trees, some rotting, some still bursting with life, created another barrier they needed to surpass. In many cases, climbing over half-rotted logs teeming with insects seemed more dangerous than scaling the huge boulders in their way.

No one spoke except Jemmy, who, as promised, not only kept up with the quick pace but chattered non-stop. Being younger, the lad had no problem climbing over boulders or half-rotten trees. Indeed, several times he caught a vine hanging from a tree limb and swung across obstacles in his way.

Half way up the steep mountain, they stopped beside another waterfall, this one smaller and less thunderous. Water poured from a hole high up in the rock wall and cascaded straight down. Years of constant pounding by the steadily flowing liquid had worn a deep, crystalline pool into the hard granite. Crevasses allowed water to escape the pond and flow into a stream they'd traversed several times.

"We'll stop here for a few moments to catch our breath." Tristan signaled to Mac. The Scotsman dutifully turned around to allow Tristan access to the leather pouch and the tin cup contained within. He dipped the vessel into the sparkling pool and passed it around. "Is everyone all right?" One by one, they drank their fill of the cool, refreshing water until Tristan stopped with a full cup in front of Mrs. Beasley. Concern made his eyes squint. "Mrs. Beasley?"

The uphill climb had affected Mrs. Beasley the most. Although perspiration trickled between Caralyn's breasts and soaked the thin corset beneath her shirt, Mrs. Beasley suffered more. One look at the woman's reddened face and a rush of sympathy rolled through Caralyn. The umbrella she carried protected her from the sun, but offered nothing against the oppressive heat and humidity.

"She's a little overheated, but she'll be fine, Tris. I'll take care of her." As Stitch helped Mrs. Beasley sit on one of the boulders surrounding the small pool, Caralyn hid a smile behind her hand. Dr. Brady Trevelyan had called Mrs. Temperance Beasley "Lovey" several times during their hike, and not once did the woman put him in his place. Indeed, she grinned at him like a lovesick fool.

"Lovey" still didn't put up a fuss when Stitch took a knife to her black bombazine gown and cut away the high lace collar and several of the buttons along the bodice. He also stripped the lace from her sleeves and demanded, albeit quietly, she remove at least one of her petticoats.

Caralyn used the reprieve to examine their surroundings. The trail continued upward and disappeared around an outcropping of more tumbled boulders. If they kept following it, they'd reach the top of the mountain, but for reasons she couldn't explain, she didn't think climbing to the summit was where they wanted to go. Another path, smaller than the one they traversed, branched off to the right and led toward the leeward side of the island. Again, she didn't think that path was the correct one to follow. They needed a cave, an entrance inside the mountain to get beneath the sleeping giant's heart.

They were close, so close. She could feel it in her bones, the excitement mingling with the hope in her heart.

Hot and sweaty, she crouched next to the crystalline pool and dipped a handkerchief into the cool water, causing the reflecting sunlight to ripple. As she rose and began to mop at the back of her neck, her gaze followed the cascading water from its source at the top of the mountain to where it stopped in the pool then finally settled on a spot where the rocks seemed to be darker. Behind the cascading water, shadows played tricks on her, and then something shimmered and winked within the darkness.

Her eyes went wide. She stopped wiping the back of her neck and stared at the curious glimmer and the inkiness around it. She squinted, trying to bring what she saw into clearer focus. A moment passed, then two; then laughter bubbled up from her chest. "Tristan," she managed to squawk. "I found it!"

Tristan stood beside her in a heartbeat. The heat of his body radiated out and beckoned her to lean close, but she resisted the call. "What did you find?"

His words fanned her ear and the butterflies in her belly took flight. She pointed toward the shadows behind the flowing water and the winking object within. "Did you see that?"

He focused on the shadows, his concentration deep. Caralyn almost bounced out of her skin when she heard his sharp gasp.

Tristan untied the bags of sand from his belt and let them drop to the ground. The machete settled atop the sand. His soft leather boots came next then his shirt. He winked as he handed the garment to her and dove into the water.

Caralyn's heart pounded so loud she could barely make out the shouts from the rest of their party. She watched his sleek body cut through the water before he disappeared beneath the waterfall where it met the pool in turbulent, misty waves. A moment later, he pulled himself onto a rock shelf behind the cascading water.

She exhaled and clutched his shirt to her chest. His scent tickled her nose. Her knees shook, and a strange warm sensation coursed through her belly. She loved the smell of him.

"Now where does he think he's going?" Graham sidled up beside her, his focus going back and forth between Tristan's watery shadow and her.

She barely glanced at him. "I think there's a cave behind the waterfall." Still watching Tristan through the veil of water, Caralyn worried the fabric in her hands. What did he find? Was it a cave? A doorway to all the treasures that awaited them? Or had the shadows simply played tricks on her? The urge to call out to him, to jump in the water after him washed over her like a wave crashing against the shore.

Graham *harrumphed* but said nothing more. Understanding dawned in his eyes, and a knowing smile curved his mouth.

"He's taking too long," Caralyn murmured, more to herself than anyone else. She took her eyes off Tristan for a second and turned to Mrs. Beasley.

The chaperone's eyes went wide in her red face, and she shook her head adamantly. "Don't you dare think such a thing, young lady."

"But—"

Mrs. Beasley interrupted her before she could finish her thought. "Have you taken leave of all your senses? You can't just blindly jump into the unknown, Miss McCreigh. That's your biggest fault in my opinion," the woman continued. "You are rash and reckless and do not consider the consequences of your actions."

Anger simmered within Caralyn and her hands balled into fists as she glared at her companion, but now was not the time to argue. She returned her attention to Tristan. Her heart leapt into her throat. He was gone!

Panic raced through her. Regardless of Mrs. Beasley's unkind words or perhaps in spite of them, she sat on the rocks and began to remove her boots just as he emerged from the water right in front of her. Relief shot through her and brought beads of perspiration with the flood of emotion. Her relief turned to something deeper and more primitive when she stared at his half-naked body covered in water droplets.

The urge to kiss every last one of them off his muscular chest caused her skin to flush hot. Caralyn knew her face had to be flaming red, but the realization could not, would not let her pull her gaze away from his beautiful, sculpted body.

Tristan rose from the water like King Neptune, sleek and graceful. A wide smile spread across his handsome face. He closed the short distance between them and pulled her into his wet, strong embrace.

Caralyn's head buzzed, the sound of thousands of exotic birds cawing and squawking in her mind. She faintly heard Mrs. Beasley's admonishment. Water dampened her clothes but did nothing to quell the fire raging within her. Trapped by his sherry-colored gaze and strong arms, she raised her head to await his kiss.

And kiss her he did.

Caralyn's toes curled inside her boots as Tristan pressed his warm lips against hers. All too soon, he pulled away and held her at arms length. "You did find something, Cara. There are steps notched into the rock behind the waterfall. They lead up to an opening. And this is what we saw shimmering in the darkness." He held out his hand. A diamond twinkled in the center of his palm. "I saw a handful of these scattered on the steps."

Tears sprang to her eyes and blurred her vision as she handed him his shirt. A thousand words filled her head, but none could get past the lump in her throat. She swallowed hard. Though only one lone diamond sat in his hand and a few more were scattered on the steps, the promise of much more made her heart pound in her chest, made everything she had planned worthwhile, made the possibility of ruining her life acceptable.

"I'm afraid we'll all have to get wet," Tristan told the group as they gathered around him. "I didn't see another way to get behind the waterfall and the steps."

There were few protests. His gaze met and held hers then swept over her head. "Where's Jemmy?"

"He was here a minute ago."

They started looking for the boy who'd been chattering non-stop until only a few seconds ago. He couldn't have gone far, and yet they all knew how fast his little legs could carry him.

"Jemmy!" Tristan yelled above the constant rush of the waterfall and the squawking of the birds. Fear and worry for his son evident not only in his expression, but also in his voice, he hollered again. "Jemmy!"

"Up here, Papa." Jemmy's sweet voice came from above.

Tristan swung around to find Jemmy about twenty feet up, standing between a slab of granite and the waterfall. "Come down from there before—" He never finished his sentence. The boy took a step to his left and disappeared from view.

"Jemmy!"

His son's blond head appeared, an impish grin on his lips. "There's a path, Papa. It goes behind the waterfall." He spun around, arms spread wide. "It's wide enough to dance and you don't even get wet."

Tristan laughed with relief, the thundering boom of it startling the birds from the trees. Caralyn jumped as well. Mrs. Beasley shook her head, her mouth open as if a reprimand hovered on her tongue.

"Come down here and show us."

While Jemmy chattered and climbed over the rocks, Caralyn took the opportunity to watch Tristan slip into his shirt, disappointed he covered the taut, muscled chest she'd been admiring. He sat on the rocks to pull on his boots then handed the machete to Mac.

Excitement visible all over his face, Jemmy skittered to a halt in front of them. "It ain't—"

"Isn't," Tristan corrected automatically.

The boy continued as if he hadn't been interrupted at all. "—hard to get into the cave if you know where to go."

Tristan tied the bags of sand to his belt and beckoned the boy closer. Jemmy did as he was told, and Caralyn held her breath. She hoped Tristan wouldn't scold his son as badly as Mrs. Beasley had scolded her. No one liked to be chastised, especially in front of others.

Once again, the captain of the *Adventurer* surprised her. His voice lowered but still rang with love and patience. "I thought I told you to stay close. I thought we agreed you wouldn't wander away without an adult with you."

Jemmy nodded with enthusiasm as he did everything else. "Yes, Papa, but—"

"Listen to me, son. There are dangers here we don't know, don't expect. You could have slipped and fallen from those rocks, and it's a long way down. I love you, boy, and it would break my heart if something were to happen to you. Do you understand?"

The boy shifted from one foot to the other. "Yes, Papa."

"Good." Tristan ruffled his son's hair then rose. "Lead the way, my little explorer."

The small group followed Jemmy through a maze of jumbled rocks, some rounded with age, some jagged and sharp as diamonds. Caralyn paused and took a deep breath. To her right, granite wall, to her left, the green expanse of tropical forest punctuated by beautiful, colorful blooms. In front of her, Tristan's broad back

… and her future. Her heart beat so quickly, she heard it over the sound of the thundering water. A fine mist cooled the humid air as she stepped into the narrow passageway behind the waterfall.

Mac cleared his throat and drew attention to himself. Face pale and shiny with sweat, he handed out the candles he pulled from the sack. He removed the lantern last and thrust it toward Tristan.

As he took the lantern from the man, concern caused Tristan's eyes to narrow slightly. "What is it, Mac?"

The quartermaster's hands shook as he struck a match and lit the lantern and the candles each person held. "Cap'n, ye know I'd sail off the edge of the ocean if'n ye asked me, but I canna go in there. I canna breathe with the walls so close."

"You don't have to go inside, Mac. You can wait for us here, at the entrance."

As captain, he could have forced Mac to accompany them or forced everyone else to stay outside while he explored the cave alone, and yet he had noticed the Scotsman's pale face and the fear so evident in his eyes and graciously offered him a reprieve. Tristan's kindness and understanding knew no bounds and Caralyn's admiration for this man grew. Drawn to his thoughtfulness and compassion, she moved closer to him and thrilled when he casually draped an arm around her shoulders.

She almost smiled when he focused on Mrs. Beasley and said, "I'm certain Mrs. Beasley has no desire to explore the cave either."

"You'd be mistaken, Captain," Mrs. Beasley muscled her way in between the two of them. "I will not allow you to be alone with her!" The woman puffed up her already ample bosom and frowned at him. "You have already taken too many liberties, sir. I go where she goes."

And with those words, Mrs. Beasley grabbed Caralyn's hand and pulled her into the cave. Tristan's startled shout of warning followed; however, Mrs. Beasley rushed forward without stopping.

Chapter 10

The passage twisted and turned, wider in some places, so narrow in others they had to slide against the walls damp with moisture. The farther along they went, the darker their path became, the ambient light from outside growing dim until there was none.

The others were behind them. Caralyn heard their footsteps, their low voiced conversation and her name echoing in the small corridor. Candlelight flickered and danced, shadows grew and diminished, only to grow again.

She held her candle higher, as did Mrs. Beasley, until the passage ended and they stepped into a long chamber. A putrid smell slammed against her and stole her breath for a moment. Her stomach lurched and tears sprang to her eyes. She held her finger beneath her nose to block out the worst of the odors, but nothing helped. Above her, the ceiling undulated like black waves on the ocean. She raised the candle for a closer look and wished she hadn't.

Bats. Thousands of them hung from the roof of the cavern. A startled scream built in her throat, but she swallowed it away. She hated bats almost as much as she hated snakes.

Apparently, Mrs. Beasley hated bats as well. The woman, still grasping her arm, stopped short. A surprised squeal escaped her, the sound enough to send the winged rodents into flight, their piercing shrieks bouncing off the walls in the chamber.

Generations of the flying creatures left their mark on the floor, but without hesitation Caralyn crouched low and brought Mrs. Beasley down beside her. "Open your umbrella."

The woman dropped her candle, snapped the umbrella open, and held it close over their heads. With only one flickering candle burning, darkness hovered, and the walls of the cavern seemed to draw in around them. The sound of wings flapping as the bats made their way to the outside world became overwhelming. Chest tight, palms sweating, the awful smell tickling her nose, Caralyn concentrated on not vomiting.

A shriek of fear escaped Mrs. Beasley each time one of the bats flew too close and bounced off the protective sunshade. Caralyn held her breath to avoid the fetid stench and silently recited the Lord's Prayer.

In moments, the melee ended. Except for the steady *plop, plop, plop* of water dripping from the stalagmites, silence permeated the grotto.

Caralyn helped Mrs. Beasley to her feet. "Here, you hold this while I find your candle."

The woman closed the umbrella with a snap and grabbed the candle, her knuckles white. In the glow of the dancing flame, Mrs. Beasley's face appeared ghostly. Tears glittered behind the lenses of her glasses and her chin trembled, but she held herself rigid. "I've never been so afraid in all my life," she whispered, her voice shaking as much as the candle in her hand.

"They're gone now and they won't be back as long as we're here." Caralyn patted her companion's hand. "You were very brave."

Mrs. Beasley *harrumphed* but said nothing more as Caralyn retrieved the fallen candle from the guano-covered floor.

Light flickered as the rest of the group joined them. Without hesitation, without the least bit of embarrassment, Dr. Trevelyan rushed to them and enfolded Mrs. Beasley in his embrace. "Lovey, are you all right?"

As she melted against him, Mrs. Beasley nodded against his chest. Her breath hitched, as if she fought off the urge to cry.

"Are you hurt?" Tristan stood not a foot away from Caralyn. Concern etched lines on his face, but his eyes still contained all the excitement of this adventure. Nothing, it seemed, not bats, not the fetid smell suffocating them, could dampen the exhilaration of being here. He moved a step closer and gently raised her face with the touch of his finger at her chin.

"I'm fine, just a little startled." Caralyn couldn't help the shiver that raced down her back, and yet the simple touch of his hand, the very nearness of him, calmed all her fears. "I hate bats."

"I'm not fond of them, either." A smile twitched the corners of his mouth. "Perhaps it would be best if you, Mrs. Beasley, and Jemmy waited outside with Mac."

Caralyn shook her head. As much as she would love to remove herself from this dark, damp cave and the overpowering smell, the lure of finding Izzy's Fortune wouldn't let her. "I wouldn't dream of it, Tristan."

"What about you, Mrs. Beasley?"

The woman shook her head. "If she stays," her voice trembled but grew stronger within the doctor's embrace, "I stay."

Though frightened, her companion displayed an uncommon amount of heart, and Caralyn had to admire the woman's courage.

"Jemmy?"

The boy slid his small hand into his father's larger one. "I wanna be with you." A lump rose to Caralyn's throat. The love between Tristan and Jemmy touched her heart and reminded her of the adventures she'd shared with her father. Daniel McCreigh would have loved this journey into the caves deep beneath the earth. She shook off the pang of loneliness and regret that her father no longer wished to search for Izzy's Fortune.

Tristan gazed at this son and finally nodded, then glanced at Graham, who stood near the entrance to the tunnel. "What about you, Graham?"

The man grinned. "I'm not fond of bats or caves, but I wouldn't miss this for the world." He gave an exaggerated bow. "Shall we explore this horrid place?"

Candles held high, Tristan's lantern brighter than all of them combined, they explored the cavern. With every step Caralyn and her companions took, they released more of the stench from the cave floor. Her boots would be ruined, as would everyone else's. Indeed, the hem of Mrs. Beasley's gown showed stains that would never be removed. Once they found the treasure, Caralyn vowed she would buy the woman twenty gowns to replace the one she now wore.

They weren't the first to be here; some of the previous visitors hadn't made it out alive. Human bones littered the floor above and beneath the coating of bat guano. An involuntary shiver shook Caralyn to her core, and the flame from her candle flickered as her hand trembled.

What had killed these people? Fighting among themselves, all for want of the treasure? Had they become lost and disoriented, unable to find their way to freedom? Would the same happen to them? She shook her head, determined that it not be so, but her stomach clenched and once again, she fought for control as she tried to step around the bones.

Others were not so cautious. The crack of bones snapping echoed in the chamber. Caralyn jumped with each sharp pop. Her throat constricted and she tasted bile, but she continued on, edging along the wall, Tristan just a short distance away, Jemmy, for once, quiet. All of this—the atrocious odor, the bats, the bones, the feeling the cave was too small and stealing her breath—would be worth it when they found the treasure.

Within the chamber, flickering candlelight created ghostly shadows that danced on the walls. Perception and distance changed. Sound echoed. Darkness beyond the small pools of light closed in around her. She gripped the candle tighter to keep her hand from shaking then took a deep breath and forced her legs to carry her forward.

"There's another tunnel." The light of Caralyn's candle shined into a gaping chasm but only for a short distance before being swallowed in inky blackness.

"I found one as well," Graham called out from the other side of the chamber, the sound of his voice close, yet far away at the same time.

"So did we," Stitch remarked from the farthest reach of the cave to the north, his hand clasping Mrs. Beasley's as they approached the opening, the flame of the candle flickering. "I feel cool air."

"Which one should we take?" Tristan asked as he held his lantern higher to cast more light.

With a shrug, Stitch replied, "You're the captain. You choose."

Tristan's gaze went to each one of them. Finally, he gave a slight nod of his head. "Since you feel cool air, Stitch, I think that might be our best bet." He eyed each member of his small group. "Is everyone ready?"

The purpose of the bags of sand Tristan carried became clear. He made a small slit in the corner of one sack and let a steady stream of white mark their progress as the small group made their way into the first tunnel. Pride at his resourcefulness swelled in Caralyn's chest as she gazed at Tristan's wide shoulders ahead of her.

Like the chasm that led to the chamber, this passageway twisted and turned as well, the walls drawing closer until no one, not even Jemmy, could slip inside the small opening. They could go no further.

A shiver snaked its way down Caralyn's back. *Is it just my imagination or is the roof of the cave coming closer?*

Tristan sighed, disappointment evident in his stance, the sloping of his shoulders, the grim set of his mouth. "It's a dead end. We'll have to turn back."

"But I feel cool air." Dr. Trevelyan watched the flame of his candle move as if carried by a breeze. "Where is it coming from?"

"Perhaps we missed another tunnel." Tristan held the lantern high. Shadows and light danced on the moist walls. "In any case, the space is too small. None of us can fit through."

"I don't like this," Jemmy whispered as he sidled closer to his father.

"You can still wait outside with Mac," Tristan suggested but the boy shook his head.

They turned around as one and this time, Graham led the way back into the main chamber.

"Since I chose so poorly, perhaps someone else would like to try," Tristan said.

Graham dug a coin out of his pocket. "Heads, we take this tunnel to the south. Tails, we take the one leading west." He tossed the coin high in the air, caught it in his hand, and slapped it on his wrist. "West it is."

Another dead end of sorts. Instead of the walls closing in, the passageway led to an opening ... and a drop of several yards to the ocean below. Though the view was nothing short of amazing and the warm air circulating around her eased some of the nausea roiling in Caralyn's stomach, they could proceed no further.

As one, they turned and went back to the main chamber.

The last tunnel led upward at a slight grade. Caralyn heard rushing water. She thought it could be the river, which fed one of the waterfalls on the island, but couldn't be sure. Strange. The sound came from above her. The sides of the cave gleamed with moisture. Small puddles of water shimmered on the ground. She glanced at the ceiling of the channel, which was so low, it seemed to scrape the top of Tristan's head. For once, she thanked heaven for her short stature.

Caralyn knew they hadn't been inside the mountain for very long and yet, between the oppressive darkness, the rank dampness, which surrounded them, and the way the passages twisted and turned, time had lost all meaning. She couldn't tell if only a few minutes had passed or if it had been hours since they first discovered the cave behind the waterfall. She closed her eyes for a moment and concentrated on the treasure—and precious freedom—soon to be in her grasp.

The passage led to another chamber, smaller than the first but high-domed with an irregular oval shape. Fresh air and a single ray of sunlight filtered in through the hole in the ceiling to illuminate the pile of bones and a small wooden chest in the center of the chamber. The skeleton of a human hand rested atop the strongbox, the bones undisturbed after all these years. Tears welled in Caralyn's eyes as hope and expectation died a painful death in her heart. This was not the treasure she imagined, for there could not possibly be a fortune in gold and jewels in one tiny wooden box. Caralyn took a deep breath and a step forward.

"Wait." Tristan commanded and grabbed her arm. "Look at the floor."

Caralyn did as he asked. All around the chest, two-inch long needle-like spears of wood littered the floor. Hundreds of them, some still stuck in the remnants of clothing in disintegrating piles.

"Poison darts?" Though she'd heard tales about natives of the Caribbean islands using such things, she'd never believed. Until now.

"It's within the realm of possibility," Dr. Trevelyan admitted as he hunched down and carefully pushed the darts around with a bone. "There are such poisons that can kill instantly. Some paralyze your muscles first—"

"Brady!" Mrs. Beasley said. The doctor glanced at her then at the young boy beside her. He continued on, but in another vein. "The chest must be a trap. Anyone who tries to move it will be struck with these darts." He rose and walked around the chamber, shining the light from his candle on the rough rock. He paused and pressed his fingers against several small slits in the wall. "I would imagine the darts come from here but I cannot see how."

"No matter, Stitch." Tristan turned up the wick on his lantern to chase the darkness away. He crouched low and inspected the area around the chest without getting too close. Caralyn admired the way his movements caused the muscles in his back to ripple.

He stood and ran his fingers through his hair. "Obviously the chest is a trap, as this poor fellow learned," he pointed to the skeletal hand atop the box, "but I see no strings or wires. The ground beneath it seems solid."

"Here." Mrs. Beasley held out her umbrella. "Use this."

Tristan grabbed the offered item. "Everyone stand against the wall. I don't want anyone hurt."

Caralyn motioned to Jemmy. "Come stand by me." The boy carefully picked his way around the bones on the floor and joined her at the far side of the chamber. He slipped his hand into hers and squeezed. "You're very brave, Jemmy," she whispered in his ear. The boy's smile lit up his entire face.

The others did as they were told as well. Once certain they were out of harm's way, Tristan used the umbrella's pointed tip and brushed the skeletal hand from the top of the box then pushed the chest an inch.

Caralyn held her breath. Nothing happened. No poisoned darts flew, no sound echoed in the small chamber.

He tried again, pushing at the coffer with the tip of the umbrella. Another inch. Then two. Still nothing.

One more time, Tristan shoved the strongbox. A metallic ping resonated in the air as the chest scrapped across the hard packed dirt. Her nerves on edge, Caralyn jumped, as did Tristan, but still, nothing happened. No darts flew across the chamber, the walls didn't suddenly collapse, the floor remained solid beneath their feet.

Tristan gave a relieved chuckle. "I can only assume the last poor fellow to touch the chest released all the darts." He glanced around the chamber at the people under his protection and grinned. "I think it's safe now." He returned the umbrella to Mrs. Beasley. "Caralyn, would you like to—"

Before he finished his sentence, Caralyn approached the chest and knelt in front of it. She held her breath and said a silent prayer. With trembling fingers, she lifted the lid. No gold coins filled the box. No fortune in loose gems either. The sweet taste of freedom, so recently acquired, turned bitter as she stared at a burlap wrapped object inside the coffer.

With great care, she untied the string and peeled away the fabric to reveal a jewel-encrusted statuette of the Virgin Mother. How she wanted to cry, to just let the tears roll down her face and give in to the painful realization that she would never be able to buy herself out of a marriage she didn't want. She bit her lip and swallowed against the lump in her throat.

"Well, what's in there?" Graham stepped away from the chamber wall. "Emeralds? Rubies? Gold?"

Caralyn took a deep breath to get her emotions under control and lifted the golden figurine from the chest. "No precious gems, Graham. No gold coins," she said, her voice tight even to her own ears. "Just this."

She held the effigy as if it were made of glass instead of gold and showed them all what this adventure beneath the mountain had brought.

"I warned you, didn't I?" Mrs. Beasley *harrumphed* and grabbed the statue from her hand. Her eyes, behind the lenses of her glasses, narrowed as she pinned Caralyn with an unforgiving stare. Her voice hardened. "I knew from the beginning there was no such treasure, that this was all a lark to avoid the inevitable. Now, perhaps, you'll listen and we can leave this godforsaken place for England."

Even a small piece of paradise couldn't please her companion. Caralyn hung her head. Her hopes, her dreams, died a painful death, and yet she wasn't willing to concede defeat. Not yet. She still had time, still had the rambling thoughts Andrew Pembrook had committed to paper all those years ago.

She shifted from one foot to the other. Angry words were on the tip of her tongue. Tired, hungry, so filled with disappointment her heart hurt, she opened her mouth to unleash those words but couldn't utter a single one.

"There's a piece of parchment." Tristan's comment grabbed her attention. Caralyn faced him as he pulled the folded note from the bottom of the coffer.

She gazed into his eyes, saw the twinkle of understanding in their depths, and knew his faith hadn't faltered, not for a moment. He believed in Izzy's Fortune, believed they would find the legendary treasure so many sought. "Read it."

A slight smile curved the corners of his mouth as he unfolded the heavy parchment. "It says, 'Take the hand of the Blessed Virgin.'"

Caralyn studied the statue Mrs. Beasley held. This Virgin Mary did not have hands which one could hold, which meant there was another statue, one that did. The disillusionment and frustration of moments before disappeared as quickly as they had come. Hope once more flooded her heart.

"There was a chapel on Pembrook's plantation," she all but whispered. "He mentions it many times in the course of his writing—I believe he spent a great deal of time there, praying—perhaps for forgiveness for stealing the treasure; perhaps so Morgan wouldn't find him and kill him. What say you?" She retrieved the golden statuette from Mrs. Beasley and held it up. "Does this warrant a visit to Jamaica?"

"Jamaica!" Mrs. Beasley exclaimed. Her entire body stiffened. Bright spots of color stained the woman's cheeks and her eyes glittered. "There is no treasure, Miss McCreigh! No reason to continue this—this farce, no logical—"

"Lovey." Stitch said the word softly and gently touched her shoulder. Mrs. Beasley's mouth snapped closed, and her lips pressed together into an unflattering line. She sniffed and her eyes grew shiny with unshed tears. With one last glare at Caralyn, she allowed the good doctor to draw her away toward the tunnel. He spoke to her softly, the words a quiet hum Caralyn could not hear, but whatever he said to the woman seemed to appease her.

"We set sail tomorrow after a good night's sleep," Tristan announced to those remaining in the chamber. "But we'll have to stop for supplies first. We'll continue on to Puerto Rico."

Caralyn glanced at the statue then at him. In the light of the lantern, his unusual eyes sparkled. A sweet smile lifted the corners of his mouth, and she wanted more than anything to touch his tempting lips with her own.

"Faith," he whispered as he tilted her chin with the tip of his finger. "Keep your faith. I believe Izzy's Fortune is out there. And it'll be more than just that gold statue in your hand."

Caralyn nodded then smiled and slid her hand into his.

• • •

They'd spent more time beneath the mountain than Tristan had realized. No longer overhead, the sun had long begun its decent into the horizon. The heat and humidity seemed to dissipate, and a cool breeze whistled through the palm fronds, making them rattle against each other. The colorful birds were silent.

While in the cave, Jemmy had been quiet and reserved, hovering close to Tristan. Now, full of renewed energy, he scrambled over rocks and fallen trees, and swung from the vines within his reach, his constant chatter a balm for the weary group trudging down toward the secluded cove.

Tristan turned his head and studied Caralyn beside him. She had grown quiet, as if lost in thought. Perhaps she still bristled from her companion's unkind words. If he could find a moment with Mrs. Beasley, he would talk to her about the way she spoke to

Caralyn. No one had the right to disparage someone else's dreams. "Cara?"

"Yes?"

"Are you all right?"

"Yes." She responded with a single word but didn't say anything more.

It didn't take nearly as long to reach the camp as it had to reach the tunnel, and the smell of roasting pork met Tristan's nose. His entire crew, except for two, were in various stages of activity. A few more canvas tents dotted the sand. Stacks of firewood rested beside the fire pit. Socrates walked the length of the beach, back and forth, the blade of his long knife reflecting the light of the fading sun, on the lookout for feral pigs, in case there were more.

Woody, Coop, and Ephraim made use of one of the dilapidated grass huts and played a game of chance. A few more of his men were lounging in the cove's crystal blue water.

Hash had cut the wild pig into four sections, each one on a spit, which Gawain Jacoby and Mad Dog turned slowly. Flames danced in the fireplace and sizzled each time a drop of pork fat dribbled into the heat. Hunger made Tristan's stomach rumble.

Mrs. Beasley, ahead of the small group, marched straight to her tent without a word and closed the flap. Tristan watched her and a slight smile curved his mouth. Judging by the way she had stomped across the sand, back ramrod stiff, perhaps Stitch had already taken care of the problem of her criticism and harsh words.

His smile grew and his suspicion proved correct as Stitch sidled up beside Caralyn. He heard the good doctor's words clearly. "I'm sorry."

Caralyn glanced at him. "For what?"

"For the way Mrs. Beasley spoke to you in the cave." His face flushed as he rammed in hands into his pocket. "She doesn't mean it, you know."

She placed her hand in the crook of his arm and smiled at him. "You have nothing to be sorry about, Stitch. Mrs. Beasley has never been afraid to speak her mind, and she means every word of it. She should take a lesson from the way Tristan reprimands his son. Never a harsh word. Always with love and kindness."

The flush on his face deepened. "I'll have a talk with her."

Again, Caralyn flashed him a beaming smile. "I appreciate your offer, but it isn't necessary. It's the way she is and I've accepted that. I realize she isn't happy being dragged from pillar to post in search of a treasure that may or may not exist. I realize I give her cause to chastise me."

"Be that as it may, Miss Cara, I shall still speak with her. Despite her tendency to chastise you, as you put it, Mrs. Beasley has a beautiful heart. When she chooses, she can be kindness itself."

"You're quite fond of her, aren't you, Stitch?"

If possible, the man's face turned even redder, the color staining his ears as well as his throat. His mouth opened several times, but no words issued forth, just a strangled groan.

Tristan couldn't help himself. He chuckled as the doctor made a hasty retreat to his own tent. "You embarrassed him," he said to Caralyn. "He didn't think anyone noticed."

"How could anyone not notice?" she asked with a laugh. "He called her Lovey. Not once, not twice, but several times."

Tristan shrugged his shoulders. He wasn't interested in Stitch and Mrs. Beasley. The sparkle was back in Caralyn's incredible eyes and the grin on her face did something strange to his heart. The urge to kiss her once again, to take her in his arms and lay her down on the sand became undeniable. His pulse picked up its pace and his heartbeat so fast, he thought his chest might explode.

"Did you find the treasure?"

"Are we richer than Midas?"

"Where is it?"

"Are we going back for it tomorrow?"

Whatever thoughts and wishes he harbored toward Caralyn quickly disappeared beneath the barrage of questions from his crew as the men accompanied the small party to the fire pit.

"Been wonderin' when ye'd be back," Hash remarked as Tristan cut a small piece of pork and slipped it into his mouth. "Been waiting fer ye. Ye find that blasted treasure?"

Tristan grinned and spoke to all the men gathered around him. "We did not find the treasure. We did find a gold statue of the Blessed Mother and a clue." He gestured toward Mac. "Show them the statue."

The Scotsman pulled the burlap wrapped effigy from his sack and released the tie that held it together with great care. The men *oohed* and *aahed* and passed the icon from one hand to the other. The parchment came next. One after another, they read the written words and tried to decipher the clue. Instead of being disappointed because there were no jewels or coins, the crew became more excited. This was their proof, and each one, to the last man, couldn't wait to begin the next part of their adventure.

"Where to next, Cap'n?" Gawain asked.

"We'll continue on to Puerto Rico for fresh supplies then Jamaica." Tristan glanced at Caralyn. The grin parting her tempting lips melted his heart. "Miss McCreigh believes there is a chapel on Pembrook's plantation."

The excitement grew and their voices became louder, gestures more animated as they dined on fresh pork and small roasted potatoes Hash pulled from the glowing ashes of the fire.

Mrs. Beasley did not join in either the meal or the conversation. She stayed in her tent, using exhaustion for her excuse, but Tristan suspected she might still be angry they were continuing their quest. Or, she was embarrassed by the clothing lent to her as her gown had been truly ruined by the excursion into the cave.

The conversation and laughter around the fire pit did not end with the meal. The hopes and dreams of every man was shared long after the moon rose high and stars twinkled in the velvety black night.

Belly full, clean and warm, and exhausted from his adventures of the day, Jemmy snuggled beside his father. He let out a long sigh and closed his eyes. In seconds, he slept, despite the loud laughter all around him. Or perhaps because of it.

Tristan gazed at his son's blond hair shimmering in the moonlight and grinned. He'd never known anyone who could fall asleep so quickly or completely.

Content, feeling the warmth of his son's heavy body leaning against him, Tristan let himself relax. The day had been long and yet, he wasn't tired. Indeed, despite only finding one gold statue in the cave, he was exhilarated. After years of searching for Izzy's Fortune, he'd finally found some proof it truly existed. His eyes roamed to the crew gathered around the fire.

This is the life! What could be better than to be surrounded by people you loved and trusted and who felt the same about you? To be on the trail of a fabulous fortune? To be on an island paradise with a beautiful woman?

With a start, he realized Caralyn wasn't among those gathered around him. Stitch and Socrates were missing as well. He glanced at the tent behind him, the flap now open. No light shined from within. Mrs. Beasley was gone, too.

He spotted Graham lounging against one of the logs that had been set up around the fire, a piece of pork in his hand. "Where is Cara?"

The man shrugged his shoulders and took another bite of the meat. "Haven't seen her in awhile," he said around the food in his mouth.

"I saw her walk over to the waterfall awhile ago," Gawain offered then gestured to Stitch, who paced the sand further down the beach.

With great care so as not to disturb Jemmy's rest, Tristan rose to his feet and lifted the boy in his arms. His son murmured but did not awaken as Tristan carried him to their tent and laid him down on a bedroll in the soft sand. He sighed deeply as Tristan covered him with a light blanket. He left the tent, spoke a few words with Hash, and went in search of the woman with the dancing sea-blue eyes.

He found Socrates standing guard atop a huge boulder near the first in a series of three glistening pools fed by the waterfall. "Sorry, Cap'n, ye can't be comin' any further."

Tristan stopped and glared at the man who impeded his progress. "And why not?"

The crewman shifted his weight from one foot to the other and a big grin spread his lips. "Miss McCreigh needs her privacy."

Tristan raised an eyebrow and folded his arms across his chest. Never before had Socrates Callahan taken such a stance. "I beg your pardon?"

Socrates lowered his voice. "She's takin' a bath. Mrs. Beasley's up there with her."

His imagination took flight. Tristan envisioned Caralyn in the moonlight, water sparkling on her skin, her hair flowing down her back. He had not forgotten about laying her down in the sand and exploring every inch of her body, of touching her skin to see how soft it truly was, of feeling the weight of her milky white breasts in his hands. Hot blood surged through his veins, and the urge to surprise her while she bathed became undeniable.

Before he could even consider acting on his desires, Socrates shook his head. "Now, Cap'n, I know ye can order me to step aside and I might consider it 'cause ye're the captain, but I don' think ye'll be doin' that. Ye have respect for Miss McCreigh and so do I." His red hair gleamed like fire in the moonlight as he took a step closer and pointed to Dr. Trevelyan's lonely figure pacing the sand farther down the beach. "Jes' like I tol' Stitch, ye'll have to wait until they're done."

Tristan bowed his head. As much as he would have liked to at least catch a glimpse of his fascinating mermaid, he wouldn't invade her privacy—not with a guard dog like Socrates on duty. "As you wish." He stuck his hands in his pocket and strolled toward Dr. Trevelyan.

Chapter 11

Caralyn shot out of the water in the small pool beside the cascading waterfall and pushed her hair out of her face. It felt wonderful to be clean, to be rid of the smell of the cave. With her stomach full of Hash's wonderful dinner, and plans in place to continue the search for Izzy's Fortune, contentment spread through her.

She treaded water and listened to the noises coming from camp. The men were in high spirits, their ribald laughter competing with the chirping crickets, the breeze that rattled the palm fronds, and the constant rush of water as it fell to the cove below her. She grinned and floated on her back. Above her, the bright ball of the moon glowed.

"Miss McCreigh! You haven't a stitch of clothing on!"

Startled, Caralyn gasped and sank to the bottom of the pool. She turned quickly and through the shimmering water saw Mrs. Beasley standing on a rock above her, arms folded across her chest, body stiff with indignation. She rose to the surface, exposing only her head, in time to hear another tongue-lashing.

"Young lady, this goes beyond what could be considered proper, beyond decency. I've never seen such heathenish behavior." The woman took a deep breath and began to tap her foot on the rock on which she stood. "Even for you, Miss McCreigh. Your family will hear of this, I assure you."

Too full of the satisfaction of finding another piece of Pembrook's puzzle, Caralyn grinned. "Tell them. Tell them everything I've done. I'll bet you a pound Father won't be upset, though Charles might be." Her grin widened and the urge to laugh tickled her. An invitation fell from her lips before she could stop it. "Why don't you join me, Mrs. Bea—Temperance? The water is warm and quite lovely. It's much better than the baths we've been taking in the hipbath. At least take your shoes and stockings off and put your feet in."

The woman sniffed but she did gaze at the water with what Caralyn thought was longing.

"It's improper," she stated, but without as much arrogance as usual. "As are these clothes I'm wearing." She gestured to the loose white shirt and tan trousers that replaced her ruined gown. The pant legs were rolled to her knees, exposing the white stockings beneath, and a length of rope, tied around her waist, held the trousers in place.

"No one can see you here, Temperance. Mr. Callahan is keeping watch." A touch of sympathy rushed through Caralyn for the ruination of her companion's clothing. "I'm sorry your gown is beyond repair, but we'll remedy that once we reach Puerto Rico. While the men are gathering fresh supplies, you and I can shop. If I recall correctly, there's a lovely dress shop in San Juan." Caralyn grinned at her. "Although, you must admit, dressed as you are now, don't you feel a bit more free? And cooler?"

For once, the pinched expression her companion usually wore eased and a slight smile graced her lips. In that moment, in the moonlight, her lips parted, she looked beautiful and Caralyn saw why Stitch was smitten with her.

"As much as I hate to acknowledge it, you're right. I don't feel quite so constricted; however, it is still highly improper." Her arms crossed over her chest again. "I have always held myself to a higher standard."

Caralyn wiped dripping water from her face. "And there is nothing wrong with that, but we are in the middle of nowhere, far away from the rules of society. I certainly won't tell a soul if you set your standards a little lower. Just for a moment."

Behind the lenses of her glasses, Temperance's eyes gleamed as she studied the water in the pool.

Yes, that is longing I see in her eyes.

Temperance bit her lip and glanced around. The only light came from the moon's glow. The third pool, high above the sandy beach, surrounded by rock, offered privacy and security. Without so much as another word, Temperance sat on the rock and removed her shoes and stockings. She eased her feet into the warm water and sighed. "Oh, this is heaven." She said nothing more, but her expression remained soft.

Caralyn made her way toward where Temperance dangled her feet and found a small rock shelf below the water's surface. It was high enough for her to sit, but still be completely covered.

She didn't want to ruin this lovely interlude. For once, Temperance Beasley seemed a little more approachable, more accepting of a break in decorum. She took a deep breath. "I realize coming on this adventure was never your idea, and you're only here because of me, but I have a request." She continued in a rush before she lost her nerve. "In the future, I would appreciate it, if you must chastise me, please do it in private."

The woman stiffened and the pinched expression returned to her face but only for a moment. She didn't look at Caralyn. Instead, her gaze settled on her hands folded in her lap. Her mouth opened and closed several times before she said, "I apologize for that." She finally lifted her head. Caralyn caught the sheen of unshed tears in the woman's eyes. "From now on, I will endeavor to keep our discussions private. I am only trying to keep you safe, Miss—"

"Please," Caralyn interrupted, "after all this time, after all we've been through, don't you think you should call me Cara?"

"Your brother paid me to keep you out of trouble. I take my responsibilities to heart, Miss ... Cara. These pirates you're so fond of—"

Caralyn giggled. "They're not pirates, Temperance. They're treasure hunters."

The woman *harrumphed.* "Be that as it may, they are still men and men, when not kept at the proper distance, can become ...

unpredictable—and dare I say it—savage. The captain especially. Beneath his air of civility lies a bold and daring man. He has taken far too many liberties, and given the opportunity, I'm certain he would take more."

Warmth spread throughout Caralyn's body as she remembered the passionate kisses Tristan had given her. In truth, she hadn't minded, not one bit. "I cannot argue. Captain Trey is forthright and self-assured but a gentleman through and through." Caralyn sighed but pushed for her argument, defending the crew she'd come to love.

"These men are the finest of any I've ever met. They are kind and considerate. Perhaps not as educated as some, perhaps a little lacking in the social graces but each and every one of them has been nothing but thoughtful and compassionate toward you." Caralyn tilted her head. "And what of Dr. Trevelyan? Is he not a gentleman? Is he not educated?"

In the glow of moonlight, Temperance's face took on a pinkish hue. "Education does not make the man, Cara, and I am quite fond of the good doctor; however, I cannot disagree with you. I have been treated kindly."

"My offer still stands, Temperance. Once we reach Puerto Rico, I can secure passage for you to return to Charleston if you wish or anywhere else you choose to go."

Her companion grew silent as she mulled over the offer. After a while, she smiled. "I will stay and continue to hunt for this Izzy's Fortune even though I do not believe it exists. Someone must watch over you to make certain you do nothing more foolish than you have already done." She sighed and adjusted her glasses on her nose. "Your brother—"

"Doesn't have to know."

Temperance just stared at her then finally inclined her head. "I'll say one more thing and then the subject is closed. Mind your heart, my girl. Too easily given, it can be too easily broken as well."

• • •

Tristan sat in the sand beside Brady, arms resting on his bent knees, hands dangling between them, and simply enjoyed the quiet solitude of the evening. His companion sat in much the same position as they waited.

Stitch broke the silence. "What will you do with your share of the treasure?"

"Invest it, like I always do. I've had my eye on another warehouse in Charleston and there's a struggling plantation in Jamaica I wouldn't mind owning. Under the right management, I'm certain Sugar Hill could be quite productive. They make a fine rum." He chuckled then sighed. "This is my last adventure, Stitch, whether we find Izzy's Fortune or not."

"Your last? I don't understand."

"Father has ordered me home to marry."

"Marry? You?" Stitch shook his head and glanced at him. "Given your feelings on the subject, I'm surprised you're even considering it."

"I have no choice. Father has made all the arrangements, including choosing the woman who is to be my wife."

"The earl is a willful man," Stitch agreed. "More than once, he's made me shake in my boots. Perhaps he has chosen wisely."

Tristan sighed again. "How could he choose wisely? He doesn't know me, doesn't know what I want." The moment the words left his mouth, he realized the truth although he couldn't say the thought aloud. *How could Father know? Up until a short time ago, I didn't even know what I wanted. All I knew is that I didn't want a marriage like his.*

"What about love, Tris? Does that enter into the equation with your father?"

"No, love doesn't matter. I will marry for money, as generations have done before me." Tristan glanced at his companion and blurted, "Quite frankly, I don't believe the earl believes in love."

Stitch said nothing for a long time as he stared at the gently lapping waves. "Perhaps, in time, you'll grow to love this woman you're to marry. It does happen. Some of the best marriages have been based on less."

"You don't truly believe that, do you?"

In the glow of moonlight, Stitch's face took on a particular rosy hue. "Yes, I do. You know how much I loved my Fannie. She was the love of my life, yet we barely knew each other when we married. Like you, my marriage was arranged for the benefit of both our families. The best I had hoped for was companionship, and yet over the years, we came to love each other. There will come a moment when you will look at your future wife and realize she is the woman you have waited for all your life." He shrugged his shoulders. "Tell me about the woman you are to marry."

Tristan laughed. "I can't. I've never met her. Furthermore, I don't even know her name, though I would imagine she's from a good family. She must be. Why else would Father have chosen her?" A long sigh escaped him as he gazed at the moonlight shimmering on the water. "I suppose I should have gone back to England and courted the woman. At least met her, but I … I wanted one last adventure, one last chance to find Izzy's Fortune. I know—very selfish on my part."

They grew silent, the only sound the whisper of a breeze through the palm trees. The silence didn't last long as Tristan commented, "You're quite taken with her."

"Miss Cara? Oh, yes. She's a lovely young woman."

Tristan chuckled. "Not Cara, although I will agree, she's quite lovely. Mrs. Beasley."

He watched as a blush deepened on the doctor's face. The man looked down and studied the sand between his bent knees. After a long silence, Tristan began to wonder if Stitch would answer, then his companion took a deep breath.

"I've never met anyone like her." He traced a shape in the sand with the tip of his finger. "Oh, I realize she's sometimes difficult and opinionated, and she's not happy with the circumstances she finds herself in, but she truly is a sweet woman." A long sigh escaped him. "I never thought, after my Fannie . . ."

He obliterated the heart he'd drawn in the sand with a sweep of his hand. "Do you think it's possible to find love not once, but twice in your life? To find a person who perfectly fills a part of your soul?"

Tristan leaned back on his elbows. He didn't have to think about the question—he knew the answer in a heartbeat as the vision of Caralyn danced before his eyes. "Yes, I think it's possible, but most of us are lucky to find that kind of love only once."

He would have said more as a shrill whistle rent the air. Tristan looked toward the rocks where Socrates kept watch. Caralyn and Mrs. Beasley stood beside him. Both had wet hair and carried their shoes in their hands. "It would seem the ladies are finished with their toilette."

He rose from his position and offered his hand to Stitch. "Shall we escort them back to camp?" The good doctor grasped his hand and stood. "About what we discussed," Tristan said before he released Stitch's hand. "I would prefer we keep it between ourselves. I will tell the crew that this is our last adventure when the time is right, preferably after we find Izzy's Fortune."

"Of course, Tristan. If nothing else, I am a man of discretion." The man grinned at him as they strolled across the sand toward Socrates and the ladies.

Tristan glanced in his direction, about to comment, but stopped when he saw the expression on the doctor's face. He'd never seen such a look and almost chuckled when he realized exactly what Stitch's serene countenance meant.

Brady Trevelyan only had eyes for one person and his gaze locked on Mrs. Beasley. The smile parting his lips was nothing less than angelic and the flush staining his cheeks confirmed it. When he approached Mrs. Beasley and took her hands in his, no one else in the world existed. Their heads were close together and snippets of their conversation floated to him as they walked toward the camp.

Lovesick, besotted fools. The thought rumbled through Tristan's brain … until he glanced at Caralyn. *And I am no better.* She looked utterly delectable in a simple gown of white with sprigs of blue flowers, her bare feet half-hidden beneath the sand. Moonlight reflected off her impish grin and all thought departed.

Blood sang through his veins, warming every inch of his skin. His heart pounded in his chest. If Socrates hadn't been standing so close to her, he would have given himself permission to lay her down in the sand as he longed to do.

"I feel so much better." Her grin widened as she tilted her head to look up at him and ran her fingers through her wet hair. The urge to reach out and touch her, to lift the heavy tresses from her shoulders and rub the silken strands through his fingers almost overpowered him. Her voice lowered, striking a cord in the very fiber of his being. "I don't reek like the cave anymore."

She smelled fresh and clean which Tristan found more alluring than if she'd doused herself in scent. He swallowed hard and tried to think of something to say but words escaped him. Indeed, thought escaped him so he took her hand and kissed her knuckles then led her back to camp behind Socrates, who strolled along the water's edge.

The camp was utterly quiet when they approached. There would be no lively reel tonight, no dancing on the small spit of beach. Most of the crew, bellies full, comforted by the warmth of the tropical evening, relaxed in small groups if they weren't already asleep on makeshift beds. A few of his men had headed back to the *Adventurer*, preferring to sleep in their hammocks. Graham hadn't moved, although he now clamped a pipe between his lips. He glanced up at Tristan and grinned, but said nothing.

Caralyn disappeared into her tent, but only for a moment. She returned with a brush and Pembrook's journal then took a seat on a blanket before the fire.

Tristan leaned back against a log and allowed himself to watch her brush her long hair. Firelight created a warm glow on her face and reflected off her light brown tresses, bringing out shades of gold and red. She caught him watching her and grinned in his direction.

Her blue-green eyes twinkled in the light of the fire. In their depths, he saw determination, courage, strength, spirit ... and passion. For adventure. For life. Exactly what he'd always wanted in a woman but never thought he'd find.

As if struck by lightning, Tristan's heart skipped a beat then resumed with a painful thump while the words Stitch had said earlier reverberated in his mind. Exhilaration surged through him, an excitement he could not deny. And yet, he could do nothing—could not take her in his arms as he longed to do, could not kiss her until they were both breathless, could not explore the softness of her body.

He turned away and studied the moon hanging over them as if suspended by a string, but even that was a mistake. He could still smell the warm freshness of her skin, the scent reminiscent of a forest after a rain.

Tristan thought about the woman he was to marry and a twinge of guilt trickled through him. How unfair he was to not meet her, court her, before they became man and wife. How thoughtless to put his own concerns first and not care at all how she felt. Did she want this marriage? Or had her hand been forced as well?

In the end, it didn't matter. If he truly wanted a successful marriage, a union different than the one his parents shared, then he certainly wasn't going about it the right way. Instead of chasing an illusive dream of untold treasure, he should be in England right now getting to know the woman he would share his life with.

He stared into the flame dancing in the fire pit and his mood soured. The excitement, the satisfaction of finding a piece of Izzy's Fortune faded as if it never existed.

Quiet laughter interrupted his thoughts and he turned to face the source. Graham regaled Caralyn with a story that had her eyes sparkling, her tempting lips spread in a smile that could have charmed the population of London. Another chuckle escaped her, filling the warm night with magic.

Tristan held his breath. Fate was a cruel master, he knew. Fickle. Unpredictable. Capricious. Like the sea he loved. Why did he have to find the woman of his dreams now when his future had already been decided? When the choice was no longer his to make?

Perhaps he still had a choice, but without returning to England right away and confronting his father, he'd never know. And he couldn't do that, not just yet. He'd given his word, not only to his crew, but to Caralyn as well. The search for Izzy's Fortune had to continue. Without a word, he rose to his feet and strolled down the beach, the words of the letter he planned to write to his father jumbled in his mind. In the meantime, he would have to find a way to keep his distance from Caralyn, as impossible as it might be.

• • •

Caralyn finished twisting her hair into a long, thick braid and let it fall over her shoulder as she watched Tristan's broad back fade in the distance. The inclination to run after him, to join him on his stroll along the beach rose in her, but the air of solitude surrounding him didn't invite company. A sigh escaped her as she turned around and faced the fire.

Beside her, Graham made a small sound and drew her attention. He made a great show of refilling his pipe and puffing it alight. Their eyes met and the charming smile she'd seen on his face so many times before flashed again. Smoke circled his head before it drifted up to the night sky. "Finding Izzy's Fortune is important to you. Why? Why would a lady such as yourself risk so much for something that may or may not exist?"

"More important than you know. I . . ." How much to tell him? Even Mrs. Beasley didn't know why finding the treasure had become so paramount. Though she couldn't remember the name of her betrothed, she couldn't forget the title of his father nor her plan to drop a sack filled with gold coins in front of the earl and demand to be released from the promise of marriage.

She glanced at Graham, who watched her intently, waiting for her answer. Instead of responding to his question, she asked one of her own. "Why is it important to you?"

He shrugged his shoulders. "It isn't. I'm a simple man. I have no need for more riches. I have more than enough to see me into old age quite comfortably. I could walk away from this search right this moment and it would not break my heart as long as I did not have to give up the sea. For me, it's the adventure, whether I find the treasure or not." He puffed on his pipe, filling the air with fragrant smoke. "You never answered my question."

Caralyn bit her lip and stalled by carefully unwrapping Pembrook's journal and opening the book to where the author first mentioned the Island of the Sleeping Man. She didn't look at him but felt his gaze on her. "If I tell you something, do I have your word you'll keep it to yourself?"

"Of course."

"I am to be married when I reach England," she blurted out, still unable to meet his eyes.

"I see."

"It's a marriage I do not want, to a man I do not know." She glanced at Graham from the corner of her eye. No emotion showed on his face.

"So you embarked on this search for Izzy's Fortune to what? Stall for time?"

She faced him, her finger marking her place in the journal. "No," she lied, then changed her mind and spoke the truth. "Yes, to stall for time, but more importantly, to find the treasure. My portion will be more than enough to replace my dowry and release me from the marriage." She took a deep breath and let her gaze wander around the camp. She and Graham were the only two around the fire. Everyone else had turned in for the night, except for Tristan, who hadn't returned from his stroll down the beach.

"What if we don't find Izzy's Fortune? And even if we do, what if this gentleman should decline your offer? What will you do then?"

Her throat constricted and unshed tears burned her eyes. Her heart beat a slow painful rhythm in her chest. "I … I … I will do what is expected of me."

His expression betrayed nothing, although the corners of his mouth tilted upward. "Then I wish you good fortune with your plan, dear lady, but for now, I must say good night." He rose to his feet, nodded toward her then headed off to his tent.

Caralyn watched him until the flap of his tent closed. She let her pent up breath escape her. The night had grown quiet. Crickets chirped, palm fronds rattled, logs crackled and popped in the fire and the constant rush of water on the sand were the only sounds to keep her company.

She stared at the flames flickering in the fire pit, but didn't see them. Her mind raced with unanswered questions and doubts. What if they didn't find the treasure? And if they did, what if the earl didn't accept her proposal? Could she truly spend the rest of her life with a man she didn't love?

The fine hairs at the back of her neck rose and her skin began to tingle. She turned to see Tristan standing behind her. Moonlight danced on the drops of water in his hair and his loose white shirt ruffled in the breeze. Her heart did a funny little flutter in her chest.

"I thought you might have turned in for the night." Tristan lowered himself to the blanket beside her. He reclined against the log, his forearm resting on his bent knee, his gaze on her.

"I'm not the least bit sleepy." The funny little flutter in Caralyn's chest grew to amazing proportions. How easy it would be to snuggle up beside him and rest her head on his chest, easier still to touch her lips to his. Though the impulse raced through her, she did neither. "I've been thinking. Perhaps we shouldn't leave for Puerto Rico tomorrow. Perhaps we should continue our search of the island. There may be another cave."

He gestured toward the book in her hand. "Have you found something that leads you to believe this?"

"No, I just … I just can't believe the gold statue is all there is on this island. I was hoping for more."

"As was I, but we do have a clue, something we didn't know before. Like you, I believe the treasure may be on Jamaica, hidden from prying eyes in the chapel Pembrook writes about, but it would make sense to search here a bit more."

Caralyn opened the journal and began to read. As she turned the page, flames from the fire showed through the paper, highlighting lines that were not on either side. Her breath caught in her lungs for a moment and she doubted what she saw. She also wondered why she hadn't noticed it before. "Look at this. Do you see what I see?"

Tristan took the journal from her and turned the pages as she had done. "There's two pages stuck together."

By the light of the fire, he tried to separate the two pieces of paper. "I can't. My fingers . . ."

Caralyn reclaimed the diary and tried as well. "I can't separate them either." Without a thought to the consequences, she tore the pages from the book and held them up to the flames. A sigh of frustration escaped her. "Nothing is clear."

Tristan rose, grabbed the lantern hanging from a post, and brought it closer. He turned the wick, shedding more light. Caralyn held the pages in front of the lantern, but still, with the papers stuck together and writing on both sides, nothing became clearer. Perhaps it was just random lines—senseless scribbles—drawn by a man who had lost his sanity. With more frustration than she realized, she folded the pages and pushed them into the pocket of her gown. Perhaps, in the light of day, she'd be able to see the lines more clearly. Or with a bit of steam, she might be able to separate the two pages.

"Tomorrow, we'll begin searching the rest of the island," Tristan said as he took her hand and helped her to rise. He grabbed the book, which had fallen to the sand, handed it to her then escorted her to her tent. "But for now, we both need our rest." He squeezed her hand and bowed slightly from the waist. "Good night."

Caralyn said nothing as she slipped through the opening of her tent and tied the flaps closed. Once she secured Pembrook's journal in the oilcloth and placed it in her valise, she crawled onto the makeshift bed. Temperance's light snores filled the interior of the canvas room. As she'd stated to Tristan, she wasn't the least bit sleepy, yet as soon as she became comfortable, her eyes closed and she dreamed not of treasure and riches, but of a man and the wonder of his kiss.

Chapter 12

From the small, secluded cove where the *Explorer* lay at anchor, Porkchop had a perfect view of ships entering and leaving Kingston Harbor. He'd spent days in the crow's nest, a spyglass to his eye, fighting his fatigue, fighting his boredom, fighting his fear the captain would find displeasure with him, but his patience paid off. Relief shot through him and he grinned as the *Adventurer* finally came into view.

Porkchop lowered the spyglass and tucked it into the sash around his waist before he climbed down from his perch. Perhaps the news would make the captain happy, although Porkchop doubted anything would ever make him happy. Entwhistle's already foul mood had worsened since they lost the *Adventurer* at sea and set sail for Jamaica to wait for Captain Trey to arrive, though there had never been a guarantee the vessel would come here. Only a simple hope shared by all those who sailed with Captain Entwhistle.

Not a patient man by any sense of the word, Entwhistle had the capacity to punish his crew out of frustration and did quite often. Porkchop and the rest of his shipmates merely had to survive his sudden outbursts of rage and cruelty for misdeeds, real or imagined.

Porkchop took a deep breath, knocked on the door, and swung the portal open when the captain bade him enter.

"Sorry to be disturbin' ye, but I thought ye might like t' know." He shifted his weight from one leg to the other and swiped his knit cap from his head as he stood before Captain Entwhistle's fine mahogany desk. "The *Adventurer* is coming into port."

The captain stopped writing in the log book on his desk and stabbed his pen into the inkwell. His body stiffened as he inhaled and glared at Porkchop.

The murderous gleam in the captain's dark eyes made Porkchop shiver. He took a step away from the desk. Not for the first time he thought about giving up life at sea. Or at least leaving Entwhistle's crew, but as quickly as the idea popped into his head, it was gone. He couldn't imagine another life, and he doubted anyone else would have him on their ship. He took a deep breath and waited for the captain's orders.

"I want you to follow him. And don't lose him this time or I'll nail your hide to the yardarm."

"Aye, Cap'n." Porkchop backed out of the cabin and breathed a sigh of relief. Once again, he had survived an encounter with one of the meanest, orneriest men on the sea. He pulled his knit cap over his head, hitched up his trousers, and said a few words as Petey helped him lower a rowboat to the water.

The harbor teemed with ships and people of all nations going about their business as Porkchop rowed the dinghy through the obstacles. Stevedores unloaded cargo as men and women, dressed in the finest clothing, disembarked the vessels and proceeded on their way in this island paradise. Hansom cabs made a nice profit ferrying passengers to their destination. Vendors selling fresh fruit, their voices raised above the din, attracted newly arrived travelers to their booths for a taste of something sweet.

Porkchop dragged his rowboat to shore away from the hustle and bustle. No one seemed to notice him, which was just as well, as he didn't want to be noticed. He wandered along the street until he found a bench under the awning of a tavern where he could watch the harbor. He pulled a clay pipe from his pocket. After filling the bowl with tobacco, he puffed it alight and made himself comfortable as he waited.

From his vantage point, he watched the *Adventurer* furl her sails and drop anchor then lower a longboat to the water.

He recognized Mr. Alcott and the boy, Jemmy, as they climbed into the boat. Dr. Trevelyan tossed several duffle bags and two soft-sided valises into the boat then climbed in to help the two women board the vessel.

One didn't give chase to another crew without coming to know who they were and, in Porkchop's case, admiring them. There seemed to be an easy camaraderie and respect between the captain and his crew, which the sailor envied. He doubted there was backstabbing as with his own shipmates, and he was certain no one called anyone else "idjit."

Captain Trey climbed into the boat last. Porkchop grinned as the captain sat beside one of the women and said something to make her laugh. The sound carried across the water and cut through the din surrounding them as though by magic.

Porkchop stiffened as the boat bumped against the dock and lowered his head. He didn't want to be seen. Just as he recognized the *Adventurer's* crew, he knew they would recognize him as well.

He needn't have worried. No one paid him the least bit of attention as Captain Trey helped the women to the dock with tender courtesy. From where he sat, Porkchop heard the discussion and grinned.

He should have known. Where else would the captain go but Finnegan's, the tavern on the hill, which had been in existence since 1685? As Trey and his party climbed into a horse-drawn landau for hire, Porkchop dumped the ashes from his pipe into a planter beside the bench, rose, and tugged up his trousers. He tucked his pipe into his pocket and trudged up the hill to Finnegan's.

• • •

Caralyn sat next to Tristan in the close confines of the landau and tried to relax, except she couldn't. Between the excitement of following Pembrook's clues and the warmth of Tristan beside her, her body and mind were in a constant state of chaos.

Time passed with amazing speed and three weeks had come and gone since their visit to the Island of the Sleeping Man and Puerto Rico. Caralyn had become more and more aware of the captain's often overwhelming presence, the heat he exuded, the controlled power he held at bay. The slightest touch of his hand made her blood race through her veins and her body quiver. As Kingston passed before her eyes, she barely noticed the many changes since she'd last visited.

The driver stopped the carriage before a two-story stone building on a hill and applied the brake. Tristan disembarked first and held his hand out to her. Her fingers tingled; indeed, her entire body tingled as she allowed him to help her from the carriage. She watched him from the corner of her eye as he helped Temperance then paid the driver while Stitch unfolded his long legs and climbed out. Jemmy jumped out of the conveyance of his own accord, barely able to stop chattering for even a moment.

Graham remained in the landau, his back against the seat, arms along the cushioned tops. "I will join you shortly." He grinned then chuckled. "Save some rum for me." He tapped the driver on the shoulder and the carriage moved away.

Caralyn waved one last time then took a moment to gather her thoughts and look around. The sign over the door swung in the breeze. In bright green letters on a white background were the words Finnegan's Crooked Shillelagh, Est. 1685. Cut through the words was a long, misshapen cane.

Dr. Trevelyan opened the solid oak door and held it while everyone passed through. Caralyn didn't miss the grin he shared with Temperance nor the blush that rose to the woman's face. Compared to the bright light of outdoors, the confines of the tavern were dark and cool. Caralyn stopped in the doorway to let her eyes adjust to the difference until Tristan laid his hand on the small of her back and ushered her farther into the huge room. Only a handful of people occupied the tables, some quietly conversing, some sharing a game of chess. Paintings, as well as brass sconces, covered the walls, mostly of ships in full sail facing the bracing waves of the ocean. Stairs, off to the left, rose to the second floor.

A woman stood behind a long mahogany bar, her back toward the door. Long, flaming red hair curled past her hips and moved as if it had a life of its own as she placed clean glasses on a shelf. "Make yerselves ta home. I'll be right with ye."

"Take your time, Fi."

The woman stopped, the glass hovering in mid-air before she carefully placed it on the shelf. She turned her head to look behind her, and when her gaze fell upon them, she let out a squeal. "Saints be praised!" She ran around the bar. "Donal! Come quick!" Well along with child, her rounded belly did not prevent her from jumping into Tristan's arms and planting a kiss on his cheek.

Caralyn watched the display with a touch of jealousy, a feeling new and alien to her. Her body stiffened. Her stomach twisted and she couldn't help wondering if the woman carried Tristan's baby. Why she would think such a thing, she couldn't explain. The thought just popped into her mind, unfounded though it may have been. By sheer force of will, she controlled the urge to pull the woman away from Tristan by her long red hair.

She shouldn't have worried. Tristan's response was that of a loving friend. He kissed her on the cheek and let her go. The knot in Caralyn's stomach loosened. "You're prettier than ever, Fi. How are you?" Tristan glanced at her stomach and grinned.

She laughed, her green eyes sparkling, her cheeks pink, but didn't respond as she turned her attention to the good doctor. "Stitch. Ye look like a man finally findin' what he wants." She pressed a kiss to his cheek but her eyes went directly to Temperance.

"Fi, my dear, once again, I am astounded by your beauty."

"Donal!" She called again. "Where is that man?"

She glanced behind her for a moment then turned her attention to Jemmy. Affection for the boy was evident in her beautiful smile and lovely voice with its strong Gaelic lilt, as if she'd just left the verdant green of Ireland. "Aye, look at ye, Master Jemmy." She pulled the boy against her for a hug. "Ye've grown a foot, I swear, since the last time I saw ye."

"Aunt Fi, you're squishing me," the boy mumbled into the woman's stomach and pulled himself free from her arms, his face bright pink. He glanced at her belly, curiosity dancing in his eyes.

"Ye kin touch it," Fi said and laid his hand on her stomach. "Young Donal is expectin' a brother but I think he'll be just as happy with a sister."

"Fi, I'd like you to meet Miss Caralyn McCreigh." There could be no mistaking the obvious pleasure in Tristan's voice or the gleam in his eyes as he said the words. Liquid heat filled her veins like warm honey as Caralyn held out her hand to the other woman. "Cara, this is Fiona Finnegan, one of my dearest friends."

"Oh, and 'tis a delight to be meetin' ye, Miss McCreigh." No simple handshake would do as Fiona pulled Caralyn into a hug.

"And this is Mrs. Temperance Beasley," Stitch said as Fiona released her and turned her attention to the woman standing beside him.

Caralyn hid her grin as Mrs. Beasley was treated to the same exuberant greeting. Her companion stiffened within the embrace then relaxed and returned the warm welcome. In that moment, Temperance seemed truly happy.

Temperance Beasley's transformation could be described as nothing less than amazing in Caralyn's opinion. Weeks at sea had changed her, or perhaps, the affection Stitch continually bestowed upon her had done that. She no longer frowned, no longer scraped her hair back into a tight bun or wore widow's black. Indeed, with the bright new wardrobe they'd purchased in Puerto Rico, and her long auburn hair flowing down her back in graceful curls, she looked like a much younger, much happier woman.

"What's all the fuss, woman?"

Caralyn turned toward the voice and stared. The man coming in through a back door was the biggest, hairiest man she'd ever seen. Broad shouldered, barrel-chested, legs as thick as tree trunks, arms rippling with muscle, he had to duck to keep from bumping his head on a chandelier made of an old ship's wheel. The two cases of rum he carried, one under each arm, seemed like no more than cigar boxes. Coarse hair covered the bottom part of his face in a thick, shaggy beard as black as midnight, his white teeth offering a sharp contrast.

"Faith and begora, will ye look at what the wind blew in!"

He placed the rum on the bar then flung his arms wide and embraced Tristan in a hug that would crush the ribs of a smaller man. After much backslapping, he pulled away then proceeded to give the same greeting to Stitch. "Ye been gone too long, my friends." He turned to Jemmy. "Come give yer uncle a hug."

The boy's face glowed as the big man picked him up and held him with a gentleness that belied his strength. "Ye've grown, lad. Soon ye'll be as big as me." He placed the boy on his own two feet then ruffled Jemmy's hair, his love for the lad obvious to all.

Caralyn glanced at Temperance and almost burst into laughter. Eyes wide behind the lenses of her glasses, her mouth opened in an "O," Temperance's expression mirrored her surprise to see so large a man.

"Donal, I'd like you meet Mrs. Temperance Beasley." Stitch grabbed her hand and brought her forward. Her mouth closed with an audible click before her lips spread into a smile.

"'Tis a pleasure to be sure." His big hand dwarfed her smaller one as he brought her knuckles to his lips. Temperance blushed to the roots of her hair and giggled.

"Cara," Tristan placed his hand at the small of her back, igniting a fire in her veins and interrupting her musings. "I'd like you to meet Donal Finnegan, proud owner of Finnegan's Crooked Shillelagh and historian extraordinaire. If it happened in Jamaica, he knows. Donal, Miss Caralyn McCreigh."

The big man winked. "There's been a Finnegan on Jamaica since before the quake in '92." He spoke in a charming mix of Jamaican, Irish, and English accents, his words lilting and musical. "1692, that is. Back in the day, most of the pirates went to Port Royal. Only the smartest ones came to the Shillelagh. Calico Jack, Anne Bonney, Blackbeard, and perhaps the greatest pirate of them all, Henry Morgan." He beamed with pride at the history of his tavern. "Look at the rafter above your head, lass."

Caralyn looked up and saw all the initials carved into the sturdy rafter. Morgan's was, by far, the largest. A shiver of excitement raced down her back as she turned her gaze to the big man in front of her. If Morgan had come here, perhaps Pembrook had as well. She held out her hand. "A pleasure to meet you."

"Ah, the pleasure is all mine, lass," he said as he took her offered hand.

As with Temperance, a giggle escaped her as he brought her hand to his lips and brushed her knuckles with his shaggy mustache. He studied her for a moment, the brilliance of his blue eyes a sharp contrast to the darkness of his skin and hair.

"McCreigh," he muttered as his eyes began to twinkle. "Be ye Daniel McCreigh's daughter?"

Surprised, Caralyn could only stare at the man as a rush of pride and homesickness flowed through her. "You know my father?"

"Oh, aye. It's me great pleasure to be knowin' yer da. A fine man," he lowered his voice to a conspiratorial whisper, "with a touch of the blarney. We lifted a few glasses together, he and I, at this verra table, while he regaled me with tales o' his treasure hunting and how he met yer mother. Tell me, lass, does he still search for Izzy's Fortune?"

She shook her head. "Sadly, he no longer believes in the treasure."

Donal finally released her hand. "'Tis a shame," he pronounced and then his eyes narrowed as he gazed into her face. "Ah, but ye still believe."

"Yes, I do."

"Good lass. I've no doubt ye'll find what ye been lookin' for, though many a scoundrel has tried before ye." His grin widened and his eyes sparkled. "Speakin' o' scoundrels, is Alcott with you?"

Tristan chuckled. "He'll be along shortly."

"Will ye be stayin' then?" Fi asked as she glanced at the pile of white duffle bags on the floor beside the door. "An' will the crew be joinin' ye?"

"If you have a few rooms available, Fi," Tristan answered and once again, Caralyn saw the fondness for this woman in his eyes and heard it in his voice. "Most of the crew will stay aboard ship, although a few have family here and will stay with them so it'll just be us."

"Aye. I'll be showin' ye upstairs after I take care of young master Jemmy." She grabbed the boy's hand. His face wreathed in smiles, the expression in his eyes one of adoration. And who could blame him? Fi Finnegan, in Caralyn's opinion, embodied motherhood personified with her patient manner and gentle smile. "Donal will be happy to see ye again and you remember Mama Annie, hmm?"

"Can I, Papa?"

"May I," Tristan corrected his speech. "Of course, but mind Mama Annie. As long as you're with her, she's the captain."

"Aye, Papa."

As Fi led Jemmy toward the windowed Dutch door at the back of the room and the courtyard and house beyond, Donal spread his arms wide to encompass a long table. "Welcome, friends.

Make yerselves ta home." He stepped behind the bar, opened one of the cases on its surface, and started removing bottles. "Can I be gettin' ye somethin' to wash the salt water from yer mouths? We have rum, rum, and more rum. Local made, ye know. We also have some very fine wine, coffee, tea, brandy, and me own verra special ale. What's yer pleasure?"

Tristan and Stitch glanced at each other and spoke at the same time. "Rum."

"Miss Temperance?"

Temperance hung her umbrella on the back of a chair then took a seat next to Stitch. "Tea, please," she said with a sigh.

"And what of ye, Miss McCreigh?"

"Wine. No. Brandy." She took a quick peek at Temperance's face and changed her mind once more. "Tea, please."

Donal made quick work of serving them. For so large a man, he moved with innate grace and amazing speed and joined them at the table with a mug of ale.

"So what brings ye to me fair establishment? Judgin' by the looks of ye, I'd say ye have a question or two for auld Donal." His eyes remained on Caralyn.

"More than questions, Donal," Tristan said as he finished the rum in his glass and poured himself another. "We need your help."

The big man's eyes lit up with pleasure. He wiped his mouth with the back of his hand to remove the foam from the ale. "With Izzy's Fortune? Have ye found a clue then, lad?"

"Show him, Cara."

Caralyn opened the valise and pulled out the statue. With trembling fingers, she removed the cloth protecting the piece then handed it to him.

"Aye, 'tis beautiful to be sure." He sighed as he turned the golden statue around in his big hands. "Look at the details, how lovingly made. And this is part of the treasure? Are ye certain, lass?"

"The maker's mark is engraved on the base. I've done enough research to know *Don* Miguel Ybarra ye Castellano cast several pieces of art for Queen Isabella in gold and silver. I believe this is one of them." Donal passed the statue to Tristan, who held it in his hands as Caralyn reached into the bag and pulled out the wooden case. Anticipation made butterflies dance in her stomach as Donal took the case from her and unhitched the lock.

A startled gasp escaped the big man as he opened the box and stared at the jewel-encrusted chalice.

"The chalice was made by him as well."

With a delicateness that seemed incomparable with the size of his hands, Donal removed the chalice from its velvet bed. Sunlight coming in through the small windows struck the jewels, casting a rainbow on the walls. He pursed his lips and whistled then placed the chalice back in its case. "Must be worth a small fortune. What else have ye got in that bag o' tricks?"

Caralyn pulled the last item from her bag, unwrapped the oilcloth, and placed the book in front of him. "This is Arthur Pembrook's journal."

Donal lifted the cover and read the first few pages. After a long time, he looked at them. "I have no doubt the chalice and the statue could belong to Izzy's Fortune, but I've never heard of Arthur Pembrook. Are ye certain this is a journal? It reads like an adventure novel. *Robinson Crusoe* comes to mind."

Tears stung Caralyn's eyes in an instant. To come this far only to find disappointment. Could it be she had been wrong? Could it be Pembrook had, indeed, written a novel and not one word of it was true? She blinked several times to rid herself of the tears blurring her vision. No, she couldn't believe all of it was a lie, fiction created by a man who'd lived in his own imagination, a man who slowly lost his sanity. She had proof Izzy's Fortune existed.

"He mentions that he changed his name. By the time he came to Jamaica, he called himself something else, though he never mentions his new name." Caralyn took a deep breath in order to still the sudden pounding of her heart. "He writes quite a bit about his wife, Mary, and a plantation called Collin's Folly."

"I know of Collin's Folly, though not this Pembrook who wrote yer journal. Let me ponder a bit and see what I can remember." Donal slumped back in his chair and steepled his fingers. He grew quiet as he tapped his lip several times in deep thought.

Caralyn wanted to jump out of her skin. She wanted to shake the big man to help him remember. She did neither. Instead, she sat beside Tristan, her hands folded on the table and waited, as did everyone else. She barely drew breath until Tristan touched her arm. She glanced at him. The expression on his face reminded her that he still believed, no matter that Donal couldn't remember Pembrook.

All at once, Donal let out a shout and snapped his fingers. "Ah, lassie, ye din't think I'd remember, did ye?" He patted her hand. Caralyn heaved a sigh of relief. "I don't know the particulars of how your Pembrook came to Jamaica, but I do know Mary Collins married a man named Andrew Pearce. As I recall, they lived quite happily on the plantation for a number of years." He took a deep breath, took another swallow of ale then continued his story.

"Mary loved him to distraction, or so it's been claimed. And the plantation produced a mighty fine rum, but that all changed one night, if I remember correctly. Mind ye, most of what I know is considered folklore, passed from one generation to another—stories me da told me, stories his da told him and so on." He took another deep breath, his eyes sparkling, his smile beaming beneath his shaggy beard.

"No one knows how your Pembrook or Pearce died. Some say he took his own life. Some say Morgan, lieutenant governor at the time, ordered his death." He raised his glass and swallowed the remainder of his ale. "'Tis sorry I am, but the plantation's gone. Parceled out and now belongin' to others."

"What about the chapel?" Hope blossomed in Caralyn's heart once more. "Does it still stand?"

"The Chapel of the Blessed Virgin?" Fiona placed her hand on her husband's shoulder. Caralyn had been so intent on Donal, she hadn't seen the woman come back into the main room. "Aye, the chapel still stands but ye canna be goin' there. 'Tis haunted."

Donal agreed. "'Tis true. Mary Collins found her husband in the chapel. He'd been shot. The pistol was still in his hand. Grief stricken, Mary killed herself to join the man she loved, or so the legend goes. They remain in the chapel where she found him and their ghosts stand upon the cliff, hand in hand, keeping watch. No one has ever dared to desecrate their resting place."

"I don't believe in ghosts, Donal," Caralyn told him. "What I do believe is that Arthur or Andrew or whatever his name was, buried Izzy's Fortune in the chapel."

The big man tilted his head as he studied her. "I hate to be disappointin' ye, lass, but there's no treasure in the chapel. There's nothing except a huge statue of the Blessed Virgin and the tombs of Mary and her husband." His smile brightened as he patted her hand. "But I understand ye must look for yerself. Fi, my love, will ye bring me the map? Ye know the one I'm talkin' about."

As Fi left the room, Tristan asked, "What's the best way to get to the chapel? Should we rent a carriage? Or can we sail?"

"No matter what ye take, ye'll end up on foot," Donal said as he stood and strode over to the bar for another draft of ale. "The chapel is on a cliff, overlooking the sea. Ye can take the *Adventurer* but ye'll have to drop anchor and take the longboats to the beach." His eyes shined and his smile beamed as he returned to the table. Fi came back with the map, and Donal pointed to the section marked "Saint James Parrish" on the opposite side of the island.

"The chapel be here, surrounded by jagged rocks. Sailors have told me ye can see a glowing light all around, especially at night." He looked up and caught Caralyn's eyes. "Is tomorra too soon fer ye?"

Before she could answer, the door opened, letting in a blaze of blinding sunlight and the rest of the *Adventurer's* crew entered the tavern amid good-natured shouts. She saw Tristan reach into his pocket and remove a small leather pouch, which he passed on to Fiona. She grinned as she stuffed it into her apron pocket. Donal made quick work of rolling the map before he jumped from his seat and greeted his old friends. The noise level grew to deafening proportions.

Caralyn gently wrapped Pembrook's journal and placed it, along with the statue and the chalice, back in the valise by her feet. Anticipation caused a flurry of butterflies in her stomach, and she couldn't keep the smile from her lips. Tomorrow, they'd find the treasure, she was certain. Tomorrow, her new life would begin.

Chapter 13

Caralyn placed the valise on the bed in the well-appointed room Fi had shown her. Downstairs, she heard the laughter of the crew, Fi's sweet voice, and Donal's baritone rumble as they renewed their acquaintance with the *Adventurer's* crew. Here, in her room, blissful silence reigned.

She took a moment to study her surroundings. Paintings hung on the knotted pine walls, again repeating the sailing ships downstairs. She stepped closer to one in particular, recognizing the *Adventurer*, captured forever in oil, then looked for the artist's signature. In the corner, on the right side toward the bottom, she found it: *Fiona Finnegan*.

A woman of many talents, it seemed.

The huge four-poster bed, draped in netting, looked inviting and much bigger than the bed she currently shared with Temperance in the captain's cabin. A colorful patchwork quilt covered the bed and pillows, plump and soft, rested against the carved headboard.

Oh, to sleep in a real bed without Temperance's constant kicking and snoring.

Delighted by the idea, she pulled her brush from her valise then crossed the room to the mirror in the corner. A smile parted her lips as she studied her reflection and pulled the brush through her hair. The woman in the mirror returned her grin.

Who is that woman? And why does she look so happy?

Caralyn knew the answer immediately. Despite the fact she was to be married to a man she didn't know and she had yet to find Izzy's Fortune, though she had no doubt she would, this had, indeed, been a grand adventure. Temperance Beasley had turned from paid companion to close friend and found love with Stitch; Caralyn had been reunited with Socrates, whom she had always adored; and most importantly, she'd met Tristan.

A finer man she couldn't imagine. Not only handsome and charming, he had integrity and honor. His word was his promise and he needed nothing more than to simply state his intention. Every man on the crew had complete and utter trust in him, as did she. He captained with compassion and kindness, much as her father had done aboard the *Lady Elizabeth*, earning the deep respect due him. This adventure wouldn't be half as exciting, half as fun, if she hadn't been with Tristan and the crew.

A knock interrupted her thoughts. "Yes?"

The door opened and the object of her musings stood in front of her, his arms laden with folded bath towels, the grin she'd come to love parting his lips. Caralyn inhaled and held her breath. Could it be possible he'd grown more handsome in the space of a few moments?

"Fi asked me to bring these to you." He glanced around the room then spotted a small table beside a hipbath and headed toward it. Caralyn exhaled in a rush as she watched him. He moved with easy grace and a sure-footed confidence that thrilled her beyond reason.

He turned after depositing the towels on the table and his gaze fell on the bed then rose to meet hers. She saw desire in his eyes—hot, raw, and utterly stark. Warmth suffused her. Indeed, heat rushed to her face and neck, and a shiver raced down her spine. She couldn't take her gaze from his, couldn't move, couldn't breathe for a moment.

Then like a little boy caught doing something he shouldn't, Tristan blushed. His mouth twisted into an impish grin. "Fi says there's plenty of hot water if you want to freshen up."

The yearning in his eyes remained. Caralyn swallowed hard to ease the sudden dryness in her throat. How easy would it be to walk into his arms and touch her lips to his? How easy would it be to fall into the bed between them and give into the rush of longing filling her? How easy would it be to forget the promises made for her and stay with this man forever?

"I'll see you downstairs." He closed the door behind him but not before he glanced at her one more time. Again, the smoldering gleam in his beautiful eyes made her heart beat faster, made the quivering in her belly grow, made her want to throw propriety out the window and press her lips to his.

She took a deep breath to quell the trembling in her body, and yet that did nothing to stop the thoughts racing through her head. Brush in hand, she sat on the edge of the bed, the mattress dipping slightly beneath her weight, the enormity of her dilemma heavy on her shoulders.

The answer remained as it always had. Find the treasure. Give the earl a bag of gold worth more than her promised dowry, and walk away from a marriage she never wanted in the first place. She wouldn't even have to meet his son—her intended—though she should so she could explain.

And then what? You can't go home again after disgracing your family.

A long sigh escaped her, but then she began to smile once more. She wouldn't have to go home. She could go anywhere with her share of the treasure. If she wanted, she could buy a plantation or an inn or open a dress shop or anything else she so chose. She could change her name, as Pembrook had done, and begin life anew. She could stay with the *Adventurer* and hunt for other treasures with Tristan, as she desired. With the proceeds from Izzy's Fortune, she could do anything she wanted. The possibilities were endless.

If she found the treasure.

Not *if. When.*

Feeling much better, Caralyn rose from the bed. Though a long, leisurely soak in the tub beckoned, she was much more anxious to rejoin everyone downstairs and settled on a quick sponge bath. She pulled a fresh gown from the valise, shook the wrinkles from it, and dressed. She finished brushing her hair, leaving the long tresses to tumble down her back. Before she left her room, she tossed her nightgown across the pillow so she wouldn't have to rummage through her bag later.

Caralyn stopped midway down the stairs and gazed into the common room. Her heart swelled in her chest, and tears misted her eyes with unexpected joy. Boisterous laughter, jokes, and bits and pieces of conversation met her ears. How fond she'd become of these men. They might be rough and tumble, but they were so true and faithful—to each other and their captain—she couldn't help admiring them and the life they led.

Graham had concluded his business and joined the rest of the crew, and now stood deep in conversation with Tristan and Donal. Rum nearly splashed out of his glass as he gestured with his hands in the midst of yet another tall tale. Fiona and another woman Caralyn had yet to meet made quick work of keeping all glasses filled while the wonderful aroma of roasting chickens permeated the air. Later, after dinner, she knew there would be music and dancing, as the *Adventurer's* crew used nearly any excuse to celebrate. And what better excuse than to be reunited with old friends and pursue a treasure reported to be beyond belief? The men who regularly frequented Finnegan's for games of chess or checkers, who'd been there all afternoon, sipping on mugs of ale, would be invited to share in the festivities.

Tristan glanced up at her then excused himself from his companions and strode to the bottom of the stairs. He raised his hand toward her, his gaze warm and inviting, his lips parted in that lovable impish grin. Within the space of an indrawn breath, Caralyn placed her hand in his. The rush of yearning coursing through her intensified. For a moment, a lifetime, she heard nothing except the beating of her own heart, felt nothing except the longing blossoming in her soul, saw nothing except the promise in his eyes.

The spell broke when Hash entered the room and announced, "Dinner is served." He carried a platter heaped high with chickens roasted to perfection. Tiny round potatoes and steaming vegetables, staples from Fiona's kitchen which Hash had commandeered, surrounded the birds. As if they'd never eaten Hash's wonderful creations before, the crew rushed to the long table in the middle of the room, jostling each other for position and the chance to be the first one to sample his fine fare.

Caralyn took a deep breath and allowed Tristan to lead her to her seat.

• • •

With more than a touch of envy, Porkchop watched the people gathered around the table. The remains of a simple dinner and bottles of rum, brandy, and wine, some empty, some on their way to being empty, littered the tabletop. Conversation from the crew of the *Adventurer*, the Finnegans, and their other guests drowned out every other sound in the tavern, the deep masculine laughter of the men punctuated by the gentler tones of the women.

He sat in the chair in a darkened corner, the same position he'd held since walking into Finnegan's hours ago, and nursed his third ale, just waiting and watching. When the woman named Cara had showed Donal the treasures in her valise, Porkchop had barely been able to control his excitement. He had wanted to jump up and steal the treasures right from her hand, but that wouldn't have been wise. And so, he waited for the most opportune time.

For the second time that day, he had been rewarded for his patience. That valise was now upstairs in the room the woman rented, unwatched, unprotected, waiting for him to take it while its owner relaxed with another glass of wine.

No one noticed when he slid out of his seat and climbed the stairs to the second floor. Anticipation and fear made his body quiver, for he'd never done what he was about to do now. He'd never stolen a single thing in his life, but the rules had changed. The items in the woman's valise were proof Izzy's Fortune truly did exist.

As quietly as he could, Porkchop crept down the hallway and let himself into the first guest room. Panic seized him. His heart raced in his chest, his body trembled. Indeed, his mouth was so dry, he couldn't swallow if he wanted to. For several moments, he stood motionless, waiting for the sudden rush of fear to disappear.

What am I doin'? The thought blazed through his brain, but he forced it away and made himself move about the room.

Moonlight gleamed in through the open French doors, and a light breeze heavy with the scent of impending rain, fluttered the sheer curtains. But this wasn't Cara's room, for he couldn't find the valise.

Porkchop inspected three more rooms until he found the treasure he sought. He spotted the soft-sided case beside the bed instantly, but it wasn't the case that grabbed his attention and held it. Rather, the white silk and lace nightgown resting upon the plump pillows on the bed, shimmering in the moonlight, beckoned him closer.

He couldn't resist the magnetic pull of the garment. Never had he seen such a beautiful thing, and his imagination pictured the woman named Cara wearing it, the whiteness of the gown a contrast to her tanned skin. Pleasure shot through him, not only from the feel of the silk beneath his fingers, but also from the earthy fragrance that tickled his nose. The vision in his mind became clearer and he could see her, light brown hair curling around her shoulders, sea-blue eyes sparkling, the smile on her lips just for him.

A noise, the scraping of a chair leg against stone floor downstairs, jarred him from his musings. He laid the nightgown on the pillows, exactly where it had been, picked up the valise, and crept toward the door. He breathed a sigh of relief to find the hallway empty.

At the end of the long corridor stood French doors leading out to a balcony and a set of stairs to the courtyard below. Treasure in hand, Porkchop held his breath as he tiptoed toward the door and the sweet escape that lay beyond.

A short time later, breathless and aching from his exertions of rowing the boat back to the *Explorer*, Porkchop knocked on the door of the captain's cabin and waited for permission to enter before he opened the portal. He stopped two steps into the cabin, startled by the vision before him. Entwhistle stood at the window, his ramrod stiff back toward the door, hands clasped behind him. Fragrant smoke rose and curled around his head and mixed with the dim light coming from the two lanterns in the room. For a moment, the sailor could have sworn he was in the presence of the devil himself. He blinked, several times, unable to move, though his bowels had no trouble twisting in his gut.

"What is it?"

Frigid air seemed to fill the cabin as the captain spoke, adding to the illusion of dread swirling in Porkchop's brain and trickling down his spine. The sailor shivered. Swallowing the fear that gripped him, Porkchop took another few steps on shaky legs and dropped the valise on the desk. "Thought ye might like to look at these. I took it from one of the woman travelin' with Trey."

The captain turned around and the haze of smoke disappeared, though the image of Entwhistle as Satan did not. Porkchop sucked air into his lungs. He shifted his weight from one leg to the other, as always, nervous in his captain's presence.

Entwhistle took a step toward the desk and lowered himself to a chair. He placed his pipe in a glass dish then opened the valise and peeked inside. Porkchop remained on his feet, his muscles taut, as the captain pulled the first item from the cloth case. With the precision of a surgeon, Entwhistle removed the cloth surrounding one of the objects to reveal the gold statue of the Virgin Mary. He inspected the icon, turning it this way and that in his big hands.

"Do you know where they got this?"

"I heared 'em talkin' 'bout an island east o' Puerto Rico. They called it 'The Island of the Sleeping Man,' but I ain't never heared of such a place." Again, Porkchop shifted his weight. He didn't quite know what to do with his hands. He wanted to wrap his arms around his chest—for comfort, for protection, for warmth against the chill in the captain's smile, and yet he didn't move, and his hands remained by his sides.

Entwhistle removed a wooden box from the valise and set it on the desk. His dark eyes glittered as he opened the case and stared at the jewel-encrusted golden chalice. He inhaled deeply as he gently pulled the cup from its bed of velvet. Emeralds and rubies reflected the meager light of the lanterns and cast their colors on the rich mahogany walls.

For the first time in his memory, the sailor saw a true smile on Entwhistle's face as he examined the goblet and read the maker's inscription on the bottom. Porkchop could only watch him with fascination as he replaced the chalice in the case with a gentleness that belied the captain's hard, cold true nature.

Lastly, he removed an oilcloth-protected bundle and untied the strings holding the cloth in place to reveal a book. With trembling fingers, he opened the leather cover and began to read, skimming over the words in his haste to learn the owner of the journal. A sharp gasp escaped him before he turned suspicious eyes toward Porkchop. "Did you read this?"

The sailor swallowed, trying to ease the dryness in his throat. "No, Cap'n, I can't read, but I be knowin' whose journal it is. Belongs to a man named Arthur Pembrook who sailed with Henry Morgan. Or so I heard."

"Where did you get these again?"

"From the woman with Trey." For a moment, Porkchop forgot who he spoke with as the memory of Cara's laughter filled his heart with lightness and joy. He'd couldn't recall a happier time than spending most of the day watching her, listening to her sweet voice, hoping she'd smile at him, look at him, the way she looked at Captain Trey.

"Have a seat, Thaddeus." Captain Entwhistle gestured to a chair on the other side of his desk. He poured brandy into a fine crystal snifter and slid it across the desk.

The simple request and offer of a drink took Porkchop by surprise. Never once, in all the time he'd been sailing with the captain had he ever been offered a chair in the captain's cabin. Never once had Entwhistle called him by his given name. Never once had he shared his supply of spirits, at least not with him. Suspicion and fear grabbed hold of Porkchop, and it took every ounce of his will power not to shudder as he swiped his knit cap from his head and lowered himself to the offered chair.

"Tell me about the women traveling with Trey." Entwhistle picked up his pipe, filled it with fresh tobacco and lit it. Smoke curled around his head and the image of the captain as the devil snaked through Porkchop's brain.

The sailor opened his mouth, but no words would come forth. He grabbed the glass of brandy as if his life depended on it and took a big swallow. The warmth travelled to his belly, unraveling the knot in his stomach and loosening the thoughts in his mind. "There's Temperance Beasley, the other lady's companion, judgin' by the way she's always correcting the younger one and tellin' her what to do."

He sighed, realizing he spoke in a rush to get the words out before the captain turned from the charming man in front of him right now to the devil he knew the man to be. "Reminds me of me own mother but the one ye be most in'erested in is Caralyn McCreigh. Ye be knowin' her father, Daniel, of the *Lady Elizabeth*.

I heared her say she found the book and the cup in an old clock her father bought from an estate here in Jamaica. It's filled with clues to find Izzy's Fortune." He pointed to the golden statue on the desk. "They foun' that on the island, which led 'em back here."

"Did you happen to hear what they're planning to do next?"

"They talked about a chapel on the cliffs on the other side of the island in St. James' Parish. Finnegan even pulled out a map to show them where it is, but I was too far away to see. They're settin' off tomorrow to start searchin'."

Entwhistle sat back in his chair and steepled his fingers in front of his face. "A chapel," he murmured and said it once again, as if repeating it to himself would jog his memory. His eyes glazed over as he stared at Porkchop. As if realizing he wasn't alone, the captain jerked in his chair, and the smile he bestowed on the sailor did nothing to inspire confidence. "You've done well, Thaddeus. Now finish your drink and toddle off to sleep. Tomorrow will be a big day."

• • •

"I like her, Tristan," Fiona said as she refilled his glass. "Not only is she beautiful, but kind and adventurous, and might I say, daring. She reminds me o' someone."

"And who would that be?"

"Ye, ye scoundrel." She grinned. "She's the kind o' woman ye always searched fer but ne'er thought existed. A far cry from yer mother, who left the raisin' of ye t' yer da. An' she loves Jemmy. I be knowin' how important that is to ye."

Tristan raised an eyebrow. He couldn't refute Fiona's words. After all, he knew them to be true. He glanced at Caralyn now and his heart skipped a beat. Perhaps it was the wine that made her eyes sparkle, her cheeks explode with color, and her smile beam as she danced a lively reel with Socrates, but he didn't think so.

"I have this for ye." She handed him a letter she pulled from her pocket. Tristan recognized the seal immediately and heaved a sigh. Another missive from his father, another command to return home and marry the woman the earl had chosen, another opportunity to realize the woman he wanted was not the woman he would spend his life with. Perhaps this letter would contain the name of his future wife. Perhaps not. At this moment, it didn't matter as his gaze swept the floor and found Caralyn once more.

"Yer da?" Fiona asked.

"Aye." He tucked the letter into his pocket. There would be time later to read his father's summons, time to regret the decisions he had no part in making.

"Aren't ye goin' to read it?"

Tristan shook his head. "I already know what it says."

"An' 'tis not what you want, is it?"

Again, he shook his head and sighed.

"Well, what is it ye be wantin'?"

Tristan knew she waited for an answer but he couldn't speak. He knew exactly what he wanted … something he couldn't have. From the corner of his eye, he saw Fiona follow his line of sight and sigh.

"Ah, I see. 'Tis her." She gave him a gentle push toward the dance floor. "Then go and get her. At least dance with the lass. Tomorra be a long way away."

Tristan needed no more urging than that. He stepped onto the dance floor and tapped Socrates on the shoulder. "I believe this is my dance."

"O' course, Cap'n." The sailor relinquished his light grasp on Caralyn's fingers and bowed.

She'd had too much wine. Tristan could tell the moment he took Caralyn in his arms, her body soft and pliant and leaning into his, although the tempo of the song did not require them to embrace. Her eyes, the color of the sea he loved so well, twinkled with merriment … and something else. Invitation? Promise? Desire? For him? Or was it the wine she had consumed and he only saw what he wanted to see?

Whatever message her straightforward gaze sent, he'd be more than willing to comply. He held her closer still and felt her heart pounding through his body. The heat of her hand on his shoulder seeped beneath his jacket and not only touched his skin, but his soul as well.

"I like your friends." Her words were slurred, just a little.

"They like you as well."

He swirled her around the floor, the warmth of her hands, the way her body moved in time to his—all conspired against his good intentions as a gentleman. The music stopped and yet he wanted to keep moving with her, wanted to keep holding her close, wanted to take her upstairs and touch every part of her body, taste the sweet nectar of her kiss, bury himself deep into her softness and feel the ardor of her response.

Instead, he whispered in her perfect, shell-like ear, "I do believe, Cara, you have had a bit too much wine. Perhaps, it's time for you to retire."

"I'm not the least bit sleepy."

He couldn't help the grin that parted his lips, couldn't help touching his lips to her ear, couldn't help delighting in the shiver that shook her. "Be that as it may, we've a busy day tomorrow and it wouldn't do for your head to be pounding."

Caralyn giggled. "Perhaps you're right. I do feel giddy and so happy, I could dance all night, but tomorrow will be a busy day." She sighed then and he felt the reverberations all the way to his toes. "I hope we find the treasure, Tristan. I have such plans."

"As do I, but nothing will happen unless you get some sleep."

He released his hold on her but caught her again as she swayed. The urge to kiss her, to taste her tempting lips once more overwhelmed him. Blood sang through his veins and thundered in his ears. In her inebriated state, he could do anything he wished, and yet that wasn't the way he wanted her.

She hiccupped and another giggle escaped her. "Ooh, perhaps I have had too much to drink."

"Come, I'll take you upstairs." He led her through the crowd of people dancing to yet another lively reel. Graham smirked at him and quirked an eyebrow. Socrates and Mac scowled and tried to impede his progress but the greatest obstacle remained Temperance Beasley.

She stood at the bottom of the stairs, hands on her hips, her foot tapping the hard wood floor. "Where do you think you're going, Captain?"

"I'm escorting Caralyn to her room." He lowered his voice. "I believe she's had a little too much to drink."

The woman raised an eyebrow as her lips pinched together. "Your services are not required. I will take care of her."

Tristan nodded once and relinquished his hold on Caralyn, trusting her to the woman who held her safety above all else. "As you wish, Temperance."

He watched them ascend the stairs, one riser at a time. Twice Caralyn lost her balance, but Temperance held her in a strong-armed grip. At the top, Caralyn turned and waved to him, her smile warm and inviting, her eyes soft as she let out another burst of laughter.

He stayed where he stood until they disappeared from view then turned, almost colliding with Socrates. The man said nothing but the expression on his face spoke volumes. The sailor would protect Caralyn with his last breath, as would any one of the crew. Tristan nodded, understanding the intent, though he said nothing to defend himself. "I think I'll turn in as well. We've an early start tomorrow, Mr. Callahan, you may want to make the announcement to the men."

Tristan wandered through the main house behind the tavern and climbed to the third floor. He found Jemmy, tucked into bed, sleeping the sleep of the innocent, hands curled beneath his chin. He kissed his son's forehead, pulled the light blanket over his shoulders, and left the house.

He took a seat in the courtyard beneath a flaming torch. Through the multi-windowed Dutch door, he saw that most of his crew had departed though a few hardy souls remained, Hash included, to help Fiona clean the mess from their feast. A grin split his lips but quickly disappeared as he pulled the letter from his father from his pocket. Turning it over and over in his hands, he took a deep breath then broke the seal and read the words.

Again, no mention of his future wife's name, only a summons to be in London on April twenty-fifth and to be at a specific address in Mayfair at noon to marry a stranger. Odd how Caralyn needed to be in London so close to when he was to be married. He shook his head, dismissing the coincidence, and thought about the letter he meant to write to his father, the words of which remained random thoughts in his head, but perhaps the time had come to take those thoughts and put them into action. If need be, he would beg to be released from his upcoming nuptials. His other option would be to meet the woman before the priest pronounced them man and wife and convince her he wasn't the man she should want. He could think of half a dozen other men who would be thrilled to be married to an heiress, but he wasn't one of them. A noise drew his attention. He glanced up toward the second floor of the tavern and his breath seized in his lungs. Caralyn stood on the balcony, her hands lightly resting on the carved balustrade. She smiled at the moon above and he could see her lips move, although he could not hear what she said.

Did she pray? To find the treasure? Or for another reason? Mesmerized, he couldn't tear his gaze away from the vision before him. Moonlight bathed her in silver and reflected off her tanned shoulders. A breeze ruffled her long hair. Indeed, the slight wind molded the diaphanous white gown against her body, leaving nothing to his imagination. She looked like an angel from heaven. One sent to torment him? Or one sent to fulfill all his dreams?

Tristan's body responded faster than his thoughts. His heart thumped in his chest, blood pounded through his veins and roared in his ears. An urgency he couldn't deny swelled within him and the desire to climb the trellis to her balcony, take her in his arms, and make love to her as he longed to do caused his muscles to tighten. And yet, he did nothing. He was, above all else, an honorable man. But that didn't mean he couldn't dream of how she'd feel in his arms. He closed his eyes and let the fantasy take hold.

Chapter 14

Tristan tossed and turned. He rolled over on his side, bringing the sheet with him. The pillow beneath his head had grown warm again but he didn't flip it to the cool side as he'd done so many times during the night. He hadn't slept well, hadn't been able to get the vision of Caralyn standing on the balcony out of his mind, and when he did sleep, he dreamt of her—in his arms, the taste of her lips on his tongue, the curves of her body perfectly molded to his hands. Every thought conspired to make one hellish yet oddly pleasant night.

The morning sun streamed through the windows as he chased the dregs of his dreams away, tossed back the sheet, and climbed out of bed. He strode toward the open French doors, bringing the sheet with him to wrap around his waist, and surveyed his surroundings. Bird song filled the morning. Palm fronds rustled in the breeze. He heard the telltale sounds of someone cooking— the quick chops of a knife against cutting board, the metal clink of pots and pans being placed on the stove, the murmur of quiet conversation. Fiona and Donal had begun their day.

He yawned and stretched then rubbed the sleep from his eyes. A smile crossed his lips as he placed his hands on the balcony railing and glanced toward where he saw Caralyn standing last night. Today, they would find Izzy's Fortune. He felt it in his bones and yet, for the first time in his life, he didn't want to find the treasure he sought. And he knew why.

Caralyn.

She would take her share and go on with her plans, her life. He'd never see her again, never touch her again, never feel the softness of her lips beneath his again. The thought, the realization, made his stomach clench but most surprisingly of all, his chest ached in the region of his heart.

"It's gone! Dear Lord, it's gone!"

Though they weren't loud, he knew in a moment who had uttered those sad, tortured words. Caralyn. Her sobs echoed in his head. Instantly, his body tensed and the pain in his chest intensified to the point where he didn't even think. He grabbed his trousers from the chair arm where he'd left them and stepped into the legs on the run. By the time he reached her closed door, he'd finished buttoning his trousers, though how he accomplished the task he couldn't begin to fathom. His hands shook so badly, he had trouble twisting the doorknob.

Without a second thought for propriety, for whatever state of undress he might find her in, he flung the door open. And stopped.

Caralyn stood in the middle of the room, dressed in the white satin and lace nightgown that had haunted his dreams. She didn't move, didn't try to cover herself.

"Cara?"

"It's gone," she whispered, her voice trembling. Indeed, her whole body trembled and yet, she remained motionless. Her whole stance conveyed disappointment, sadness, utter disbelief.

"What's gone?" He stepped into her room and slowly approached her.

"Everything. The chalice, the statue, Pembrook's journal. It's all gone." She turned to him. Seeing such misery reflected on her face, Tristan drew in his breath sharply. "Someone took my valise."

He thought his heart hurt before, but he'd been mistaken. One look at the tears streaming down her cheeks, and pain blossomed in his chest.

"Who would do such a thing? How will we find the treasure?" Her voice held such sadness, he could think only of comforting her, not of the answers she sought.

Tristan gathered her in arms. She leaned against him, her tears wetting his bare skin, her body warm and alive and shaking.

"Don't cry, Cara mia, it'll be all right." The fragrance uniquely hers tickled his nose as he kissed the top of her head. "We can still find Izzy's Fortune. We don't need Pembrook's journal."

"Are you certain?" She hiccupped and huffed in air.

"Of course." He released her so he could gaze into her eyes, and his heart skipped a beat. Even with tear tracks on her face, she remained the most beautiful woman he'd ever known. With a tenderness he didn't know he possessed, Tristan wiped the wetness from her cheeks with the pad of his thumb then touched his lips to hers in the gentlest of kisses. "Have faith, Cara mia. Where was your valise?"

"Beside the bed."

"Was it here last night? Did you see it before you retired?"

Caralyn sighed. "I don't remember. I was a bit in my cups, if you remember, and didn't notice anything except the moonlight coming in through my window." Her breath hitched. He thought she might start to cry again but she didn't. Instead, she took another deep breath.

Tristan's heart hurt even more as he watched her gain control. He pulled her into his embrace and just held her as he longed to do. She felt so perfect in his arms, so right. Now, if she could stay there forever, he'd be a happy man.

"It doesn't matter, Cara," he whispered against her hair. "You've read Pembrook's journal so many times, you know it by heart, but the last true clue led us to the Island of the Sleeping Man. What he wrote after that were the ramblings of a man slowly giving way to insanity."

"Captain!" Temperance entered the room with a sharp reprimand. "What have you done to this poor girl? Release her immediately!"

Heat flashed through his veins and his face warmed at the sound of Temperance's sharp command. Tristan relinquished his hold on Caralyn and stepped back. He turned toward the woman who tried her hardest to ruin every private, tender moment between him and Caralyn and he wanted to shout at her to leave them alone. He swallowed his anger when he realized what she thought—considering their current states of undress, holding Caralyn as he did, he might have drawn the same conclusion. "It's not what you think."

The suspicion in her eyes remained undimmed and color bloomed on her pale cheeks. She stomped the rest of the way into the room and insinuated herself between them, forcing Tristan to take several more steps backward.

"And what am I to think, Captain? Look at yourself. Standing here, half naked." She leveled a piercing stare at him. Her breath came in short gasps as her chest heaved with righteous indignation. "Look at her with tears on her face!"

She whirled and faced Caralyn. "And you, young lady, your behavior is most unbecoming and unseemly. I should have never taken my own room, never allowed you to have this opportunity. What am I to tell your family?"

"There is nothing to tell, Mrs. Bea—Temperance," Tristan insisted. "I was—"

"Oh, I know what you were doing, Captain. How dare you take advantage of my charge."

Caralyn glanced past her companion and met his gaze. A smile twitched the corners of her mouth and her eyes began to twinkle, but not with tears. They sparkled with humor.

Tristan gazed at her, once again amazed by her resilience, her spirit. Just moments ago, she'd been crying with disappointment, but not now. He began to see the humor as well, despite Temperance's unrelenting stare and obvious anger, despite the fact the woman believed him to be the worst kind of cad.

"Temperance, please. It truly isn't what you think." Caralyn gently grabbed her companion's hand, forcing Temperance to look at her. In a voice strong with conviction, she said, "I remain unsullied, my virtue intact. Someone took my valise. The captain simply tried to comfort me."

It took a moment, perhaps two, before the words Caralyn said registered with the woman. "Oh!" Temperance's anger deflated in an instant. Indeed, she seemed to shrink right before their eyes. "My apologies, Captain."

"Apology accepted, Temperance. We will speak of it no more." He caught Caralyn's eye. "Will you be all right?"

Caralyn nodded but her gaze remained on him. What he saw in their depths made him regret Temperance's interruption and not for the first time.

"If you'll excuse me then?"

"Of course. We'll meet you downstairs."

Tristan inclined his head and left the room, only to meet Stitch in the hallway.

"Everything all right? What happened?" The doctor's eyes raked him from the top of his head to the tips of his bare feet. An eyebrow raised in question. "Did you—"

The urge to defend himself and his actions overwhelmed him. "Of course not! I would never take advantage of a woman. You should know me better than that," he snapped. "Caralyn's valise has been taken. She was upset. I offered comfort and reassurance. That is all. Now, if you'll excuse me?"

Stitch gave one short nod then grinned as they both heard Temperance offer the same kind of comfort colored with a berating in almost the same breath.

Tristan slammed the door to his room and took a deep breath to still the pounding of his heart. His hands shook, indeed, his entire body shook with suppressed anger. Temperance's attitude he could understand, but his own shipmate? How could a man he'd sailed with for the better part of ten years doubt his honor? His intentions?

He supposed he could understand. The circumstances they'd found themselves in were a bit unusual to say the least and if he admitted the truth, he *had* thought of making love to the delectable, tempting Caralyn. More than once. But she wouldn't be in tears when she left his bed.

Tristan took another deep breath and felt his ire diminish. He finished dressing, donning a flowing white shirt that laced up at the neckline then pulled on his boots. While tucking his shirt into his trousers, he caught a glimpse of himself in the mirror and chuckled.

"I do look like a pirate, as Temperance says."

In better spirits, he made his way down to the common room. The smell of bacon made his stomach growl as did the fragrant aroma of coffee. None of the other patrons of Finnegan's arose this early, so the room was empty except for Stitch, who sat at the long table and looked a bit . . .contrite?

"Come. Join me." The good doctor raised his coffee cup high and gestured to the chair across from him.

Tristan quirked an eyebrow and smirked at his friend as he joined him at the table.

"My apologies, Captain, for thinking the worst." He grinned. "I fear some of Temperance's vigilance has influenced me. You are right. I do know you better than that."

For the second time this morning, Tristan opened his heart and accepted the apology but before he could voice a word, the door to the kitchen opened. Fiona and Donal carried chafing dishes of the delicious food he'd been smelling and rested them on the long buffet table.

"Help yerselves, gentlemen," Fiona said as she wiped a small spill from the counter.

Tristan needed no second invitation. He rose from his seat and surveyed the selection. Slices of ham, browned from their turn over a high flame, fluffy scrambled eggs, crisp bacon, fruit, breads and muffins, and a pan filled with something he couldn't quite identify, though the heavenly aroma tickled his nose and made his mouth water.

He filled his plate with a sampling of each and went back to the table but before he could taste anything, a noise drew his attention. He looked toward the stairs and saw Caralyn, dressed in the same blue gown as last night. Her earlier tears had left her eyes glowing with warmth though not a trace of those tears remained on her face. Indeed, she smiled at him and his heart lightened. Temperance followed closely, her eyes on Stitch and Stitch alone, so much so she almost lost her footing and grabbed the banister for stability.

As one, Tristan and Stitch rose from their seats and waited.

"Are you all right?" he asked when Caralyn joined him at the table, searching her features, looking for signs of distress, but none remained. He determined, in that moment, to never let her out of his sight again. This time, someone had taken her valise. The next time, if he allowed a next time, someone could take her. And though he had no proof, he could only think of one man bold enough, insane enough to risk stealing right under their very noses. Entwhistle. But how had he known?

Caralyn laid her hand on his arm and the heat of her innocent touch made the blood in his veins flow like warm honey. "Oh, yes." She took the chair Tristan held for her. "You were right. I know Pembrook's journal better than the man who wrote it. We'll find the treasure, I have no doubt." Concern made her frown. "Do you know who took my things?"

"I have my suspicions, but you are not to worry. Nothing like this will ever happen again." Her perfume swirled in his brain, making it difficult to think, and yet, he had the presence of mind to promise her she'd be safe then to pour her a cup of coffee and give her the plate he had prepared for himself. As he made another plate, he caught a glimpse of Stitch and Temperance. He grinned, realizing they treated each other like a comfortable, married couple—a very much in love couple.

Graham joined them moments later, not from upstairs but through the front door, and one could only guess where he'd spent the night, although the satisfied grin on his face left no doubt he'd been with a woman. Or two. Or perhaps even three. He headed straight for the buffet lined up on the table and filled his plate before sitting down with a groan that could only be described as pleased.

Jemmy entered the common room escorted by Mama Annie, his sleep tousled hair standing up in places. Young Donal trailed behind, his hair, too, standing up. "Are we gonna hunt for treasure, Papa?"

"Of course. After you eat breakfast." Tristan leaned back in his chair and sipped at his coffee as his son scrambled onto his lap. The boy reached for a glass of milk then picked up a crisp slice of bacon from the plate and popped it in his mouth.

Tristan glanced around the table, pleased and oddly humbled he had such good friends, until his gaze met Caralyn's over Jemmy's head, and for a moment, as if in a dream, they weren't in the common room of Finnegan's as partners in a treasure hunt. They were in the dining room of the Winterbourne estates, a warm and loving family, the likes of which he'd never known. He closed and opened his eyes, but the vision remained, and he wished with all his heart such an image could come true.

• • •

The chapel Pembrook built came into view exactly how Donal had described it—high on a cliff top, bathed in an ethereal light, both beautiful and eerie at the same time. Waves crashed against the rocks at the bottom of the escarpment, a constant explosion of sound. Tristan inhaled deeply, astounded by the stark splendor of the small building, and though he saw no ghosts of Pembrook and his wife, wondered if perhaps they shouldn't interrupt their rest.

He studied the faces of his crew and knew they thought the same. Superstitious by nature, his men might not be inclined to enter the haunted sanctuary. Caralyn, on the other hand, seemed more than anxious to bother sleeping ghosts. She stood beside him at the wheel, her body fairly vibrating with anticipation.

"Isn't it beautiful?" she breathed on a sigh.

Tristan didn't answer. He couldn't. His gaze remained on her face and once again, he found her to be the most remarkable, captivating, and beautiful woman he'd ever met, even in the trousers and loose shirt she'd changed into on the ship. Her disappointment, indeed, her frustration and tears over finding her valise missing did nothing to dampen her excitement or drive to find this treasure. In fact, she'd become more determined.

They sailed past the chapel and followed the shoreline until Tristan found a small beach then released the wheel to Mad Dog's confident hand. "Mr. Anders, blow the whistle for me."

The bosun tooted several times on his whistle and the crew jumped into action. In moments, the sails were furled and the anchor splashed into the crystal turquoise water. When the men were finished, they lined up on the quarterdeck.

"I need volunteers to explore the chapel."

Not one man raised his hand. Tristan wasn't surprised.

Mac stepped forward and pulled the knit cap from his head. "Beggin' yer pardon, Cap'n, but I believe I speak for everyone. We won't be disturbin' no ghosts."

Tristan nodded. He understood. "No one will be forced to go into the chapel."

"Be that as it may, we'd rather stay here."

Again, Tristan nodded. "Of course." He glanced at his men then met Caralyn's eyes. "Caralyn?"

"I'm ready." She grinned at him as she twisted her hair into a tail at the back of her head, her eyes sparkling. "Just say the word."

Temperance shrugged and sighed. "If she goes, I go," she stated, although her features were pale and worry clouded her eyes behind the lenses of her glasses.

"If she goes, I go," Stitch echoed her sentiments as he moved closer to Temperance and slipped his hand into hers.

"I'm in," Graham said as he grabbed the burlap sack filled with lanterns and sturdy ropes and other tools they might need.

"Can I go, Papa?" Jemmy tugged at his father's hand.

"May I," Tristan corrected then crouched down so he could be eye level with the boy. "Not this time, son. We don't know what we'll find. I want you to stay with the crew."

Disappointment radiated from the boy. His head drooped and he shifted his weight from one bare foot to the other, his hands shoved into his pockets. "Aye, Papa," he whispered.

Tristan ruffled the boy's hair. "Next time. I promise."

"Aye, Papa," he repeated but this time, the disappointment seemed less, his voice much stronger.

"No other volunteers?" Tristan asked as he rose to his full height. Not a man among them raised his hand. "Mr. Callahan, please lower the longboat."

The sailor was quick to obey but not before he said a word or two to Caralyn, who simply nodded and gave him her brightest smile. Moments later, the five of them climbed into the longboat where Tristan picked up the oars and began rowing toward the small beach.

• • •

Caralyn took a deep breath in an effort to still the excitement bubbling within her as she followed Tristan up the torturous dirt and rock path twisting perilously close to the edge of the escarpment.

The chapel loomed ahead awash in sunlight. Wild flowers, blooming in brilliant colors, surrounded the house of worship. She glanced to her right and saw nothing except a broad expanse of blue and the white crested waves in perpetual motion. One false move, one false step could find her dropping to the jagged rocks below.

She pulled her gaze away from the dizzying sight and concentrated on the sea of trees to her left. Perspiration beaded on her forehead and yet the constant breezes from the ocean kept her cool. Palm fronds rattled overhead and dried leaves crackled beneath their feet. Birdsong filled the air, as did the constant surge of the surf. *We don't need Pembrook's journal. The treasure is here. I know it.*

She looked up and sighed. From the sea, the chapel had been beautiful, but upon closer inspection, the small structure was even more so. Despite time and hurricanes, the structure itself seemed as sturdy as the day it had been built. Moss left a rich patina on the pale stones and flowering vines clung to the walls but left the stained glass windows untouched and intact.

Perhaps, as rumored, ghosts protected this sacred place.

Caralyn studied the windows as she hiked closer. They were not portrayals of saints as she would have expected. Indeed, the colored glass depicted the Island of the Sleeping Man as well as the two other islands beside it. How odd to see such things on a chapel, but how like Pembrook, who seemed to be a most unusual man.

"Are we ready to meet Pembrook's ghost?" Tristan asked as he moved toward the thick wooden door in the center of the building.

"There are no spirits." She grinned at him. "But even if there are, we're not truly troubling them."

The door screeched on its rusted hinges as Tristan pushed against it, further evidence no one had come here in a very long time. Rainbows of light from the windows filled the small room and illuminated the finely patterned cobwebs in the corners. Dust covered the stone floor of the nearly empty chapel though not a human footprint disturbed the fine layer of dirt. The ornate marble resting places of Arthur and Mary were side-by-side, peaceful, untouched in decades, the effigies carved into the tops of the sarcophagi reaching out to touch each other's hands.

In front of the tombs, a *prie dieu*, the bench where one knelt, covered in tattered burgundy velvet … and a statue of the Virgin Mary on a foot-high pedestal, her arms outstretched, palms up. Made not of plaster or carved from marble, but of wood, the paint faded and peeling, though kindness and serenity still radiated from the Blessed Mother's face.

A haunting moan echoed through the chamber, becoming louder then fading into silence only to become louder again. Caralyn grinned at Tristan although goose bumps broke out on her skin and a shiver raced down her back. "There's your ghost. It's just the wind."

Undaunted, she took a deep breath and strode up the aisle while Stitch and Temperance inspected the inscriptions written on the marble caskets. Graham pressed his palms against the walls in various locations and twisted the brass sconces, looking for hidden passageways.

Without hesitation, Caralyn knelt before the statue and began to pray.

She crossed herself and stood when she finished. "What did Pembrook's clue say?"

"Take the hand of the Blessed Virgin," Tristan replied as he stepped up beside her. Dust swirled and covered his fine black boots. A mouse skittered across the floor, drawing a small screech from Temperance, but other than that one tiny sound and the constant moan of wind, silence permeated the chapel.

Caralyn moved to her left, away from the *prie dieu*, and reached for the statue's outstretched hand, as instructed. She didn't know what she expected—a secret panel in one of the walls revealed perhaps—but nothing happened.

She took a deep breath and moved to the right side, once again placing her hand on the Virgin Mary's. It moved, ever so slightly, the wood possibly rotted by time. She squeezed tighter and pushed down a bit, but the hand in hers still only moved a fraction. She stepped closer and inspected the icon, noticing that the statue was not carved from one single piece of wood but by several pieces joined together.

"Be careful," Tristan said as he took a step closer as well.

Again, she placed her hand in the Virgin's, but this time, she didn't push down. This time, she twisted. A solid click echoed in the silence, followed by a deep rumble. The stone slate beneath her feet began to tremble. Indeed, the whole room seemed to shudder.

A startled gasp escaped her as she released the statue's hand and Temperance gave another small shriek. The woman moved toward the door, ready to flee the building should the need arise. Stitch stood beside her, his hand in hers, whether to offer comfort or to help with a hasty exit, Caralyn didn't know. Graham backed himself into a corner, the expression on his face one of doubt ... and perhaps fear?

More excited than frightened, Caralyn remained where she stood, in front of the Virgin Mary. Anticipation surged through her. Laughter bubbled up from her chest and threatened to pour from her mouth.

She reached for the statue's hand once more and twisted again. The deep rumble continued to grow louder until it became a horrible roar. Caralyn jumped as another shudder shook the floor. She tried to take a step away but not soon enough. The large stone beneath her dropped several feet. A surprised scream escaped her as she fell with the stone ... until a strong hand caught her wrist. She looked up to see Tristan, his face set with determination as she dangled above the gaping black maw that had once been solid stone.

As if she weighed nothing, Tristan pulled her to safety and gathered her in his arms.

"You need to be careful, Cara mia," he whispered in her ear. She felt him tremble as his arms tightened around her.

"I'm all right. Truly." She pressed her hands against the hard planes of his chest, the muscles beneath his flesh tense. That tension reflected in his eyes and the tightness of his lips.

"Be that as it may, you still need to take care. Finding the treasure wouldn't be half as exciting without you."

Though she loved being in his arms, and his words warmed her to the tips of her toes, curiosity made her pull away. She knelt in front of the black hole in the floor and peered into the darkness. "Graham, please bring me a lantern."

The soft glow of the lantern expelled the inky blackness and Caralyn held her breath. "There's a cavern beneath the chapel."

"Graham, toss me the rope." Tristan held out his hand but instead of receiving a coil of rope, Graham handed him a rope ladder, complete with metal hooks to hold said ladder in place.

"I'll go first," Tristan said as he secured the hooks of the ladder on the pedestal beneath the statue and flung the rest of the rope into the hole. His gaze held Caralyn's, the warmth of his eyes mesmerizing. "Wait until I give the all clear before you start down."

Caralyn nodded even though anticipation swept through her. In truth, she didn't want to wait. She wanted to see what lay beneath the floor of the chapel, what treasures had been stored for almost two centuries, untouched by human hands. She watched his head disappear as he lowered himself into the passage, the glow of the lantern he held diminishing.

"It's safe," he called up from the depths. "Send down the other lanterns then join me but be careful. It's amazing down here." His words ended on a sigh.

Graham made quick work of tying a length of cord to the burlap sack and lowering the bundle into the hollow. Soon, a warm glow dispelled the darkness and jewels, tossed carelessly in the dirt, caught and reflected the light. Caralyn released her breath in a huff of air. A multitude of colors twinkled below her. She recognized emeralds and lapis lazuli, amethyst and topaz, rubies and diamonds, the gems scattered as if Pembrook had spilled the contents of a small chest and hadn't bothered to retrieve them.

She climbed down the ladder and waited for Temperance, Stitch, and Graham to join her and Tristan. Cold, clammy moisture seeped into her clothing; indeed, it seemed to seep into her bones, but didn't dampen Caralyn's excitement one bit. Nor did the fact that no other chests filled with jewels or gold lined the walls of the chamber.

From her position, she couldn't tell how far the cavern extended in either direction; however, the constant breeze and dull roar of the ocean led her to believe the grotto began where the sea crashed against the cliff, hidden from prying eyes unless one knew where to look.

More determined than ever to find the blasted treasure and live her life as she chose, Caralyn raised her lantern high and started walking toward where the thunder of the ocean sounded loudest.

"Have a care, Cara," Tristan called after her. "We don't know what we'll find. Better yet, wait for me."

"I'll be careful," she responded but as soon as the words left her mouth, the promise left her brain. The cavern twisted and turned, the floor sloping downward at a sharp angle. Her feet sank into sand and her fingers traced the wet walls on her left. Strange, she had no sensation of the walls closing in on her, no fear the low ceiling would fall upon her head. The constant breeze smelling of brine ruffled her hair. Sunlight and shadows played over the rocks ahead as she explored the long corridor. A crab scuttled toward the opening in front of her, its pinkish shell glistening. Caralyn stood at the entrance of the cave and breathed deeply. She felt small and insignificant as the vastness of the turquoise sea spread before her. Waves crashed against the tumbled rocks below her, sending up a fine spray that settled on her skin, and she imagined when the tide came in, this entire cave became flooded.

She turned around and almost slammed into Tristan.

"I thought I asked you to wait for me."

"I'm perfectly safe, Tristan."

He quirked an eyebrow. "You almost fell into the hole in the floor. You could have broken your fool neck." His voice lowered to a growl. "It was only by the grace of God I was able to catch you."

He took her in his arms and smoothed the wispy tendrils of hair that escaped the tail at the back of her head. "I meant what I said. Finding this treasure wouldn't be half as satisfying if you weren't with me."

Caralyn acknowledged his feelings with a slight tilt of her head and pressed her hands against his chest. How she loved being in his arms, the way the heat of his body warmed her all the way to her soul. "I will endeavor to be more careful."

"And you'll wait for me from now on?"

"Yes, I'll wait for you."

"Good." His voice rumbled in his chest and vibrated against her fingertips before his head dipped and his lips touched hers in the gentlest of kisses. For a moment, for a heartbeat, Caralyn ceased to think. The crashing of the waves died away, leaving just the rush of blood to pound in her ears. His mouth slanted over hers and his tongue pushed against her lips, begging entrance, begging permission. With an eagerness that surprised her, Caralyn complied and drew in her breath as his tongue explored every inch of her mouth. Her knees grew weak beneath the tender onslaught and her hands stole around his neck, pulling him closer.

Tristan broke the kiss with a chuckle, his smile brilliant. "Let's see if Pembrook really stole Izzy's Fortune and hid it beneath the chapel." He took her hand. The warmth of his touch, combined with the heat of his kiss, made her clumsy and awkward and she tripped twice as they followed the twisting passage back to rejoin the rest of their party.

Caralyn resisted the urge to giggle when she saw Stitch and Temperance. They were busy picking up all the jewels scattered in the dirt and dropping them into the burlap sack Graham held. If they found no other treasure here, at least they had those jewels.

They continued walking in the opposite direction, Caralyn's small hand in Tristan's until the tunnel ended in a small chamber. No treasure chests were piled in the middle of the hollow, no gold displayed for the taking, although a sprinkling of gems sparkled in the light of the lamp. Caralyn let go of Tristan's hand, raised her lantern, and gasped as the glow revealed a mural painted on the wall.

"Oh my!" Her voice echoed in the chamber. Her heart pounded within her chest and excitement made her stomach clench. Within moments, Temperance and Stitch joined them, as did Graham. "Pembrook didn't come here to pray. He came to paint, to remember." She stood back so she could see the entire image. "There's the Island of the Sleeping Man and its sister islands. Look at this." She moved closer and her fingers grazed the wall of the cave, over the mural, and came to rest on lines of jewels embedded into the rock. Rubies and lapis lazuli marked the paths they had already explored on the Island of the Sleeping Man, however, there was another path, this one outlined in brilliant emeralds, on the island in the middle. A heart-shaped emerald glistened at the end.

"The map was a ruse, as we know. Pembrook never hid the treasure on the Island of the Sleeping Man, he just wanted everyone to think he had." Caralyn traced her finger along the line of emeralds. "It's here." She turned and caught Tristan's grin. "Will you take us back to this island?"

He gave an exaggerated bow, the lantern in his hand reflecting light on the path of jewels. "As my lady wishes."

Euphoria filled her. Though the cave was not filled with the treasure she sought, she *would* find Izzy's Fortune. The certainty of it strengthened her resolve.

• • •

"Well?"

Porkchop jumped, dropped the spyglass from his eye, and shivered as Captain Entwhistle sidled up beside him. He'd been so intent on watching Caralyn, he hadn't heard the captain, hadn't felt his presence until it was too late.

"Nothin' te report, sir," he said and raised the glass to his eye once more. "They're leavin' same way they went in. Only carryin' one burlap sack. I'm thinkin' Izzy's Fortune weren't in the chapel like they thought."

The captain grunted and held out his hand. Porkchop placed the spyglass in it and remained silent as Entwhistle peered through the glass. He grunted again and returned the spyglass. "Don't let them out of your sight." He started to walk away then stopped and said over his shoulder, "If you value your life."

Chapter 15

After leaving Jamaica, a pod of dolphins took up residence beside the *Adventurer*, racing with the ship, their sleek bodies hurling out of the water and flying through the air with amazing agility and speed. To every sailor on board, the dolphins brought with them a sense of good fortune.

As the sun began its slow descent into the horizon, the reddish gold rays bathed the sails in color so vibrant, the normally white sheets appeared to be on fire. A light breeze filled them and the *Adventurer* glided through the waves. With a firm grip on the ship's wheel, Tristan couldn't be more content. This was where he wanted to be, what he chose to do. His gaze fixed on Caralyn and a trickle of anxiety whispered through his veins.

They were running out of time.

In truth, he was glad they hadn't found the treasure in the chapel, but only because it allowed him to continue the search with Caralyn. As he studied her now, listened to her laughter, watched the bright smile light up her face as she watched the dolphins with Jemmy, he knew, despite the fact they only had a few handfuls of jewels, she was happy.

And what her happiness did to him simply amazed him. Joy surged through his veins and brought a smile to his face.

His gaze slid to Temperance and Stitch. They, too, watched the dolphins. They stood at the rail, hand in hand, the warm glow of the sun washing them in pure light, but perhaps it wasn't only the sun that had them glowing. Perhaps it was love. The fondness between them had grown to something more, something that couldn't be denied, something evident to every man who saw them together.

Tristan grinned, happy Stitch had found that elusive prize, and yet, regret and jealousy tinged his happiness. He witnessed the tender kiss Stitch placed on Temperance's forehead, the lingering touch of his hand on hers before the ship's surgeon headed toward the helm. Envy tightened Tristan's gut, made him grip the wheel tighter, and yet, he couldn't begrudge any man who'd found love, especially since that was what he wanted.

"Beautiful evening, isn't it?" Stitch said as he stepped beside him at the wheel.

"Yes, it is." Tristan lifted his cup of coffee and took a big gulp.

"Temperance and I want to get married." The words spilled from Stitch without hesitation.

Tristan swallowed the mouthful of coffee so he wouldn't choke, but a strangled cough escaped him anyway.

"We would consider it an honor if you would preside over our vows."

Rendered almost speechless, Tristan grinned. "Of course. When?"

The man grinned in return then shifted his weight from one leg to the other. He clasped his hands behind his back. "I can't think of a better time than right now. Temperance and I don't need anything fancy. Just a few simple words from the Bible. Everyone we care about is already here."

"Do you have a ring to give her?"

A blush stained Stitch's face and the smile he gave reminded Tristan of Jemmy's when caught doing something he shouldn't. "No, not yet, but when we were at the chapel, I found a beautiful emerald that I'll have made into a ring for her."

"I'm happy for you, Stitch. She's a wonderful woman." He turned and looked at the sun lowering in the sky. "I think a sunset ceremony would be lovely. Go tell your future bride the good news." Stitch would never know how much Tristan wished the ceremony could be his, that he could marry the woman of his choice instead of the nameless, faceless woman waiting for him in England. His gaze swept the deck and settled on Caralyn once more. His vision misted as she smiled at him.

The doctor walked away, a jaunty bounce to his normally dignified step. Tristan watched him as he kissed Temperance then gave her the good news. She glanced in his direction and mouthed the words "thank you" before she and Caralyn left the deck amid happy squeals.

Tristan signaled to Graham and beckoned him closer then nodded toward Stitch pacing the deck. "The good doctor wants to marry Mrs. Beasley."

The man followed his line of vision then quirked an eyebrow and grinned. "I have long suspected as much. Any fool can see he's beyond smitten with our young widow. And she with him. They make a good pair."

"Yes, they do." He didn't realize he'd said the words with a touch of wistfulness until Graham shot him a glance, his eyebrow raised almost to his hairline. He ignored the expression and asked, "Do we have any champagne to toast the happy couple?"

"I think we have several cases, but I'll double check. If not, we have plenty of rum, wine, and brandy." Though he said he'd double check, Graham didn't move for the longest time, his sharp eyes searching Tristan's face. "Are you all right with this?"

"Of course. Why wouldn't I be?" he snapped, his tone more brusque than usual.

Graham shrugged. "I was just thinking about your own upcoming nuptials and wondering if you're still planning to go through with them."

Tristan said nothing, although his stomach twisted and left a sour taste in his mouth. What could he say? Graham knew he had no choice, knew whether they found the treasure or not, his father had committed him to marry and he wasn't in the position to refuse.

Again, Graham shrugged. "I'll go check on that champagne." Ten minutes passed before the navigator returned, a case of champagne in his arms. Dust and cobwebs covered both the wooden crate and Graham's fine clothing. "Found it."

"Good." Tristan took the case from him. "If you'll take the wheel for a bit, I'll bring this to Hash, then I need to find my Bible."

As soon as he stepped into Hash's galley, his mouth began to water from the incredible aromas, and his stomach growled, reminding him he hadn't eaten since breakfast. He watched the big man chop vegetables and toss them into a pot on the stove. Over the years, other captains, having heard of Hash's culinary mastery, had tried to entice the cook away from the *Adventurer*. Hash, to Tristan's gratitude, never even considered their offers.

He placed the case of champagne on the table. Hash didn't jump, didn't even turn away from the stove as he dropped a bit of green bean toward Smudge. The cat gobbled up the tidbit and meowed as he rubbed up against the man's legs. "How can I help you, Cap'n?"

"You didn't happen to bake a cake for desert tonight, did you?"

Hash turned around and wiped his hands on his ever-present apron. Sweat and flour dotted his round face. "As it happens, Cap'n, I did not." A frown creased his forehead. "Beggin' yer pardon, but did ye want cake?"

"Well … .uh … I hadn't even thought about it until a few moments ago. Stitch and Temperance are getting married and I thought a cake would be nice."

"That sly fox." Hash shook his head and grinned. "Earlier today, I received a special request from the good doctor. He asked for rice pudding with rum raisin sauce." He used the apron to swipe at his forehead then stepped over the cat still winding his way between his thick legs and leaned against the table in the middle of the room. "Miss Temperance's favorite dessert, I was told." His grin widened and he slapped the tabletop. "Gettin' married, is he? Well, I'll be damned." He gestured to the crate on the table. "An' I suppose this champagne is for the celebration?"

"You suppose correctly. The wedding will be at sunset on the quarterdeck."

Without another word, Hash turned toward the stove and removed the pot then untied his apron and threw it on the hook behind the door. "I'll be seein' ye on deck, Cap'n. Wouldn't miss this for the world."

For a man as large as Hash, he moved with speed and grace. Smudge followed, his long, sinewy body weaving between the man's legs. Hash didn't seem to mind. Indeed, his stride lengthened to accommodate the cat. Before he disappeared into his cabin, he stopped. "Beggin' yer pardon, Cap'n, but could ye ask Mr. Callahan, Mr. Jacoby, and Mad Dog to meet me in the galley?"

"Of course," Tristan said then shook his head, amusement making him grin as he watched man and beast disappear. He took a deep breath and went to his cabin.

He heard giggles coming from behind the closed door, the excited chatter of Caralyn and Temperance as they prepared for a shipboard wedding. A surge of jealousy struck him again. For a moment, his stomach twisted into a knot and a heaviness settled in his chest, the same debilitating weight as when he realized Caralyn would leave him when they found the treasure. He forced himself to breathe, inhaling and holding it before releasing the lungful of air slowly. The tightness in his stomach eased, but his chest still felt heavy. He raised his hand and knocked.

Caralyn answered the door, her eyes sparkling, her cheeks filled with color, her hair piled on her head in loose curls. The smile on her lips made his heart beat a bit faster. She'd changed from the pale yellow gown she'd worn earlier into an amethyst one shot through with silver threads. A row of tiny pearl buttons went from the neckline to her waist, and he wondered briefly if they were just for show or if they functioned as they should. He had an incredible inclination to find out.

He couldn't speak over the lump that rose to his throat. She'd never looked lovelier, never more beautiful, and again, he wished this ceremony could be between the two of them. He swallowed. "Sorry for the interruption. I just need to find my Bible." The door opened wider and he stepped through.

"Temperance, you look lovely." And indeed, she did. Her long auburn hair hung loose and curled wildly down her back, the chestnut tresses gleaming in the lamplight. A simple strand of pearls adorned her neck and glowed against the midnight blue of her gown. Behind the lenses of her glasses, her eyes twinkled with excitement. "Uh, I'll be out of your way in a moment."

He went to his desk, opened the side drawer and retrieved a well-worn, much loved Bible. "I'll see you on deck," he said to both of them, but his gaze remained on Caralyn as he closed the door behind him.

With his step heavier than usual, Tristan trudged up the stairs and signaled to Mr. Anders. "Would you assemble the crew?"

The bosun tooted on his whistle and the crew immediately paused in their activity to assemble on the quarterdeck.

"Gentlemen," he said, his voice rising over the excited rumblings of the men, "tonight, we have the honor of witnessing the marriage between our own Stitch and Temperance Beasley. Go wash yourselves up, but be back here in five minutes. Mr. Callahan, Mr. Jacoby, Mad Dog," he addressed the sailors, "Hash requests your presence in the galley. However, I suggest you clean up first."

"Aye, Cap'n," all three responded in unison before they raced to their own quarters, jostling each other with well-connected elbows and shouts.

Tristan stood on the quarterdeck as he waited, motionless, torn between happiness and misery.

He felt a tug on his sleeve and looked down to see Jemmy. Someone had taken him in hand as well. Perhaps it had been Stitch. The boy sported his finest clothing, his hair slicked back with pleasant smelling pomade. "Why is Stitch marrying Miss Temperance?"

"Because he loves her and she loves him."

With all the innocence of a boy who'd seen much being raised by a roughened crew of men, and who remained naïve yet knowledgeable at the same time, he asked, "Does that mean you're going to marry Miss Cara? You love her, don't you?"

Startled by the simple question, Tristan stiffened. What could he say? Though he wished it to be so, that didn't necessarily make it so. And love? He didn't know if what he felt for Caralyn could be considered love. Then again, what would he know of it, having never felt this way before. True, he enjoyed her company and found her intelligent, fascinating, and adorable, but he wasn't certain if that equaled love.

Instead of answering, he said, "Let's just celebrate one wedding at a time, shall we?"

The boy nodded, although questions remained in his eyes, questions his curious son did not voice, questions Tristan would rather not answer. He watched, Jemmy's hand in his, as Mr. Callahan and Mad Dog created makeshift tables made of planks of wood. He'd never seen either of them move so quickly, but then Hash was right behind them, carrying a cast iron pot, which lent a heavenly scent to the air. Amusement tickled him as the men rushed, almost tripping over themselves, in their haste to have everything prepared.

Glasses, plates, and silverware were added to the table along with napkins and baskets of bread, the crate of champagne, and the large pan of rice pudding drizzled with rum raisin sauce. Candles, surrounded by protective glass, flickered as Mr. Jacoby lit them against the coming night.

He turned and studied the horizon behind him. The sun was sinking quickly. He figured he had less than ten minutes to perform the ceremony before the sun set completely. "Mr. Anders, please sound the order."

The shipman gave three short blasts on his whistle. The crew came running from all directions, dressed in their finest clothing, hair wet and slicked back, hands damp, some still buttoning their shirts or adjusting their trousers.

"Are you ready?" Tristan asked as a nervous Stitch walked up the stairs and stood in front of him.

"Yes." One simple word was all he could utter.

"Mac, would you ask the ladies to join us?"

The Scotsman nodded, his kilt swishing around his legs as he rushed to follow orders.

A few moments later, a collective sigh went up from the assembled crew as Temperance joined Brady and slipped her hand in his. Tristan shared their awe. She'd never looked more beautiful and it wasn't the gown or her hair. It was the expression of love and happiness on her face. Caralyn motioned to Jemmy and they both stood a few steps behind the bride. Tears shimmered in Caralyn's eyes, making them a more crystalline blue. She smiled at him and his heart grew heavier than it had before.

Tristan dragged his gaze away from Caralyn then cleared his throat and opened the Bible. As he read one of his favorite passages, he glanced at Temperance then at Stitch. He'd never seen a couple more in love than these two, and though he'd never presided over a wedding before, his words rang out with confidence. "If you'll both place your hands on the Bible." When they did so, Tristan spoke again. "Do you, Temperance Beasley, take this man as your lawful husband, to have and to hold, for better or for worse, for richer or for poorer, in sickness and in health, to love and to cherish, from this day forward until death do you part?"

"I do." Her voice, quiet but strong, conveyed her conviction.

He repeated the same question to Stitch and received the same answer, also spoken with conviction and a great deal of love.

"If there is any among you who believe Brady and Temperance should not be joined in marriage, speak now or forever hold your peace." The crew remained silent, as not one objected to the union, and as the sun disappeared into the horizon with a last flash of brilliant color, Tristan pronounced Stitch and Temperance man and wife. "You may kiss the bride."

A cheer rose from the crew as Brady Trevelyan leaned forward and placed a sweet kiss on his wife's lips.

Champagne flowed, the hastily prepared feast enjoyed and exclaimed over, and music filled the silence of the night.

The sound of feet stomping on the deck as the men danced to the music drowned out the beat of Tristan's heart. He watched Caralyn as she dipped and swayed, her skirt lifted to reveal lacy petticoats as she danced with one man after another. Patient, though he wanted nothing more than to steal her away and into his own arms, he waited until it was his turn.

Laughter bubbled from Caralyn's throat as she landed in his embrace, the buttons of her dress, the ones in his mind since he first saw them, pressed against his chest.

• • •

Caralyn didn't know how it happened. Or when it happened. One moment, they were dancing on the deck, swaying to the music, the next they were in the captain's cabin. Tristan's hands molded her body to his, his lips on hers as they leaned against the door, his knee pressed between her thighs.

Perhaps it was the champagne that had flowed so freely, though she'd only had one glass, or the romance of a sunset wedding. Perhaps it was *him*, and the heady mix of emotions surging through her, the intoxicating touch of his mouth to hers, the taste of him, the feel of his powerful body so close, the smell of spindrift surrounding her. All she knew was that kissing him, holding him, had become more important than breathing.

I shouldn't be doing this. The thought rambled through her head, and yet she didn't want to stop the amazing sensations racing through her, didn't want to end this perfect moment. He pulled the pins from her hair and the heavy weight fell to tickle her shoulders as his fingers threaded through her curls.

I should tell him.

"I'm promised to another," she blurted as her lips met his, the first time she admitted the secret she'd been hiding. She felt him stiffen and pull away slightly, but only for a moment before he gathered her closer.

"As am I," he whispered against her cheek.

Shock whispered through her, but she chose to ignore it. There would be time enough later to agonize over his admission and her own. For right now, she didn't want to think at all.

"But we're alone now in the middle of the ocean. We can pretend the world and our obligations beyond this do not exist." The tone of his voice sounded almost tortured to her ears as his arms tightened around her. "Just let me hold you, Cara mia. That's all I ask."

Darkness engulfed the cabin, except for the beams of moonlight that caressed them. Caralyn settled into his arms and reveled in the warmth he exuded, the gentle strength of his embrace. His breath fanned her neck, just below her ear, as he placed tender kisses along her throat and jaw line. Goose bumps pebbled her skin and a strange though pleasant tightening stirred between her legs.

She couldn't help herself. Being held in his arms was not enough, couldn't satisfy the growing need that made her feel flush, made her shiver, made her want what she didn't know. She touched her lips to his while her hands splayed on his firm hard chest. His heart beat a steady cadence beneath her fingertips. He drew in his breath, made a slight noise in the back of his throat, a cross between a moan and a groan as his chest expanded beneath her hands.

That gentle kiss turned to something more demanding, more passionate, as his mouth took possession of hers and his hands— dear God, they seemed to be everywhere at once—crushing her to him, caressing her back through the material of her gown, stroking her hair, her face, warming her from the inside out.

He led her away from the door, his mouth locked on hers, tongue caressing hers, hands touching every inch of her. Breath mingled, the sound erotic to her ears. They settled into an overstuffed leather chair near the small stove used to heat the cabin. Caralyn sat on his lap, her legs slung over the arm of the chair, her gown hiked up to expose her stockings to her knees. She could feel the strength of his arousal against her backside even through the layers of clothing and a thrill raced through her.

Tristan's lips touched hers, sliding over them, tasting her, sending more heat to flood her veins, as his fingers slid over her collarbone then down to the décolletage of her gown. His fingers made short work of unbuttoning her dress to expose the corset cover beneath. A quick tug on the ribbon and the garment loosened. He lowered the short puffed sleeve of her gown and brushed his lips along her shoulder as his hand slipped beneath her corset and chemise to gently cup her breast. The nipple puckered into a hard nub as he whispered in her ear all the things he wanted to do to her.

In that instant, Caralyn ceased to think beyond the surge of yearning taking control of her, beyond the pleasurable tightening between her thighs. Heat suffused her. Indeed, fire seemed to blaze in her veins, igniting an inferno she didn't think she could survive.

She moved against him and he groaned deep in his throat, his chest rumbling beneath her hand, but then it was her turn to moan as his kisses dropped lower, from her shoulder, to the tops of her breasts exposed by corset and chemise. Supported by his arm behind her, Caralyn's head tilted back, granting him more access. A small sound escaped her as he complied with her silent wish and the spiraling heat within her grew. Within moments, the clasps at the front of her corset were undone and the chemise pushed aside.

She had an irrational desire to cover herself and brought her hands up to do so, but Tristan stopped her. "Don't, Cara mia. Let me look at you." He sighed as his gaze touched every inch of bare skin glowing in the moonlight. "You're beautiful."

His words alone were enough to convince her, but one look at the expression on his face, at the longing and appreciation in his eyes, made her cast aside all her uncertainty. She wanted this, had wanted this from the moment they met. The hunger for him had only grown stronger the more time they spent with each other. Caralyn caressed his hair and brought his head down to her breast.

The first touch of his tongue against her already hardened nipple made her gasp, indeed, made her jump as the warmth of his mouth surrounded the straining bud. The heat inside her doubled, the tightening between her thighs growing in unexpected surges.

Her shoe fell to the floor and her gown rode higher as Tristan slipped his hand beneath the hem and caressed her leg, smoothing along the silky stocking from her ankle to her calf to her knee before finding the sensitive skin of her thigh beneath her drawers. While his mouth and lips continued their leisurely exploration of her breasts and played havoc with her senses, Caralyn felt the ties holding her stocking in place slip free. With an expertise that surprised her, he slid the stocking from her leg and then the warmth of his hand replaced the silk.

Caralyn gasped as his fingers brushed up against the mass of springy curls between her thighs. No one, except herself, had ever touched her there. Moisture seeped from that secret place, making her slick, making it easy for him to part the swollen flesh and find the key to her release. As his thumb gently caressed her, the tightening pressure built, spiraling out of control. He glided a finger into her moist heat, stroking her sensitive skin as his thumb continued to draw light circles on the hardened nub.

"Come for me," he whispered against her lips. Her eyes opened and her breath came in short gasps of surprise as her body responded to the simple words and exploded.

Now Caralyn knew why men chased women and women allowed themselves to be caught. This pure rapture, this unbridled passion, this pleasure had no equal.

Tristan continued to caress her swollen flesh while his lips took possession of hers. He rose from the chair, bringing her with him as if she weighed nothing and maybe she did weigh nothing. She felt light, boneless, a quivering mass of pulsating nerves and flesh, her body ablaze with sensation, her mind unable to hold a coherent thought. He placed her on her feet, which was a mistake. With her knees weak, she wobbled and fell against him, her breasts crushing against his hard chest. Gooseflesh pebbled her skin as the gown and petticoat fell away, leaving an amethyst and white puddle on the floor. She stood in a beam of moonlight in her underclothes, one stocking still covering her leg, unashamed.

He said nothing but no words were needed. Indeed, she probably wouldn't have understood or remembered, caught as she was in the spiraling passion his touch evoked. And touch her he did—with his lips, his mouth, his hands. He made removing each piece of clothing a new experience in sensation. His eyes reflected his own need and yet, he remained gentle, patient.

Thoughts spun in her mind, but not one made sense as she helped him take off his shirt, her fingers clumsy with nervousness. The muscles in his chest and arms rippled with his movements, causing another stir of excitement within her. She couldn't resist running her hands over his hard muscles. His body stiffened beneath her touch. His wide chest tapered to a lean waist, slim hips, and long legs, and when he bent over to remove his boots, she was treated to the sight of his well-developed backside.

Anticipation grew as his trousers dropped to the floor and he stood before her, naked, unadorned, fully aroused, and so beautiful. Caralyn drank in the perfection of his body. Her mind memorized every powerful line of him, but her eyes were drawn to the heat of his gaze. In the depths of his sherry-colored eyes, she saw a promise of what was to come as he laid her gently on the bed.

Caralyn opened her arms and welcomed him. His weight pushed her further into the mattress. The fine hair on his chest pricked her already sensitive nipples and the rush of expectancy coiled like a spring in the very core of her being. Every nerve in her body came alive beneath the onslaught of his touch, every sense heightened. The smell of the sea clung to him and filled her nose. The taste of champagne on his tongue became a heady elixir within her brain. The warmth of his skin beneath her hands, the roughness of his whiskers against her face, the tenderness of his kiss all conspired to make doubts, fears, and obligations disappear.

The brief stab of pain when he entered her body for the first time startled her and she stiffened beneath him, but only for a moment. He stopped, his breath coming in short gasps, the muscles in his arms bunching from self-control.

"I'm sorry. I didn't mean to hurt you," he whispered as he planted gentle kisses on her face. Caralyn felt the tension in him, the control he exerted. She trusted him and relaxed her stiffened muscles. Tristan began to move in her slowly, the length and breadth of him filling her until she became lost in the rhythm older than time.

Poised on the edge of another jarring climax, Caralyn lifted her hips to meet his. She met him stroke for stroke, her hands clutching his backside, pulling him closer as her legs wrapped around his.

Tristan groaned as the world around her shattered into a million stars. She felt the warmth of his seed fill her, felt her own body throbbing around him, felt the tension in him ease as his mouth claimed hers once more.

A chill made her shiver as his warmth left her and he rose from the bed. She watched him, fascinated by his rippling muscles and tight, round backside as he poured water into the washbasin and grabbed a clean cloth from the drawer beneath it.

She'd known him to be gentle, to be tender. She'd seen with her own eyes the loving way he treated Jemmy and tonight, he was no different with her. He sat on the side of the bed, the washcloth in his hand. "The first time is always painful and I'm sorry. I should have been gentler, should have taken my time."

Caralyn stiffened and heat rose to her face when she realized what he was about to do, but the way he looked at her, the tenderness in his voice put her at ease and she let him bathe away the telltale proof of her virginity from her thighs. He tossed the cloth into the water basin and crawled back into bed.

Tristan caressed the side of her face, pushing her perspiration damp hair away from her cheek. "It'll never happen again. I promise."

What wouldn't happen again? Making love? Sharing a passion that seemed all consuming and just so right, she could have cried?

He kissed her then his lips moving over hers with such sweetness, tears stung her eyes. "Sleep now, my sweet." He cradled her in his arms. Caralyn let the warmth of his body surround her as she drifted into sleep, her limbs heavy with satisfaction, her heartbeat returning to a much more normal pace. The last thing she heard was his tortured whisper, "Ah, Cara mia, why did I have to find you now?"

Chapter 16

Tristan woke to the same sounds as yesterday and the day before. The creaking of the ship as it cut through the ocean waves, the sails snapping in the constant breeze, the muffled voices of the crew on deck. And something new—the light breathing of Caralyn as she slept in his arms.

His belly tightened in surprise. Never before had he woken with a woman in his bed. Granted, he'd had his fair share of women, but none had ever stayed for more than a few hours, none had been invited to stay. *This* new experience made him smile. He rather liked waking up with Caralyn. She nestled against him, her back pressed to his stomach. A low growl rumbled from him when she snuggled her backside tighter against the curve of his groin. The innocent-in-sleep move speared the warmth of her body straight through his skin to heat his blood. Indeed, waking with her in his arms gave him a thrill he'd never known. The thought dawned on him he'd never realized how lonely he'd been until she stepped onto his ship and made him an outrageous offer.

Last night had been a revelation. Making love to her changed him, made clear in his mind exactly what needed to be done. First, find the blasted treasure, then make Caralyn his for eternity. His father and the demand to marry some other woman be damned. The weight on his shoulders to carry on the family name sat like the *Adventurer's* anchor, but he would meet his obligations—on his terms … and with the woman of his choice.

The object of his thoughts sighed and snuggled closer against his chest. Tristan inhaled her scent and his muscles tensed as doubt and questions filled his mind. There had been more than one revelation last night. Caralyn had surprised him with her admission she was promised to someone. Why had she not mentioned her betrothal before now? Did she love this man she was to marry? Or was her hand being forced as Tristan's was? Could she resolve her own commitment? If she were free to be his, would she want him?

He had too many questions with no answers and yet, his heart swelled with hope, with desire. He couldn't imagine his life without her. He loved the sound of her laughter, the impish grin she usually wore, and the mischievous twinkle in her eyes. He loved her spirit and determination and her kindness. He loved how she'd grown so fond of his son.

He loved . . .her.

The realization struck him like lightning, like the green flash he sometimes saw on the horizon when the sun dipped into the ocean. He wanted to laugh with the pure pleasure of the knowledge, not only in his mind, but in his heart.

Filled with wonder and awe, with unbridled joy and a new resolve, Tristan leaned up on his elbow and watched her sleep. He smoothed her curling tresses away from her features, the glossy strands sleek and soft; the alluring fragrance drifted to his nose and made him smile. She seemed more beautiful now and he couldn't resist reaching out to caress her cheek with the back of his hand. Her skin felt like warm silk. She sighed and her backside pressed more firmly against his manhood. His smile widened.

He nuzzled the back of her neck, his breath fanning the fine hairs residing there. He watched, fascinated, as goose bumps pebbled her skin.

The sheet covering them both exposed her tanned shoulder and he traced his fingers along the smooth expanse of skin. He caressed her shoulder, collarbone, and side of her throat. His lips followed the imaginary path as he pressed light kisses on her dewy flesh. Caralyn moaned deep in her throat, her body moving against his, arousing him more than he thought possible. Blood surged through his veins. His heart pounded in his chest and pulsed in his ears so he no longer heard the sounds around him.

He pushed the sheet further down, grazing her arm with the lightest touch of his fingertips, caressing her ribs and her stomach before cupping her breast. Her nipple sprang to life, puckering beneath the subtle scraping of his thumb.

Caralyn released a startled gasp and turned her head on the pillow. Her body tensed within his embrace, and her eyes opened wide as a blush colored her face. "Oh, Tristan! What have I done? What have we done?"

Her voice held pure anguish, and for a moment Tristan read her emotions so clearly, he felt them within himself. Passion and desire radiated from the deep blue of her eyes, but remorse and perhaps a little guilt reflected there as well. He understood. He truly did. She *was* promised to another. Honor dictated she should have gone to her wedding bed pure and untouched, and yet, she'd given herself to him, fully, unconditionally, with an enthusiasm and a passion that equaled his own.

"You … you must go. I . . ." She tried to slip from the bed, but he tightened his arms around her.

"Let me stay, Cara mia," he whispered against her temple. "Just let me hold you for a little while longer." He traced the line of her jaw with the tip of his finger. "We cannot undo what we have done nor can we deny what is between us. I don't regret for one moment what we shared, but I'll go if you want me to." He kissed her then his lips capturing hers, showing her, telling her he would leave as he promised.

When Tristan raised his head and gazed into her eyes, he knew she'd made her decision. Right or wrong, she would allow him to stay. She turned toward him, her body pressing against his, her breasts crushing against his chest, the taut nipples burning his skin.

"Make love to me," she whispered, her voice shaking, her arms trembling as they wound around his neck, pulling him closer so she could touch her lips to his with a tenderness that tugged at his heart. Elation such as he'd never known thundered through him and he did as she asked.

Last night, in the glow of moonlight, their lovemaking had been driven by an urgency that could not be denied. Now, in the warmth of the sunlight streaming into the cabin, the urgency was gone, replaced by a desire to touch and be touched, to learn, to feel. Tristan explored her body as if it were new, as if he'd never touched her before.

He started with her mouth and the softness of her tempting lips. He couldn't imagine kissing another woman like this, couldn't imagine anyone else responding to his touch the way she did. Indescribable joy surged through him, making him tingle all the way to his toes. He shifted on the bed, rolling her under him so he could feel the heat of her body beneath his.

His lips traveled along her throat, planting little kisses along her velvety skin, leaving a trail of moisture in their wake. Her head tilted back, pressing into the pillow, exposing more of herself to him and he complied with her silent demand. Tristan kept up his leisurely discovery, his hands caressing her as his lips and mouth touched her face, her ears, her throat. Her breast swelled within the palm of his hand and he kissed a path to the straining peak, settling his waist between her thighs.

Though it drove him insane with need, Tristan took his time. He teased her, touched her, drew the rigid peak into his mouth, and swirled his tongue against the hard nub while his fingertips gently caressed her other breast. Her heart pounded beneath his hands. She shivered, her body writhing under his.

Caralyn's soft moan filled his ears, spurred him on, encouraged him, and his body hummed with anticipation. How he yearned for her. He kissed his way down her body to the tips of her toes. A giggle escaped her and she jumped when he slid his tongue along the arch of her foot then pulled a toe into his mouth. Her laughter trailed into a moan of pure bliss as his lips and tongue smoothed along her ankles, calves, and knees.

Her legs opened a little wider but when his lips touched her at the apex of her thighs, she snapped her legs closed.

Tristan glanced at her face and saw her embarrassment.

"Don't hide yourself, Cara. You're beautiful here, too." He continued to caress her skin, rubbing his fingers against the curls between her legs. After a moment, she relaxed, granting him access, granting permission for what he wanted, for what he hoped would please her.

A startled cry escaped her when his tongue caressed the swollen folds of flesh where his fingers had been. Her nails dug into his hair, pulling his head closer as her hips moved against his mouth. He teased her with his lips and tongue, loving the taste of her, loving the way she responded to his touch until her breath came in short gasps and her body tensed. Her thighs tightened against his ears and he couldn't hear her moans of pleasure, but he knew by the bucking of her hips, the clenching of her muscles, she'd found her bliss.

But he wasn't done teasing her, exploring her, finding new ways to make her shudder in exquisite joy.

"Tristan!" she gasped as his lips traveled across her stomach, over her breast and tight nipple. She shivered as he took the straining bud into his mouth and suckled gently. Caralyn pulled on his hair, bringing him up so she could kiss his lips.

She held his face between her hands and captured his gaze with her own, the warmth of her touch burning his skin, indeed, searing into his heart, his soul. "Take me," she whispered, her voice raw, her body squirming with need beneath his.

Tristan needed no second urging. He dipped his head and plundered the richness of her mouth as he sank himself into her slick, hot sheath. The heat of her, the tightness of her body around him threatened his sanity. Her legs wrapped around his hips, drawing him deeper. A whimper escaped her as her hips rose from the bed and she met him, stroke for stroke, thrust for thrust. Her eyelids fluttered, exposing the dark blue of her irises for brief moments at a time. The whimper turned to a cry of intense pleasure before her body tightened around him, a cry Tristan stifled with his mouth. Her hands smoothed along the rigid muscles of his back, his shoulders, until her back arched beneath him and he felt her quiver from within.

Sweat beaded on his forehead as he struggled for control, the muscles in his arms bulging as he supported his weight and plunged into her soft, yielding flesh. He smothered the urge to laugh. The pleasure he experienced from her was like nothing he'd ever felt. Caralyn bit his shoulder and cried out once more as ecstasy took her in its grip. Her slick sheath throbbed around him, squeezing and releasing the length of his rock-hard shaft until Tristan could resist no longer. With a groan of triumph, he thrust into her one last time and stiffened, spilling his seed into her in a hot surge.

"Oh, Tristan," she cried and held his face in her hands, bringing his mouth to hers. "Will it always be this way between us?"

Tristan chuckled. He couldn't help it. Her question tickled him, made him feel as if he owned the world, but also made him wonder. Would they have an always? "No, Cara mia, it will be better."

"Better?" Her smile widened even though tears appeared in her beautiful blue eyes, making them twinkle. "I don't think I could stand better."

"Don't cry, my sweet." Tristan slid from her body and held her close. He closed his eyes, reveling in the warmth of her, reveling in the joy filling his heart. She sighed as she nestled against him.

Around them, the sounds of the crew once more met his ears, the bosun's whistle blasting out several short toots. Tristan wanted nothing more than to stay here with Caralyn, but knew he should be up on the deck, guiding the *Adventurer* toward Izzy's Fortune and his future. A future with Caralyn.

He sighed against her neck. He had a duty to perform as Captain. He didn't let his men shirk theirs so he wouldn't evade his own no matter how much he wanted to. "I hate to leave you, Cara mia, but I have a ship to command." He rose from the bed then leaned down and kissed her. "And a treasure to find."

He dressed quickly, pulling on the same clothes he wore yesterday, but his gaze kept coming back to her, time and again. She snuggled beneath the sheet, her hair tousled around her shoulders, a warm glow staining her features, a satisfied smile spreading her swollen lips. A slight redness stained her cheek from his whiskers, but it was her eyes that drew him. They fairly danced in her face, the warmth in them changing their color to indigo. She looked so tempting, so adorable, he nearly changed his mind, but knew he couldn't. He sat on the bed and kissed her again, his lips moving over hers, loving the response she gave, loving the softness of her arms as they wound around his neck, drawing him closer.

"If you keep kissing me like that," he chuckled, "I'll never leave this cabin."

Caralyn grinned. "That is my intention, Captain."

"Hmm, if that is your intention, then I'm more than willing and able to comply." He touched his lips to hers, unable to resist another taste. "But I'm sure someone will be knocking on this door before too long." He stroked her cheek then stood and strode to the door. "I'll bring you a cup of coffee and a biscuit in a moment." His hand rested on the doorknob, but he didn't turn it. Reluctance to leave her swelled in his heart and his gaze remained on her. He wondered what she thought, what ideas were going through her mind, but her countenance revealed nothing. He sighed, gave a slight nod then finally left the cabin.

• • •

As soon as the door closed, Caralyn scrambled from the bed, slipped into her robe, and rushed to the small mirror hanging on the wall. Her reflection stared back at her. She hadn't changed. Except for a rash of redness on her cheek where his whiskers had chafed her skin, a glow to her features, and slightly swollen lips, she looked exactly like herself. No sign hung around her neck to proclaim her a loose woman, no tattoo stenciled across her forehead said she'd given herself to him.

She may look the same, but she certainly didn't feel the same. *Oh dear God, what have I done?*

Remorse and shame made her stomach clench, made her face flame with embarrassment as she remembered how uninhibited she'd been, allowing him to touch her, *taste* her in the most intimate of places. Last night, she could understand her actions. Almost. She had been carried away by her emotions, but this morning when she'd had the opportunity to make him leave, why had she let him stay? And why had she begged him—*begged* him—to make love to her?

"It's senseless to ask yourself these questions," she spoke aloud to her reflection. "You know exactly why you did what you did."

His touch was magical, the heat of his breath on the back of her neck thrilling, the warmth of his lips as they brushed against her skin oh, so delicious, the feel of him inside her too wonderful to describe, the emotions too powerful to forget. If she never felt this again, she would always keep these memories in her mind.

She turned away from the mirror, away from the blush that stained her cheeks, dumped the rust tinged water from the basin, refilled it then bathed. The cool water did nothing to eliminate the flush heating her skin, nor did it help to stop the reprimands swirling around her brain or the memory of their shared intimacy.

She dressed in a white cotton frock with swirls of green and gold then cleaned up the cabin, her face growing warmer as she picked up the pile of clothes from the floor and put them away. She glanced toward the bed, the rumpled sheets, the pillow indented where her head had been, and quickly adjusted the bedding, hoping to erase all signs of their lovemaking.

With the cabin spotless, Caralyn paced the floor, unsure of what to do next. Afraid the crew would take one look at her and *know* what she'd done, she didn't want to go up on deck, not yet, but staying in the cabin wasn't an option. Tomorrow would bring the same worries, the same sense of guilt, and her parents hadn't raised a coward. She sat on the bed, remembering what had occurred on the mattress, then rose and flounced into the chair beside the stove only to realize the chair held memories, too—his mouth on hers, his hands caressing her, her body responding to his every touch. Warmth heated her cheeks. Indeed, her entire body felt as if flames raced through her veins instead of blood.

She rose and began to pace.

A knock sounded on the door. Caralyn opened the portal but it wasn't Tristan with the promised coffee and biscuit. Temperance stood in his stead, her eyes sparkling behind the lenses of her glasses, her skin glowing. Marriage agreed with her.

"What's wrong? Are you unwell? You're usually on deck before the rest of the crew, having your coffee as the sun comes up." The woman studied her from head to toe. "What happened?"

Caralyn felt her cheeks grow hot and she wondered, though she wore no sign, no tattoo, if the woman saw all her secrets. She took a deep breath to still the frantic beating of her heart. "I'm fine, just a little tired," she lied as she opened the door wider and allowed Temperance to enter.

"I'm moving my things into Brady's cabin today." The woman swept into the room, her sharp gaze missing nothing, which made Caralyn glad she'd cleaned the cabin. Her eyes flitted toward the bunk. Neatly made, the bed bore no evidence of her night—and morning—of passion.

Temperance chattered about the plans she and Brady had made but Caralyn wasn't listening as she helped pack her friend's belongings in the trunk they'd purchased in Puerto Rico. She held a frilly petticoat in her hand with the intention of folding it neatly, but stopped and stared into space. A lump formed in her throat. Tears stung her eyes and blurred her vision. Her fingers gripped the petticoat and twisted.

"Caralyn."

"What?"

"You're ripping my petticoat." Temperance grabbed the garment, folded it quickly, and placed it in the trunk. Hands on her hips, she faced Caralyn, eyes unblinking behind the lenses of her glasses. "Tell me what's wrong."

"I … Nothing."

Temperance quirked an eyebrow. "I think I know you well enough to know when something isn't right," she said then reached out and took Caralyn's hand. "You can tell me, Cara."

There were some things Caralyn couldn't bring herself to admit and making love to Tristan was one of them, but there were other worries she could discuss.

"We're running out of time, Temperance," she said, though she found it difficult to speak over the constriction in her throat. "If we don't find Izzy's Fortune, I'll have to—"

"Have to what?"

"Marry that stodgy old earl's son. I don't want to. I don't know him, don't love him. How can I let him … how can I share the marriage bed? How can I spend the rest of my life with a complete stranger?"

"Come. Sit." Temperance led her to the bed and forced her to sit then sat beside her. Caralyn stared at the floor, her hands twisting in her lap until Temperance demanded, "Look at me."

She glanced at her companion, her friend, and saw compassion and sympathy reflected in her eyes, which made the lump in her throat grow larger, almost choking her.

"You're not the first woman to find herself married to a man she doesn't know. Arranged marriages happen all the time. From what I've seen, they seem to work and you'll grow fond of each other over time."

"Fond? Over time?" Caralyn rose from the bed and began to pace. "I want much more than mere fondness, Temperance. I want love and passion, like my parents. I want what you have found with Stitch."

And I think I've found it. With Tristan. She didn't say the words aloud, but they flitted through her head and she realized they were true. The constriction returned to her throat and she grew dizzy. When had she fallen in love with him? Was it last night when he'd brought her to the heights of passion? Or this morning, when she'd given herself to him once again?

Caralyn shook her head and tried to clear the fog from her mind. She attempted to pay attention to the advice Temperance offered but the questions kept coming. With a painful thud of her heart, she realized she'd been falling in love with the captain from the moment she met him. He hadn't swept her off her feet as she always thought she wanted a man to do, hadn't whisked her away on horseback from the steps of the church as her father had done with her mother. There were no thunderbolts of realization, no bright flashes of light. Falling for him had been far more subtle.

"What does finding Izzy's Fortune have to do with anything? That blasted treasure. If not for this search, you'd already be in England, getting to know the man you're to marry."

"What?"

Temperance inhaled deeply and made a face, one filled with frustration. "I asked what finding Izzy's Fortune has to do with getting married."

"It has nothing to do with getting married. Izzy's Fortune is my salvation."

"Your salvation?" Her brows drew together in a frown. "I don't understand."

Caralyn sat on the bed beside her companion and lowered her voice. "My plan is to take my share of the treasure and buy myself out of the betrothal."

Temperance gasped and her face took on a rosy hue. She blinked several times in quick succession then shook her head. "Oh, Cara, I hate to be the one to tell you this, but I don't think that's possible. The promise your father made on your behalf is binding." She caught her bottom lip between her teeth as she thought, then released it. "Who told you such a thing was possible?"

"My father," she said. "He told me as much. If I can replace the dowry he agreed upon, I can be released from his promise." She hugged herself, excitement bubbling within her veins. "I can't wait to see the look on the old earl's face when I drop a bag of gold in front of him." She took Temperance's hand in hers and squeezed. "You'll help me, won't you, Temperance?"

"Yes, of course," she agreed, but the tone of her voice held skepticism and uncertainty.

Caralyn ignored the niggling doubt in the back of her mind and rose from the bed. "You mustn't tell anyone. This must remain our secret. Agreed?" Temperance nodded but said nothing. "Good. Let's finish packing later. I'm dying for a cup of coffee. And one of Hash's biscuits."

Chapter 17

"Land ho!" Mad Dog shouted from the heights of the crow's nest. With those two words, excitement bubbled through Caralyn and made her belly quiver.

She stood on the quarterdeck but glanced behind her to see Tristan at the helm, the wheel in his confident hands, the same hands that brought her so much bliss. She held her breath as her anticipation increased ten-fold.

The *Adventurer* had become too small, the nearness of Tristan too close. Since the night of Stitch's wedding to Temperance and the awakening of her desire, she couldn't stay away from the captain. The heat in his eyes warmed her blood, the magic of his touch stayed with her even after he stopped, the intense pleasure they shared, too much to deny.

She had no willpower, no strength where he was concerned. The days were filled with warm breezes, beautiful sunshine, and the vast expanse of ocean but the nights—oh, the nights—were full of white-hot passion. Whatever shame she'd felt had long since disappeared in his warm embrace.

After the confession they were both promised to others, they'd spoken briefly of the obligations made for them by their respective families and the unhappiness with decisions not in their control. Each knew they had no choice and would marry the people chosen for them whether they wanted to or not. Caralyn did mention, in jest, that she often thought of buying her freedom with her share of Izzy's Fortune. After that, they'd made a mutual agreement not to discuss their future plans and for once in her life, Caralyn was living for the moment and the moment alone.

He grinned in her direction and her entire body tingled with expectation. With effort, she turned away from his devastating smile so full of promise and shaded her eyes against the sun. Tiny dark dots on the horizon met her stare and grew larger as the wind-filled sails brought them closer.

Caralyn left the quarterdeck and ran to the captain's cabin, her pounding heart filled with hope. She prayed, with every ounce of belief in her soul, the treasure would be here—had to be here. She changed out of her gown and donned the familiar, comfortable trousers and loose shirt.

By the time she returned topside and joined Tristan at the helm, the islands were in full view and as beautiful as she remembered. They sailed past the Island of the Sleeping Man with its thundering waterfall and hidden cove to the next—the island indicated on Pembrook's mural.

Waves crashed on a long white beach. Sand gave way to rows of palm trees, which swayed in the breeze. Beyond the palms: lush, dense jungle. Cedar, mahogany, and rosewood trees filtered the sunlight, their limbs full of colorful birds. Supple flowering vines and woody lianas twisted and climbed around thick trunks toward the leafy canopy above and life-giving sunlight. Vibrant ferns in every shade of green imaginable covered the forest floor. Orchid, hibiscus, and Poinciana blossoms punctuated the unending field of dark brown bark and shiny leaves, but not one path dotted the landscape, at least not that she could see. Time and nature had played a cruel trick and the trail in Pembrook's mural had disappeared, overgrown with ferns and smaller trees vying for their little patch of sun.

Caralyn's heart sank, and yet a shiver of anticipation raced down her spine as Tristan gave the order, "Mr. Anders, blow your whistle for me."

The young man complied and the crew sprang into action. Sails were furled and the anchor dropped with a splash into the crystal blue waters. The ship bobbed in the waves. Another toot on the whistle and the crew gathered on the quarterdeck.

"Are you ready?" Tristan asked as his gaze met hers. The sparkle in his sherry-colored eyes warmed her to her toes, the smile on his face made gooseflesh break out over her entire body.

Caralyn grinned. "Oh, yes!"

He took her hand in his as if he didn't care who saw them and together, they walked across to the deck. Caralyn's face flushed beneath the curious scrutiny of both Socrates and Temperance, but neither said a word.

Tristan paced as he addressed the crew, his hands clasped behind his back. Caralyn watched him, fascinated by the strength in his stride, the expression he wore.

"This is it, men. Our last chance to find Izzy's Fortune," he said as he strutted across the deck, his hard-soled boots clicking with each step. She detected a note of sadness in his voice. It mirrored her own.

Time had run out.

If they didn't find the treasure now, she'd have to give up her search, go to England ... and marry. The realization increased her determination.

"How will we find the treasure?" Mac stood before him, hands on his hips, his mustache a brilliant white slash across his upper lip.

"I wish I knew how to answer, Mac." Tristan stopped his pacing and studied the Scotsman. He drew in a deep breath and let it out in a sigh of frustration. "The painting on the wall beneath the chapel showed a path that ended with an emerald. I can only assume that's where the treasure is but I see no such trail. Changes have occurred since Pembrook was last here."

He sighed again and stuck his hands in his pockets. "We'll have to search the island, step by careful step. Izzy's Fortune could be anywhere, hidden in a cave, buried beneath the ground."

"If it's here, we'll find it," Mad Dog said, and the men gave a shout of agreement. Tristan smiled. Indeed, his grin lit up his entire face and Caralyn's heart thudded hard in her chest.

Tristan turned to Hash. "If you don't mind, I'd like you to stay here on the *Adventurer*."

The big man looked almost relieved as he nodded and continued to pet the cat in his arms. "'Course, Cap'n. Smudge and me'll keep the stew simmering and the coffee hot."

"Good man," Tristan said with a grin then addressed the crew. "Get our supplies and fill the longboats."

Caralyn stood back, Temperance on one side of her, Jemmy on the other and watched the activity on deck. Though she longed to help, she knew she'd only be in the way.

The quivering in her belly had not lessened. In fact, it had grown. Excitement, anticipation, and eagerness to finish this quest and find Izzy's Fortune surged through her veins.

"Are we gonna hunt for treasure, Miss Cara?"

Caralyn glanced at the boy she'd come to adore and grinned. He looked so sweet, so grown up as he stood beside her, his hand in hers. The cowlick at the back of his head stood straight up, and she resisted the urge to smooth it down.

"Yes, Jemmy, we're going to search for Izzy's Fortune."

"Can I help?"

"May I," she corrected him, having picked up the habit from Tristan. "Of course you may."

He grinned at her with all the enthusiasm and energy of a little boy, and Caralyn's heart swelled with love.

"What if it's not here?" Temperance whispered.

"It's here," Caralyn said. "It has to be."

"But what if it's not? What if—"

"Temperance, stop!" Caralyn drew in her breath and held it while she mentally counted to ten. "I cannot allow myself to believe this journey has been for nothing. The treasure is here. It must be."

The woman nodded but remained silent, although the expression on her face mirrored her doubt. With a conscious effort, Caralyn ignored her companion's skepticism and gave her attention to the activity on deck.

Within a short span of time, the boats were loaded with every thing they'd need—shovels, pickaxes, machetes, lanterns, candles, ropes, and pulleys. The boats were lowered to the water.

White-crested waves propelled them toward the shore with ease. Socrates and Mad Dog jumped from the bobbing vessels and pulled them onto the sand with the swell of the surf.

Once on the beach, Tristan offered her his hand to help her from the boat. Caralyn smiled at him, the heat of his touch warming her soul. She studied the tree line then closed her eyes and pictured Pembrook's mural in her mind. When she opened them again, she saw exactly where the path had been, or at least, where Pembrook had placed it in his painting.

"We should start there," she said as she drew Tristan's attention and pointed toward a spot directly in front of them.

"Are you certain?"

"As certain as I can be. If you close your eyes and remember the mural, you'll see it, too."

He did as she requested. A grin spread his mouth as his eyes flew open. "You're right." He chuckled then grabbed her around the waist and brought her closer to plant a light kiss on her nose.

Caralyn giggled and pressed her hands against his chest, leaning into him, although she knew she shouldn't. She felt, rather than saw Temperance watching her with disapproval, and yet the solid hardness of Tristan's body against hers infused her with desire. Despite her companion's censure, the promise in his eyes made heat rush to her face. She pulled away, although with great reluctance. "Later," she whispered for his ears only. Oh, yes. Later.

Tristan quirked an eyebrow, perhaps already thinking about later, then turned from her. "Gather around, men." He and Graham started handing out shovels, ropes, lanterns, and other tools. He saved a small gardening trowel for Jemmy and pressed it into his son's hand, much to the boy's delight. "I want you to stay close to me," he said. "Do I make myself clear?"

"Aye, Papa." The boy grinned, his smile beaming in his little face.

Tristan ruffled his son's hair and returned his expression, then directed his attention to the men around him. "I believe we've found the path—or what's left of it—that Pembrook depicted in his mural. Stay close. Stay alert. If you see something, anything at all, we'll check it out."

Caralyn's breath caught in her throat as he held out his hand, despite the glare Temperance sent their way. "Ready?"

"Lead the way, Captain."

Armed with machetes to cut their way through the thick underbrush, the crew followed behind Tristan and Caralyn in single file. Graham brought up the rear, as was his wont. The voices of the men carried in the breeze, and Caralyn smiled at the dreams they had once they found the treasure. Socrates planned to open a tavern sometime in the future when his body could no longer tolerate life at sea. Mad Dog wanted a ship of his own. He'd make an excellent captain, she knew. Coop dreamed of making and selling barrels and crates from his own shop, preferably on one of the islands in the Caribbean where balmy breezes kept the temperature perfect. Graham, not surprisingly, wanted to search for other treasures.

Birds squawked, and startled from their perches, flew off to find sanctuary against the intruders of their green world. Rustling noises in the dead leaves underfoot led Caralyn to believe snakes or feral pigs or other dangerous creatures inhabited this island, and a shudder shook her body. She took a deep breath and concentrated on keeping her eyes straight ahead.

Patches of blue sky appeared more visible as the tropical jungle receded. In due course, the forest opened into a verdant valley full of tall, wavering grasses, a multitude of colorful flowers and the palm trees that were so prevalent in the Caribbean. More cedar, mahogany, and logwood trees dotted the landscape, their limbs creating leafy canopies and offering shade to the sweaty, thirsty explorers. Mountains rose to the north, east, and west, their craggy cliffs impossible to scale.

A small lake shimmered at the base of the mountains like an emerald glimmering in the sun, just like the painting in the cave, but there was nothing else here—no statues, no chapels, no arrows pointing to the treasure—just an open plain interrupted by huge masses of jagged black and rust-colored rocks.

Caralyn's heart hammered in her chest. Though beautiful, the landscape before her was nothing less than overwhelming. "Where do we start?"

· · ·

"Porkchop!"

The captain's voice rose to the crow's nest where Porkchop stood watch . . .and daydreamed. For three days, he'd barely moved from his perch except to take short meals and relieve himself, but his time being at the top of the mast didn't bother him much. After all, he had the chance to watch Caralyn aboard the *Adventurer* when she returned from the day's excursion. Though exhaustion overwhelmed him, the sight of her lifted his spirits immensely. She, at least, gave him reason to keep the spyglass to his eye.

He sighed and wondered why in hell he continued to obey the captain's orders. In Porkchop's opinion, Entwhistle had gone daft, and he feared what the man had in mind for Trey, the girl, and the crew when, and if, they found Izzy's Fortune.

His eyes, dry and gritty from lack of sleep, worry wrinkling his brow, he folded the spyglass, stuck it in the sash around his waist, and climbed down to the deck. "Aye, sir."

"What have you to report?"

"Nothin'. They ain't found the treasure, least not that I kin tell. They're lookin' tired an' dirty, an' they ain't dancin' or celebratin'." He sighed and shifted his weight from one foot to the other. If Trey and his crew didn't find Izzy's Fortune, what would the captain do? Porkchop had done his best to keep Entwhistle on the *Explorer*, but he wondered how long that would last. The man seemed hell-bent on taking the longboats to the island and searching himself. And he wasn't above hurting someone to get what he wanted.

Porkchop wasn't concerned as much for Trey's crew as he was for the women, especially Cara. Spirited and feisty, he imagined she would stand up for herself if Entwhistle confronted her. She couldn't know about the captain's cruel streak, wouldn't realize crossing him could result in her death.

He watched the captain pace in front of him, his quick steps revealing his impatience and frustration better than words ever could. Red-faced, a muscle ticked in his cheek and his hands balled into fists. Porkchop's belly twisted with worry.

"Get back up there!" he ordered after a long time, his breath wheezing in and out of his chest.

Porkchop climbed back to the crow's nest with haste, grateful to be out of the captain's line of sight. He settled himself, raised the spyglass to his eye, and waited for the lovely Caralyn to once again appear and make his miserable life a little more bearable.

• • •

One day turned to two, then four, then before Caralyn realized, a full week had come and gone. Every rock formation had been checked for caves, every small indention in the earth dug into with shovels and picks and long wooden poles, and still they were no closer to finding the treasure.

Frustration and fear ate at her like the insects that left welts on her body. Tired, aching not only in her body, but also in her soul,

Caralyn pushed and persevered, as did the rest of the crew. The men were losing faith as was she, and yet she couldn't stop herself from searching until each rock had been overturned, every inch of ground had been explored.

The only ones who hadn't lost faith, the only ones whose bodies did not throb with pain were Jemmy and Hash. While Hash kept a kettle full of hot, filling stew aboard the *Adventurer*, Jemmy, full of energy, dug here and there in the earth, wherever his little heart desired, happy to play in the dirt.

"This is impossible," Temperance whispered, her voice full of the frustration Caralyn shared as she tossed another shovelful of dirt to the side. "How are we ever going to find the treasure this way?"

Caralyn closed her eyes for a moment. Her back, shoulders, and hands hurt from shoveling. Indeed, several blisters on her palms had broken and now screamed with pain. Perspiration soaked her clothing. She took a deep breath, opened her eyes and looked at her companion.

Temperance hadn't fared much better. Perspiration mixed with dirt smeared her cheeks, forehead, and the clothes she wore. Wispy tendrils of auburn hair escaped the bun at the back of her head and were plastered to her face. Panting from her exertions, her hands wrapped in the bandages Stitch had applied for her, she stuck the shovel into the dirt and pushed on it with her foot the way she'd been shown.

Caralyn leaned against a tree and took a sip of water from the jar Hash had so thoughtfully given each of them. She glanced over at Tristan and Stitch several yards away as she tilted the jar to her lips. They looked as exhausted and as filthy as she. The rest of the crew were scattered throughout the valley, their voices rising now and then over the sound of shovels meeting rich, loamy soil.

Tristan glanced up. Dark circles ringed his eyes, and yet he smiled at her. That smile warmed her to her toes. Renewed energy crackled through her, and she moved away from the tree to stick her shovel in the earth once more.

"Miss Cara! Miss Cara! Look what I found!" Jemmy darted through the tall, wavering grass and slid to a stop in front of her.

Caralyn grinned. She couldn't help it. Not a spot on his clothing or his body remained clean. Indeed, he seemed to have found a mud hole and bathed in it.

"Where have you been?"

"Diggin'," he replied, the ever-present smile on his face widening. He held up the small garden trowel he'd been given.

She ran her fingers through his dirt-encrusted hair and tried to wipe the mud from his face, but the boy was having none of it. He stepped out of her way with all the agility and enthusiasm of an eight-year-old.

"What did you want to show me?"

"This." He held out his hand. A ruby the size of a peach pit twinkled in the middle of his grubby little palm.

Caralyn bent down on one knee to be eye level with the boy. "Where did you find this?"

"Is it special? Did I do good?"

"Yes, Jemmy, it's very special. You did well. Can you show me where you found this?"

"Uh huh." The lad eagerly nodded then shoved the ruby in his pocket and grabbed her hand. "Come on."

Caralyn followed the boy through the grass, her heart pounding as she tried to keep up with him. Though he'd only found one gem, it still might be proof Izzy's Fortune was here.

"I found it right here." Jemmy pointed to a hole he'd dug in the earth beside a huge outcropping of uneven, rough rock. Dreams of riches beyond her belief making her hands shake, Caralyn slammed the point of her shovel into the small pit he created and continued to dig, making the hollow wider and deeper.

Twenty minutes later, breathless, the sores where the blisters had broken on her palms now bleeding, she stopped and wiped her brow with the back of her hand. She leaned against the rock, the jagged edges scratching her back. She'd found ... nothing. She wanted to cry at the impossibility of ever finding Izzy's Fortune, not with acres and acres of lush, grassy plains to search. They didn't have time. They only had a day or two at the most before they had to set sail for England.

Heart heavy with the knowledge she'd have to honor her father's promise to marry a stranger, tears stung her eyes and blurred her vision.

Then everything changed in an instant. Hope and faith returned to her heart as she gazed into the valley. The landscape shimmered through the veil of moisture in her eyes and the outlines of the rocks and trees became somehow familiar. Recognizable. She'd seen them somewhere before.

Caralyn's body shook, trembled so violently, she thought she might be physically ill. The tears disappeared as quickly as they'd come.

With her last ounce of energy, she climbed to the top of the rocky ridge. She stood motionless as she tried to reconcile the image before her with what she remembered.

"Miss Cara?" Jemmy called to her then clambered up to join her. He stuck his hand in hers and squeezed. "Miss Cara? Are you all right?"

She swallowed over the lump in her throat then leaned down and kissed the boy on the cheek.

"What are you kissing me for? I didn't do nothin'." Jemmy made a face as he tried to wipe her kiss away.

"I kissed you because I'm happy. Because I think I know where the treasure is. Let's go get your father." She scrambled from her perch and jumped the last three or four feet then caught Jemmy in her arms as he jumped too. "Tristan!" she shouted as she started running through the tall, wavering grasses, Jemmy's hand in hers. "Tristan!"

Tristan dropped his shovel and turned as Caralyn launched herself into his arms, almost knocking him over in her exuberance, but she didn't care.

"Are you all right?"

"I'm fine," she giggled as she kissed him over and over. "I am wonderful, in fact." She planted more kisses on his face, on his lips as her arms wrapped tighter around his neck.

"What happened?" Temperance joined them, breathless, her red face full of concern and censure. She raised an eyebrow as her gaze swept over Caralyn in Tristan's embrace, but she said not a word.

Caralyn related the events that lead her to climb to the top of the rocks and what she'd seen when she got there. "I think I know where the treasure is." Caralyn returned her attention to Tristan, released her hold on him and asked, "Do you remember the pages from Pembrook's journal? The ones that were stuck together?"

Tristan shrugged his shoulders as he studied her. "Vaguely. What about them?"

She couldn't keep the excitement from her voice if she tried. Happiness swelled within her, making her heart beat faster, making her words come out in a rush. "Those lines we could barely make out? They show where the treasure is. It *was* a map. We just needed the key to decipher it."

As he leaned on his shovel, Tristan sighed with all the weariness he could no longer hide. "We don't have Pembrook's journal anymore."

"Yes, but I have those pages. I never put them back in the book. Remember, I folded the papers and put them in my pocket." She grabbed his hand. "We have to go back to the ship. Now."

He tilted his head as he gazed at her, the sparkle in his eyes returning. "All right. We'll go back to the ship but we'll be losing daylight soon. We'll have to move quickly. Will you be able to keep up?" Tristan asked, concern for her wellbeing evident in his expression.

"Yes, I'll keep up."

Tristan nodded as a grin slowly spread his lips. He turned to Stitch. "Please keep an eye on Jemmy. The men can rest until we get back. They deserve a break. And have Mr. Anders here when Cara and I return."

"Of course." Stitch nodded and replied, even though he hadn't taken his eyes off his inspection of Temperance's hand and the bloody blister in the middle of her palm.

Caralyn had never run so fast in her life. Her breath hitched in her chest but the pain in her side had disappeared. Indeed, renewed energy revitalized her, made her legs pump harder as she kept up with Tristan's long-legged stride. Branches smacked at her face, her hair, her clothing, stinging her skin as they traversed the newly cleared path, but they didn't stop her progress.

"Boat or swim?" Tristan asked as they broke through the trees and skidded to a stop on the beach. Panting heavily, Caralyn bent over and rested her hands on her knees, struggling to catch her breath. "Boat," she wheezed, though swimming might have been faster as the *Adventurer* wasn't far off shore. She just didn't think she could do it after running the way she had.

She helped Tristan push the boat into the water then climbed in beside him. The muscles in her arms felt like overcooked noodles as she rowed along with him for the short trip to the ship. Days of shoveling and using the pickaxe had left her much more sore than she'd realized, but she resisted the urge to groan with her efforts.

The boat bumped up against the ship where a hanging rope ladder waved in the breeze. Where Caralyn found the strength she didn't know, but she managed to ascend the ladder, climb over the railing, and fall to the deck.

Hash came running from the galley, Smudge trailing behind him. "You're back early. Is everything all right?"

"Yes, everything is fine," Caralyn told him, although her voice came out breathy and hoarse. "I just needed something from my cabin."

"And I need food for the men," Tristan said. "Bread, cheese, whatever you have that I can easily carry. Fruit. And something to drink."

"Aye, I can have everything packed for ye by the time yer ready to leave again." Hash went back to his galley as Caralyn led the way to the captain's cabin.

Though she remembered clearly putting the pages from Pembrook's journal into her pocket, she couldn't remember which gown she had worn. One by one, they all came out of the cabinet built into the cabin wall. Frustration tore through her, making her fingers tremble as she stuffed her hand into yet another pocket and came up empty.

"Please, please, be here," she prayed as she pulled a white gown with sprigs of blue flowers printed on the fabric from the closet. Her lips spread into a grin as her fingers touched the pages. "Got it!"

"Let me see." Tristan's voice betrayed his excitement.

She handed him the pages. He unfolded them and held them up to the window in the cabin. Sunlight illuminated most of the lines between the written words, though they weren't much clearer than when they'd first looked at them.

"I don't see what you see," he admitted with a sigh then glanced at her. "You're a mess." He folded the pages and handed them to her before he started pulling leaves and bits of bark from her hair.

"Tristan, we don't have time for that," she said, though a small chuckle escaped her. She put the pages in her pocket. "We need to get back before we lose the sunlight."

"Are you sure you don't want to stay here and rest?"

"Rest? Are you—oh, you're teasing me."

He kissed her then—a long, searing kiss that made her heart pound harder than when she'd dashed through the forest. When he broke away, he smiled and caressed the side of her face with his thumb. "Even with dirt all over your face and leaves in your hair, you are still the most beautiful woman I've ever met." He kissed her again, his lips lingering over hers but only for a moment. "Let's go find the treasure."

The last rays of sunlight peeked over the craggy crest of the mountain, casting a golden hue to the west as Caralyn and Tristan ran across the open field. Mr. Anders, Stitch, Temperance, and Jemmy were right behind them, yelling questions neither one of them had the energy or breath to answer. Her lungs bursting, her legs now heavy with fatigue, Caralyn dropped the burlap sack filled with food and scrambled to the top of the rock formation. She held the pages up to catch the dying rays as the hazy light before sunset started to fall. The dots and dashes Pembrook had drawn so long ago became amazingly clear.

She moved the paper lower until the pen strokes aligned perfectly with the palm trees surrounding the lake in the near distance. With the exception of one slash not having a corresponding tree, the match was perfect.

Tristan climbed up beside her, though he said not a word. He breathed heavily from his race through the trees, his chest heaving, but the smile on his face was the most beautiful thing Caralyn had ever seen.

"The palm trees." She nodded toward the trees then the paper in her hand. "See how they're leaning against each other? Almost forming an 'X'? I think that's where Pembrook hid the treasure."

"Mr. Anders," Tristan called down from the top of the rock. "Toot your whistle for me."

The bosun gave a long, piercing blast. All over the valley, the crew rose from where they'd been resting on the ground and looked toward him. Tristan waved his arms and pointed toward the small lake and the palm trees. Almost as one, the men headed in that direction.

After a few moments, lights from several lanterns glowed in the near distance and soon, a blazing fire chased away the growing darkness.

The small group walked toward the palm trees and the rest of the crew. They were silent, except for Jemmy, who chattered non-stop. Caralyn glanced at the boy who ran circles around them and grinned, amazed by his inexhaustible amount of energy. She wished she could bottle his enthusiasm and save it for herself.

When they joined the men, some leaning on the handles of their shovels, some sitting cross-legged on the ground, Tristan explained why he'd moved them all beside the lake.

Caralyn broke away from her companions and strode toward one of the palm trees that formed the X. Her breath caught in her throat when she saw the initials carved into the trunk. She traced her fingers over them and wondered about the man who'd etched them in the wood. Pembrook had led them on a merry chase with his barely there clues, but everything they'd been through would be worth it—if this was, indeed, where he'd buried the treasure.

She climbed one of the more prominent rocks and gazed down at the space between the palm trees. The ground seemed sunken in, the depression lower than the surrounding area, as if the soil had been disturbed long ago and settled back into place over time.

She turned her attention back to Tristan and grinned. More than the adventure, despite the hardship of the past few days, she'd found exactly what she'd been looking for. Him. Now, if only she could keep him. Caralyn jumped from the rock and strode up beside him. She touched his arm. "Pembrook's initials are carved in that tree over there and the ground between the trees dips a bit."

Tristan grinned, dipped his hand into the burlap sack, and passed out the yeasty rolls with the hunks of cheese Hash had packed. "Eat up, men. We have more digging to do, but this will be the last of it. If the treasure isn't here, well, we've done our best. No one can say we didn't give it our all."

She listened to him as she handed out the bottles, some filled with wine, others with rum, one with brandy, one with water, and the last one with milk for Jemmy.

Finished with their makeshift meal, the crew picked up shovels and pickaxes and started digging in the area between the two trees, starting where the ground first dipped and working their way inward to form one huge hollow.

Caralyn caught Tristan's unwavering gaze on her as she, too, picked up her shovel. Though the palms of her hands were raw, she still wanted to do her part. But Tristan didn't agree. His eyebrow rose and his lips pressed together in a thin line. He shook his head. "Oh, no. You're done for a while." He took the tool from her hand and marched her toward a relatively smooth rock.

"Now, I want you to just sit here and rest. Do I make myself clear?" Tristan handed her another roll.

Too worn out to argue, Caralyn nodded and made herself comfortable. In truth, she was so far beyond exhausted, she couldn't hold a coherent thought. Pain radiated through her body from her exertions over the past few days. Everything hurt—head, shoulders, back, arms, legs, everything except her heart. Her gaze met and held Tristan's. Despite the pain, despite the dirt encrusted on her clothing, she wouldn't have given up this adventure for anything in the world.

"And that goes for you, too, young man," he said to Jemmy.

"Aye, Papa." The lad obeyed and crawled onto Caralyn's lap. He leaned his head against her chest and finished the piece of cheese he'd been given. The bottle of milk rested against his thigh, and he lifted it to take a long swig then belched as only a little boy who practiced could.

"And you as well, Lovey," Stitch said as he re-bandaged his wife's hand and made her sit on the rock beside Caralyn.

Caralyn leaned back against the trunk of the tree and watched the men dig. Except for the sounds of shovels hitting dirt, they were silent. She knew her own exhaustion. She could only imagine theirs.

Crickets chirped. Wind sighed through the trees and palm fronds rattled.

"I have never been so tired in all my life," Temperance groaned as she lifted a bottle to her lips and took a sip of wine. Caralyn glanced at her and grinned.

"I bet you've never been this dirty, either," she remarked as she studied the woman who'd become so much more than a paid companion.

Temperance's lips twisted into a wry grin. Her glasses reflected the light of the fire as she glanced at the filthy trousers covering her legs. "No, but it's been a grand adventure and I daresay I would do it all over again. Whether or not we find Izzy's Fortune. I've already found my treasure."

Tears misted Caralyn's eyes. "I'm happy for you, Temperance. It's a wonderful thing to find your heart's desire." She turned her attention back to the excavation, her gaze drawn to Tristan. He kept up a steady pace, the muscles in his arms bulging with effort, hair slicked back from his forehead with sweat and dirt.

Her heart swelled within her chest as she watched him stab his shovel into the hole he'd dug. A metallic clang rang through the air. It didn't sound like a stone or a tree root. Caralyn held her breath and sat up. Tristan looked at her, his lips parting in a smile of wonder and awe. He dropped the shovel then sank to his hands and knees, his head disappearing into the hollow. Caralyn nudged Jemmy from her lap and stood, taking the boy's hand in hers.

"I got somethin' here, Cap'n!" Socrates yelled as his blade made a solid thwacking sound on an object hidden beneath the soil.

"Me, too!" Mac said as he tossed his shovel aside and jumped into the hole. He started pushing dirt away with his hands before Gawain leaped into the opening beside him and helped.

"My God! It's a trunk!" Mad Dog was the first to pull his metal chest out of the ground.

"I've got one, too!" Woody bellowed.

All around her, the men were shouting, their excitement a rising tide, but Caralyn kept her gaze on Tristan. When he finally pulled the trunk out of the hole, she let out her breath in a *whoosh* and watched, paralyzed, afraid to move lest she wake up and realize she'd been dreaming as he broke the lock on the latch with a single blow from his shovel. He said not a word as he lifted the lid, but his warm gaze held hers.

Caralyn's eyes opened wide to catch all the colors of the jewels filling the trunk as the fire light danced on them. She blinked in an effort to clear her vision, not sure if she actually saw what she thought.

Fifteen chests in all, some as long as a man was tall, some smaller than a loaf of bread, some made of metal, others made of wood. So much more than Caralyn had expected, so much richer than she ever dreamed. Gold, in the form of coins and chains, plates and cups, and bars stamped with the queen's mark, filled several of the trunks. Precious and semi-precious gems in every hue of the rainbow glittered in the firelight. She saw emeralds, sapphires, and rubies. Lapis Lazuli, amethyst, and topaz and jewelry fit for a queen.

Overcome with raw emotion, Caralyn walked into Tristan's arms and held him tight. She couldn't speak, couldn't utter a sound as his arms wrapped around her. Tears filled her eyes as a lump rose to her throat.

Izzy's Fortune truly did exist. And they'd found it.

Chapter 18

Belly full from the bowl of stew he'd just eaten, Porkchop stood at the rail and relieved himself. For a moment, as his stream hit the water, he found peace, but it wouldn't last and he knew it. He dreaded the idea of going back up to the crow's nest, but feared the repercussions from the captain if he did not. Finished, he gave himself a shake then tucked himself into his trousers and turned around. And almost lost the contents of his stomach.

Entwhistle stood in front of him, a scowl distorting his face. In the glow of the lanterns, Porkchop could clearly see the murderous gleam lighting the captain's eyes. He shuddered as the frigid finger of panic traveled down his spine. Unbidden, the image of Entwhistle as Satan rumbled through his mind.

He couldn't resist exclaiming, "Cap'n!"

"Why the hell are you on deck? Why aren't you up in the crow's nest?" The low menacing tone of Entwhistle's voice struck fear in the seaman's heart. An icy coldness settled in his belly and his stomach twisted with anxiety, nay … worry. What possible reason could the captain have to be up and about at nearly midnight? Whatever the reason, no good would come of it.

Porkchop shifted his weight from one foot to the other and tugged on the waistband of his baggy trousers. "I … I … came down for somethin' ter eat." Disgusted by the whine in his own voice, he straightened himself and looked the captain right in the eye. "They ain't come back to the *Adventurer*. They ain't found no treasure."

"Be that as it may, I am tired of waiting," Entwhistle said. "Wake up Petey, Toothless, and Sanchez."

Porkchop didn't move. He couldn't. Muscles tense, mouth dry, the contents of his stomach curdled into one sour mass and left a bad taste in the back of his throat. He eyed the cat o' nine tails in the captain's hand and tried to swallow. "Sir?"

"Don't make me repeat myself." That low tone, the implied threat behind the words, made Porkchop stiffen in alarm, especially when the captain's hand, the one holding the whip, moved, just a fraction of an inch.

Porkchop needed no second warning. He tugged up his trousers and ran as fast as his feet could carry him.

"Petey," he whispered as he approached the man's hammock and shook him. "Wake up. Cap'n wants you."

The man mumbled in his sleep and tried to push Porkchop away. "Sleepin'. Go 'way."

"Get up, ye worthless scum," Porkchop exploded, his voice raising the rafters as well as rousing some of the other men sharing the small space below decks. "Cap'n's in a foul mood an' I ain't takin' no whippin' fer ye."

Petey's eyes flew open. In the dim light of the lantern turned low for the night, Porkchop could see his fear, which mimicked his own. Petey scrambled from the hammock, almost falling out of the makeshift bed.

"Get Toothless an' Sanchez an' come topside, an' be quick about it. Cap'n ain't a patient man."

Porkchop climbed the stairs to the deck on legs that felt as heavy as the *Explorer's* anchor. He stopped to catch his breath and squelch the terror rising in him. Entwhistle paced, hands clasped behind his back, his hard-soled boots loud as they struck the deck. With every fall of his foot, Porkchop cringed. *This ain't good. Ain't good 'tall.*

"Where are they?"

"Comin', sir."

Entwhistle said nothing, although the scowl on his face deepened and his thumb gently caressed the braided leather handle of the cat o' nine tails in his hand. Porkchop sucked air into his lungs and took a step back, hopefully out of reach of the whip. He couldn't stop the prayer to rush his shipmates from repeating in his mind.

Petey, Toothless, and Sanchez joined them, wiping sleep from their eyes and buttoning up hastily donned trousers. All three seemed confused, not fully awake, although they snapped to attention in front of the captain.

"Lower the dinghy, Bing." The man smiled, revealing pearl white teeth between the shagginess of his black beard. The smile did nothing to inspire confidence. Indeed, it had the opposite effect. "We're going treasure hunting and if we don't find the treasure, we'll take something else."

Porkchop swallowed hard at the captain's words. He knew exactly what Entwhistle threatened. If he couldn't get his hands on the treasure, he'd go after Caralyn and God only knew what he would do with her. His belly, already cramped with fear, rebelled completely, loosening with a speed that made him hold his breath. He prayed he wouldn't soil himself in front of his crewmates as he rushed to obey before the cat o' nine tails reached out to cut his skin and remind him who captained this ship.

Moonlight guided their way and made the whiteness of the sand glow as Toothless and Petey rowed toward the island, careful to keep the *Adventurer* within view, but far enough away so they wouldn't be heard. The surf grabbed the small boat and pushed it toward shore, away from the *Adventurer's* longboats.

Porkchop stepped onto the sand and looked around. Wind whispered and moaned through the trees. Boughs creaked. Leaves rattled against each other. A shudder shook him. More than ever, he didn't want to do this, didn't want to be part of such a tyrant's crew.

He glanced toward the captain and swallowed hard. Entwhistle stood motionless, his arms crossed over his chest, the cat o' nine tails still in his hand. A muscle twitched in his jaw. "Where is this trail they've been following?"

"It's over there." He pointed down the beach.

"Lead the way, Bing."

The four of them took off toward the path, Porkchop in the lead. He thought about the woman whose magical laughter filled his heart with longing, whose smile lightened his life, and wondered if he could fool the captain into taking the wrong path, perhaps even losing him in the forest. His feet sank into pristine white sand at the same rate his depression deepened. Oh, to be a stronger man, one with integrity like Captain Trey, one who could live his life as he chose without having to obey orders from someone else. He sighed. He was not that man and he knew it.

"Now what?" Porkchop asked as he stopped at the mouth of the footpath. He desperately wanted something to drink, something that would warm the coldness in his belly and erase the madness he saw before him. No such liquor existed and he swallowed hard against the bitterness in his throat.

"We wait."

Time lost all meaning as they crouched within the ferns covering the forest floor. Moonlight peeking through the canopy of trees cast shimmering light on his companions, making them look like ghosts.

"I hear somethin'," Petey whispered, and poked him.

"Shut yer yap, ye twice-damned fool," Porkchop whispered back. He tilted his head and listened. He heard it then, too, the magical sound of *her* laughter, the soft, sweet tones of *her* voice. From the moment he'd heard them, they'd haunted his dreams. Other voices joined hers, and he knew she traveled with her companion and the boy, but no one else. They were alone. Perfect for Entwhistle's plan. Porkchop's stomach dropped and once again he prayed he wouldn't soil himself, although the possibility remained real.

Every muscle in his body tensed and his mouth opened. He wanted to tell her to run, to hide, and would have but Entwhistle's long, bony finger stabbed him in the back.

Porkchop glanced at the captain behind him and flinched. In the shifting beams of moonlight, the smile on his face appeared more demented and crazed than ever before. All he needed were horns growing from each temple, and the portrait of the devil would be complete.

The captain gave a slight nod of his head but said nothing. He didn't need to; his meaning clear without words. They were to capture the women and the boy.

Despite his misgivings, despite his own sense of honor, Porkchop obeyed Entwhistle's silent order and rushed from the shelter of the ferns, Toothless and Petey right beside him, Sanchez coming up behind him. He grabbed Caralyn around the waist, one hand covering her mouth to stifle any scream she would have uttered, the other digging into her tender flesh. She dropped the lantern in her hand. It bounced on the sand and rolled, casting a strange yellow glow on the pristine white. Toothless grabbed the other woman. Petey and Sanchez tried catching the boy, but missed. Agile and nimble, Jemmy darted through the trees, completing his escape. With a rough curse, the seamen took after the lad.

With surprise on his side, Porkchop didn't expect the petite, filthy woman in his arms to fight as hard as she did. She bit his hand covering her mouth and kicked his shins. An elbow connected with his stomach as she wriggled and writhed to get out of his grip. "Settle yerself, Miss. I mean ye no harm." He tightened his hold on her until she calmed.

"Who are you? What do you want?" Her body trembled with terror as she turned her head. The fear in her eyes struck his heart and he loosened his grip a little. Perhaps too much. Caralyn slid from his grasp onto the sand and tried to crawl away, back into the trees.

A black-booted foot appeared in front of her and pressed against her shoulder, stopping her progress, forcing her to sit back on her haunches with a sharp cry of pain.

Porkchop flinched.

Her eyes were wide with horror as Entwhistle roughly grabbed her by the arms and hoisted her to her feet. Her mouth opened and her chest expanded as if she prepared to scream, but not a sound issued from her throat. Porkchop cringed, seeing how hard the captain's fingers dug into her flesh.

He glanced behind him and saw Toothless struggling with the other woman. A quick fist to the woman's chin and she slumped in his arms. Petey and Sanchez had not returned with the boy, but he could hear the sounds of their pursuit through the lushness of the forest floor, hear the muttered curses of his crewmates.

"Who are you?" Caralyn asked, her voice low and shaking as she wrestled her arms free of his grip.

Entwhistle smiled, though it wasn't pleasant. Indeed, Porkchop shuddered, having been on the receiving end of such a smile. He wanted to warn her, caution her against rousing the man's ire in any way. "Winton Entwhistle, captain of the *Explorer*."

The woman closed her eyes and drew in her breath. In an effort to stay calm? He didn't know, but admiration for Caralyn McCreigh grew in Porkchop's heart as she squared her shoulders. For one so petite, she had gumption. Courage. Nerve. But very little common sense.

"What do you want?"

"Why, Izzy's Fortune, of course."

"There is no treasure." Though she said the words without a hint of guile, Porkchop knew she lied. Entwhistle knew she lied as well, judging by the glower on his face and the stiffness of his body.

She shouldn't be talkin' to him that way. The thought crossed his mind. One never knew what the captain would do, although most assuredly, whatever the consequences, they'd be sure to include pain and degradation. He prayed the captain would let her indiscretion pass but couldn't help his involuntary jump or his shout of alarm as the scoundrel smacked Caralyn across the face, knocking her to the sand with the force of his action.

"Stop!" Porkchop shouted the word, unable to tolerate the captain's cruelty one more moment. It was one thing to terrorize the crew of the *Explorer*, but another matter entirely to abuse a defenseless woman, a woman who'd found a place in his heart.

Entwhistle glared at him, surprise registering on his angry, ugly face. His eyes squinted, the gleam in them promising retribution and punishment for this outburst.

Porkchop didn't care what penalty would come. He'd been whipped before and had the scars to prove it. He'd been deprived of food and sleep and companionship, held prisoner in the dark hole in the bow of the ship the crew called hell. And he had survived. But this, this was different. For once in his life, he wasn't going to be browbeaten, demoralized. If it took every ounce of fortitude in his heart, Porkchop was going to protect someone other than himself, no matter the consequences.

He ran toward Caralyn and helped her to her feet. His back stiffened and his hands balled into fists as he pushed her behind him and faced Entwhistle. "Ye'll not be hurtin' her," he said, although his voice shook with fear. "I'll not let ye."

Entwhistle laughed, a cruel, demonic cackle that frightened him deep down in his soul. "Have a soft spot for the girl, do you?" he asked, his eyes blazing with rage and insanity before he released the cat o' nine tails with a flick of his wrist. The thin leather straps, nine in all, each with a metal ball attached to the end, snapped in the air, cutting his ear and laying open the flesh of his neck.

Porkchop screamed, as did Caralyn. They both fell to the soft sand. Warm liquid seeped through the fingers he held to his neck. Blood. He glanced at her and saw the whip had caught her as well. Bloody gashes stained the sleeve of her shirt. Tears of pain filled her eyes and rolled down her cheek to drop onto the sand beneath her face and yet, she uttered not a word. Rage against the captain flared in Porkchop's heart. He trembled with the force of it, and promised, at least to himself, Entwhistle's cruelty would not be forgotten.

"Defy me again, either of you, and you'll wish you'd never been born."

• • •

Tristan and Stitch followed the path they'd trod so often in the past few days, one of the long trunks between them. The rest of his crew were far behind them as his quick pace and long-legged stride outdistanced them. He couldn't seem to lose the smile pasted to his face. After years of searching, Izzy's Fortune was his, and it was more than he ever dared dream. Caralyn would be his as well, damn the promises his father had made.

His Cara mia.

Without her, none of this would have been possible. His grin widened. He couldn't wait to get back to the ship and show her, in so many ways, how much he loved her.

The decision to send her, Temperance, and Jemmy ahead to the *Adventurer* had been hard to make but had been the right one, if for no other reason than their utter and complete exhaustion. Indeed, the lad had been falling asleep on his feet. Caralyn, despite her excitement, couldn't stop yawning, and Temperance, well, one look at her face and the grim set of her mouth expressed more than words ever could.

Tristan stepped out of the trees first, Stitch pulling up the rear, and stopped short, the long trunk bouncing against the back of his knees. The tableau on the beach took his breath away, made his heart thump in his chest. Every muscle, tendon, and sinew in his body tensed. Caralyn was in Entwhistle's clutches, helpless against the man's strength. Tears rolled down her pale face, reflecting the moonlight falling upon her. Blood stained her shirt, and pain radiated from her features.

Temperance lay on the sand a few feet away, a man's foot on her chest, holding her still. She didn't move, didn't make a sound.

Another man lay on the ground, moaning and crying, blood staining the sand beneath him.

And Jemmy?

Nowhere to be seen.

"Temperance," Stitch yelled, his voice sharp with fear, and dropped his end of the trunk. He sprinted across the sand, his breath coming in short gasps. With one smooth motion, he punched the man in the throat, pushing him away from his wife. The pirate dropped to his knees, clawing at his throat, coughing and gasping for air. Stitch glanced at the man, his hands still fisted, the threat clear before he bent over his wife and gently slapped at her cheeks. "Wake up, Lovey."

"I see you have my treasure, Trey." Entwhistle seemed to pay little attention and cared even less for his crewman. He stared at Tristan and squeezed Caralyn's arm, his fingers digging painfully into her soft skin. Caralyn gasped. The tortured sound went directly to Tristan's soul. "And I have yours."

"You bastard! Let her go!" he managed to grind out between gritted teeth, and yet he didn't move, couldn't move. He knew Entwhistle, knew his capacity for cruelty, for brutality and malice. One false move on his part could see Caralyn suffering more pain, perhaps even death.

Entwhistle shook his head, his shaggy hair flying out in all directions, reflecting the moonlight, creating a strange kind of halo around his head. All he needed were some cannon fuses, lit and tied in his unkempt beard, to resemble Blackbeard. "Not until you give me what I want." He tilted his head and grinned. "You see, I know you, Trey. You have honor, integrity, and veracity. I have none of those things, and yet I still don't trust you."

He squeezed tighter on Caralyn's arms. She gave another gasp of pain and her knees gave out. She sagged against him, his bony fingers digging into her soft flesh, the only thing stopping her from falling at his feet.

What that sight did to Tristan! Rage made him see through a red haze. His fists as well as his stomach clenched. Bile rose to the back of his throat. Muscles, already taut and rigid with the need to move, to end this stalemate, tensed even more. And yet he hesitated. It wasn't cowardice or lack of courage that stopped him from rushing to her rescue. It was concern for her, fear of what Entwhistle might do.

The crackling of dead leaves behind him drew his attention. He didn't turn, didn't make a move, but his pulse raced. Had the crew caught up? Did they wait in the darkness beneath the heavy canopy of trees for his signal? He listened harder and heard Socrates's unmistakable voice lowered to a gruff whisper.

"We're here, Cap'n. Jemmy's with us. And we got Entwhistle's men."

Those words made all the difference for Tristan. Assured his son was all right, he knew what he could do. He glanced at Stitch, Temperance in his arms, and gave a slight nod. The man quirked an eyebrow, making it clear he understood. His gaze scanned the beach, marking the position of each one of Entwhistle's men. One lay on the ground, crying, blood staining the ground beneath him. The other also lay on the ground, clutching at his throat, still coughing and gasping. Neither of them had pistols, although the knives shoved into sashes or sticking out of their boots gleamed in the moonlight. He didn't think either one was a threat now. Entwhistle, though he had no pistol or knife, had a cat o' nine tails and Tristan knew of his skill with the whip. At last, his eyes fixed on Caralyn. He stared at her … and winked. Her eyes widened.

Tristan drew breath into his lungs. "Here! You want it? You can have it!" With every ounce of strength in his possession, he tossed the long trunk in the opposite direction. The chest exploded upon impact with the ground, raining precious and semi-precious gems all over the sand. Entwhistle screamed a curse, one of the most foul words ever uttered, and did exactly what Tristan hoped he would do. He released Caralyn from his iron grip and ran toward the treasure, dropping to his knees as he scooped up emeralds and rubies from the sand while Tristan's crew burst through the trees.

Tristan ran toward the *Explorer's* captain; rage made his heart thunder in his chest, his hands ball into fists. His foot connected with the man's side, the sound of a rib cracking and the scream that erupted from Entwhistle's lips filling him with satisfaction. The man did not get up, did not even try to defend himself as Tristan punched him in the mouth. Blood spurted from his split lip.

"Tristan! Watch out!" Caralyn screamed.

Tristan stopped and peered toward his left. Surprised and amazed, he saw the man who had been moaning and crying on the sand leap to his feet and run toward him, a huge rock in his hand. Aware that Entwhistle could attack him from behind, Tristan took a few steps away from the captain. Muscles tense, fists positioned to throw the first blow, he prepared to fight this newcomer, but the sailor wanted nothing to do with him. He ran past Tristan, growled once, and brought the rock down on the Entwhistle's head.

Entwhistle didn't utter a sound as he tried to crawl away, but the sailor couldn't seem to stop himself. Again and again, he smashed the rock against the Entwhistle's skull until the captain stopped moving completely. The crewman took a step back, gasping for breath, and kicked the man twice for good measure. Tristan doubted Entwhistle would ever move again as the sailor dropped to his knees, seemingly drained of energy and the taste for revenge.

Tristan tore his gaze away from the bloody mess that had once been a man and ran toward Caralyn. "My God, Cara! Are you all right?" He breathed, the rush of air filling his lungs, hoping the simple action would calm his shattered nerves. He drew her into his arms and held her tight, his chin resting on the top of her head. She trembled within his embrace and burst into tears.

Seeing her in Entwhistle's clutches, knowing the man was capable of anything, had stopped his heart from beating. And now, though his heart pounded in his chest, he still couldn't shake the devastating emotions coursing through him. Relief that she was safely in his arms coursed through him, making him tremble as much as she. "If anything had happened to you, I don't . . ." He couldn't finish the thought. "I love you, Cara mia."

She held him tighter, her body shuddering. Wetness seeped through his shirt, and he knew it was from her tears, but her voice was strong as she whispered, "I love you, too." Those words filled his heart, made his blood sing through his veins. He pulled away and gazed into her eyes. "No one will ever hurt you again. I give you my word."

"Papa! Papa!" Jemmy raced out of the forest, his feet flying over the sand. Tristan turned just in time as the boy launched himself into his father's arms. Tristan's heart swelled even more. "I did good! I didn't let him catch me, an' I found Socrates!"

Tristan laughed with pride and relief as he hugged his son. "Yes, my boy, you did good."

"Well done, lad!" Stitch said to Jemmy as he and Temperance joined them. The woman had a colorful bruise forming along her jawline but otherwise seemed fine as she embraced Caralyn and held her tight. Tristan saw the tears shining in her eyes behind the lenses of her glasses.

"I have never been so afraid in all my life," she said, her voice shaking. "When can we leave this godforsaken island? I long for civilization."

"Let me look at that arm." Stitch took Caralyn's hand in his. With a well-practiced move, he ripped the sleeve of her shirt, tearing it along the seams until it came off in his hands. He inspected the raw gashes in her flesh, *tsked* a few times, and then walked toward the shoreline and dipped the torn sleeve into the water. He came back, wringing the piece of cloth between his hands then snapping it open. "Now, this is going to sting a bit."

Caralyn yelped as the salt water did more than just sting as he started cleaning the bloody stripes. She gasped and kept her gaze on Tristan while Stitch tore her other sleeve and used it as bandage. "That should hold until we get back to the *Adventurer*."

"Beggin' your pardon, Cap'n, this man would like a word with you." Mad Dog, his face a mask of anger, a cut over one eye still trickling blood, held one of Entwhistle's men by the arm.

Tristan glanced at the man Mad Dog held in his grip, the same one who'd repeatedly slammed the rock against Entwhistle's head until he was dead. His eyes widened as recognition became clear. He knew this man. Or at least he'd seen him before. At Finnegan's. And at the Salty Dog so long ago. Entwhistle's henchman. Now he knew how Entwhistle had found them.

The man lowered his gaze and shuffled his feet. "I'm sorry, Miss," he whispered, his words slurring from the fat lip he'd received from one of Tristan's crew. "I never meant ter hurt ye." He raised his head. Tears shimmered in his eyes as he addressed Caralyn directly.

"It were me who stole yer book, but I were followin' orders, Miss, from the captain over there." He glanced behind him toward the dead man on the beach and shuddered. "He ain't never gonna come after ye again, ain't never gonna hurt anyone again." The man sighed. "I be humbly beggin' yer forgiveness."

Tristan glared at the man and scowled. He felt no pity, no remorse or mercy for the sailor, even though he had killed Entwhistle. Death would be a blessing to him.

Caralyn lightly touched his arm. Tristan said nothing as he gazed into her eyes, but knew in his heart, she had more compassion and sympathy in her than he ever would.

"He did try to help me," she said, her voice soft and full of understanding.

She turned toward the sailor and smiled. Tristan groaned, his hands balling into fists, his muscles tensing once more as he moved closer to her. Stitch and Mad Dog flanked her as well, offering protection. "What is your name?" she asked.

"Thaddeus Bing, Miss." He returned her smile with a shy one of his own. "But they call me Porkchop."

She nodded once then reached out to touch his round face with the tips of her fingers. "I forgive you, Thaddeus, but you must promise me you'll be a good man, a kind man, from now on."

"Thank you, Miss." Fresh tears filled Porkchop's eyes as he gazed at her with adoration. "I knew ye were an angel the firs' time I saw ye."

"Cara," Tristan started, but she held up her hand and stopped him.

"It's all right, Tristan. He won't hurt me or come after us, will you, Porkchop?"

The man shook his head. "No, Miss. Ye has my word."

Again, she nodded, and then her eyes narrowed and her voice lowered as she took a step closer. "If you do come after us or try to harm us in any way, then what you suffered at the hands of your captain will be nothing compared to what you'll suffer at mine.

This man," she pointed to Tristan, "would just as soon kill you for what you've done as would these men." She gestured toward Stitch and Mad Dog and the rest of the crew who had gathered around. "Do not make me regret my kindness, Thaddeus."

The man flinched and bowed his head but mumbled his compliance and understanding. Tristan watched her, amazement and awe swelling his heart as she walked away, her back rigid, her shoulders squared.

"Are we just going to let them go?" Socrates asked.

Tristan grinned, his gaze still on Caralyn as she reached for Jemmy's hand and strode down the beach. "No, we're going to scuttle their boat then bring the rest of the *Explorer's* crew here. We'll leave them on the island. There's plenty of food and water so they won't starve. It's better than they deserve."

Chapter 19

Tristan stood on deck, motionless, his hands clasped behind his back, and stared at the night sky as Mad Dog, his hands firm upon the wheel, guided the *Adventurer* into the mouth of the mighty Thames. Except for the wind snapping the sails around him and the familiar creaking of the ship, silence met his ears.

Sadness filled his heart and a long sigh escaped him as their journey neared its end. By the time the sun rose in a few short hours, they'd be in London.

Keep sailing. The words repeated in his head. More than ever before, Tristan considered the possibility. They had time. No one knew they'd returned. He drew in a deep breath and let it out slowly then closed his eyes against the ache that took his breath away.

As much as he wanted to keep sailing, as the voice in his head demanded, he couldn't. Honor bound, not only to his father but to the promise he'd made to Caralyn, he couldn't shirk his duty. In four days' time, he would be married—he only hoped he could convince his father to allow him to marry the woman he desired and not the one chosen for him.

He turned toward Mad Dog. "Keep her steady."

The sailor nodded, but didn't take his sight from the familiar landmarks, which were just hazy blurs on the horizon.

Tristan strode across the deck, his boot heels clicking on the hard wood, echoing in the eerie quiet. He headed toward the cabin he shared with Graham then changed his mind and went to his own. He and Caralyn only had a few more hours to be together—a few more moments he could hold her, touch her, before they parted ways.

Oh, how the knowledge hurt. The persistent pain in his chest grew and he almost stumbled from the devastating force of it, as if someone had punched him in the gut.

He entered the cabin and inhaled deeply. Caralyn's perfume permeated the room with its subtle fresh, clean scent, like the forest after a rain. He stood in the doorway, watching her as she slept in the glow of the lantern lit against the darkness, her hair spread out on the pillow, her body curled beneath the blanket against the cool chill.

In silence, he removed his clothing, folded his garments on the chair beside the small stove then slipped into the bed, careful not to wake her.

"Where have you been?"

"Topside," he replied in a hoarse whisper, surprised she was not sleeping as he thought. "We'll be in London in a few hours."

"So soon?"

"Aye, the winds were with us." He held her closely and inhaled the fragrance of her hair. "Or against us."

She turned to him, snuggling into his warmth, her body pressed tightly against his, the lace and silk of her nightgown teasing his skin. Her breath puffed against his chest, heating his flesh, fanning his desire as he reveled in her softness. Indeed, she need do nothing more than look at him, and his body responded in an instant, blood singing through his veins, heart pounding with an urgency to possess her.

"Run away with me. We can lose ourselves in the Caribbean where no one can find us. Others have done it. Hell, Pembrook did it. Why can't we?" His words startled even himself and the possibility they could do such a thing made hope blossom in his heart, but Caralyn stiffened in his arms. She rose up on her elbow and looked at him. Tears welled in her eyes and shimmered on her lashes. Such pain reflected on her beautiful face, he couldn't bear it.

"Oh, Tristan, you know we can't," she cried, her voice tight, her body trembling. "We have obligations, the both of us. The scandal would ruin us, not to mention what it would do to our families."

She took a deep breath then reached out to touch his face, as if memorizing every line, every curve, every whisker.

Tristan let out his breath in a long sigh. He knew she was right, but still, he had to try, had to stop the ache in his chest, the sorrow filling his soul. "If we were free of our commitments, would you stay with me?"

Her eyes twinkled in the dim light as her hand lowered to smooth over his bare chest. The sweet caress, so tender, nearly stole his breath. "Are you asking me to marry you?"

His heart thumped and his body tensed. "Would you have me?"

She nodded, though sadness flickered in her eyes beneath the sheen of tears. "If I were free. Yes."

"We could petition our fathers." Even as he said the words, he knew it wouldn't work—once given, his father's promise was never revoked.

She said nothing, though the expression in her eyes spoke volumes, and the hope that blossomed so briefly in his heart died just as quickly.

And still, he persisted. His arms tightened around her, holding her closer, the softness of her skin like velvet beneath his fingers. "I love you, Cara mia. I want you by my side as we sail the oceans, searching for lost treasure. I want your smile to be the first thing I see in the morning and the last thing I see before I sleep. I want to hear your laughter until I take my last breath. We must try, Cara."

Caralyn nodded, her eyes sparkling in the lamplight. "Do you think our family's would allow us . . ." she started to ask but didn't finish the thought. Instead, she whispered, "We have a few more hours. We can live a lifetime in those hours. Let's not waste a moment." Her lips touched his in a kiss that seared his soul. Despite his grief, pleasure jolted him to the tips of his toes. Blood sizzled through his veins and his heart, his broken, aching heart, thudded painfully in his chest.

She planted light kisses on his face, his neck, his chest, the warmth of her lips singeing his skin. He pulled her atop him so she straddled him, the silk of her nightgown tickling his thighs and chest, the moist heat of her pressing on his hard shaft. He weaved his fingers into her hair and pulled her closer to plunder her mouth, imprinting the taste of her in his memory.

He wanted to feel all of her, touch every inch of her, memorize the softness of her dewy flesh. He pulled the thin gown over her head and tossed it to the floor. Her breasts fit his hands perfectly, the taut nipples burning into his palms.

Caralyn gasped and arched her back as he drew first one pebble hard nipple into his mouth then the other, his tongue swirling around the dusty rose peak, making it harder, more rigid as his hand slipped between her thighs. His fingers found the source of her pleasure, the silky wetness making her slick as he caressed her between the swollen folds.

Caralyn cried out as her body rocked with the force of her climax. Tristan almost grinned, loving the quickness of her response, the reckless abandon and enthusiasm of her loving. As she slumped over him, her hair fell forward, tickling his skin, the fragrance reaching his nose and filling his brain.

"Oh, Tristan," she whispered in his ear and he finally smiled. He'd only begun to tease her, caress her, make her forget for a short time what lay ahead when the sun rose.

With his hands on her hips, he shifted her slight weight and guided her onto his shaft, slowly, drawing out the movement until he thought he could bear it no more. Caralyn released a long sigh as her hips moved over him. Heat and moisture surrounded him, the tightness of her sheath thrilling him beyond words, beyond thought. He closed his eyes, but only for a moment. He wanted to watch her face, see her emotions as she rode from one climax to another.

She threw her head back and tensed. A moan of pure pleasure escaped her as her body pulsed around him.

He could feel his own release building, his body stiffening beneath her, and yet he cautioned himself to take his time, to be patient. He rolled her beneath him, his shaft still imbedded in her moist heat. Her legs wrapped around his hips, drawing him closer as her hands smoothed along his face, bringing his head toward hers for a kiss.

He moved in her slowly, drawing out almost completely only to drive into her welcoming flesh over and over. The intensity of his pleasure doubled then tripled. Her nails dug into his backside as she caught his rhythm, her hips rising up to meet his, stroke for stroke, until Caralyn stiffened beneath him, her breath coming in short gasps. Her legs tightened around his hips. He studied her face as her eyes fluttered open and held her gaze with his own, fascinated by the changing colors. He knew she rode the crest of another climax, could feel her sheath tightening around him, and he quickened his pace.

Her sighs and moans of pleasure drove him, yet urged him to hold back, to give as much as she gave, but when her body exploded around him, he could restrain himself no longer, the joy too intense.

Tristan smothered her scream of bliss with his mouth then groaned as the power of his own climax hit him. Drained yet vitalized, sapped of strength yet full of energy, he continued to move within her warmth, delighting in the shudder that rippled through her.

Sweat beaded on his forehead, his arms ached from holding himself above her and yet, he did not want to leave the heat of her. Caralyn sighed beneath him, her legs still wrapped around his hips, holding him prisoner within her body, her hands smoothing along his back. He captured her mouth with his own, his tongue tangling with hers. Elation surged through him, and if he had his way, he'd make love to her again. And again. But sorrow permeated his joy, and he slowly withdrew from her.

He gathered her in his arms and kissed her temple.

"I love you, Tristan."

"And I love you," he whispered when he really wanted to shout the words. "Sleep now." He held her until her breathing deepened and her lashes fluttered on her cheek. Tristan watched her slumber, reluctant to leave her warmth, unwilling and unable to let her go. He smoothed a lock of her silken hair between his fingers and realized all the treasure filling the hold didn't mean a thing when the only treasure he wanted was her. He slipped from the bed and dressed in silence, his heart breaking a little more with every move he made before he left her to head up on deck. As much as he wanted to stay with her, he still had his duties as captain.

He strode the stairs to the deck and stood, not at the helm, but at the rail, his hands gripping the brass so tightly, his knuckles whitened. A muscle jumped in his clenched jaw. How long he remained in that position, he didn't know, but he couldn't seem to move. Familiar landmarks drifted by and the sun rose in the east as it had done since the beginning of time, but he barely noticed. He could still smell her perfume, hear her whispered cries of ecstasy and the ache in his heart grew ten-fold. The few hours they shared were not enough, and yet they would have to be. His father would never let him out of his commitment and he doubted hers would either.

The lump in his throat threatened to choke him as sudden tears filled his eyes and blurred his vision, surprising him. He hadn't cried since he was a young boy, but this, the thought of her walking out of his life, cut him to the core. He blinked then quickly wiped the tears from his face with the back of his hand.

The smell of Hash's coffee, much improved since Caralyn had been onboard, drifted to his nose, but the thought of having a cup twisted his stomach. He had no interest in food or drink, just her.

He felt the stares of the crew as they gathered on deck to begin their daily chores. Not one spoke to him, not one dared to invade his privacy, for which he was extremely grateful. He took a deep breath then another and another, in an effort to numb the sorrow in his heart. He sensed rather than saw someone behind him then felt the small hand of his son slide within his. He glanced at the boy. Despite his grief, the corners of his mouth twitched.

Jemmy's hair stood straight up, having not seen the benefit of either comb or brush. His clothes were wrinkled and looked slept in, which, of course, they probably were. "Is that the same shirt you wore yesterday?"

The boy nodded with enthusiasm.

"And you didn't comb your hair, did you?"

Again with eagerness, the boy shook his head.

Tristan crouched down to be eye level with his son. "I bet you haven't brushed your teeth either, have you?"

Jemmy tilted his head and stared at his father for a very long time. Instead of answering the question, he asked, "Are you sad, Papa?"

"Yes, I am."

Not understanding the reason, the boy grinned. "But we found the treasure."

"Yes, son. Yes, we did," Tristan replied, but without returning the boy's smile. They had indeed found Izzy's Fortune, but he'd found a treasure far more worth keeping. Except he couldn't keep her. "But that doesn't mean you don't have to brush your teeth or your hair or dress in clean clothes, like a young gentlemen. After you do those things, you may come back on deck and have breakfast with the crew. Would you like that?"

Jemmy threw his arms around his father and hugged him. The feel of the boy's arms was the balm Tristan needed. He closed his eyes and held him tighter, as if his sanity depended upon it.

Which it did.

"I love you, lad," he whispered, saying the words his father very rarely, if ever, said to him.

"I love you, too, Papa," Jemmy said as he pulled out of his father's embrace and scampered to his quarters.

Tristan watched him, his lips pressed into a thin line. How would he ever tell his son that Caralyn would be leaving? Would it break the boy's heart as the knowledge broke his own? Unless he could convince the earl to free him of his promise.

"Here's your coffee, Cap'n." Hash pressed a ceramic mug into his hand. Fragrant steam tickled his nose. "Breakfast will be ready shortly."

Without realizing he did it, Tristan brought the cup to his lips and sipped while he waited for Caralyn.

However, Caralyn did not have breakfast with the crew this morning. Though Mr. Anders tooted on his whistle to call the men, she remained absent. Tristan missed her lively presence, but he understood and respected her wishes. He himself found it difficult to listen to the men laugh and carry on around the table while his heart was full of grief and sadness.

He returned to the deck, his belly empty except for the coffee he drank without tasting it. He could still shout the order to set another course, to keep sailing, but the words were stuck in his throat.

Mr. Anders's whistle cut through the noise of the London docks, loud and brash after the comforting sounds of the sea, and the crew rushed to follow orders. Sails were furled and heavy ropes were tossed to the men waiting along the pier.

"I'll hire a carriage and make sure her trunks are loaded into the boot," Stitch said. Tristan jumped, startled. He hadn't seen the man approach, nor heard his footsteps. "Temperance and I will accompany Cara to her destination then return to the ship." The good doctor held his gaze, his head tilting to the side. "Are you all right?"

"No." The simple word escaped him before he could stop it. "She's leaving, damn it, when all I want is for her to stay."

Stitch nodded his understanding. "She has no choice, Tris, and neither do you. I know you're both promised to others. You'll have to forget her."

Tristan raised an eyebrow. "Forget her? How the hell can I do that?" He gestured to Temperance, who trailed behind Caralyn a step or two. "How would you feel right now if Temperance were leaving? Could you forget her?"

The doctor's eyes darted to his wife. He swallowed hard, his Adam's apple bobbing as he watched her. He bowed slightly. "Forgive me. I … I wasn't thinking. Indeed, she would be impossible to forget. They both would."

He turned at the sound of her sweet voice and stared. *My God, she is beautiful.* She'd dressed with care, the bright blue of her gown reflecting in her eyes, making them bluer and matching the reticule, which swung from her wrist. She carried the valise they'd retrieved from the *Explorer* in her hand. She'd pulled her hair away her from her face so that it fell in a shining mass down her back, and all he wanted to do was run his fingers through the glossy strands one last time. Her cheeks were pale except for the two spots of color high on her cheekbones, and though she smiled, sadness reflected in her features.

He couldn't take his eyes from her as he watched her say goodbye to the men. His heart, if possible, broke even more and thudded painfully in his chest.

"Hash, I want you to keep Smudge," Tristan heard her say she as she scratched the cat behind the ears. Smudge closed her big yellow eyes and purred but didn't try to escape the tender embrace in which the cook held her. "She's grown very attached to you."

The big man nodded, his smile beaming and held the cat a little tighter. "Thank ye, Miss Cara."

She moved on to the next person and the next, giving them hugs or pressing her lips against their cheeks. She stopped in front of Socrates, dropped the valise, and wrapped her arms around him.

"It's been a pleasure to sail with ye again, Miss Cara." If he wasn't mistaken, Tristan thought he heard sobs in the man's voice and knew he wouldn't be the only one to miss Caralyn.

"Take care of yourself, Socrates, and when you open your tavern, I'll be sure to visit."

"Aye, I'd like that."

She hugged him again then stood in front of Graham. She held out her hand, but the navigator grabbed her in a bear hug and squeezed. They spoke for a few moments, words Tristan couldn't hear above the sounds around them, but there were tears in both their eyes when the embrace ended.

She stopped in front of Mac. "Keep well, Mac."

The Scotsman, the one who'd been most vocal about having a woman on board, blushed, his bushy mustache a slash of white on his scarlet face. He looked down at his feet then back at her. "It's been a pleasure," he said and took to his heels, his body tense with embarrassment that anyone should see his softer side.

Tristan almost smiled. Almost.

She approached Jemmy and held out her arms. The boy rushed into them. "And you, you little monkey, be a good boy. Learn your lessons well." A lump rose to Tristan's throat, bigger than before. He couldn't speak if he wanted to. "I expect to see you sailing this ship in a few years."

"Aye, Miss Cara." The boy grinned, his eyes full of adoration; then he scurried away to climb the rigging, not the reaction Tristan had expected at all. Perhaps he didn't understand Caralyn wouldn't be coming back.

Tristan waited, his muscles tense, his mouth set in a grim line as Caralyn picked up her valise and slowly walked toward him.

This was it. She'd saved her last goodbye for him. He didn't think he could bear the sorrow filling his heart.

"I must go. I . . ."

She couldn't finish the sentence and he didn't want her to. Her eyes, the color of the deep blue sea, sparkled with unshed tears as she kissed his lips one last time, oblivious to anyone who might be watching. For once, Temperance, right beside her, remained silent, the expression of censure she usually wore gone from her face.

He'd been so wrong. A woman's touch, *this* woman's touch, could and did compare to the spray of spindrift on his face, the thrill of battling the elements in the middle of the ocean.

My God, what will I do without her?

"Don't go," he blurted out, unable to help himself.

"I must." Her voice lowered then cracked as she said, "But I will come back, if I am able. You have my promise."

"I'll wait for you."

Tristan watched her leave the ship and climb into the hired carriage. How deeply he'd fallen, so deeply he was willing to give up everything for her, his Cara mia. Once again, the thought of renouncing his title and letting his younger brother take the reins and the responsibility flashed through his mind. His father would never allow it. As the first-born, the earldom belonged to him.

"Is she gone?" Graham sidled up beside him and gripped the rail.

Tristan said nothing for a long time as the carriage bearing his happiness rolled over the cobblestoned street. "Yes. Stitch and Temperance are accompanying her."

"What now?"

Tristan turned to him. A persistent pain ripped through him from the region of his heart. He stiffened against the ache and wondered, briefly, if the sorrow would ever subside or if it would remain with him for the rest of his life. After all these years, he'd finally found the woman he knew was meant for him—and he had to give her up, had to let her go. "Take the ship. Burn it. Sell it. Sail it around the world. I don't give a damn. She's yours to do with as you will."

He left the deck and sought sanctuary in the cabin where they'd spent so much time together, but the fragrance of her perfume hit him with all the weight of an anchor being dropped into the water.

He could go after her, could steal her away from the man she was promised to marry, and yet, he did nothing. He slumped into the chair and held his head in his hands. "Goodbye, Cara mia," he whispered. But even as he said the words, hope still dwelled in his heart. She said she would come back and if—when—she did, he would be ready.

He grabbed paper, ink, and a pen and dashed off notes to his father.

• • •

As the wheels of the hired carriage rolled over the cobbled stone, Caralyn sat in the corner of the coach. She hadn't looked back after she left the ship, afraid her resolve would soften and she'd tell Tristan of her plan to drop a bag of gold in front of the earl and demand to be released from her father's promise. But she couldn't tell him, not until she knew for certain the earl would accept her offer.

She didn't speak to her companions, who sat across from her now, didn't even look at them. She couldn't. Unshed tears stung her eyes, tears she couldn't release, fearful that if she started crying, she'd never be able to stop.

She twisted her gloved fingers around the silk ropes of her reticule and called herself every kind of fool.

She shouldn't have fallen in love with the captain, but how could she help herself? The man was everything she'd always wanted—handsome, gentle, and compassionate, full of integrity and a spirit for adventure that matched her own.

Not only had she fallen in love with Tristan, but with his son as well. Jemmy reminded her of her brother, Charles, when he was younger—so much so it hurt. She closed her eyes, forcing the tears away, calling upon every fiber in her being to give her strength.

Caralyn wasn't even aware the carriage had stopped, so lost was she in her own misery.

"Cara." Temperance reached out to touch her hand and Caralyn jumped, startled by the light touch. "We're here."

The door opened and the driver placed a wooden box beneath the portal. He held out his hand. Caralyn grabbed it as if her sanity depended on it and stepped down to the street in front of an imposing brick building. A wrought iron fence surrounded a small flower garden where roses bloomed in a profusion of red, pink, and yellow, but she didn't see any of the colors, only the massive iron gate that led to a flagstone walkway and the two crouching lions that flanked it.

Caralyn let out her breath in a huff as the driver deposited her trunks beside the door. He nodded to her, touched the brim of his hat then climbed into his seat. The carriage creaked as he took up the reins and settled himself.

"Will you be all right?" Stitch leaned out the carriage window, drawing her attention away from the stone lions.

Temperance's head poked out beside his. As a last moment decision, her companion was refusing the salary Caralyn's brother had promised her. Between her share of Izzy's Fortune and Stitch's, neither one would ever have to worry about money again. "I can stay, if you'd like, Cara. Brady will stay as well, won't you, dear?"

"Of course," the man answered. "For as long as you need us."

Unsure and nervous, questions rumbling through her mind at breakneck speed, Caralyn's entire body trembled with apprehension. Whose home was this? What kind of reception would she receive? She should have been here months ago; how could she explain she'd gone on an adventure without telling a soul? And how could she tell her companions her stomach was one giant knot, that if she let herself think, she might run screaming into the fog-shrouded street? She shivered, but it had nothing to do with the chill air.

Temperance and Stitch had plans. Within the next few weeks, they'd be moving to an estate the good doctor had purchased years ago but had never resided in. He planned to finish the book he'd been writing about searching for hidden treasure. "No, I'll be all right, but thank you both. For everything."

"It is I who should be thanking you," Temperance said, her voice hoarse. Tears sparkled in her eyes, making them luminous behind the lenses of her glasses. "If it weren't for you, I'd never have met Brady."

Caralyn swallowed hard over the lump in her throat. "It was a grand adventure, wasn't it? I shall miss you, but I'll enjoy reliving our time together once your book is published, Stitch. And I have your address. We'll write to each other, and of course, we'll visit once we're all settled."

She kissed them both then tapped her hand against the side of the carriage, signaling the driver. The conveyance pulled away. Bereft, frightened so much her entire body shuddered, Caralyn faced the imposing front door of the manse. Ornately carved, with knockers made to resemble lion's heads, the twin portals were at least twelve feet in height. She took a deep breath, raised her hand, and grasped the handle hanging from the lion's mouth, but she couldn't bring herself to knock.

Her heart beat a swift cadence in her chest. Though encased in soft kid gloves, her palms were damp. Indeed, despite the coolness of the fog shrouding her surroundings, perspiration trickled between her breasts. Torn between her desire to return to Tristan and her duty, she stood in perfect stillness for a moment longer before she let the handle drop.

The door swung open to reveal a man who stood so stiffly, Caralyn wondered if a pole extended up his back.

"I am Caralyn McCreigh."

"Yes, milady. We've been expecting you." He bowed then smiled as he gestured to a footman to take her trunks. "If you'll follow me, please." He bowed again then led her into the great hall and guided her into a small parlor. "If you'll wait here a moment, Her Grace will be with you shortly."

Caralyn tossed her reticule on the settee and looked around the room decorated cheerfully in reds, golds, and greens in the richest brocades and softest velvets. Flames crackled and popped in the fireplace, lending warmth to the room, a warmth she didn't feel. She glanced at the portrait above the mantle and gasped.

Confusion created a deep furrow in her brow and made her eyes squint as she studied the portrait. With certainty, she knew she'd never posed for it so the question remained, how was it done and why was it here?

She felt a presence behind her but couldn't take her eyes away from the portrait. Without knowing whom she addressed, she had to ask, "Why is there a portrait of me here in a home I've never been?"

"My dear child," the voice shook the slightest bit but still rang with authority. "That is not you. I had this portrait commissioned as a wedding gift for my late husband, the Duke of Lion's Mead. I was just a few years younger than you are now." The voice came closer and a hand rested easily on Caralyn's shoulder.

Neither alarmed nor frightened, but extremely curious, Caralyn turned around. Her eyes widened as she took in the vision before her. She could have been looking in a mirror for staring back at her were her own eyes, her own smile, though the hair piled on her head was snow white.

"The resemblance is uncanny, wouldn't you agree, Cara?" The woman quirked an eyebrow and took a slow step away.

"Who are you?"

"Of course. You wouldn't know, would you? I am Caralyn DeMarshe, dowager duchess of Lion's Mead. You were named for me. You may call me Grandmama."

"You are my grandmother?"

"Yes, I am."

No sooner had the duchess said the words than the room started to swirl and tilt, colors passing before Caralyn's eyes in a kaleidoscope as a wave of dizziness overwhelmed her. Actually, it all overwhelmed her—finding the treasure, saying goodbye to Tristan and Jemmy, leaving the ship. Tears blurred her vision even as the room seemed to grow darker.

"Oh my. I never thought … it's almost too much, isn't it?" the duchess asked, her voice kind as she led Caralyn toward a chaise lounge beside the fire. "But a DeMarshe woman never faints." She crossed the room to a small round table, pulled the stopper from a crystal bottle, and poured a small splash of brandy into a matching cut crystal snifter. "Drink this," she said and handed the glass to her.

Caralyn swallowed the liquor, feeling the warmth settle in her stomach. The room stopped spinning. She took a moment and studied the regal woman before her, but hardly had time to gather her shattered wits when she heard the familiar quick footsteps and the sweet, dulcet tones of her mother's voice.

"She's here?" A moment later, the door swung open and her mother swept into the room, a huge smile on her face though her lovely eyes shimmered with tears. "Cara!"

Caralyn jumped from the chaise lounge despite feeling lightheaded and ran into her mother's open arms. "Oh, Mama!"

"So much as happened since you left me that horrible note and ran away!" Elizabeth said as she grabbed Caralyn's icy hands and led her toward a settee. "Your father, bless his irritating heart, arranged all of this. I didn't agree with what he had done, but I have forgiven him, just as I've forgiven you." She glanced toward the duchess. The smile on her face lit up the entire room as she held out her hand. "Your grandmother and I have been reunited. We've been making up for lost time while we waited for you, and now you are here. Three generations of DeMarshe women in one room. I never thought I'd live to see this."

"Where is Papa?"

"He went hunting, of all things! I have never known the man to hunt. He's always been a sailor. But he'll be back very soon. Now, tell us everything! Was it a grand adventure?"

Chapter 20

"Ouch!" Caralyn yelped and jumped as yet another pin jabbed her.

"Please, Miss, you must try to stay still," the seamstress plying the pins admonished her.

Properly reprimanded, Caralyn concentrated on not moving a muscle, yet every time a door slammed or she heard a male voice, she wanted to bolt. Waiting to speak to her father had become an exercise in utter frustration, and her patience had worn thin.

Caralyn took a deep breath and kept her eyes closed as a team of seamstresses, hired by the duchess, pinned and pulled fabric, dressed and undressed her. She didn't want to see any of the elaborate gowns, didn't want to participate in the experience that only reminded her how much her heart hurt.

A sigh did escape her, though. Not a moment belonged to her. This dress fitting was just another example. From dawn until hours past midnight, the duchess delighted in introducing Caralyn to aunts and uncles and cousins she never knew existed. And all seemed to conspire to keep her from doing as her heart desired most—finding the Earl of Winterbourne, gaining her freedom, and returning to Tristan.

Three days had come and gone since she stood on the steps to her grandmother's house—three days of regaling relatives with her search for Izzy's Fortune and her high adventure. And with each passing moment, her heart broke a little more. She had tried bribing the household staff to give her an address for the earl's estates, but none would give her the information she needed. The staff adored the duchess and wouldn't risk raising her ire. Caralyn's one attempt at leaving the house and hiring a carriage had failed miserably. She'd been caught by none other than the duchess herself and quickly whisked away to another tea.

Time had become her enemy. She needed to talk to her father, but the man remained suspiciously absent. She hadn't seen him at all. Hunting, she'd been told, when she asked.

Another sigh whispered through her lips. She missed the easy, carefree days of their search for Izzy's Fortune, missed the crew and Jemmy. She even missed Temperance, but most of all, she missed Tristan. The taste of his kiss, the feel of his body pressed against hers, the exquisite moments of passion shared. Her heart ached when she thought of his sherry-colored eyes gazing into hers, the crooked smile she loved so well on his face.

"*C'est magnifique!*" one of the seamstresses gasped.

Caralyn's eyes flew open and her gaze landed on her reflection in the mirror. She couldn't help herself. She glared at the woman in the beveled looking glass and struggled to catch her breath. The ivory satin and lace gown she would wear tomorrow when she vowed to honor and obey a man she had yet to meet made her look like an angel. An angel with a broken heart. An angel not quite so pure. Lord Ravensley, her intended, remained suspiciously absent—did he not wish to marry either?

Her chin trembled, her throat constricted and her body began to shake, as if stricken with fever. The tears she'd been holding at bay released in a torrent and rolled down her cheeks. She didn't even try to stop them.

"What's wrong, *ma cherie?*" the seamstress in charge asked in her lightly accented English. "You do not like the gown?"

Caralyn glanced at her mother and tried to speak over the lump in her throat. "I … I . . ."

"Leave us, please." Elizabeth rose from the settee where she'd been offering suggestions on fit and style. The women left the room, chattering among themselves and closed the door behind them.

"Cara, dear, what is wrong?"

"I can't do it, Mama," Caralyn managed to say, although the constriction in her throat threatened to choke her. She blinked tears from her eyes as she gazed at her mother. "I've finally found the man I've been looking for all my life, the one I can love until I die. I love Tristan with all my heart." Determination straightened her spine and she sniffed. Elizabeth handed her an embroidered handkerchief and she wiped the tears from her face. "I won't marry someone else. I can't. Papa promised me I wouldn't have to if I found Izzy's Fortune."

"But Cara—"

Caralyn didn't wait to hear what her mother was about to say. She stepped down from the foot high platform in front of the mirror and rushed to one of the trunks beside the wall. She slipped the lock and flipped the lid to expose an array of gold and jewels. "Well, I found it, Mama. I found the treasure and where is Papa?"

Elizabeth's eyes opened wide as she strode across the room to look inside the chest. "Oh, Cara," she sighed then took her daughter's ice-cold hands into her warm ones. "You must follow your heart, my love, as I once did, but remember, the choices you make will be the ones you must live with for all your days. Is your captain worth ruining your father's reputation as well as your own? Is he worth the scandal?"

"Was Papa?"

A beautiful smile crossed her mother's lips and her eyes glowed. A blush stole across her face. "Yes, he was, Cara, and still is. I loved him then, I love him still, and I have not once regretted my decision. Do you feel the same about your captain?"

"Yes, Mama. I don't want to live without him."

"Ah, she is like all the DeMarshe women, is she not?"

Caralyn gasped and whirled around. The duchess, whom she'd come to know and adore, stood in the doorway.

"Headstrong," she said as she closed the door and strode across the room to join them at the chest, her cane tapping the carpeted floor with each step. To Caralyn, the rhythmic beat sounded like the constant ticking of the clock, telling her time had run out.

The duchess glanced into the trunk. One eyebrow rose as a smile crossed her lips. "Willful. Rash and reckless, with a weakness for men of the sea." She grasped Caralyn's chin between finger and thumb. "But knowing her own heart."

"What am I to do?" The tears fell. She couldn't help it.

"Life is long. You cannot go through it with sadness as your constant companion." The duchess sighed then glanced at her daughter. Elizabeth raised a perfectly shaped brow as she held her mother's gaze then slowly nodded. "As your mother did so long ago, as I once did, you must follow your heart. Go to him. Find this captain of yours and tell him you love him."

"I can't." Caralyn scooped up a handful of gold coins and let them drop back into the chest one by one. "I can't go to Tristan if I am not free. I must speak with the Earl of Winterbourne and try to convince him to set me free of Papa's word. I can pay him the dowry Papa promised, but I have no idea where to find him."

"So that's why you've been trying to bribe my staff and sneak out of the house." The duchess chuckled. "Why did you not just ask me?" She laid cool fingers on Caralyn's arm. "By the time you change your clothes, I can have a carriage ready to take you where you need to go."

• • •

She's not coming back.

The words echoed through Tristan's mind as the ticking of the clock reminded him of exactly how long Caralyn had been gone. Three days, four hours, twenty-four minutes. Twenty-five minutes. Twenty-six.

He paced the length of his cabin, back and forth, unable to sit still for more than a moment, unable to concentrate on the captain's log he needed to complete before he transferred ownership of the *Adventurer* to Graham.

Twenty-seven minutes.

He'd yet to receive a response from his father, either. The messages he'd sent after they sailed into port had gone unanswered. He could and should ride out for the Winterbourne estates and confront his father, but where was he? The London townhouse? The estates in Swansea? One of the other estates? The hunting lodge? And what if Caralyn came back after he was gone? Would she think he'd given up waiting for her?

Twenty-eight minutes.

Most of the crew had gone to town to spend their portion of the treasure. Only Stitch, Temperance, Hash, and Jemmy remained onboard. The creaking of the ship and the ticking of the clock were simply repeated reminders of the time he wasted, the time Caralyn was not in his arms.

Tristan sighed, sat at his desk again, and tried to record the details of his journey to find Izzy's Fortune but every word, every fact reminded him of Caralyn. Indeed, her perfume permeated the cabin. He inhaled, letting the scent he associated with her fill his mind.

"When is Miss Cara coming back? I miss her."

Tristan looked up from the captain's log on his desk to see his son in the doorway of the cabin. His eyes were wide, red-rimmed, and glowed in the pearly light coming in through the window. He looked as if he'd been crying. "Come here." He opened his arms wide. The boy flew across the room and settled onto his lap.

"I miss her, too, son," he said, "but I don't think she'll be able to come back. She . . ." He stopped himself from saying too much. Only eight, Jemmy wouldn't understand the obligations of adults, couldn't understand the circumstances he and Caralyn had found themselves in—to find the perfect mate, the perfect person only to be promised to others, but the boy deserved to know.

Before he could explain, Jemmy whispered, "I wish she could be my mother."

The words were spoken so softly, so wistfully, Tristan wasn't sure he'd heard them correctly, but they touched his heart. He held the boy tighter. How unfair he'd been, never realizing how much Jemmy had grown to love Caralyn, never realizing how his actions had affected his son. Guilt raged through him and his own eyes misted, blurring his vision. The ache in his chest, his constant companion, exploded. He held his breath against the pain, and as much as he hated to hurt his son more, he had to tell him. "She's to be married to someone else."

"She can't," the boy blurted as tears filled his eyes. His voice cracked. "She loves you, Papa. And you love her. *You* have to marry her."

Tristan sighed and closed his eyes, unable to bear the anguish he saw reflected on Jemmy's face, anguish that mirrored his own. "It's not possible, son. I'm sorry. We both, she and I, have responsibilities and commitments, duties to fulfill." The words sounded weak, even to his own ears. His voice lowered as he uttered, "I am to be married as well."

"No, Papa!" Jemmy squirmed out of his embrace. Anger stiffened his little body as he stood in front of his father, red faced, hands balled into fists. "You can't marry someone else! You can't!"

"But I must."

"I want Miss Cara! You have to find her and bring her back!" Tears flowed freely from Jemmy's eyes and ran down his cheeks.

"I can't."

"I hate you, Papa!" His son shouted the words and fled from the room as fast as his feet could carry him.

Tristan closed his eyes against the sorrow filling his soul. Jemmy had never said those words to him before and God help him, they hurt. He resisted the urge to chase after his son. For now. He knew no matter what he said, no matter how he tried to explain, Jemmy wouldn't understand. The boy was too upset to listen. It was the second hardest thing Tristan had ever done. The first had been watching Caralyn leave the *Adventurer*.

"What's wrong with Jemmy?" Stitch stood in the doorway, concern etched on his face. "He ran past me as if the hounds of hell were on his heels, his eyes full of tears. Temperance is trying to comfort him, but she isn't doing much good. The boy is inconsolable."

"I had to tell him Caralyn isn't coming back … had to tell him she's getting married to someone else, as am I." He scrubbed at his face then raked his fingers through his hair. His breath hitched in his chest as he revealed the hurtful words his son had thrown at him. "He told me he hated me."

Stitch shook his head. "I'm sorry. That must have been very hard for you." The doctor entered the room and headed for the liquor cabinet. He poured a healthy draught of brandy into snifters and handed one to Tristan then pulled a chair closer to the desk. He took a sip of the cognac. "He doesn't mean it, you know. Children will say things when they're upset. They don't realize how hurtful words can sometimes be, but he'll calm down."

"I don't know, Stitch." Tristan let out his pent up breath. "If you could have seen the hurt on his face, the way he looked at me." He closed his eyes against the pain, against the sympathy in Stitch's expression. "He said he wished Caralyn could be his mother."

"I see. He grew very fond of her very quickly and she of him, I think." He leaned back in his chair, crossed his legs, and then took another sip of brandy. "What about you?"

"What about me?" His words were curt. He didn't mean them to be, but he didn't want to talk about this, didn't want to share the sadness in his heart about Caralyn. He didn't offer an apology, although he knew he should. The lump in his throat made it too difficult to speak.

The doctor's eyebrow lifted, but he remained silent for a very long time. When he finally spoke, he said, "You know, I still have the address where Temperance and I brought Caralyn. I would presume she's still there. She isn't married yet, Tristan, and neither are you." He finished his brandy then rose from his seat. He laid his hand on Tristan's shoulder and squeezed. "Sometimes, a child's simple view is the right one. Adults always make things more complicated than they need to be. Perhaps you should listen to Jemmy and follow your heart."

He left the cabin, closing the door behind him. Tristan leaned back in his chair and steepled his fingers in front of his face, his thumbs resting under his chin, fingertips touching the tip of his nose. The advice Stitch gave him to heed Jemmy's words whirled in his mind.

Dare he follow his heart?

He closed his eyes. The memory of all of them sitting down for breakfast at Finnegan's flashed through his mind. How happy he'd been at that moment. How content. How much he wanted that to be real.

"Yes, damn it, I dare!" He said the words aloud and his heart pounded in his chest, not with pain, not with sorrow, but with hope. He stood, tossed back the brandy, and rushed from the cabin. Stitch was the only one in sight, although he could hear Jemmy's sobs. The good doctor paced back and forth on deck, his hands clasped behind his back, deep in thought.

"Ah, you've come to a decision, I see."

Tristan grinned. "If you'll keep an eye on Jemmy, I'll take that address."

Stitch nodded and handed him a slip of paper. "Bring her back to us."

Excitement pulsed through his veins as he left the ship and hailed the first carriage he saw. His foot tapped the floor in an effort to convince the driver to go faster. He sat back against the cushioned seat and twisted the signet ring around and around on his finger. He stopped twisting and stared at the symbol on it, a smile spreading his lips. He could only imagine the look on his father's face when he introduced Caralyn as the only woman he'd consider marrying.

Tristan didn't wait for the carriage to come to a complete stop or for the driver to climb from his perch and place the wooden box beneath the door. He jumped to the cobblestoned street and tossed a few coins to the driver then stood for a moment to catch his breath as the carriage pulled away. Hawthorne House and the carved lions flanking the wrought iron gate greeted him with stony silence.

He strode toward the door, lifted the heavy lion's head knocker, and waited. And waited. He shifted his weight from one foot to the other, pushed his hands into his pockets then removed them again. He stared at the door, willing it to open, willing it to disappear. Unable to stop himself, he lifted the knocker once more and let it drop.

Once the door finally opened, every rule of decorum and propriety left him. He pushed past the startled butler and rushed into the house.

"Cara! Cara!" Tristan's voice echoed through the cavernous great hall, the chandelier above his head tinkling in response.

"Sir, if you would please—" The butler tried to grab his arm, but Tristan shook him off.

"Cara!" He strode toward the sweeping staircase, expecting to see Caralyn come flying down the stairs. Instead, he saw a young girl, a child of no more than four or five. She stood on a step midway down the staircase, a rag doll clutched in her arms. Masses of light brown hair curled around her head. She grinned at him.

Tristan couldn't help himself. He grinned back. "Hello, sweetheart."

The girl giggled and scampered down the remaining steps. She looked at him with the biggest, bluest eyes he'd ever seen. "Who are you?"

"My name is Tristan." He bowed before her, completely enchanted. If he and Caralyn were ever to have a daughter, this was what she would look like. He crouched down to be eye level with her. "And what is your name?"

"Elizabeth Caralyn McCreigh."

His heart pounded in his chest as he looked at her. He could see Caralyn in her sparkling blue eyes, her mass of bouncing curls, her mischievous grin, and assumed she was either niece or sister.

"How old are you, Elizabeth?"

"Four and a half. Almost five," she told him, her voice full of pride then showed him the doll she carried. "This is Apple Annie. She's almost five too."

Delighted by this little elfin creature, charmed by those flashing blue eyes, Tristan asked, "Do you know where Caralyn is?"

"Aunt Cara?"

"Young man!"

Tristan turned at the sound of a woman's commanding voice and stared, his mouth open. Except for the whiteness of her hair piled high upon her head, the resemblance to Caralyn astounded him. Her mother, perhaps?

He rose from his crouched position and watched the woman come closer. Spots of color highlighted her pale cheeks as she crossed the marble floor, her cane tapping with each step she took. The butler walked several steps behind her, back rigid, thin lips pressed together in anger.

"Betsy, go and find your grandmother. Ask her to meet me in the salon," she ordered. Once the girl scurried back up the stairs, she turned to the butler. "It's all right, Crandall. You may go."

The butler hesitated for a moment then bowed. "Yes, Your Grace."

Your Grace?

Crandall left the great hall, but not before scowling at Tristan, his intent clear. He didn't go far, either. Tristan almost grinned, realizing the butler's footsteps ceased once the man was out of sight.

The woman faced him once again and Tristan found himself the subject of the boldest assessment of his person he'd ever experienced. Disconcerted, surprised, he returned her frank stare with one of his own.

An eyebrow lifted and her head tilted to the side. "Now, young man, what is the meaning of this? Who are you? Why have you come barging into my home, bellowing at the top of your lungs like a fishwife hawking her wares?" she demanded, her voice full of authority, an authority he recognized.

"My apologies, Your Grace." He bowed before her, recognition finally dawning. Of course. Hawthorne House. The lions crouching beside the gate. The lion's head knockers. The woman before him was the dowager duchess of Lion's Mead.

"I sometimes forget my manners. As captain of the *Adventurer*, I am accustomed to giving orders, not taking them. I want—" he began then changed his mind when he caught her expression. "Pardon me, Your Grace. I am Tristan Youngblood, Lord Ravensley. With your permission, I would like to speak with Caralyn."

The duchess continued to scrutinize him, her eyes missing nothing. She let out a sigh and the hint of a smile crossed her lips. "So you are Cara's captain." She hooked her hand into the crook of his arm. "There is much we need to discuss, young man, beginning with what happened between you and my granddaughter. Crandall, please bring a bottle of our finest cognac."

Granddaughter? Caralyn McCreigh was the duchess's granddaughter? His heart sank. No matter what he and Caralyn felt about each other, he knew he'd never be able to convince her father to allow her out of her impending marriage … unless he had this formidable woman on his side, and he wasn't sure he could be successful. On legs as heavy as wooden blocks, Tristan allowed himself to be escorted into a very lovely salon, the duchess still holding his arm.

"Please, sit down, Lord Ravensley." She pointed to a chair upholstered in red, green, and gold as she took the one opposite.

Tristan sat on the edge and looked around the room. The portrait over the fireplace caught his eye and he stared as he spoke. "Tristan, please. I've been away for a long time. The title of lord does not sit easily on my shoulders."

The grand lady bowed her head as the door opened. Crandall entered, carrying cognac and crystal snifters on a silver tray. Another woman followed, younger than the duchess, but bearing the same resemblance to the woman sitting across from him, the woman in the portrait and Caralyn. She must be Caralyn's mother. Tristan rose to his feet. The woman stopped and simply stared, her mouth open as the butler responded to the duchess's summons.

After a word or two with Crandall, the duchess turned to Elizabeth and said, "May I present my daughter, Elizabeth, Caralyn's mother. Elizabeth, this is Cara's captain." One brow cocked over a blue eye as she smiled.

"Oh! But she's—Oh!" Her paralysis broken, Elizabeth stepped forward and extended her hand. "A pleasure, Captain. Caralyn has told us so much about you."

"If I may, I'd like your permission to speak with Caralyn then her father," he insisted as the duchess poured cognac into a crystal snifter and handed it to him. He remained on his feet, anxious, every nerve in his body poised to search the manse from top to bottom until he found her.

"You have my permission, my dear man; however, neither one of them is here at the moment." The duchess took a sip of her cognac but her eyes never left him. "Caralyn left about an hour ago."

"Where did she go?" He put his glass on the tray, the cognac untouched. "Will she be back soon? It is of the utmost importance that I see her, Your Grace. Please."

"I remember you, Tristan," the duchess said, her voice full of fondness. "The last time we met, you were about ten. You were in a hurry then, too." The duchess leaned forward and pierced him with her stare. "Do you love my granddaughter?"

"Do you love my daughter?"

Both women spoke in unison then grinned at each other, as if they shared a secret, a secret that somehow concerned him. And Caralyn.

Startled by the question, Tristan opened his mouth then closed it. The circumstances he found himself in were the most unusual. Uncomfortable, his uneasiness and suspicion growing, he knew honesty would be best. "Yes, I love Caralyn. More than life itself. More than I ever thought possible."

"And do you promise to cherish her for the rest of your days?" The question came from Elizabeth.

Puzzled and confounded, Tristan nodded. "Of course. It is my deepest wish."

"Good." The duchess rose and walked to the door. Elizabeth followed. Crandall waited outside, a note in his hand, which he passed to her.

Stunned by the unexpected reaction to his honesty, his declaration of love for Caralyn, Tristan rushed toward the door. "But I ... I don't understand. Please, I must see Caralyn. You must tell me where she is."

The duchess winked at him and handed him the paper. "This is the address where you will find Caralyn. Crandall has had my fastest horse saddled. Go. Now." She winked at him again.

Confused, bewildered, feeling as if too much liquor addled his thinking, though he hadn't touched the brandy she'd offered, Tristan opened the folded paper. Tears misted his eyes and his throat constricted in an instant. Joy filled his soul and made his heart thunder in his chest. The address was his own. Or rather, his father's London townhouse.

"I am the man Cara is promised to marry?"

. . .

The front door of the earl's home was almost as impressive as the massive portals to her grandmother's town house. The duchess's carriage had broken all records for slowness as it rolled through the streets of London, but now waited in the drive along with the maid and footman her grandmother had insisted accompany her. Caralyn quashed the tide of nausea twisting her stomach and let the iron knocker fall. The sound carried through the manse.

Dogs barked in the background as the door opened to reveal an older, slightly stooped man, his ginger hair liberally streaked with grey. He looked at her and tried to straighten, but age had done its damage. "Yes, Miss?"

"I'd like to see the earl." Despite her fear, despite the urge to cry or run away, her voice remained strong.

"Of course." He opened the door wider and allowed her to enter. Caralyn tightened her grip on the handle of the valise. Heavy with gold coins and various pieces of gem-encrusted jewelry to replace her dowry, its weight pulled at her shoulder. "Please wait while I see if his lordship is receiving visitors. May I tell him who is calling?"

"Caralyn McCreigh," she said. Her voice echoed in the great hall as did the butler's footsteps, reminding her of the cave where they'd found the statue of the Blessed Mother. Caralyn gazed around the large room where she waited. Unlike her grandmother's great hall, which was light and airy, the earl's hall seemed dark. Unable to help herself, she strode to the window and opened the heavy draperies, allowing weak sunlight to flood the area where she stood. She shivered but didn't know if she did so because of her fear or the dampness seeping into her bones. Oh, how she missed the warm bright sunshine of the islands.

The butler touched her arm. "This way, Miss."

Caralyn jumped, startled, and followed the man into a massive library. He closed the door behind him, leaving her alone in the room.

Two stories high, bookshelves and curio cabinets lined the walls. A spiral staircase rose to the second floor where, in a corner flooded with pale sunlight, a grouping of deep, comfortable chairs flanked the wide window. She saw someone's foot bobbing, but the person sitting in the chair, his back toward her, did not rise.

"Well, this is certainly a surprise," the earl greeted her warmly. He came down another set of spiral stairs to her left, a book in one hand, his other hand gliding along the railing. "I didn't expect to see you until tomorrow when you married my son."

Her stomach clenched as he reached the bottom step and came toward her. She clutched the handle of her valise tighter, gripping the wooden rings with fingers that had suddenly turned to stone.

"I am Rayne Youngblood, Earl of Winterbourne." He kissed the tips of her fingers then stood back. "Ah, you are lovelier than I hoped. Your father said you were, but you know how fathers can exaggerate." He chuckled lightly. "Please." He gestured to a chair while he seated himself behind a mahogany desk.

Caralyn sat on the edge of the chair, placed her valise on the floor beside her, and fidgeted with the pleats in her skirt. Now that she was here, words failed her. She didn't know how to begin, didn't know how to say what she needed to say. She glanced at him and decided he had a kind face. Perhaps he would understand.

"Though this is a pleasant surprise, my dear, I am curious about the reason for your visit." He looked at her, his bushy white brows raised as he twisted the onyx signet ring around and around on his finger. "I feel you have something important on your mind."

As she watched him, Caralyn's heart beat triple time in her chest. She had the strangest feeling she knew this man, but for the life of her, she didn't know how.

"Forgive my boldness, milord," she said before she lost her nerve, "but I've come to ask that you release me from my father's promise. I do not wish to marry your son."

"I see." He twisted the ring a little more then, as if trying to break his own habit, stopped, leaned forward, and folded his hands on the desktop. "May I ask why?"

Caralyn swallowed hard. Her father had always instilled in her the valor of honesty. "I've met someone."

"This man you've met," he said as he took off his glasses and held them by the earpiece.

Those eyes! She knew those eyes! But . . .

"Are you in love with him?"

Caralyn forced her attention away from his sherry-colored gaze and sighed. "Yes. I am in love with him, and I want to marry him if he'll have me."

"I see." He drew a deep breath. "And what of my son, the man you're promised to?"

She rose from the seat unable to sit still and began to pace. "I apologize, sir, but I cannot, will not, marry your son. I will meet with him and offer my apologies in person but nothing will change my mind." She stopped before his desk, her direct gaze meeting his. "Do you not want your son to be happy? Do you not want him to have a successful, loving marriage?"

He didn't answer. Instead, he returned her stare, unrelenting, unblinking. "What if I insist? What if I hold you to the promises made on your behalf?"

"I would beg you to reconsider." Oh, how she hated the pleading tone in her voice, and yet she couldn't help it. "I can replace the dowry my father agreed upon." She lifted the valise from the floor, opened it, and shook the contents onto the shiny surface of his desk. The earl jumped and gasped, whether from the thundering explosion of sound as the treasure hit the desktop or the surprise of seeing such a fortune, she didn't know. And didn't care.

His eyes opened wide as he picked up a gold crucifix. The emeralds embedded in the gold twinkled in the weak light coming in the window. "Is this what I think it is?"

"Izzy's Fortune," Caralyn said. "It's yours if you will release me from my father's promise."

The earl sighed and shook his head. He inspected the piece in his hand. "Let me think on this for a moment."

Caralyn sat, her eyes boring into him, her heart pounding. She twisted her hands in her lap and resisted the urge to run her damp palms on her gown. She didn't blink, didn't take her gaze from him for one moment. And she prayed. Oh, how she prayed.

Again, the earl sighed. "Very well, Miss McCreigh. You've shown a great deal of courage coming to see me as you have. I will—"

He never finished the sentence, never said the words she so wanted to hear. Instead, she heard the door behind her open and close and the earl grinned as someone walked into the room. "Son, you're just in time."

Caralyn cringed. Her stomach, already twisted with fear and unease, clenched, as did her jaw. Finding whatever dregs of courage she could, she rose from her seat and turned to face the earl's son, hopefully, for the first and the last time.

She gasped. Tears filled her eyes. She trembled. Indeed, she shook so badly, she thought her knees would buckle. Joy such as she'd never known flowed through her veins. Her heart raced, her pulse pounded in her ears.

Tristan opened his arms. Without hesitation, without a second thought, Caralyn flew into them. His lips met hers in a kiss so gentle, so tender, she felt as if heaven had blessed her. "Oh, Tristan," she whispered, amazed. "I'm so glad you're here but I don't understand."

"Neither did I until I met your grandmother. I think your father and mine," he glanced at the earl, "have something to tell us." His arms tightened around her. "I'm never letting you go again, my love," he whispered as his lips found hers once more.

The earl chuckled and looked toward the chairs flanking the window on the second story. "Daniel, you can come out now. I do believe it's time to confess to our plan."

Caralyn looked toward the chairs as her father slowly stood, a sheepish grin on his face. He held up his hands in surrender. "Forgive me, Cara, but I wanted for you a love like your mother's and mine, and a man who could understand your passion for adventure." He stepped down the spiral staircase and strode to the desk.

Rayne took off his glasses and wiped his eyes as he addressed his son. "And I didn't want for you the marriage your mother and I had. I wanted better for you, Tristan. I wanted you to find love, and I believe you have."

"I knew from the moment I met Tristan, he would be the one for you, Cara. I knew, or rather, I hoped, given the opportunity, you would fall in love with each other. Forgive us our deception. We are but old men who only wanted happiness for our children," Daniel said as he put his arm around his oldest friend.

Caralyn didn't know what to say as she stared at them. She should be furious, and yet as Rayne and her father stood together, the both of them hopeless romantics and matchmakers extraordinaire, she couldn't be. She glanced at Tristan, the man of her dreams, the one she could love until she took her last breath, and grinned. "Should we forgive them?"

Tristan held her gaze. In the depths of his sparkling, sherry-colored eyes, she saw the promise of everything she ever wanted. "I think we should." He lowered his voice and whispered in her ear. "Because they were right. I do love you, Cara mia. Will you marry me?"

"Oh, yes."

Epilogue

"Wake up, sleepyhead."

The words whispered in his ear caused gooseflesh to pebble his skin. Tristan roused from sleep slowly as only a contented man can. Warm fingers tickled the thick mat of hair on his chest and caressed lower. His whole body came alive. He caught Caralyn's hand and opened one eye. Bright sunlight streamed through the window and fell upon the impish grin on her face.

How he loved this woman. With every beat of his heart, every breath he drew, he knew how lucky he'd been to find someone as passionate, as beautiful, as adventurous as she.

"Now, you know what will happen if you continue to do that."

Sleep tousled hair brushed against his chest as she nodded. "I know." Her grin grew and a wicked light danced in her sea-blue eyes. "Happy anniversary, my love," she murmured before she kissed his cheek.

Startled by her words and the fact he may have forgotten such an important date, Tristan mentally went over the calendar in his head and realized she must be mistaken. He smoothed his finger along the soft skin of her jaw. "Cara mia, today is not our anniversary."

Caralyn nodded. "Ten years ago today, I offered you an outrageous proposition. I hired you to help me find a treasure." Her eyes darkened to an even darker blue. "I fell in love with you the first time you kissed me, and when you played your violin, I knew my heart would always be yours."

His heart swelled in his chest—with pride, with love. A lump rose in his throat and he couldn't speak, but his lips could convey what he felt in his heart and he tasted her mouth with the sweetest of kisses as his hands caressed her through the silkiness of her nightgown.

"I have something for you." She broke the kiss and stretched across him. Her breasts pressed against his chest and he groaned before he reached for her.

"Do you know what you do to me?"

She giggled and slapped his hand away as she dug in the bedside table drawer and withdrew a thick envelope.

"What is it?"

"Open it and see."

Tristan sat up in bed with his back against the cushioned headboard. Caralyn settled beside him, her hand resting on his chest as he opened the envelope. A sigh escaped him as he read the letter from the lawyer.

"It took me almost ten months, but I finally tracked it down. This is a map to Calico Jack Rackham's last treasure. Or at least a map attributed to him before he was put to death."

Tristan closed his eyes against the sudden moisture that made his vision blur. Beyond the privacy of their bedchamber, Winterbourne Manor burst at the seams. Friends and relatives converged on the manse to celebrate two amazing events. The release of Dr. Brady Trevelyan's third book, *Adventures of a Treasure Hunter*, and Graham Alcott's marriage.

The bigger surprise had to be the upcoming nuptials of Graham and Irene Baker. Graham said she reminded him a great deal of Caralyn. He met her, of all places, on the beach in Long Island, New York, while she dug for Captain Kidd's buried treasure. It had been love at first sight.

He heard servants scurrying here and there, heard the voices of his guests, but above it all, he heard and reveled in the laughter of his children.

His children.

Jemmy, the child of his heart, home from school for holiday, chased his younger siblings up and down the hallway. His first born, Rayne Brady—all of eight and as serious as his grandfather had been—recited the rules of the game of chase. With his natural inclination for figures and finances, he would be running the

Winterbourne estates before long, much to Jemmy's profound relief as the boy had no desire to be landlocked.

Daniel Graham was thirteen months younger than Rayne and full of the same spirit of adventure Tristan never lost. He and Jemmy talked constantly of sailing the seas to find lost treasure.

A shout from the hallway made him swivel his head toward the door.

Temperance, a miniature version of Caralyn with snapping sea-blue eyes and light brown hair that curled around her little face, peeked through the bedroom door. Even at three years old, his daughter knew exactly what she wanted. He couldn't help the grin that tugged at the corners of his mouth. Last week she'd told him, quite emphatically, definitely no to peas and carrots, but yes to Papa's kisses. Again, his heart swelled almost painfully in his chest as she squealed, "Papa!"

"Good morning, my little sprite." Tristan grinned as his daughter burst into the room, leaving the door wide open, and jumped on the bed. She snuggled between him and her mother, her little body warm. Caralyn wrapped an arm around her and nestled closer as Temperance grabbed the letter from his hand and pretended to read.

It didn't take long for her brothers to follow her. Rayne and Daniel perched at the end of the bed and Jemmy, at nineteen, too old to climb into their bed, slumped in one of the chairs flanking the fireplace, his leg swinging over the arm.

Tristan glanced at each one of his children then turned to Caralyn, the woman who'd been the answer to every dream, every desire he'd ever had. "It's a wonderful gift, Cara mia, but I don't need it." He smoothed his finger over her cheek and drew in a breath in an effort to keep the emotions threatening to overwhelm him at bay. As it was, he had to swallow—hard—to remove the lump from his throat. "I have everything I want right here. I don't need to hunt for treasure because you, my love, and our children, are the only treasures worth keeping."

About the Author

Marie Patrick has always had a love affair with words and books, but it wasn't until a trip to Arizona, where she now makes her home with her husband and two furry, four-legged "girls," that she became inspired to write about the sometimes desolate, yet beautiful landscape. Her inspiration doesn't just come from the Wild West, though. It comes from history itself. She is fascinated with pirates and men in uniform and lawmen with shiny badges. When not writing or researching her favorite topics, she can usually be found curled up with a good book. Marie loves to hear from her readers. Drop her a note at *Akamariep@aol.com* or visit her website at *www.mariepatrick.com*.

A Sneak Peek from Crimson Romance
(From *One Day's Loving* by Rue Allyn)

Boston Massachusetts, Late June 1870

"I regret, Mr. Van Wynde, I cannot accept your proposal. You will understand that with my grandfather's passing last week I could not entertain any offer of marriage."

Persephone Mae Alden of the Boston Aldens stared wide-eyed at the man kneeling before her on the floor of the manse's formal parlor. Thanks to her parsimonious grandfather's belief that women were sin personified, she had never entered the social scene. Nonetheless, skepticism came easily after living, since childhood, with the cruelest hypocrite on earth—almost as easily as the knowledge that the way to survival lay in dissembling and avoidance. *Never, never, risk telling a man exactly what you think—* it wasn't safe.

Still on his knees, Charles Otto Van Wynde, III looked up, calf-eyed, at Mae. "Had I not wished to give you my support during this sad time, I would never have spoken. Please tell me I may hope for a different answer in the future."

Mae was torn between the urge to giggle and the need to flee. Until today, she had never met Mr. Van Wynde, though she'd read of him and his nine sisters in the social columns of the *Daily Advertiser*. Despite his Brahmin name, Mr. Van Wynde had no money to speak of. The inappropriate timing of his offer had much more to do with obtaining the support of her grandfather's fortune for his unmarried siblings than with any inclination to offer her solace. Mae wished for Edith and Kiera. With her older sisters' help, she might have avoided this encounter. But Kiera had run off to San Francisco. Then newspaper reports of a murderer matching Kiera's description hit the Boston streets, so Edith left to find Kiera and bring her home. Mae had promised to lie to protect their whereabouts while Grandfather remained in a coma. That he would die just five days after Edith's departure was bad luck.

Like it or not, Mae was on her own.

"Please get up, kind sir. I cannot bear to look down upon one as considerate as you." To name him considerate was to push dissembling to its limits. Heavens, the will had not even been read before Van Wynde came knocking on her door, offering condolences and heart in the same money-seeking breath. Mae told herself she was doing him a favor. She doubted very much that Grandfather would leave more than a pittance to any of his three granddaughters.

Van Wynde straightened his spare form, bringing his oddly round face to eye level with her. "Can I say anything to change your mind?"

"Your request honors me. However, I do not wish to mislead you. My heart is given elsewhere." She would not tell him her heart was given firmly to the principle that marriage was a trap to keep women in servitude to men. Such a statement would only encourage him to try to prove otherwise and lead to embarrassment for them both. She had no desire to prolong this absurd encounter and suffer unwanted attentions simply to assuage his male pride.

"Then I will wish you happy and say farewell." The young man bowed and departed.

Mae sank into a chair. That had been the second proposal in as many days with the funeral only three days before. She was to appear at the offices of Collins & Collins, Attorneys at Law tomorrow for the reading of the will. Two weeks after, it would clear probate and become public record. Pray heaven she would not have to endure any other pleas to marry before then.

Soon, everyone would know she had little or no inheritance. She could sink into the safe obscurity of poverty to await the doom Grandfather dictated in his last will and testament. Whatever he ordered would be a cruel, thoughtless attempt to punish her and her two older sisters for the crime of being born female.

. . .

Light seeped under the porte cochere of the manse the following soggy afternoon, as Mae moved from the door to the Alden town carriage. Grandfather was too stingy to pay to have a coachman on staff, so the hired driver handed her into the vehicle.

"Please hurry," she told him. "This rain has made the unpaved streets a morass, and I've no wish to be late."

"Yes, miss." The man's voice had the quality of pebbles crunching under boot heels. He tugged at the brim of his hat then laid her umbrella on the rear-facing bench before closing the door.

Seconds later, the carriage set off with a jerk that sent her sinking into the unaccustomed comfort of the deeply cushioned seat—before the funeral, she had always walked if she needed to go anywhere. Grandfather had believed indulgence was a sin for everyone but himself. He and he alone had earned the Alden fortune through shrewd investments and ruthless business economies. Comfort was his earthly reward, and his alone, for his ability to buy and sell with an eye to making a profit. He'd given little thought to the workers on whose backs he'd built his empire and even less to the granddaughters he despised.

Now Grandfather was dead, and Mae could experience some of the luxuries denied her. But for how long? She'd been surprised when a note from attorney James W. Collins V had informed her that she and her sisters were included in the will. Given the ferocity of Grandfather's misogyny, she'd expected to be tossed to the street with nothing but the clothing on her back.

She was due at the attorney's office by one o'clock. Mr. Collins—James as she thought of him privately—was a busy man and shouldn't be kept kicking his heels. So busy the few times he'd come to the manse on business in his father's place, they'd exchanged only the smallest courtesies. Now that his client had passed on, Mr. Collins would have little inclination to humor a graceless dab of a woman. His insistence that the reading take place in his office merely indicated he thought her insignificant.

She didn't mind, she told herself. She'd be spending a long hour in the presence of a man she admired, perhaps too much. Unlike Mr. VanWynde, James was a striking example of a Boston Brahmin. Tall, square of jaw, broad of shoulder, with long legs and narrow—heavens she'd been raised better than to think of a man's physique, let alone the span of his hips.

If she must daydream inappropriately, better to dream of his fine, glossy, black hair and the humor she'd always imagined in his shining, hazel eyes. She dared not ponder the texture of his fingers. She had no idea if his fingers were rough or smooth. She'd never had the temerity to approach him or offer her hand in hope his palm would clasp hers for a few moments.

There she went, letting her mind lead her astray. Thoughts of James's hands should be forbidden because that led to fantasies of where he might place those fingers. Safer by far to think of his voice, deep and musical, or the enchanting aroma that lay beneath the sandalwood of his cologne. What might it be like to wake to such a scent every...

Obviously she could not be trusted to think of James at all without imagining the most improper events. Impatient with herself, Mae glanced at the watch fob pinned at her waist.

The timepiece showed five minutes before one o'clock. What in the world was taking so long? They'd been moving at a spanking speed despite the mud and mire in the streets.

Did the coachman know the way to Collins & Collins's offices? She pushed aside the curtain and looked out the window. The rain sheeted down so hard she could make out no landmarks.

Fearing to be late and anger James, she leaned forward and slid back the small door that would allow her to talk directly to the driver. He was already speaking, which was odd, since she did not have an outrider. About to ask with whom he spoke, she finally realized what he was saying. Her words froze in her throat.

"What do we do with the Alden woman when we get to the ship?" asked an unfamiliar nasal twang.

"I told you," answered the gravel-voiced driver. "We put a bag over her head and carry her aboard. The captain'll pay us for her. Then we go back to the Burying Ground and wait for the ransom to be delivered."

"Don't you think they'll put the coppers on us for not giving her back once we got our piece of old man Alden's fortune?" queried Twang. "Nice of him to pop off when he did. From what I hear, he never would have paid a penny for his granddaughter. Bet that lawyer will be more generous."

"He'd better be. Either way, they'll have the coppers on us. But we'll be away before they can figure out where we're going. We'll stay a step ahead of the law, and soon we'll be in Cuba smoking cigars and living the high life." Gravel laughed.

Mae clapped a hand over her mouth to keep herself from crying an alarm then quietly shut the small door. She was being abducted.

In all her twenty one years she'd never been so frightened. She had to escape before they reached their destination but how? For the past sixteen years of her life, she'd run and hid at the first sign of trouble. Where could she run, and how could she hide in the middle of a Boston downpour with no idea where in the city she was? She couldn't just wait to be sold into some terrible fate.

Kiera would go on the offensive—attack her abductors, counting on surprise to even the odds. With more guile and often more sense, Edith would jump from the carriage and run.

Mae could smell the bay mixing with the rain, indecision carrying her closer to doom. If she was to escape, she had to act. She unlatched the door of the carriage closest to the boardwalk, poising herself to jump. When driver began to guide the horses around a corner, she leapt, landing in the mud with a breath-stealing thud. The carriage door banged shut.

"What the—" shouted Gravel. "She's getting away! Go after her while I get this coach turned around."

Mae sucked in air, then rose, gathered her muddy skirts, and ran as fast as she could. She had to find a hiding place. She dodged around the corner of the nearest building.

Footsteps pounded on the boardwalk, passed the building where she sheltered, and then faded in the distance.

Heart racing, she found herself in an alley with fences and high gates on either side. She ran to the first gate. It was unlocked; God bless luck. She wrenched the portal open, slid through, and latched it securely behind her. Looking around she saw large crates and huge barrels—tuns, some with lids askew—that from the look and smell of them once contained wine or whiskey.

"Did you check down this alley?" shouted Gravel.

"Didn't see it," stated Twang. "Why would she go down there anyway?"

"Fool. She'd want to hide. Go look for her. I'll check the alley across the street."

Will the gate keep my pursuer out? Maybe he'll climb over? Indecision became panic.

Moving quickly and quietly, she forced open the loose cover on one of the huge kegs. The fumes were awful, but it was empty, with enough room for her to squeeze inside, bustle and all.

The process was awkward; nonetheless, she managed to pull the lid shut moments before scraping sounded outside near the gate. A thud followed, and Twang cursed. "If I get my hands on that bitch, she'll wish she'd never been born. It's her fault I tore me good pants climbing that gate."

He continued to curse as he stomped around the yard banging on crates and barrels. He hit the tun where Mae hid, and she smothered a yelp.

"Ain't a hollow piece in the place. Too bad I can't take a keg with me. I could use a drink."

The scraping sound came again, followed by a more distant thud.

"Well?" Gravel questioned.

"She ain't in there or any of the other yards in this alley."

"Damn. We need that ransom. We don't get out of Boston tonight, we're dead meat. We owe too much money to the bookies."

"Then we better start walking, 'cause we ain't getting no ransom this night."

"We got a carriage. We can ride out of town then sell the coach when we're far enough away. The money won't get us to Cuba, but at least that bitch was good for something." Gravel added his curses to Twang's as their voices faded away.

Mae waited, shivering with shock and fear that the men would return. *How long should I wait before emerging to see if they are truly gone?*

Kiera would check now. She'd take a barrel stave as a club and whack anyone opposing her on the head. Edith would wait. She'd plan while she waited. Like Kiera, she'd probably find a weapon. Then she would determine her location and decide the best means of getting home. Or would she go to James's office first?

Mae looked at her bedraggled dress and sniffed the whiskey-soaked air. She wanted to go home, but if James's office was closer she should go there. She needed help more than she needed to repair her appearance.

She listened a few moments more and heard nothing save the distant bark of a dog. Had she waited long enough? What would she do if the men lay in wait for her? Filled with trepidation, she pushed open the cover of the barrel.

An unaccustomed and oddly pleasant tension shivered through her. Not more fear, that emotion was too well known. No, this sizzling tension was more like anticipation combined with apprehension.

She couldn't possibly be exhilarated by the risks she'd taken. Could she?

• • •

At 2:30 p.m. James W. Collins V examined his pocket watch for the fourth time before he opened the door to the outer office of his law firm. "Harry, has Miss Alden sent any word as to why she's late or let us know if she's canceled our appointment?"

"Not that I know. . . Oh, I forgot. I found a letter on the floor about an hour ago. I must not have heard the messenger, and he slipped it under the door, thinking we were closed for lunch."

James bit his tongue to keep from shouting his irritation at the old clerk. Harry had been with the firm since the doors opened thirty years ago. While he had occasional lapses in memory and saw less well than he once did, he knew everything about every case and client in the firm's history. His knowledge was invaluable; putting up with minor lapses was a small price.

"Let me have it."

"What, sir?"

"The letter you found on the floor."

"Oh, yes. Now where did I put that?" Harry spent long moments searching and finally found the document on the seat of his desk chair.

"Here you are, sir."

The paper was warm and slightly creased, but James took it anyway and tore open the envelope.

Mister Collins,

We have Miss Alden. Place $100,000.00 inside a carpet bag. Leave the bag behind Mr. C. Alden IV's headstone at the Central Burying Ground. Then walk to Boylston Street. A boy will find you with instructions on how to get Miss Alden back. If the money is not given on time or you call in the police, Miss Alden will disappear from Boston forever.

"Harry, get the police here at once."

"Why?"

"I will explain later."

"Yes, sir." Harry donned his coat and hat then searched for and found his umbrella.

"Would you hurry, man? Miss Alden's been abducted."

"What? When? How? I'd better go for the police."

James ground his teeth. "Excellent idea."

Harry made for the door, but it opened before he could touch the knob.

Huffing as if she'd run a great distance, a woman stood framed in the doorway. Her rain-sodden hair dragged down her face and across her shoulders. Her dress was muddy, crumpled, and her neckline askew. She smelled like a violet-strewn whiskey factory.

"This is no place for the likes of you. Get on your way," ordered Harry. He shifted to block her path into the office. "I'm going for the police."

"No, please. You don't understand." She stopped for breath. "I'm Persephone Mae Alden."

Her elocution was at odds with her odor and appearance. Tremors shook the timid voice, and James noticed the shivers racking the woman's small frame.

Harry snorted. "I doubt that. Miss Alden is a well-bred miss and would never. . ."

James finally recognized the delicate bone structure obscured by the mass of wet hair and moved Harry aside. "Forgive my clerk, Miss Alden. He's somewhat overprotective."

"Sir!" objected Harry. "You cannot believe this drab."

"If you wore your spectacles, you would see that Miss Alden is no drab. I'm surprised you didn't hear her identity in her voice. Come into my office, Miss Alden. I gather you escaped your captors. Harry fetch some tea."

"Mae, please. With all that's happened, standing on ceremony is more effort than I can manage. I did escape, but how did you know, Mr. Collins?"

"If I am to address you as Mae, you must call me James." He ushered her into his office and settled her near the pot bellied stove, placing a woolen lap rug around her shoulders. "I just received the ransom note. Excuse me a moment. I'll have my clerk send for your maid and a change of clothing then he will go for the police."

"Tell him to ask for the second housemaid. Most of the staff at the manse are ill with colds. I would not have any of them exposed to this wretched weather."

James stared at her a moment. He'd never met a woman more concerned for her servants than her appearance. Perhaps there was more to Miss Mae Alden than their few previous encounters led him to believe.

In the mood for more Crimson Romance?
Check out *How to Wed an Earl*
by Ivory Lei at *CrimsonRomance.com*.

Printed in the United States
By Bookmasters